W9-BZA-146

"This moving story of a young soldier in the Civil War has been researched with great care. Mary Hennessy vividly recreates the texture of life on the land and the rigors of military service in mid-nineteenth century America."

—Laurie Nussdorfer
Professor of History and Letters
Wesleyan University

Major H.W. Sawyer (center, seated) and Staff, 3d Division, Cavalry Corps, Department of Washington. Camp Stoneman, November, 1864. (Photo courtesy of Henry Washington Sawyer IV Collection.)

His Hour Upon the Stage

The Story of a Civil War
Horse Soldier and the Woman
·Who Fought to Save His Life

Mary Hennessy

Illustrations by Leila Sawyer

VANTAGE PRESS
New York

FIRST EDITION

Published by Vantage Press, Inc.
419 Park Ave. South, New York, NY 10016

Manufactured in the United States of America
ISBN: 978-0-533-15673-3

Library of Congress Catalog Card No.: 2006909759

0 9 8 7 6 5 4 3 2

For the great-grandchildren of Henry Washington Sawyer

Rebecca   Jonathan   Hal

and their families

Elizabeth, Gideon, Ben and Layla
Leila, Zoë and Arden

and in memory of his grandson, Henry Washington Sawyer III, who first told me the compelling story of his grandfather and inspired me to write it.

Acknowledgments

To Allison Holt Smith, my gratitude for her enthusiasm and technical expertise in the preparation of the manuscript.

To Murray, my deepest appreciation for his devotion and eagerness to make good things happen in my life.

To Elizabeth, whose blithe spirit nourishes us all, my thanks for her never-failing willingness to help me in the writing of this book by employing her native literary talent to untangle all manner of editorial problems, always with heart-warming patience and encouragement.

To Jonathan, my gratitude for his patient help with everything related to computers and for his knowledgeable perspective on illustrations, maps, photographs, and history. I have appreciated his readiness with a reassuring word, his sense of humor and unparalleled good taste.

I am indebted to Donna Diller Ballenger, my steadfast friend for more than sixty years, whose loyalty and generous spirit have helped me through countless vicissitudes of life.

Civil War scholar Herb Kaufman at the Civil War and Underground Railroad Museum in Philadelphia has been generous with his time in sharing his profound knowledge and in guiding me to books and other helpful sources for research.

To Alice Norton, my appreciation for valuable suggestions offered from her wealth of experience in public relations and libraries.

To Leila, I am indebted for her insightful illustrations enlivening each chapter, for drawing the map highlighting important action in the story, and for her gracious willingness to be of help always.

His Hour Upon the Stage

1

The horse was dead. He lay on his side with his head resting heavily on the body of his rider. Dust swirling in the fury of battle the previous day had mixed with sweat, smearing the glistening black hide, and the hot June sun had dried the blood oozing from the shell wound on his bulging flank. Flies buzzed around it and fought to get at the blood that had trickled down his nostrils. Even in death the powerful sinews in his legs and the luxuriant mane spreading over the curve of his neck lent a majesty given to steeds of noble lineage.

On the horse's head lay the motionless outstretched arm of the Yankee officer who had fallen with him and whose love for the animal was expressed in the manner in which the fingers were entwined tenderly about the black mane.

The officer and his horse were not alone. Intermingled on the battlefield were bodies wearing blue and gray uniforms and contorted grotesquely in varying throes of death. Bloody parts of arms and severed legs were bestrewn over the ground, and lying in the enormous shell hollows were fragments of human remains and dead horses with gaping holes in their sides. In the stillness of the early morning moans of pain and weak cries of thirst hummed softly, while the stench of death from the swollen corpses, their blood blackened by the sun, hung in the air above the buzz of thousands of hungry insects frenziedly at work.

Into this scene two Confederate soldiers made their way slowly across the field. They were barefoot, their uniforms filthy and torn exposing patches of grimy flesh on arms and legs. From under dirty caps their tousled hair hung askew. Gaunt hunger lodged in their eye sockets above beards untrimmed and full of briars. Slung over their stooped shoulders were haversacks and muskets. There was about their haggard frames an overpowering weariness as they stepped over bodies inspecting each carefully, deliberately searching.

One reached down and tugged at a leather belt from the blue uniform of a dead Yankee, rolling the body over as he did so. "This'll do me jes' fine," he said, holding up his prize. Yanking the frayed and knotted cord that held his trousers up and tossing it over his shoulder, he threaded the newly acquired leather belt through the loops, patting the good fit.

They trudged on and their eyes lit upon a shiny sword lying next to the carcass of the black horse. "Shore that *was* a fine horse," one of them said. "A real gentleman's horse, I'd say."

The other picked up the sword and squinted at the engravings: *E pluribus unum.* "What's that?" he asked his companion.

"Prob'ly some kind of motto or somethin'." They ran their dirty fingers over the engraving of oak leaves and acorns, an eagle, a tent with a flag on top, and an Indian with a hatchet in one hand and a quiver full of arrows. Turning the sword over, they examined the inscription on the other side: 1st New Jersey Cavalry. Henry Washington Sawyer.

"The gentleman also had a fine pair o' shoes," exclaimed one with a smile bordering on a leer. He thrust his dust-covered bare foot with the toenails full of grime alongside the shoe of the officer. "He won't be a-needin' these no more," he said, kneeling down and beginning to unlace the officer's shoes. As he was about to slip the shoe off one foot, the officer stirred and moved his hand away from the horse's head to his own forehead.

"Water," he whispered, "Water . . ."

The Confederate soldier blanched and jumped back, dropping the foot. "Ach!" the looter exclaimed. "He's not a total goner after all!"

The wounded man opened his eyes slightly, lifting his hand shakily to shield them from the sun. "Water," he repeated. "Water . . . Prince, boy. . . ." He turned his head to look at his horse. "Oh, no," he groaned.

It was then that the two plunderers saw the wound on the side of the man's head. "He musta been in the thick of it yesterday," one said. "Short time ago I'd have given 'im up for dead. The way his head's been bleedin', he may not make it."

"He got shot in the leg too," said the other, pointing to the dried blood on the trousers.

They turned away from the officer when they heard a mule-drawn Confederate ambulance wagon bumping across the field with wounded lying on its bunks within. They hailed it, motioning to the man on the ground. "Do ye pick up Yankees?" one called out.

The driver left the ambulance and approached the spot where the wounded man lay. He knelt on the ground just as the latter opened his eyes again and whispered: "Water."

"Sure ye kin have a leetle drink," he said, shoving a canteen to the man's lips. Raising his head painfully to the canteen, he drank in long, slow draughts, then fell back on the ground with a sigh.

One of the soldiers called the driver's attention to the inscription on the sword.

"Yeh," the driver answered. "The 1st New Jersey were in the battle on Fleetwood Hill yesterday. Gave ole Jeb Stuart a poundin'. Lots of dead on both sides." Then, eyeing the two bedraggled soldiers, he continued: "How'd you two manage to come through it?" His voice was edged with suspicion.

The two soldiers looked furtively at each other, wondering which one should answer the question. Finally one spoke up: "Oh, we wuz carryin' our wounded back to our lines. All day long with grape flyin' over us and shells fallin' all 'round us. Oh, we wuz in the thick of it, all right."

"Yessiree," agreed the other hurriedly, nodding a little too energetically. Their faces were so encrusted with dirt that only the eyes carried any expression, and the ambulance driver stared at those long and hard to discern any hint of guilt.

From the ambulance, the groan of a young soldier with a leg missing jarred the driver from his judgment of the two. Looking

3

down at the fallen Yankee, he spoke. "Seein' as how he's an officer, I'd best take him along to Culpeper. He might be of some use to our officers—that is, if he even makes it to Culpeper with that bleedin' head."

He motioned to the two soldiers to help carry the man to the ambulance. They lifted him roughly and he winced and cried out as they jostled him across the battlefield up and down the shell holes. Laying him on one of the bunks amidst the wounded, they placed his sword on top of him. The mules' muscles grew taut as they strained to pull their load over the rough ground. Each hole in its surface brought an outburst of cries of pain from the wounded passengers. Most were unconscious but the anguish they suffered vent itself with every turning of the wheels.

The two soldiers watched the ambulance lumber out of sight. "Wahl, I lost me a fine pair o' shoes," drawled one.

They walked back to look at the black horse once more. "Yep, that sure was a fine horse, like the ones our officers at home rode in peaceful times," the other commented. They lingered momentarily before continuing their search for booty.

Soon they had discarded their muskets for quick-loading Spencer carbines, playing with them like boys, aiming them and squinting at a make-believe target. They sat down then to inspect the boots of two dead Yankees.

" 'magine foot soldiers havin' boots as good as these!" exclaimed one. " 'Reckon they were new to the war. Hadn't seen much walkin' or fightin' to be in this good shape."

The boots resisted leaving their owners' stiffened feet, and the two men knelt by the bodies and tugged with some degree of exasperation lest they be denied their prize again. When the boots finally slipped off, socks came with them. "Wahl, I'll be a stinkin' polecat if the Yanks didn't have socks too! I ain't had socks on since the Battle o' Kelly's Ford a coupla months ago. The last I seen o' them they was floatin' away along the Rappyhannock while a Yankee was tryin' to bayonet me."

He took a stick and dug a clod of dried mud out from under his big toenail, then pulled the socks on over his grimy feet whose soles were the color and texture of leather. Next came the boots. "Reckon these'll walk until the end o' the war."

While lacing up the pair he had taken from the second dead soldier, the other announced proudly: "My feet ain't *never* felt boots like these, not even back home in G'o'gia." He stood up and walked, gloating at his new acquisition. "When onc't I git back home, I kin tell the folks this was my award for fightin' the Battle o' Brandy Station way up in Virginny. Wot is the date, I wonder?"

His comrade, looking through the personal possessions of a soldier's haversack on the ground, announced: "This here 'un has a calendar right in with some letter writin' paper. Kin you-all read the dates?" he handed it across the body to his friend. The latter studied it.

"Wahl," he drawled, "we wuz in Chancellorsville the first part o' May when ole Stonewall got his. I remember the moon was full that night he got shot. Ah still cain't understan' why his own men couldn't see 'im in the light o' the moon. It was bright as day. They musta been crazy or skeered to death in the fightin' to shoot him dead. Terrible." He shook his head in disbelief. "Last night the moon was 'bout full agin, so I reckon it's along about the first week o' June 1863." He stopped momentarily, deep in thought. "That makes the war over two years old. An' we wuz told back in the beginnin' that the fightin' 'd be over in a matter o' weeks, that the Yankees'd run as soon as they seed our army." He laughed sardonically.

The Reb sorting through the contents of the haversack pushed the stationery towards his friend. "This ain't no use to me. Kin you-all write?"

The other nodded, taking the paper and stuffing it in his pocket, while his comrade continued his search. A packet of needles, a spool of thread, a pair of scissors, a bar of soap, a comb, a family photo of a young woman with an infant on her lap, and some letters were filched from the sack. "He won't be needin' any o' this," he said, cramming everything into his pocket except the letters, which he threw over his back.

"Di'n't he have no food hidin' in thar?" his companion wanted to know.

5

The arm dug deeply into the sack and withdrew two lemons. "One fer each of us," he said, dividing the spoils.

They stood up with their newly acquired arms slung over their shoulders, walking gingerly with a tip-toe step as they flexed the new boots, stopping at another body in a Yankee uniform. Kneeling down, one of them put his hand on the gold wedding ring on the cold finger. He pulled and pulled but the ring would not budge.

"Leave it be," ordered his accomplice, his hand inside the dead man's jacket. "Lookee here," he announced, bringing forth a pocket watch. "He went through the battle, got hisself shot to hell, but the watch come through unhurt." He was about to take his other hand out of the dead man's pocket when his fingers grasped a letter. Pulling it out to read the name of the man, he looked puzzled at the writing. To his friend, he said: "Lookee here what I've found. One of our boys fakin' it, dressed in Yankee blue. This here was Nathaniel Jeremiah Jackson, Private, Army of the Confederate States of America."

"Wahl, mebee the uniform's better'n the first one he had, but it di'n't protec' him no better when the fightin' got started. Pore dead Johnny Reb. I wonder where he come from."

His friend looked at the envelope. "The letter came from Alabamy."

"A long walk from Alabamy to die on the fields of Virginny," answered the other.

"We'd best be gettin' back or lieutenant'll be callin' us stragglers."

"'Cain't pass this up," his companion objected as he pulled a suspender off a dead soldier's pants. "This here leather'll make me a fine canteen strap. And I can use this here button, too." They passed again the body of the black horse. "I wonder what manner o' man would have such a fine horse," one of them mused, staring at the animal. "He called 'im Prince. A good name for 'im too. Anyone who knowed anythin' 'bout horses would say he had 'ristocratic blood."

Two slain Yankee officers rested near the spot where Henry Washington Sawyer had lain. "The Yankee cavalry shore did lose a heap o' officers in that there battle," remarked the one who could read, squinting at the swords of each dead man: John H. Shelmire. Virgil Broderick.

"And a heap o' horses too," responded the other. Dead horses with bloated bellies were strewn across the field, lying near their fallen riders. "Pore animals. They jes' did as they wuz made to do. No way to defen' theirselves. Animals is animals no matter what side they's on."

Suddenly they heard voices from an approaching Confederate burial detail. Slipping quickly behind two trees, they watched from afar as the men came into sight, about twenty of them, marching along with shovels carried over their shoulders. They stopped at the edge of the battlefield to survey the work that lay ahead of them. For a few moments they silently counted bodies. Then they moved as a team to begin the grim task of digging a trench. The hot sun shone mercilessly on their bent backs as they dug down through the dried out earth. The dirt piled up on either side of the trench as they threw up one shovelful after another. The workers stopped frequently to wipe sweat from their faces and to lean on their shovels.

The sun rose to its highest point and the workers shed their jackets. "What was the count?" one man asked the leader of the detail.

" 'bout 60 dead," was the reply. "And 'bout the same number wounded. The ambulances'll be along to pick up those. Most of them are nearly dead. They'll be goners if the ambulances don't get here quick."

By afternoon the trench was deep enough and the burial detail climbed out on hands and knees, parked their shovels in the mounds of dirt alongside it, and set to the labor of filling the long trench. Silently, they went by two's to lift the corpses from the field and to carry them to their final resting place. The blue and the gray were laid side by side, face up and face down, arms and legs intertwined, seeming as one nameless army, united in death, the young with their boyish faces and straw-colored hair, the older with deeply lined foreheads and graying beards.

Even when the bodies had been covered with the earth from the trench, the burial was not finished. The men gathered fence rails and placed them in a pile. Setting them ablaze, with great effort they dragged the carcasses of horses to the flames. The fire and sparks flew skyward and the stench of burning flesh hung heavily in the air while a nauseating greasy smoke rose in a cloud above. While attention was riveted on the gruesome scene, the two soldiers hiding behind the trees made their way stealthily back towards Confederate lines.

2

When the ambulance wagon arrived in Culpeper, Virginia after covering miles of bumpy terrain jostling its occupants painfully, it pulled up in front of a church which had been turned into a hospital. It was dusk when the mules came to a halt before the darkened building where two men with bandaged heads sat on the doorstep taking the cool evening air.

"These here are from Brandy Station," announced the driver. "It's a mix o' Yanks and our boys. Most of 'em are pretty far gone."

One of the men sitting on the steps answered, "We're full up. No room for anyone. Only one doc here. Operated all night and all day."

The second man added, "We've been here since early May. We got ours at Chancellorsville. In the best shape of anyone here. We do what we can to help. No other staff here."

Suddenly, a man with sleeves rolled up above his elbows and wearing an apron spattered with blood emerged from the darkness of the church. "How many do you have?" he asked the ambulance driver.

"Twelve" was the reply. "Can't vouch for 'em all bein' alive, though."

The man with the soiled apron mopped the sweat from his brow with a hand that bore the stains of his labor. Turning to the two bandaged orderlies, he ordered, "Bring 'em in, boys. We'll have to make room for 'em." Then, aside to the driver, he added, "Don't know when I can get to 'em. Two ambulances from Brandy Station came last night loaded with wounded real bad. That musta been a big battle."

The two men stood up with difficulty holding onto the wall and with wobbly legs descended the steps. Helped by the driver, they lifted the wounded off their bunks, one at a time, and struggled up the steps into the church.

Reaching the door, they paused momentarily to let their eyes adjust to the darkness within. In the suffused candlelight, bodies of wounded could be distinguished lying head-to-toe on the pews and on straw spread out on the floor. From the eerie gloom in the nave of the church came groans of pain and supplications for water. The two men carrying in the new arrivals wound their way down the center aisle approaching the altar.

"We'd best leave 'em right here," said one, lowering the wounded soldier they were carrying. "Doc prob'ly won't get to 'em 'til tomorrow. Maybe not 'til evenin'."

When Henry Sawyer was laid on the floor of the church with his sword beside him, he was still unconscious of his surroundings, but inside his feverish head whirled a carousel of memories. He lay there for a night and a day. While he awaited attention from the overworked doctor, his brain plucked at various chapters of his life. One moment he was a Union cavalry officer skirmishing before a battle, and the next he was a young farm boy growing up in Pennsylvania with his mother and father and brothers around him.

*　　*　　*

Henry Washington Sawyer was eighteen years old the day he read the advertisement in the newspaper that would change his life. He had ridden his horse from the farm to the shop in the Village for some worm medicine for the dogs, and after selecting the powder from the shelf he browsed through the newspapers on sale. As he turned the pages of the *Philadelphia Gazette,* his attention was arrested by a prominently displayed box:

<u>Master Carpenter in Cape Island, New Jersey</u> seeks apprentices to build homes in this rapidly growing community. With its harbor as fine as any on the New Jersey coast, this established town is destined to become the most popular resort on the eastern coast of America. For immediate hiring, contact Ezekiel Eldredge, Cape Island.

Henry stared at the words, reading them through again slowly, then looked at the date on the front page: February 1, 1848. He turned back to the advertisement and read it once more. "Where is Cape Island?" he wondered to himself.

Swinging up into the saddle on his handsome white stallion, Beauty, waiting outside, he turned the horse towards home, and as they jogged along the eight miles through the Pennsylvania countryside to the farm he could think of nothing else but the advertisement.

That evening, seated between his brothers, Thaddeus and Silas, at the supper table, he was lost in thought and did not even hear his mother offer him a second piece of apple pie.

"Ye're very quiet, Henry," she commented. "Are ye ailin'?"

Startled from his thoughts, he assured her that he was not ill and accepted her offer with enthusiasm.

Henry glanced at his father at the head of the table, longing to tell him about the advertisement, to ask questions and to solicit advice, but he hesitated, knowing only too well what his father's reaction would be to any suggestion that he might leave the family farm. He remembered the occasion when he turned eighteen the previous spring and his father had approached the subject rather casually.

"This farm will be yours and Thad's and Si's some day," he'd said. "It's rich land, Henry, and you boys can have a good life here."

Henry had not wanted to hurt his father, nor did he know how to express his feelings exactly about his own future, so after a silence all he had said was, "Yes, Pa, it sure is a beautiful farm." His father had turned to study his face momentarily before leaving the subject.

Nine months had passed since that brief exchange and spring was approaching. Long after his brothers fell asleep that night in the big bedroom they shared in the farmhouse, Henry lay awake thinking. He tried to imagine the New Jersey coast, the harbor, the smell of the ocean and the sound of the waves as they rolled in in a winter storm. He had never been anywhere near the sea, and all the scenes he pictured were creations of his imagination. He saw himself riding his horse on the sand in the early morning hours and again in the twilight as the sun set over the shining water. Doubts crowded in as well. Did he know enough about tools and how to use them to qualify him to be an "apprentice carpenter" who could actually build houses and earn enough to support himself? Where would he live? What would town life be like? He had never lived anywhere but on this farm.

Normally, the heavy manual farm labor put him to sleep within minutes of his laying his head on the pillow, but tonight sleep did not come. Moonlight was shining through the open curtain and Henry was wide awake, his hands behind his head and his eyes staring up at the ceiling. His mind was in turmoil. Emotions he didn't fully understand churned his thoughts. Questions kept protruding and he couldn't find the answers. Was it wrong to feel this way about life on the farm, this place that had nurtured him and given him security for eighteen years? Why was he not satisfied with his life? Why was he searching for something else? He loved his family. They were not the problem. But even though Si and Thad had always been close to him, he could not bring himself to discuss his feelings with them. They were so different from himself. They had no desire to leave this place where they were born and raised. They knew everything about farming that twenty and twenty-one years of hard work could teach them and they liked rural life. Towns and cities held no lure for them. How could Henry expect them to understand the restlessness that called him away from the farm to seek his livelihood? How could he explain to them his desire for adventure when they appeared to be so contented with the even tenor of life on the farm whose surface was ruffled only by the change of seasons?

Why had he turned out this way? Perhaps he would find the answer if he looked back through his life. He closed his eyes.

*　　*　　*

Henry could not remember a time in his life when he had not loved horses. As a little boy his fondness for all the animals in the barnyard was a natural part of growing up. In the springtime he played with baby lambs and laughed at their wobbly legs and twitching tails as they nursed their mothers. He stroked the soft coats of newborn calves, rubbed the noses of spindly legged colts, and watched litters of piglets suckle enormous grunting sows stretched out full length.

But the happiest times were those days in the spring when his father hitched Rob and Willy, the Percheron team, to the plow and Henry could skip alongside them feeling the deliciousness of the sun-warmed earth under his bare feet. The squeaky rubbing of the leather harness and the snorting of the great animals as they strained to pull the plow through the earth were sounds that he would always associate with his carefree boyhood. When the team reached the end of the field and Henry's father turned them around for the return trip, Henry would reach up to pat a sweating rump and rub his fingers in the white foam glistening on the gray and white hides. Their immense muscles were strong and pulling, and he felt awed at the strength in the enormous furry hooves as they were raised and lowered in perfect synchronization.

Always at the end of a day of plowing his father unhitched the horses and held their halters as they drank from a watering trough in long, slow draughts. Then, lifting Henry up high and placing him astride one of the huge sweating bodies, his father would ask, "How does the world look from up there, my boy?"

Henry would grasp the shaggy mane of the animal and hold on tightly, all the time his short legs hugging the warm body under him. "Oh, Pa, it's great! I can see clear to the end of the farm, all the way to the big elm tree."

He was not frightened at being so high above the ground.

13

There was nothing about these largest of all farm animals that provoked anything but a sense of security and happiness in the small lad. Had he ever stopped to think about it, there was nothing at all to be afraid of on the farm.

As the summer days and winter months went by and became the passing years, Henry learned everything that life on a farm in early 19th-century America could teach a youth. As he grew, so did his knowledge about horses of all kinds—riding and carriage and draft animals. He learned how to take care of them, the grooming with brush and curry comb, and the trimming of hooves, and he accompanied his father to the blacksmith's where the horseshoes were hammered out on the anvil. Breaking horses to the bit took hours of patience and steadfast love of the animals.

At age six he started to school, walking the four miles there and back with Si and Thad and carrying his sandwich wrapped in newspaper. Boys were needed for farm work in the spring so they attended school for only six months, leaving it in late February when the days began to grow noticeably longer and milder and the frozen ground turned to mud. Formal schooling stopped at the end of the eighth year when he was fourteen. Nobody continued beyond that year unless he was from a rich family that could afford private education. All the boys Henry knew came from farms and there was never any question but what eight years of schooling sufficed for young boys destined to become farmers.

When Henry learned to read he became fascinated with stories about early American history and explorers' adventures that piqued his interest in places he had never seen. His teacher loaned him books of her own which he read avidly in the long winter evenings before the fire. Often his mother put down her needlework and read with him, helping him with strange words. His teacher encouraged him to keep on reading even in the months when he was not in school and could avail himself of the books at the new library just established in the village. Miss Hannah Olsen, the librarian, took especial interest in youngsters who came to her for assistance in selecting books. Henry rode his pony, Flash, to the library regularly to bring books home, and Miss Hannah smiled watching him fasten them tightly with the leather strap to hold them securely in the saddle.

From the kitchen window Eliza Ann Sawyer watched her son returning from the library one evening, swinging the books as he walked along. Over the years as the boys were growing up, it had not been difficult for her to discern the differing attitudes of her three sons towards scholarship. Si and Thad were indifferent to school; there was no burning desire in either of them to prepare himself for any livelihood other than the ready-made one—the family farm. Secretly, in her heart she nourished a yearning that one of her sons would break the bonds the farm had on all of them. Years ago she had had a dream for herself while growing up in the aftermath of the Revolutionary War: she had wanted to become a teacher. But during that time in the country's history young girls were not permitted the luxury of dreams, and so she had married young and the dream had died. Perhaps there was a chance for Henry to have a dream and to follow it, "like reaching for a star," she thought. His love of books pleased her and inspired her to talk to him about his future.

"What would ye like to be when ye grow up?" she asked him when they were alone in the kitchen before supper.

Henry looked puzzled by her question. "What do ye mean, Ma? I'm going to be a farmer just like Pa, I guess."

"Well, that's fine if ye <u>want</u> to be a farmer," she answered, "but ye needn't be one if ye'd rather be somethin' else."

He looked at her strangely, thoughtfully. "What else <u>could</u> I be, Ma?" he asked.

"Ye could be <u>lots</u> of things," she said firmly. "Ye could study to be a doctor or even a teacher. Ye might even like to be President like General Washington," she added with a laugh. " 'Course, that would take a heap o' studyin' but at least ye have his name. That's a good start."

Henry gazed into the crackling fire in the fireplace and thought about what his mother had said. He saw cowboys and Indians leaping up in the flames, soldiers on horseback, sailing ships with captains, trains with engineers driving locomotives. It seemed as if the pages of a book were turning before his eyes. The world was opening up wide to him. Suddenly, he looked at his mother and said, "But, Ma, how would I do something like that? How would I start?"

She came to the fireside and sat beside him. "Well, first off, ye have to have a dream. That's the beginnin' and then ye have to follow it, and ye can't let <u>anythin'</u> get in the way of it. That's the hardest part. Things always seem to get in the way of dreams," her voice trailed off wistfully. They sat together awhile longer, each deep in thought, staring into the fire. "Try to find your dream, Henry, and steer your ship right for it. Don't give up. I'll help ye all I can," she finished, with a pat on his back.

Henry assumed more and more responsibilities for the farm work as he grew older and stronger into his teens. He fed the horses and cows, cleaned their stalls, pitched manure out the barn door to the rising manure pile, forked fresh straw into the stalls. On cold winter mornings it was dark when he pulled on his overalls and walked through the snow to the barn to milk the cows and carry the pails of foaming milk back to his mother in the kitchen. Often when he was seated on the milking stool with his head resting against the warm flank of the cow, he would think about the book he had read the night before and wonder if he would ever be so fortunate as to travel to those faraway parts of the world. Should a Pennsylvania farm boy even <u>want</u> to do such a thing? Perhaps this was the dream his mother had spoken of.

Springtime brought long days of sowing and planting. Lambing time was in March and sheep-shearing followed in May. The family vegetable garden near the kitchen was Henry's special responsibility. In the late spring he pushed the hand cultivator through the clods of earth, then followed it with a hoe to prepare the soil for planting. He dug individual holes for planting beans, covering the seeds with soil he pushed in with his bare feet. Once when he was planting beans he began a mental tabulation of how many holes he had dug in his life already and how many he would dig if he lived to be sixty years old, and when the sum came to over 3000 holes he leaned on the hoe and gave a long sigh, "Do I <u>want</u> to dig 3000 holes?"

All through the hot summer he weeded the plants as they pushed through the ground, hoed the rows and watered them by hand with a sprinkling can. While thinning carrots on his hands and knees one day, he counted the little wisps of green shoots which he had pulled from one row and discarded. There were more than 500. It was tedious work and took a long time to get to the end of the row. Sitting on the ground and looking back at the row he had just finished, he wiped his brow and said aloud, "Guess this must be why I don't like carrots!"

In the winter months when farm work was slack he learned how to build and repair things. Under his father's instruction he learned how to swing an ax and to fell a tree, and from his father also he learned about the great variety of trees and how to choose the right wood for carpentry jobs. There was much he needed to know about tools of all kinds: how to sharpen a saw correctly so the shape and slant of the teeth produced a clean sweep gliding easily through the timber, how to plane wood straight, how to use a hammer properly to avoid missing the nail and leaving an indentation of the hammer in the wood, and how to handle a chisel. When a stonemason came to the farm to build the milk house, Henry watched how he laid the foundation of field stone. Repairing gates on the farm was an annual chore requiring considerable skill, and there were many gates for many pastures.

Gradually, in his teenage years Henry began to be aware of his liking for building and making things with his hands. Nothing on the farm interested him quite as much as using tools with good-smelling timber. There was variety in this work and he took pleasure in creating things that were useful and beautifully crafted. Absent were the monotony and drudgery of the day-to-day farm work he had been caught up in all his life. This discovery about himself worried him not a little because there seemed to be an unspoken assumption in his family that he and Si and Thad would all remain on the farm together for the rest of their lives. At least, it was his <u>father's</u> wish, of that he was certain.

*   *   *

And now it was February 1848 with his life on the farm stretching out before him, year after year the same as those that had passed. Henry rolled over in his bed and looked at the moon-

17

light. In a few months he would be nineteen. He must not put off talking to his father any longer. He would speak to him soon. This spring, in fact.

And, with that decision arrived at, sleep closed his eyes.

3

The next morning Henry's father announced that a trip to Lancaster was in the offing for any of the boys who wanted to go along. Farm work was slack in February making it the appropriate time for his annual trip to the thriving market town with its shops and businesses attracting visitors from miles around.

Since the travelers would be gone two days, Thad elected to stay at home with his mother and do the farm chores. His father would take the team and wagon. Henry's mother packed them a

basket of food to see them through the journey, and the three set off in the bright sunshine tucked inside warm coats and wool caps to ward off the wind chill. Henry's father drove the team from his seat at the front of the wagon while Si and Henry shared their space at the back with two Holstein bull calves born that winter.

As the wagon jolted along the lane, the boys settled down deeply in the soft straw. "What're ye aimin' to buy, Pa?" Si asked.

"Mostly tools," he called back from the front of the wagon. "And some iron ware. We need nails and a new hammer. I want one with a long adz-eye that holds the head firm and the handle doesn't splinter when you pull nails. Need hinges for fixing the pasture gates and a sliding bolt for the barn door. Some hasps and hooks. 'Reckon I'll just drop in at Jeremiah Johnson's to have a look 'round. He's sure to have all the new-fangled inventions."

The wagon creaked along through the Lancaster County rolling farmland, by pastures and woodlands covered with snow.

There was little activity around any of the farm buildings, only barnyards where stood horses with heavy, furry winter coats warming themselves in the sunshine, their breath steaming in the cold air, and piles of manure that had grown high during the winter cleaning of stalls waiting to be spread on the fields in the spring.

Long before they reached the outskirts of Lancaster the spire of Trinity Church could be seen silhouetted against the sky. The road followed the winding Conestoga River for a time and then left it at the foot of the gentle hill on which the town was situated. That afternoon the approach was crowded with carts and traps and wagons of all descriptions jostling pigs, cows, horses, sheep and goats on their way to the big livestock pens. It was a noisy procession with bleats of the animals combining with the squeaking of wheels. The wagon groaned its way laboriously up the hill as they followed the lead wagon toward the central open square.

From his place in the wagon Henry watched the buildings passing by: red brick houses and buildings of gray stone, taverns with colorful signs swinging before their doors. Riding slowly by the "Sign of the Red Lion" Henry could hear the loud laughter from within blending with the smell of ale. Farther up the hill were "The Bull's Head" and "The Sign of General Washington," and between the two taverns were a tinsmith and a coppersmith where a good deal of loud tapping-on-metal could be heard. A tailor's shop displayed a fine black suit in the window, which prompted Henry to point and say to Si, "Looks like something you'd wear to a funeral, right?" Next was a watchmaker's establishment where a huge clock with a pendulum chimed the hours. They were conscious of the pungent fragrance of leather issuing from a saddler's shop. A few horses were hitched at the hitching post near the entrance. Henry studied them carefully and felt a rush of pride at the superiority of his own Beauty at home in the barn.

They rode by the imposing buildings holding the Lancaster County Bank and the Lancaster Savings Institution and Henry called Si's attention to the English names of the streets: King Street and Queen Street and Prince Street and Duke Street. Their eyes boggled at the array of business establishments, one after another: printers, bookstores, druggists, gunsmiths, cabinetmakers, physicians, confectioneries, tobacconists, coachmakers and oystermen. There was everything here that anyone could want. Henry felt the exhilarating vitality of the town. It was pulsing with life. So much color, so many people and so much energy in the air. His senses were titillated to the breaking point. Sitting up tall in the wagon he stretched his neck up high so as not to miss any of the sights passing by. There was an exuberance about the scene that filled him with excitement and fueled the plans for his future that were ever churning inside him.

Henry's father turned the horses into North Queen Street where the railroad station loomed up. A shiny new locomotive stood on the tracks, steam belching from its stack. Nearby was Michael McGrann's White Horse Hotel with its sign reading: "Rest and Refreshment. All Travelers Welcome."

At the open market square, the bull calves were unloaded and Henry's father led them away by their halters to be sold, leaving Si and Henry free to go about the town on foot. They strolled slowly up one side of North Queen Street looking into all of the shop windows until they came to the Lancaster Court House, pausing there to look up at the bell tower and the dome.

Nearby was a confectionery and cake bakery. The two boys looked into the window longingly, appraising the candies and frosted cakes. Never having set foot in such a place before, they hesitated momentarily before entering, wiping their boots off before stepping inside.

"What would ye like?" the pretty girl behind the counter queried as the two boys approached rather self-consciously. Her blond curls were held neatly with a plaid ribbon and her cheeks were the color of Eliza Ann Sawyer's pale pink sweetpeas, Henry thought.

21

"What have ye got for five cents?" Si asked, a little embarrassed at revealing the small sum in his pocket.

Her smile put him at ease. "Oh, lots of things. There are these white cakes with lemon icing, raisin buns with sugar icing, apple tarts with raisins and walnuts, buttermilk biscuits and . . ."

"I'll have one of the apple tarts," he interrupted her lengthy spiel which showed signs of just getting underway.

"And you?" she addressed Henry.

"A tart for me too," he replied, smiling shyly.

The boys paid their five cents each and took their purchases in hand.

"This your first visit to Lancaster?" the girl asked with a smile of bewitching radiance that showed her fine white teeth.

"The first in a long time," Si answered a little bashfully, her prettiness overwhelming him. "We're just here while my father sells some livestock. Got to go home t'morrow. Too bad, too. There's lots to see here." He lifted his cap slightly as they turned to go.

"If ye haven't anythin' special to do this evenin' there's a lecture at the Lutheran Church hall," the girl called after them. "And there's a social hour afterwards. It's free," she added with a knowing smile.

"Thanks," the boys responded together. "We might just do that."

Crossing the street with caution to avoid the mud-splashing wagons, they wended their way down the other side of North Queen Street. Nothing missed their keen inspection. There were hardware stores displaying 9-plate stoves for wood and coal, plow plates, single and double-barreled shotguns, and fine window glass. A cabinetmaker was selling sideboards, marble-topped washstands, hat and umbrella stands, and coffins. They stared long and hard at enormous threshing machines made to be powered by one, two, three or four horses. A bootmaker was selling children's boots from 37 1/2 cents to $1.12. They looked in on a brushmaker and the grocery and liquor store that advertised its willingness to barter its goods for country produce.

Turning a corner they found themselves looking up at a

plaque designating the office of Senator James Buchanan. Loud talking and bawdy laughter came through the open door of the Leopard Tavern, but all was quiet at Markley's Temperance House. At the butcher's establishment whole carcasses of animals hung from hooks. From the background came telling squeals and throaty protests. They were fascinated by the display of scythes and grain cradles for sale in the hardware store. Next came a ropemaker and a jackscrew maker. The smell of the saddlery filled their nostrils, and Henry lingered long over the variety of bridles, martingales and full accouterments for horses.

They walked by the General News and Publication Office which had a magazine for sale entitled *American Phrenological Journal.* Si, curious to know what that was all about, turned the pages. Skulls and more skulls.

Religious books and hymn books were on view, and the works of Shakespeare could be had for twenty-five cents. Henry bought a James Fenimore Cooper story for his mother.

At the printing establishment of the *Lancaster Examiner and Herald* and the *Lancaster Union and Republican Sentinel* they bought a copy of the *Workingmen's Press* and for their father a German language paper called *Der Volksfreund.* From a German immigrant family, he had spoken German as a young boy and even now he occasionally lapsed into the language when he needed to express something precisely.

A gunsmith shop caught their attention. Never before had they fingered a Leman rifle or seen the Leman northwest Indian guns, dueling pistols and shotguns. The yeasty odor emerging from a nearby brewery assailed their nostrils as they looked in at the door of a coachmaker where the noise of metal being pounded greeted their ears.

The streets were thronged with people hurrying in every direction, pulling their wool collars up around their necks to ward off the February chill. Snow and mud mixed to a slush underfoot, and horses and carriages driving through it splashed pedestrians mercilessly. Si and Henry leaned up against the wall of the Farmers' Bank of Lancaster to watch the world passing by. Farm-reared, they had acquired at an early age a keen sensitivity to their surroundings. Their awareness of differences was sharp. Here, before them, was a kaleidoscope of sounds and sights and smells. For a few moments they savored the scene, their bodies responding to the energy electrifying the air.

They moved on shortly to a cabinet and chair manufactory. An ornate French bedstead provoked Henry to comment, "Ma would sure like that."

"And Pa would like that," added Si pointing at a rocking chair.

The drug store displayed bottles of horse embrocation, sperm oil, and perfumes alongside candles, fishing tackle, paints and shoe soles. Henry read the label on the horse liniment carefully.

Nearing the Eastern Hotel the youths heard strains of music, and as the door opened emitting a noisy group of revelers from within, they took advantage of the chance to slip inside. It was warm and brightly lit and cheerful in the lobby; it felt good to be out of the cold. In one corner a garishly dressed woman of ample proportions was playing an organ. They had neither seen nor heard an organ, and they stood completely transfixed by the instrument and its music. Their gaze came to rest on the woman herself. They stared at the rings on her fingers as they glided over the keys, at the baubles swinging from her ears and at the glittering combs holding her auburn locks in place. A feather wound its way around one ear and encircled her head. Her smooth silk dress fitting tightly over her bountiful bosom shone with black sequins, and even her feet were adorned with colored beads sparkling on the tiny buckles of her velvet shoes. The music that she was calling forth from the massive instrument reverberated through the lobby to its high ceilings, drowning out the chatter and laughter of the visitors thronging the room. Henry's eyes were glazed in wonderment and Si's jaw was ajar as they stood mesmerized by the organ's tremendous volume and tones sending shivers down their spines.

The organist turned momentarily to look at them, smiling rather coquettishly as she launched forth with a rendition of the favorite "Columbia the Gem of the Ocean," gilding it with an infectious swing. The two youthful visitors had never heard a performance quite like this before and were obviously impressed by the entertainer herself who, relishing the delightful naiveté of the farm lads, gave out with her best efforts, lifting her hands high off the keys with a flourish, all the better to display the flash of bejeweled fingers.

"What's that stuff all around her eyes?" Henry queried Si.

"Paint, I guess," was the reply.

"<u>Real</u> paint?" Henry pursued. "Like the stuff on the barn?"

"No, of course not <u>real</u> paint! But paint for faces, like actresses use to make them look pretty."

Henry continued to study her face. "Does it wash off?"

"I don't know. I s'pose so."

Henry took a last look at the woman, and as he turned away slowly she gave him a wink with one of the blue eyes encircled with the black make-up. A slight chuckle came forth quite spontaneously from him.

In a rack on the lobby wall were displayed the advertisements of local shopkeepers and town events. One such poster featured a drawing of the entertainer who had just performed for them. "Belle" was her name and the drawing portrayed her physical attractiveness with exaggerated brush strokes.

"Look, Si!" exclaimed Henry pointing at the picture. "Let's take it home to Thad. Just to show him what he missed by staying home!" he added with a mischievous twinkle in his eye as he put the drawing of Belle into his pocket.

Outside again in the chilly afternoon, the boys pulled their caps down and their collars up as they gazed at some containers in a drug and dental establishment window: Stainburns Vegetable Extract and Oakley's Depurative Syrup and Wild Cherry Balsam. The proprietors claimed they could perform operations on artificial teeth and insert artificial eyes. They also sold horse and cattle powders.

It was almost dark when the boys met their father at Jeremiah Johnson's carpentry shop where they found him examining tools. He was deeply absorbed in inspecting a new tool—a double-bitted ax. "Look, boys," he said, running his hand along the straight wooden handle to the blades on either side of it at the end. "Just invented. <u>Two bits.</u> When one goes dull you just turn the handle over and use the one on the other side. When you're working in the woods you don't have to stop and sharpen the bit in the middle of the job."

Henry was struck by the design of the ax. "Pa, that would save a lot of time, wouldn't it? The job'd go much faster if we didn't have to sharpen bits until the end of the day. That inventor must be a lumberman himself. He really knows the problem a man faces when he's out felling trees all day."

His father was deep in thought. "Yes, Henry, he was a smart one all right. I think we ought to have one of these on the farm. It'd be good to have somethin' that's brand new in the country."

After further consideration and serious discussion of the merits of the new ax, the important purchase was made and they wended their way back to the wagon where the three hungry travelers opened the basket of food that Eliza Ann Sawyer had packed for them.

"How'd you like to go to a lecture, Pa?" Si ventured when the food had been eaten. "There's one at the Lutheran Church social hall tonight."

"How'd you hear about that?" his father wanted to know.

"Oh," Si answered with attempted nonchalance that did not escape his father's notice, "we stopped in at a confectionery shop and the girl there told us about it."

"Oh, I *see*," responded his father. "Will she be there, I wonder?"

The crimson flush across Si's face amused his father. "Well, I reckon we'd better look in at the social hall then. I haven't heard a good lecture in I don't know how many years."

The Lutheran Church was brightly lit when the three visitors walked up the steps. Gathered inside were all kinds of folk: farmers in muddy boots, local merchants, smiling politicians with grandiose gestures flinging their arms around members of the local populace, and women holding their cloaks tightly around them. The seats were filled so the three stood at the back of the hall.

Seated on the dais was the Mayor of Lancaster, and next to him was a Negro lady. The buzz of conversation throughout the hall softened when the Mayor rose and held up one hand to the audience. "Ladies and gentlemen of Lancaster City and County and all visitors from our glorious State of Pennsylvania," he began with sweeping grandeur. "I extend to all of you assembled here a warm welcome. Tonight the City of Lancaster is indeed honored by the presence of a lady who comes to us from the city of Philadelphia to enlighten us about the work of the Philadelphia Female Anti-Slavery Society." There was a muffled undertone throughout the hall, private commentaries on the information just offered.

When the speaker of the evening rose, all became quiet once again. "Thank you, your honor, for your interest in this great cause which enables me to speak to the people of Lancaster this evening," she began.

Henry and Si had never seen a person of color. There was none in the farm country where they lived and the opportunity to mix with people outside the farming community was almost non-existent. They were engrossed in studying the speaker and listening to her message.

"The state of Pennsylvania has a proud history in upholding human rights. From the time of our country's conception Pennsylvania has been the leader in fighting for freedom. In 1780 the state's assembly abolished slavery and repealed discriminatory codes. Emancipation of slaves within our state has come gradually and we can say that slavery has been virtually abolished.

"But slavery outside our state's boundaries continues to oppress thousands of folk who fell under its cruelty only through circumstances of Fate—the accident of their forefathers' birth in another continent, the color of their skin, and human greed that has preyed on them.

"Hatred is growing in our land. Hatred and violence. As a free state bordering slave states, Pennsylvania has become a haven for fugitive slaves who, by their courage and through physical hardships, have sought asylum within our boundaries. Fugitive slaves are hunted down like animals. They need our help and our protection. We must stand together for right. We must unite in our refusal to return them to their bestial owners.

"The Philadelphia Female Anti-Slavery Society supports the work begun long ago by the Quakers who founded the Pennsylvania Abolition Society to aid the Negro community and to promote abolition of slavery. The Underground Railroad needs your help. Southeastern Pennsylvania and this beautiful valley of the Susquehanna offer hope to colored folk who want only a stopping place on their way to freedom in Canada. They ask only for a safe place to hide, a shelter from their pursuers who hunt them with dogs and wreak vengeance on them if captured."

The speaker's plea set Henry to thinking. After the lecture he asked his father: "What is this Underground Railroad, Pa? Have you ever seen it?"

"No, son. It's not right out in the open for folks to look at. It's just like the speaker said: it's hiding places for Negroes escaping from southern slaveholders. Most of them are trying to get to Canada where they'd be safe from their masters." He was silent for a moment while Henry pondered his explanation. "Ye see, there's a feeling in the southern states that anyone who captures a runaway slave is bound by law to return him to his master because it is considered a return of property."

Henry thought long and hard. "Seems to me like that's unfair. The way I see it," he said, "if a man goes to all that trouble to run away—just to be free—he oughta be given the chance. It'd be a dirty trick taking him all the way back to a man who's going to treat him meaner than ever because he tried to escape."

His father gave him a firm slap on the back which seemed to Henry to be an endorsement of his own feelings.

They turned to see Si talking to a pretty girl with blond curls held by a bow of ribbon. "Si has found a friend," was Henry's father's dry comment. "The confectionery shopkeeper, perhaps?"

Henry nodded. As they watched, another girl joined the couple.

"Probably her younger sister," his father said, gently nudging Henry in the direction of the young people. "I'll meet ye both back at the wagon," he added and left the hall.

Later that night as the three travelers bedded down on the straw in the wagon, Henry had much to think about. Memories of everything he had seen and heard that day whirled around in his head, all mixed up with the talk by the lady from Philadelphia. He did not want to fall asleep right away; he enjoyed the time for reflection and savored all the experiences the day had brought.

Looking up at the black sky filled with stars, he was supremely happy that he had made the decision to embark on an adventure when spring arrived.

4

With the coming of warm weather and the longer days of spring, Henry knew it was time for him to be on the move. It was mid-May and he was restless. He had hesitated long enough, he reasoned with himself, about bringing up the subject of the newspaper advertisement with his father. He was going to do it today—on his nineteenth birthday.

First, he would talk it over with Beauty. As he groomed the white mane and pulled out a handful of prickly burrs, he proposed the idea: "Beauty, how'd you like to go live near the ocean? It's a long ways from here. Probably 'bout 150 miles. A long walk, fella." He slid the curry comb along the smooth back and down the warm flank, then lifted each hoof to examine the shoe. "You're in fine condition," he said proudly with a resounding slap on the rump.

At that moment Henry's father was standing with his foot on a rail of the barnyard fence, sucking a long piece of sweet grass as he looked out over the green fields of his farm. Henry came up to him, drew a deep breath and blurted out, "Pa, I think I'd like to become a carpenter. There's a builder in New Jersey who's lookin' for apprentices to build houses in a place called Cape Island. A resort town. I reckon it'd be a good place to start." He paused momentarily before adding, "I've been thinkin' about this for a long time, Pa."

His father continued to look out over the farm for some time before replying: "You can be a carpenter right here in Pennsylvania—if you want to be a carpenter, that is." He paused a moment before asking what Henry knew was the inevitable question: "Why don't you want to stay here on the farm with your brothers? There's a good life waiting here for you for sure."

Henry shuffled his feet. "Pa, farming's O.K. for Si and Thad. Their hearts are right here on these 200 acres. But I," he hesitated before trying to explain, "I want somethin' . . . somethin' different. I've never been anywhere 'cept on this farm, and I'm itchin' to have a look 'round some place new."

His father stared at him thoughtfully. "Well, son, that New Jersey place sure would be new. Nothin' like eastern Pennsylvania, I'll betcha. A long ways to go to find a job." He stopped, buried in his thoughts. "We'd sure miss you on the farm."

"Si and Thad are good farmers, Pa. The best. They'll get along O.K."

"New Jersey is a long ways from your mother too, son. She'll miss you sorely—you bein' her youngest and all that." He waited a moment before adding, "And her favorite."

There was a brief silence between them before his father asked, "When are you aimin' to leave?"

"I reckon I ought to be off right soon, Pa. The buildin' season ought to be goin' strong 'bout now. The weather's fine. I'll start in a day or two, I guess."

"You'll be takin' your horse?"

"Yes, Pa. He's in fine shape. Good and strong. Hooves firm."

And so, on a bright morning in May 1848, Henry packed a saddle bag with his clothes, a little money his mother had given him, a long rope halter, brushes and curry comb, and a canteen of lemonade. His mother filled a haversack with food, including some special baked goods she had made for his journey. When he came into the kitchen for the last time she looked up at him with a brave smile. "Be sure to write to us and tell us how ye're farin'. Ye've grown up awful fast. It seems like it was only yesterday ye were a little lad playin' with the orphan lambs." Henry put his arm around her shoulder and together they walked out to the barn.

"Ready, Beauty?" he greeted his horse brightly in a bold attempt to cover up his own feelings of uncertainty at leaving home. He laid the red saddle blanket on Beauty that his mother had made for him one Christmas, hoisted the saddle on top of it and tightened the girth. Leading the horse out of the barn, he stopped by the watering trough to give him one last drink. His father and brothers helped him tie the saddle bag and his bed roll to the saddle, and then stepped back as Henry mounted.

They were quiet and undemonstrative as they said goodbye. His father made a pretense of checking the saddle girth again and when he had tightened it one more notch he looked up at Henry and said, "Remember, if things don't go well for you, son, you can always come home. Good luck, boy."

"Thanks, Pa."

Si reached into his overalls pocket and drew out a jackknife which he pressed awkwardly into Henry's hand. "This may come in handy," he said, a trifle embarrassed at his own show of affection.

Thad approached with something in his hand as well. "This'll tell you which way you're goin'," he laughed a little self-consciously. "You can't depend on ole Beauty knowin' where New Jersey is." Henry reached down and took a compass from Thad's hand. He admired both gifts and slid them into his saddle bag pocket.

"Thanks. Thanks a lot," was all he could say when an inexplicable shyness swept over him. He was overcome with an urgent need to be on his way and not to prolong the farewells to his family.

The road from the farm led eastward to the Bethlehem Pike, a dirt road just wide enough for a horse and wagon. Henry loosed the reins and gave Beauty his head. Sensing his rider's excitement, the horse started out at a fast gait, tail swishing and neck bobbing up and down. Henry smoothed out the snow white mane and rubbed the warm neck. "Yippee, Beauty!" he exclaimed. "Can you believe it? We're on our way. You're actin' like you're as keen as I am. Now, don't you be too eager and tire yourself out the first mile 'cause we've got a long ways to go. You gotta take it nice and easy, boy. There's no rush. Nobody is waitin' on us."

Henry was aware of his own exhilaration. He felt strong and sat up tall and straight in the saddle breathing deeply the fresh spring air heavy with the fragrance of apple blossoms. The sun was warm on his face and he rolled up his sleeves.

"Beauty, boy, just think. We're startin' out on a big adventure. Just you and I together. It's like we're beginnin' a new life. Today is the first day. It's like we're writin' a story and this is the first page. And what'll happen on all the pages comin' up, who knows? Isn't it excitin' just to be alive?" Henry patted the heaving rump and brushed away a fly. In answer to Henry's voice, Beauty quickened his step and trotted a few paces.

On both sides of the road were acres of low green tobacco plants spreading their leaves over the dark earth. They were not alone on the road. Two horses pulling a wagon piled high with manure passed them. The man driving the team was a neighboring farmer and he hailed Henry as he went by. Henry reflected that spreading manure in the spring was one job on the farm he would definitely <u>not</u> miss. Along came six Guernsey cows stretched across the road being herded by a frisky collie and a boy brandishing a stick over their golden backs. Behind the cows was a cart bearing four fat lambs and being pulled by a mule. The wool stuck out through the slats of the cart. Following closely was another cart filled with straw on top of which lay an enormous grunting sow. The boy riding the horse pulling the pig cart waved to Henry. He lived on a nearby farm where Henry had helped with haying every summer.

He stroked Beauty's neck. "No more haymakin' and no more spreadin' manure, for awhile anyway. There's plenty I've got to learn, though, before I can earn a livin' for both of us."

As the sun rose high in the sky, they stopped beside a stream for a long cool drink and to rest. Sitting on the grass, Henry ate his bread and cheese and his mother's cakes while Beauty grazed on succulent green shoots at the edge of the stream. By evening they had ridden about twenty miles. That was what the farmer estimated when Henry rode up to a big barn a short distance off the road to ask if they might bed down there for the night. "Where you headin'?" the farmer wanted to know, studying them closely.

"New Jersey."

"You got a far piece to go. A good horse you got there. Young?"

"About four. Had him since he was a colt. Broke him myself."

The farmer pointed to an empty stall. "You can bed him down there. Water's 'round to the side," he added, turning to walk to the farmhouse.

Henry pulled off the saddle and blanket, led Beauty to the watering trough and watched him drink long, deep draughts. Then, bringing him back to the empty stall, he slipped the bridle over his head and patted his neck. "Now you cool down and take it easy," he said while lifting each hoof and examining it closely.

He sat down on a wagon in the open barn door looking out over the hills as the sun set. From his haversack he took some more bread and meat his mother had packed for him, and he found some apple pie wrapped up in the bottom. That made him smile. His mother knew how much he liked apple pie. He thought about his mother just then and wondered if she was worrying about him. Because he was the youngest of the boys Henry had always felt a special love from his mother. It showed up in countless ways. Take the saddle blanket, for instance. The day Beauty was born on the farm and was pronounced "his," Henry's mother had said: "He'll grow up white as snow and he should have a red blanket." On winter evenings she sewed on the blanket by the light of the oil lamp and the log fire. With black thread she embroidered BEAUTY in large letters on the scarlet wool background, and above his name was the figure of a white horse carefully stitched. Along one edge of the blanket she sewed the name in black letters HENRY WASHINGTON SAWYER, OWNER. The gift, made by her own hands and especially to please him, had filled him with pride. He had tacked it on the wall above his bed in the room he shared with Si and Thad. Now he hung the blanket over the door of the stall to dry.

Henry reached down into the saddle bag to bring out the gifts from his brothers. He examined the jack-knife, opening and shutting it several times and running his finger along the shiny steel blades so sharp and new looking. He played with the compass, fascinated by the needle as it turned and wobbled and came to rest. Henry slipped it in and out of the soft case which protected the glass. He stowed the gifts away carefully in the bottom of the saddle bag, undid his bed roll and stretched it out on a pile of hay near Beauty's stall.

Lying on his back with his hands clasped under his head, Henry thought about his brothers and the years they had all grown up together. Si and Thad had been almost like twins, so near in age were they. Now, at twenty and twenty-one, they were dedicated farmers. There had never been any doubt, it seemed to Henry, that they would remain on the farm all their lives. They were strong and muscular and liked the seasonal farm labor, always ready for the plowing and cultivating, the corn planting and the grain threshing. They were capable of hours of hard work, day after day, without growing tired of the monotony and the drudgery of their daily lives. Henry reasoned that it was only a matter of time before both of his brothers would marry and "settle down."

Well, he was only nineteen and he thought differently about a lot of things. Maybe someday he too would come back to the farm and marry and live there forever after, but before that he was going to see something of the world.

The following morning he was saddling Beauty when the farmer came down the path from his house. "Are you aimin' to ride the whole way to New Jersey?" he asked.

"Yes'm. I 'spect to ride about twenty miles a day."

"I hear there's a ferry over on the Schuylkill. That'd make the trip faster—that is, if you're hurryin'."

Henry was adjusting the stirrup and he turned to the farmer. "No, we're not hurryin' but thanks for tellin' me about the ferry. We might look into it. How far is the river from here?"

"Oh, 'bout twenty miles, I'd say. You'd turn southwest at Hopkins Corners. The road'd take you right to the landing."

"Any idea how much it'd cost?"

The farmer thought hard as he looked down at the ground. "One man and one horse. Well," he drawled, "I reckon a few dollars. Depends how far down river you go." He paused, looking at Beauty. "How d'you figure he'd take to travelin' on the water?"

Henry patted Beauty's neck. "I think he'd be O.K. Somethin' new for him. New for me, too," he added with a smile.

The day grew brighter and warmer as they rode and when they came to the crossroads, Henry dismounted and tied the reins to a hitching post outside a small shop. Inside he bought candies for himself and some apples and large carrots to share with Beauty. Outside he filled his canteen at the pump and watered Beauty at the watering trough.

Sitting on a bench in the shade was an old codger who impressed Henry as someone who might be knowledgeable about the countryside. "Howdy," Henry greeted him. "Is this the way to the Schuylkill ferry?" He pointed down the road.

"Shore is," drawled the man. "Down there about ten miles. You aimin' to ride it?"

"Maybe," answered Henry.

"Wahl, it don't go every day," the man continued. "Only when there's a load o' logs for Philadelphia. You might hafta wait a day or two."

"That'd be O.K.," Henry replied. "Much obliged to you."

He offered a carrot and an apple to Beauty who crunched them noisily. Swinging up into the saddle, Henry talked to the animal in a confidential tone. "Well, boy, what d'you say? Shall we try the ferry? D'you think you'd like ridin' on the river? It might be bumpy at times. It'd give us a good look at the countryside without doin' any work! How'd you like travelin' all those miles and never movin' a foot? Sure would be a different way to get where we're goin'. Shall we go for the adventure?" He patted Beauty's neck and the horse quickened his step as if in agreement with the proposal.

Twilight found them on the banks of the Schuylkill at the ferry landing. There was no ferry in sight. Nor were there any people or houses. The whole river scene was quiet and deserted. Woods came to the edge of the river on both banks. There were no lights or signs of human habitation.

Henry dismounted and led Beauty to the river's edge for a long drink. The animal started at the sight of his own reflection in the glassy surface. "How'd you like a swim?" he laughed, pulling off the saddle and blanket. He took the horse's reins and walked cautiously into the river, slowly feeling for his footing. Beauty held back. "C'mon," Henry cajoled him. "Cool off in this nice water. Come, boy." He tugged gently at the reins. Very slowly Beauty ventured forth, stepping gingerly out into the water away from the safety of the riverbank. When the river reached his belly, he flopped down and began to swim, splashing noisily. Henry laughed. "I've never seen you swim before. Isn't this the life? Who'd have thought you and I'd be swimmin' in a big river only two days away from home? This sure beats takin' a bath the old way."

Together they splashed and swam around in circles, Henry holding the reins at full length. "This is a good way to wash clothes, too," he chuckled, jumping up and down vigorously in the water. "But, of course, you don't need to worry about that!" His laughter and shouts carried across the river breaking the profound silence of the scene.

When they emerged from the river Beauty shook himself like a wet dog, and Henry rubbed him down. He let him graze in the sweet grass along the bank of the river while he rolled out his bed roll, fished out some bread and cheese from the depths of the haversack and drank from his canteen. As darkness descended he took the bridle off Beauty and tied him with the halter to a nearby tree.

"Sure is peaceful, isn't it, boy?" Henry sighed as he lay back on his bed roll and looked up at the night sky. "Aren't we havin' the best adventure any lad with a horse ever had?"

As he closed his eyes and breathed the cool night air, Henry heard two bullfrogs having a conversation in the river. He wondered what they were saying to each other about the swimmers who had just left their river. That the two unseen observers were discussing the antics of a swimming horse Henry was certain. These two days had been good ones, and tomorrow? Tomorrow was tomorrow. All the days stretched ahead pleasantly as far as he could see. Each one would bring its unexpected adventure. He went to sleep thinking about his good fortune.

The next day no ferry appeared on the river. Henry saddled Beauty and rode back the way they'd come, stopping at a farm a few miles down the road. He rode up to a barn where he found a farmer about to shear some sheep. "Need a hand there?" Henry called to him. "I'm waitin' on the ferry, I could do a day's work."

The farmer was agreeable to the offer of help. "You come from around here?" he wanted to know, eyeing Beauty with interest.

"Near Allentown. My father's farm," Henry reassured him. "We just did our shearin' last week."

The farmer looked satisfied and pointed to an empty stall in the barn. "You can leave your horse in there for the day."

Sheep shearing was a job that called for strong arms to hold the animal while the thick wool was cut. It was hot work, too. The sheep strained and balked at the clippers. By noon a flock of thirty ewes stood in the pen, completely shorn of their fleece. The farmer took Henry into his house for the noonday meal. It was the first hot food he had eaten since leaving home and it tasted good. There was fried chicken, biscuits with gravy, potatoes, and apple pie with cheese. The meal was served by the farmer's wife and his daughter who looked about Henry's age. Back home he never thought much about girls. He didn't know many his age and hardly ever had a chance to talk to one. The farmer's daughter looked at him rather shyly as she put the plate of food in front of him, and Henry thought she was rather pretty, especially her warm brown eyes.

"Where are you headed?" the farmer asked him.

"New Jersey. Cape Island, to be exact. I'm aimin' to be a carpenter."

"Been there b'fore?"

"No. I 'spect to apprentice to a carpenter there. I hear there's lots o' buildin' goin' on. A big resort."

"I been told the state is more south than north. Slaves there too. Different from Pennsylvania," he said. "Folks in the south have different ideas about things, I guess." He paused, seeming to wait for a response from Henry, then continued: "You 'spectin' to ride the ferry down the Schuylkill to the city?"

"Yes. How often does it come by the landin'?"

"Every three or four days. Probably tomorrow. Mostly logs for the city." He pushed back his chair from the table. "I'm plantin' corn this afternoon. Have a new planter. Have you seen one?"

Henry shook his head and said that he'd be glad for the chance to see one at work. He thanked the farmer's wife for the meal and smiled at the young girl who watched him as he followed her father out of the house.

The new corn planter had two seats close to the ground. A team of horses pulled it, and two people riding in the seats alternately slipped shelled corn into the furrow which was quickly covered by earth. Henry sat in one seat and the farmer was next to him. Each planting received a cup of water from a tank carried on the planter. Henry thought the new invention was splendid the way it could plant a whole field with such speed and efficiency. He thought of the years he had planted corn by hand with his father and Si and Thad, just one of many back-breaking jobs on a farm.

Back at the barn at the end of the afternoon the farmer's daughter stood in the doorway with a pitcher of lemonade and two glasses. The two workers wiped the sweat from their foreheads and climbed out of their seats on the corn planter.

"Thanks, Melindy. Nothin' like cold lemonade after a day plantin'," her father said.

Henry thanked her too. When she smiled he looked down at the ground. "You sure have a pretty horse," she began timidly.

Henry looked up then and felt at ease with her. "Want to ride him? He's smart and very quiet."

Overcome with shyness, Melindy flushed.

"Come on," he urged, leading Beauty out of the stall. "I'll hold him for you."

She approached a little fearfully and lifted her left foot to the stirrup. As he helped boost her into the saddle, he realized it was the first time in his life he had ever touched a girl's body. Melindy's was warm and soft and the feel of it sent a pleasant sensation through his frame.

While leading Beauty by the reins around the farm buildings, he allowed his thoughts to dwell on the whole subject of girls and how little he knew about them. He recalled how he felt with the salesgirl in the Lancaster confectionery. It was the same now with Melindy. He felt at a loss to know how to talk to a girl. He was awkward, all hands and feet, and tongue-tied when he was face to face with one and needed to say something. Exasperated with himself, he kicked at the powdery dirt in the farmyard.

The sun was low in the sky and he was about to leave for the river when Melindy's father offered some oats to Beauty. Henry thanked him and rode out onto the road. When he had gone only a short distance, he turned to look back. "Good luck," the farmer called and Melindy waved her hand.

The following morning when the ferry glided alongside the landing with its load of logs, Henry proposed to the ferryman that he and Beauty would ride it down to the city. There was just room for them both; he sat on top of the logs and held Beauty's reins up short, steadying him.

At the end of two days, they reached Philadelphia and, on firm land once again, Henry asked for directions to the pike and they continued on their way to New Jersey.

5

Beauty paused on the bridge to look out at the ocean. Raising his handsome head, he shook it and snorted. Henry patted his thick mane while they gazed out across the expanse of sun-lit waves to the horizon. It was early June and seagulls were dipping in and out of the breakers, riding them with an easy nonchalance, and smaller birds were pecking in the sand where the rollers broke on the shore.

The horse raised his head repeatedly, nostrils flared to the fresh salt air, and then flung it from side to side. Henry rubbed the animal's neck. "Hey, Beauty, take it easy, boy," he said soothingly. "You've never smelled salt water before."

It was true. The salt was strange to nostrils accustomed only to the scent of new-mown hay in barns and clover-filled pastures in Pennsylvania.

The bridge where they stood now led onto Cape Island at the southern tip of New Jersey. Henry slid out of the saddle and led Beauty across the sand to the water's edge, crunching seashells as they went. The horse sniffed an incoming wave and extended a pink tongue towards it, then backed up abruptly when it broke over his furry hooves. Henry laughed at him. "You can't drink that. I am tellin' you now you won't like it."

41

He laid his head against Beauty's warm neck and drew in deep breaths of the brisk sea air which smelled wild and strange. Henry spoke into the animal's ear as he fingered it: "Beauty, isn't that quite a picture? It's worth ten days of travelin', isn't it, just to see that ocean?"

The two strolled north along the beach together keeping the land on the left and the ocean on the right, making their way through bits of seaweed and shells and tiny fish, the horse inspecting carefully every clump of sea grass, sniffing and pawing all that was strange. Henry loosed the reins and held them lightly. Beauty nudged his elbow occasionally. They approached what appeared to be a long narrow strip of land running parallel to the mainland but separated from it by a channel of sea water. Virtually an island, the strip continued as far as he could see but there appeared to be no habitation on it. It seemed to be a kind of barrier reef. Looking across to its ocean side, he could make out waves pounding on the far shore. Henry was intrigued with the wild loneliness of the place and its inaccessibility. Visible from his position were low scrubby trees twisted and gnarled by the wind. But no houses. No people. Only wild sea birds dipping in the soft warm breeze.

Henry wondered if at that moment the tide was high or low. A farm boy needn't know anything about tides, but here in Cape Island that knowledge would be essential. He would have to become aware of all these features of seaside life. As he studied it now, the channel lying between the mainland where he stood and the barrier strip was of an indeterminate depth. He would have to come back another time for comparison. When the tide was at its lowest point, perhaps it would be possible to get a horse across the channel to explore that lone strip of land which appeared so near and yet was tantalizingly out of reach. He could see the sand blowing and hear the cries of undulating sea birds. His heart leaped with a sense of adventure. "Oh, Beauty," he sighed, "we will have to explore, you and I together."

As he stood there mesmerized by the challenge, a herd of some twenty cattle appeared over the headland being driven by a man and two boys on horseback. Henry watched, spellbound, as the cattle were herded down to the edge of the channel. There followed a whooping and hollering and a wild waving of arms and caps as the beasts were urged into the water, the horses pursuing them closely, pushing them along over the objection of bleatings and throaty groans of protest. The animals found their footing and continued to walk slowly out into the channel. Following closely behind and flanking them came the horseback riders. Henry watched in awe as the lumbering animals walked beyond their depth and began to paw the water and swim for the shore of the island. They reached it in a few minutes of rather ungraceful swimming and splashing and clambered ashore, all twenty of them, as Henry counted their rumps emerging from the water.

His jaw dropped and he clapped his hands on his knees. "Well, I'll be! Didya ever see anythin' as *spectacular* as that, Beauty?"

As he watched, dumbfounded, the three riders turned their horses back towards the mainland and plunged into the channel once again, leaving the cattle on the shore behind them. Shortly they came ashore not far from where Henry stood. He walked Beauty along the sand to have a word with them. "Howdy," he greeted them, smiling. "Your cattle sure are good swimmers."

The man returned the greeting. "Yep, they don't like it at first but once they get out to their summer pasture they settle down."

Henry could not hide his astonishment. "You mean they stay out there all <u>summer</u>? You don't have to feed 'em?"

"Plenty of feed out there," the man answered. "Grass and salt hay and lots o' scrub. Feed's no problem."

"Can't they get away? Get lost?" Henry was curious. "What keeps 'em together?"

"Wahl," he drawled, "there's no place for 'em to *go*. They're surrounded by the sea. Next autumn we'll go out again and round 'em up and bring 'em back for the winter. Saves us looking after 'em all summer. Folks have been foraging cattle on these barrier islands for over a hundred years. Takin' cattle over started back in the days o' the whaler yeomen. Sheep and horses too used to come over for the summer months. No need for fencin'. The inlets kept 'em on their own islands."

"How many are there?" Henry asked.

"Five. Stretchin' the whole way up the peninsula. The islands protect the mainland. Rough sea on the other side, though. Lots of ships wrecked in the winter storms." He eyed Henry and Beauty closely. "You must be new around here."

"Yep," Henry replied. "We just arrived today, Beauty and I."

"Come far?"

"From Pennsylvania. I reckon close to 150 miles."

"You got people here?"

"No, nobody. I'm lookin' for work. Apprentice carpenter, I hope."

"The place is growin' fast," the man offered. "You won't have any trouble. Hotels goin' up all the time. More people coming here every summer. Not enough places for 'em all to stay."

His two sons were listening to the conversation. One of them spoke finally: "Sure is a fine horse. How old is he?"

Henry responded with warm pride: "Four. I've had him since he was a colt. Broke him myself. He's real smart. But he has a lot to learn about the ocean and this country." Then grinning he added: "So do I."

"What's your name?" was the question of the older boy who looked about Henry's age.

"Sawyer."

"Nobody by that name around here," the man said.

"What's yours?" Henry asked the boy who had spoken to him.

"Eldredge. Lots of us here. We go back a couple hundred years, I guess, don't we, Pa?"

His father nodded and then laughed heartily: "Yes, the Eldredges came on the *Mayflower*—or greeted it when it landed. We go back a long ways! I'm Jeremiah Eldredge. These are my boys, Nathaniel and Jacob."

"Do you know Ezekiel Eldredge?" Henry asked eagerly. "He's the master carpenter I heard was lookin' for apprentices to build houses."

"He's my brother," Eldredge replied. "Lives next to my farm."

"Is your farm close by?"

"A couple of miles up the Old Cape Road." He was turning his horse in that direction when he stopped momentarily to ask: "Where are you stayin'?"

"Don't know yet. 'Reckon I'll find a place all right. I haven't looked."

"You can stay tonight at my place," he continued. "You can bed your horse in my barn. Plenty o' room now the cattle are gone."

"Thank you kindly," answered Henry as he followed Jeremiah Eldredge and Nathaniel and Jacob up over the headland from where they had come.

"Do you know anythin' 'bout the history o' Cape Island?" Eldredge called to Henry over his shoulder.

"No. And I'd like to," Henry replied, riding up alongside him.

"The first settlers here—about thirty-five families, one o' them was Eldredge—were all whalers or those that worked for the whalers, like coopers and cordwainers and carpenters and blacksmiths. It was about 200 years ago when pirates prowled around the bay and sea coasts. One story goes that Captain Kidd buried his treasure in the beach at the Point. The thirty-five families stuck together and as years went by married each other. They lived along the creeks and sounds and the bay instead o' organizin' themselves into a town. A lot o' them died from a plague. Some o' the families died out totally. It was the whaler yeomen who took to farmin' that first got the idea o' takin' their cattle over to the barrier islands where we left ours today. To keep the animals from gettin' mixed up, the farmers cut earmarks in them."

Henry listened attentively to everything Eldredge told him. "Was there good whalin' off Cape Island—enough for thirty-five families to make a livin'?" he asked.

"No. That was the problem. Sometimes they'd launch their boats and fish for two months without ever seein' a spout of a whale. Some years all they'd get was two whales. When they weren't whalin' or farmin' they were lumberin'. Cuttin' cedar logs in the forests and swamps and cuttin' them into shingles to send to Philadelphia. There was a sawmill powered by the tide. The wooden planks went to the early shipbuildin'. But land-ownin' has always been most important because there's not much of it that's good for farmin'. Too much swamp land and salt marsh and beach. Not so long ago there were lots of disagreements and fights over who would own land on the Cape. The thirty-five whalin' families kept control, though, by gettin' the positions of land surveyors. That was the most important job around. My piece o' land was passed down to me from several generations of Eldredges. And it'll go to Nathaniel and Jacob next. Why, I reckon 200 years from now there'll still be Eldredges here farmin' this same piece o' ground, raisin' cattle and sheep and plantin' corn and grasses."

"I wonder what it was like here durin' the time of the Revolutionary War," Henry mused.

"Well," Eldredge continued, "in those days there were salt works here up and down the coast. The government needed salt for provisions and to make gunpowder for the Continental Army. The Leamings and Jesse Hand and John Holmes found salt-makin' a very profitable business. But they weren't the only ones who made money durin' that war, either. The privateers captured schooners and cargoes along Great Egg Harbor and sold at auction. Such things as sugar, molasses, cotton and coffee brought good money. Fact is, the Cape men on the militia rolls went to sea as privateers rather than into the Continental Army. Road-buildin' took off right after the war and, along with that, bridges and causeways. A lot o' the buildin' was at Cape Island which made this here part grow into a resort. It was already known to be a healthful seaside place before the Revolutionary War!"

The four riders turned in at the farm gate and Eldredge led the way into the barn.

The following morning was Sunday and Henry was anxious to have a look at the town. He saddled Beauty and rode him back towards the ocean road. Eldredge had mentioned the big hotels and he wanted to see for himself just what these structures looked like. Riding along the seafront, he could make out in the distance a building of several stories that seemed to ramble along to some length facing the ocean. As he drew near he read a sign MANSION HOUSE, 1832. A few guests were sitting on a verandah running along the front of the hotel overlooking the sea and supported by slender wooden posts and there were two upper stories where several other faces could be seen at the windows looking out at the expanse of shining water. The building was about 150 feet long, he guessed. Henry had never seen anything quite like this. Was this really what a mansion looked like? It did not seem very attractive at all. Except for its gabled roof, it looked something like a shed, and the rather plain wood exterior gave an impression of unfinished rawness to the whole. He stared and stared at the building.

He continued riding and came across another which introduced itself quite boldly to passersby by spelling out THE NEW ATLANTIC HOUSE in story-high letters across its front. Painted white and with four stories, it looked quite new with its large verandah screening the entire facade. The whole effect was an architectural pleasure to the eye.

Henry also found the CONGRESS HALL whose mish-mash design brought a smile to his face. Built in 1816, a sign said, it appeared to be the product of one addition after another over a period of time resulting in irregular rooflines, balconies devoid of symmetry, and doorways of varying sizes.

The houses he passed were all very similar to one another and plain. He studied their design: simple, box-like rectangles with pitched rooves, framed in wood and clapboarded. Not many people were about; the "season" for summer tourists would not begin until July 1. A wind was whirling up the sand on the beach and sifting it through the air as he rode along. Beauty tossed his head and snorted.

The dirt road left the cluster of buildings and wound down to the southern tip of land where the Delaware Bay converged with the broad Atlantic. It was a spot that stirred the senses and he reveled in the experience: the purity and freshness of the breeze stroking his face, the warmth of the sun on his arms, the smell of fish and salt in the air and the wild taste of it, the cry of seagulls over the confluence of bay and ocean where tides rippled and churned the waves to a froth. Henry sat in the saddle breathing deeply and absorbing the deliciousness of his surroundings. He felt strong and energized. Looking out across the water he could see waves breaking on the shoals and sand bars that Eldredge had described.

They rounded the cape and Henry turned Beauty towards the west, in the direction of a distant lighthouse. They rode toward the light, keeping on the wet sand of the Bay that edged the dry white sand of the beach. Beauty's hooves crunched on seashells and stones and sometimes squashed dead fish and other marine creatures that had drifted in. The beacon of the lighthouse beckoned them. He rode until he was in the shadow of the white tower itself. He looked up at the light shining out to sea and for a few minutes he sat and thought about the ships that depended on that welcome to guide them to safety from a storm-tossed sea.

Rounding the base of the great tower to its western side, they came upon a tidy cultivated garden where a girl was bending over rows of potato plants pulling weeds out of the dark soil. As if in greeting, Beauty snorted and she looked up, startled at the sudden appearance of strangers. Henry, noting her expression, said quickly: "Sorry if we frightened you." He smiled uncertainly. "We were just takin' a ride out from town. A pretty day. Never been this near a lighthouse before. Never even seen one before."

Her long blond hair was tied with a ribbon at the back of her neck, and when she looked up at him he reflected that her blue eyes were not unfriendly even though he had surprised her. He guessed she was about his own age or perhaps a little younger.

"You must be a stranger to these parts, then?" she answered softly, standing up and shielding her eyes from the sun with her hand.

Her manner put Henry at ease. "Matter of fact, 'been here just a bit longer than twenty-four hours," he said.

Her eyes opened wide in amazement. "Where'd you come from?"

"Pennsylvania. My father's farm."

She walked slowly between the rows of vegetables towards Beauty who was nibbling a tall weed at the edge of the garden.

"You're beautiful!" she remarked, extending her hand towards his muzzle. The horse chewed up the plant and she held her hand flat, palm upwards for him to lick it with his warm, slobbering tongue. Her laugh came easily.

"That's his name. Beauty." Henry sat up very straight, throwing his shoulders back proudly.

She looked straight into Beauty's face and patted his nose. "Would you like a drink of water?" she asked. "If you've walked all the way from Pennsylvania you must be thirsty." Her voice was so gentle and her manner so warm that Henry forgot his initial embarrassment and slid down out of the saddle. Standing next to him she was scarcely five feet tall. He had not been conscious of his own height before now but he seemed to tower over her blond head which came up only to his shoulder.

"It's very kind of you. I'm sure he would like a drink. We've come clear out from town and there's nothin' but salt water between here and there."

Turning away she walked toward the lighthouse and disappeared behind its door. When she emerged she was carrying water in a pewter bucket that she placed on the ground in front of Beauty.

Henry's face mirrored his wonderment. "You live here?" he asked in astonishment.

"Yes, my father's the lighthouse keeper." They were silent watching Beauty drink. "This is our garden," she went on. "It's mine, really. It takes a lot of time keeping the weeds down."

Henry was impressed with her poise and self-assurance. They had a way of making him feel comfortable in her presence. "It's a fine garden," he complimented her, then added, grinning: "I've pulled a good many weeds myself back in Pennsylvania!"

She smiled at him, all the while patting Beauty's neck. "Are you staying here long?"

"Plan to," answered Henry. "Tomorrow I'm startin' to look for work."

"What do you do?"

"Carpentry. I'm just learnin' the trade," he answered a trifle apologetically. "I'll just be apprenticin'."

"You shouldn't have any trouble finding work in Cape Island," she announced with great certainty. "So much building going on. Hotels and guest cottages going up all the time. The place is growing so fast, why it's becoming the most popular resort on the east coast of America!"

49

Henry laughed, "That's just what the advertisement said—the one I read back home that made me decide to come here straightaway."

She was quiet then, a little shy, looking down at Beauty finishing the last of the water.

Henry pulled the reins together. "Well, I guess we'd better be goin'. Much obliged for the water. Been nice talkin' to you." He was about to put his foot in the stirrup and then hesitated. "I don't even know your name," he said turning towards her. "Mine's Henry. Henry Sawyer. Pleased to meet you." He extended his hand.

"I'm Harriet. Harriet Eldredge."

Henry registered surprise. "Eldredge is the name o' the folks I stayed with last night. On a farm north of town."

"That must be my Uncle Jeremiah and Aunt Abigail. Nathaniel and Jacob are my cousins," she said. "You'll find a lot of Eldredges here. It's an old name in Cape Island."

"Then Ezekiel Eldredge the builder is your uncle too?" Henry asked.

"He is," she replied. "Uncle Ezekiel and Aunt Tabitha. They have two sons, John and Robert. He builds houses for summer guests. I'm sure he could use an apprentice like yourself."

The sincerity in her manner was reassuring to Henry and helped erase the niggling self-doubts about his skills.

"Good luck," she added as he put his foot in the stirrup.

"Thanks." He turned Beauty around and called to her: "Maybe I'll see you again sometime."

A wave of her hand was her answer.

All the way back along the sand Henry thought about Harriet. He had never paid much attention to girls when he was growing up. On the farm there had been no opportunity to meet any, and his school days were so long ago he couldn't remember anything about girls in the eighth grade except that all the boys liked to tease them. But this girl had made a definite impression on him. He asked himself questions about her and tried to answer then. What was there about Harriet that appealed to him? He was conscious of a subtle understanding between them, a kind of immediate bonding. It had happened so easily and inex-

50

plicably. He tried to fathom the mystery. Was it her gentleness? Her sincerity? There was about her a straightforward honesty that made him like her. And trust her.

Lost in thought, Henry loosed the reins and gave Beauty his head. The horse jogged along retracing his steps on the shore line. The late afternoon sun behind them cast a special golden light on the water. An enormous jellyfish floating in toward shore on a wave washed over Beauty's hooves. He shied away from the balloon-like creature of the sea suddenly and jarred Henry from his reverie.

"Whoa! Take it easy, boy!" he exclaimed, grabbing the saddle with his knees. He laughed at himself for his carelessness in guiding Beauty. What *could* he have been thinking of?

Turning the horse back in the direction of the hotels, Henry stopped to read a notice posted on a building: "Carpenters, skilled and apprentice, needed. Apply contractor Peter Hand."

"Beauty, this has been a good day," he said, rubbing the animal's neck. "There's plenty o' work here. Tomorra' we'll start earnin' our keep."

Back at the Eldredges' farm he watered Beauty at the horses' trough and led him into his stall.

In the farmhouse the family were sitting down to their evening meal and motioned to him to pull up a chair. "Did you see some of the town today?" Jeremiah Eldredge wanted to know.

"Yes. Sure did. I rode by the Mansion House and the New Atlantic House and the Congress Hall. I rode all the way around the Cape clear out to the lighthouse." He paused, waiting. "Sure is pretty out there by the lighthouse." He said no more.

In bed later that night he thought a lot about what the morrow would bring in the way of a job for him. He was anxious, even a little nervous. It was a "first" for him—the first time he was out on his own needing to prove himself. His thoughts drifted along to Harriet. He pictured her again standing in her garden and looking up at him with those clear, blue, honest eyes. A serenity spread over him and the nervousness of a few moments ago floated away. He could not recall a time in his life when thinking about another human being had brought him such peace of mind.

51

6

"Have you done much buildin'?" was Ezekiel Eldredge's first question when Henry arrived at his place very early the following morning.

"Just on my father's farm, sir. I helped him with barn sidin', buildin' fences and gates, and grain hoppers, that sort of thing. We repaired things. Some masonry and roofin'. He taught me a lot about tools."

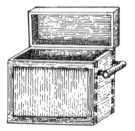

"Got any tools?"

"No, sir." He paused. "I came on my horse."

Eldredge studied him carefully. "You'll need tools. And a tool chest," he said. "I can fit you out to start with, but you'll be wantin' some of your own—that is, if you're plannin' to stay." He eyed Henry questioningly.

"Oh, yes, sir!" was the quick reply. "I aim to stay a long time. I want to learn the trade."

Eldredge continued: "Wahl . . . I guess if you rode all the way from Pennsylvania you probably mean what you say. You can work off your tools a few at a time. How's that?"

"Oh, that's fine, sir," Henry answered eagerly.

Eldredge was resting his foot on the cart wheel. "I start apprentices at six dollars a week, includin' Saturday work. So with your tools, that'd be five dollars clear, every Saturday night."

"Agreed, sir," Henry replied with enthusiasm.

"I'll see how you do. I'm a fair man. If you work well and if I can count on you doin' a good job, you'll earn more."

"Thank you, sir. I'll do my best."

"Want to start today, then?"

"Oh, yes, sir! Right away."

He led Henry into an out-building and pointed to a wooden tool chest in the corner. "Put that on the cart," he instructed. As Henry lifted the chest by the wooden handles at either end, he took note of the dovetailed joints at the four corners which gave it a sturdy, solid feel. The lid was hinged and rested exactly on the rectangular box. Fine craftsmanship, he thought.

Eldredge brought tools from a work bench and explained them as he dropped them into the chest. "We're shinglin' and clapboardin' a roomin' house, gettin' it ready for July. The clapboards come from the sawmill all cut and the shingles from the cedar swamps up at Dennis Creek. We season them over the winter. We cut 'em to fit. You'll need a draw knife to feather 'em, a shinglin' hatchet and shinglin' nails, an auger, a jack plane for the clapboards, clapboard gauge, claw hammer, a saw, brace and bits, chalk and line. That'll be all for now. Later on I'll fit you out with a moldin' plane, some chisels and other gauges."

The two-wheeled cart was pulled by Eldredge's horse along the ocean drive to the work site. As they rode, side by side, Eldredge said: "I've got two men on this job. Done lots of buildin' for me. You can learn from 'em. One's Joseph Leamin'. The Leamin'ses been around here as long as Eldredges. The other's Ambrose." He turned to look squarely at Henry when he asked: "Have you got any objections to workin' alongside a black man?"

"I don't think so," replied Henry slowly. "I've never known any."

"Ambrose's family are freed slaves from over on Thomas Hughes' place. A good worker. Smart too. Trustworthy." He was silent for a moment, then continued: "I don't know what the feelin' is in Pennsylvania but here you'll run into folks who feel pretty strong about black people. Lots o' the folks who stay at the

53

hotels in the summer come from southwards and they speak their thoughts pretty openly sometimes. Guess they don't much like the idea of black people movin' around free. They get kinda annoyed at bein' served in the hotels by them that aren't slaves. You see, all the hotels hire 'em durin' the summer."

Henry remained thoughtful the rest of the ride. He was curious to meet Ambrose.

At the work site the rooming house construction appeared to be well along. The two men were at work on the clapboarding.

"This here is Henry Sawyer. A new apprentice," Eldredge called up to them. "Not sure how much he knows. He'll need some showin', I reckon."

Henry acknowledged their greetings and with Eldredge's help lifted the tool chest off the cart. Eldredge drove off to another job without further ado.

This was how Henry made the acquaintance of Ambrose—the first day of a friendship that would last throughout his life. Joseph Leaming was hammering on the clapboard while Ambrose held the board in place. Henry watched the whole process, then took his turn. They worked for several hours, the sun beating down on the three of them, and at noon Joseph took a break and walked to his nearby home for lunch. Ambrose sat down in the shade of the building, mopped his forehead with his sleeve, and drew some corn pone out of his pants pocket. Henry stood, awkwardly, then turned to move away.

Ambrose looked up and held out a piece of the bread. "If you-all didn't bring no vittles, have some o' ma mammy's pone."

Henry acknowledged the offer but refused it.

Ambrose insisted. "You-all know what the Bible says 'bout Jesus feedin' the multitude with the loaves and the fishes. There's plenty o' good pone here for two."

Henry sat on the ground next to Ambrose and accepted the offer of food. He was hungry and the cornbread filled the gnawing void inside. He decided that since the two of them would be working closely together he ought to enlighten Ambrose a little about who he was and why he was here. Perhaps, then, Ambrose would feel like telling him about himself. So, as they ate pone together, Henry told him about his family and the farm and about

mented one day: "You sure are a happy man now'days." Even Beauty seemed to sense the eagerness with which Henry approached their home in the evening as the sun went down behind them and, accordingly, quickened his gait.

In his absence Harriet did all the things a new wife does to turn a house into a home. Her tools were needles and threads, homespun materials and yarns, and with them she created the simple furnishings for their cottage. She baked bread in the brick oven in the cellar, made soap, pumped water at the well and heated it in the big fireplace to wash their clothes. As she went about her chores, the purity of the child-like happiness in her heart came out in song. Sometimes she would stand and run her hands along the windowsills, lovingly feeling their smoothness where Henry had planed them.

Her dowry was small. They had begun their married life with the barest of household essentials and these had come from the lighthouse transported on her Uncle Ezekiel's wagon: her bed and her grandmother's quilt, a small dining table, two straight wooden chairs, some cooking pots and pans, a few dishes and some cutlery.

Late December brought shorter days and gray skies, flakes of snow and cold winds blowing over the bluff. She looked out the window and planned the garden she would plant there when spring arrived, mentally seeding rows of peas, carrots, beets, lettuce and beans. There would be herbs and plants for dyeing wool. She smiled thinking of the hot summer months when the cellar would be cool for all the produce she raised and where on its shelves she would place the preserves for winter.

When her daily chores were finished, Harriet pulled on her heavy walking boots and wrapped herself in her warm cloak for a walk which oftentimes took her miles from the cottage. Upon her return she would look in at Beauty's stall and with a pitchfork shake some clean straw down and then put a measure of oats in his box to welcome him in the evening.

Coming into the cottage with her cheeks aglow from the blustery winds, she made sure that the fire in the fireplace was crackling for Henry's return. She lit the oil lamp and the candles to greet him. All day long she looked forward to the moment

87

when she would hear Beauty's hoof beats and presently Henry would open the door and she would see the beloved smile on his boyish face. Every evening as he came in from the darkness he held out his arms to fold her in his strong embrace. They would stand before the blazing fire, their arms clasped around each other, holding on tightly, not wanting to let go.

When the housekeeping chores of the evening were finished, they sat before the fire, dreamily watching the embers burn down, sometimes talking softly, oftentimes not talking at all as they enjoyed each other's closeness.

"I am so happy," she said to Henry, looking up at him like a little girl while the firelight played on her cheeks. Stroking his arms she commented on how strong they were becoming. "It's all the hard work you do."

She spoke with such pure sweetness that he bent down to kiss her. Her cheek was hot from the flame glow. "I love you, my dearest," he whispered.

Time stood still on those winter evenings, suspending the young lovers in a bliss of such perfection that there was no beginning and no ending to their joy.

From the warmth of the hearthside Harriet carried a candle to their bedroom and drew the curtains across the dark pane. Beside her Henry lovingly untied the ribbon at the back of her neck which held her blond hair in place. As it fell to her shoulders he fingered it and gazed at her beautiful profile that the candlelight cast as a shadow on the wall. Drawing her gently to him, he caressed her back with his hands and kissed the top of her head. They lay down together on the bed that she had slept in all her life underneath the old patchwork quilt. He did not blow out the candle just yet. "I never knew I could be so happy," he whispered to her, looking into her eyes. She lifted her lips to his and he stroked her head tenderly as she nestled within his arms.

* * *

Their first child was named for Harriet's father: Thomas Eldredge Sawyer. The infant was not given to robust health and Harriet worried about his weak start in life. To strengthen his

88

frail body she carried him on long walks by the sea so that he might be invigorated by breathing the bracing salt air.

When he was but a year old, his sister, Louisa Eldredge, was born. The joy of her arrival was overshadowed by the constant anxiety they felt for little Thomas whose small frame was wracked by respiratory difficulties. Harriet spent long hours sitting by his bed watching helplessly as he grew weaker and his coughs more threatening. One night as she kept her vigil, he opened his feverish eyes momentarily and struggled for breath. She stroked his brow comfortingly and placed a cold compress on it, resting her hand lightly on his forehead. For a few seconds her eyes closed with the fatigue of keeping watch over the sickly infant for endless hours, and when she opened them again, life had gone out of his tiny body. A convulsive sob rose up from the depths of her being. A cry of anguish brought Henry to her side in the darkness. She picked up the little body and held it close to her own as if to keep it warm. Rocking the infant back and forth, she cried softly, the hot tears anointing the baby's head. Henry put his arms around her and little Thomas, and they stood together until Harriet's quivering frame grew quiet.

Thomas Eldredge Sawyer was placed in a coffin made by his father and was buried in the cemetery of the Cold Spring Presbyterian Church less than two years after his birth.

It was only while planting her garden in the springtime that Harriet found any solace from her grief. Little Louisa toddled about the warm grass while her mother knelt and placed the seeds leftover from the lighthouse garden carefully in the ground. Every now and then the child picked up a tiny stone or twig and tottered across the grass to place it in the hole her mother had dug. When the planting was finished, Harriet sat very still and looked out across the sea. Thomas's death had left her thin and pale and she had become very pensive. Her heart ached and she could not think of the child without the hurt rising in her throat to choke her. Henry longed to see her smile again. He was gentle and patient, keeping faith in her ultimate recovery.

89

One warm day in May when she went to look at her garden and saw the pale green shoots of the peas she had planted emerging from the warm earth, she bent down over them and felt tears rolling down her cheeks onto the seedlings. She knelt there, releasing the pent up anguish in her heart, giving thanks for the new life she saw there and gaining strength from the rebirth. Louisa came running towards her, stumbled and fell into her arms. Harriet kissed her and held her close. The little girl looked up at her mother's face and rubbed her tiny hand in the tears on her cheek. Taking a corner of her frock, she wiped her mother's face dry. Harriet's surprise was so complete that she laughed aloud.

When Henry returned that spring evening it was still daylight and he saw the two of them walking to meet him and Beauty. It was the first time that they had greeted him in this way. He felt his heart lift when Harriet raised Louisa in the air and into Henry's arms so that she could ride in the saddle in front of him the rest of the way home. The child squealed with delight when Beauty, nearing his stall with its waiting oats, broke into a bouncy trot.

Henry's overalls were covered with dust and he was weary from his day's work, but he slipped out of the saddle with Louisa in one arm and approached Harriet. Putting his other arm around her shoulder, he looked down at her tenderly and asked: "How are you, dear?"

She did not answer immediately but walked with him towards the bluff to look out across the ocean. Then, very simply, she said: "The peas are up."

10

Harriet was coming back from Beauty's stall one morning when she looked up to see the familiar figure of the tin peddler approaching. He was pushing a bright red two-wheeled cart on whose end was painted: "Nathan Springer, Manufacturer of Tin Ware." It rolled along easily over the rough ground and came to rest in front of her door.

"Good day, ma'am."

She returned his greeting warmly as he began to unlock the padlocks on the two small lids covering the compartments where his wares were stored. Harriet looked forward to his annual visit and especially so this year because of the order for merchandise she'd given him a year ago which he was now delivering: two dozen cans in which she would preserve the vegetables and fruit from her garden. She peered into the deep compartments of the cart at the various items for sale: pie plates, tin cups, graters, milk pans, dippers, buckets and pails, wash basins, lard cans, pastry molds, pastry cutters, dish pans, coffee pots and tea kettles. Harriet was intrigued by all the things he had made with his own hands and fingered them and examined them carefully while he chatted about all the people he had met on his way through the countryside. He was especially loquacious about the muddy roads he had traveled that morning and the swollen streams he had forded, wading through them in his high rubber boots that came up to his hips. He brought news from the other side of the cape—a few facts with a generous sprinkling of rumor and gossip.

"I was by the lighthouse last week," he said. "The keeper was tellin' me 'bout a shipwreck off the Delaware coast. Full of escapin' slaves. Some drowned. Some were caught and sent back."

Harriet listened attentively but said nothing. A shiver went through her as she wondered silently if the fleeing slaves had been with Harriet Tubman. There had been no word of her since the night when Ambrose had driven her and her family members away from the lighthouse. "How is everything at the lighthouse?" she inquired rather plaintively.

"The new keeper he told me there's talk o' buildin' a new light."

"A new light?" she asked, a hint of shock in her voice. "One with a flashing beacon."

"I see," she answered quietly. "That would be a change. I suppose it would be an improvement over the old light," she added wistfully.

"Would you like some newspapers?" the peddler offered cheerily. "I gathered 'em up at the shop last week. The news is old, but out here I s'pose old news is still new, right?"

She smiled. "You're right. Thank you very much." She took the bundle of newspapers from him. "I'm sure you'd like some lemonade?"

Harriet went into the house for the drink and brought it out to the peddler, her other hand clutching a little purse out of which she drew some coins for the two dozen cans he had delivered. "When you stop by next year I'd like a coffee pot," she said, picking up Louisa who kept standing on tiptoes to see inside the cart. The child watched, fascinated, as he closed the two-hinged doors over the compartments and proceeded to padlock them. Before doing so, however, the peddler reached inside and drew out a toy for the little girl: a tiny tin horse with a tail and ears that moved. With a squeal of delight, Louisa wriggled out of her mother's arms and began to run, making the toy horse gallop in the air.

"See you next year 'bout this time," the peddler said as he waved goodbye and pushed his cart back the way he had come.

Harriet was eager to read the newspapers that were the first she had seen in months, and while Louisa played with her new toy she settled herself comfortably into a rocking chair by the window. The sun was shining in brightly lighting up the rich colors in the braided wool rug at her feet that she had made that winter. Sitting in the chair she took pleasure in her handiwork, noting again the braids, which had come from discarded woolen clothing from her own family and that of her close relatives—an old gray coat belonging to Uncle Ezekiel, Uncle Jeremiah's trousers, and Aunt Tabitha's blankets—and which she had painstakingly cut into strips, braided and sewn together with her own hands.

"May 30, 1854" was the date on the newspaper she held in her hands. She began to read the front page and became so absorbed in the reporting of the news that she was unaware of the passage of time and that the sun had moved away from the window. Louisa's voice finally interrupted her concentration and when she looked up her expression was so serious and troubled that the little girl's face clouded over.

"Mommy sad?" the child said, patting her mother's face with her hand.

Startled by her daughter's keen perception, Harriet broke into a smile quickly. "No, my sweet, Mommy is happy, very happy with her Louisa," she reassured the tot, stroking her curls.

Still, as the day wore on to the time when Henry would return from his work, Harriet's mind was not at ease and the news she had read in the papers continued to absorb her thoughts and worry her.

When Henry came home that evening he was full of talk about the new Mt. Vernon Hotel almost completed. "It's going to be the largest resort hotel in America!" he said excitedly. "Rooms for 2500 people! Think of it, Harriet! Cape Island will be the most famous resort in the whole country. The Mt. Vernon is 306 feet across the front and the wings at either end are 506 feet long and

66 feet wide! Can you imagine a hotel that large? It will bring in hundreds more visitors every summer. We're becoming a boom town!"

Harriet relished his boyish enthusiasm for his work on the new hotel. He was proud of Cape Island and its progress to which he had contributed his strength and steadfastness for the past six years of his life. He had been working hard for as long as he could remember, but now at age twenty-five he was experiencing the satisfaction resulting from that industry and he could foresee a bright future as well.

"I'm so proud of you," Harriet assured him, her hand on his as they sat on the rug before the hearth. "Our lives seem to be full of blessings." Suddenly her face tightened and became serious as she continued: "The tin peddler left some newspapers with me today. There is trouble in the country, Henry. *Real* trouble. Cape Island is so peaceful and remote that one tends to forget that the rest of the country is not enjoying the same tranquility."

She stopped momentarily and when she looked up at him he saw in the firelight that her eyes were filled with fear. "I read all the papers thoroughly," she continued, "and the news is alarming. The union has become so divided on the issue of slavery that its very life is in danger. There is terrible hatred in the land. It has spread to the West where there is bitter wrangling over whether slavery should be allowed in the new territories acquired from France in 1803 by the Louisiana Purchase. It is hard to understand why, with all that unsettled land out there, people can't just go there and live peaceably. I cannot even visualize in my imagination how much land that is. Hundreds of thousands of acres just waiting for settlers. Now slavery has become a sickness creeping over it. Who would have thought that it would spread over such a large area of land stretching all the way from Canada south to the Gulf of Mexico, and from the Mississippi River west to the Rocky Mountains? All these parts of our country we have never seen. The newspapers traced the history of the problem and I read it very carefully . . . every word."

Henry urged her to share it all with him.

"The fighting of the politicians over whether the territory should be free or allow slavery became so rancorous that it was-

94

n't quieted until 1820 with the Missouri Compromise that allowed Maine to come into the union as a free state and Missouri as a slave state. But after that there was to be no slavery allowed north of Missouri's southern boundary.

"Well, that compromise didn't contain the trouble for very long. Not even thirty years. Trouble erupted again in the West, this time after the Mexican War when another large territory was acquired and the same problem came to the surface: would it be slave or free? If you remember, Henry Clay tried to solve it a few years ago with the Compromise of 1850. It really only added fuel to the fire because the worst thing that came out of that was the Fugitive Slave Law. You know what disruptive legislation that was and how it only created more ill will between the North and the South.

"And now, in these papers, I read that only a few days ago Senator Stephen A. Douglas of Illinois put forth something called the Kansas-Nebraska Act that is supposed to be the final remedy. It makes territories out of Kansas and Nebraska and says that only when they become states must the settlers decide whether or not they will be free or slave. Senator Douglas called it the 'right of popular sovereignty.' So, you see, this most recent legislation will repeal the Missouri Compromise of 1820, which said there'd be no slavery *allowed* that far north. A whole flood of controversy has been unleashed now! Where will it all end?

"When one reads the reports carefully one feels that we are being carried along by an unstoppable current towards open conflict. The newspapers predicted that the Kansas Territory is in for some desperate fighting between the two factions.

"And Harriet Beecher Stowe's book, *Uncle Tom's Cabin,* which appeared two years ago has sold thousands of copies, the papers reported, and has aroused more fury between the two sides. Add to this the hatred spilling over from the Fugitive Slave Act and one is conscious of the violence sweeping through the country."

Harriet stopped as a choking sob rose in her throat. "Oh, Henry," she went on, "I am so afraid. We are bringing another child into a world that seems to be tearing apart."

He put his arm around her and they sat quietly as he tried to think of what he could say to comfort her.

"For some time," he began, "I've been aware of increasing agitation on the outside over the slavery question. We don't hear too much in Cape Island because we're rather in the middle: we aren't in the South and we're not really in the North either as far as political sentiment goes. But I do listen to what people around the work site are saying and you're right, there is trouble brewing. But we must trust our leaders, Harriet, and have faith in their resolve to guide the country through these troubled times. What else can we do?"

She looked up at him with the most terrified expression on her countenance. He could not bear to see her so pained but still he knew that her native intelligence was so strong that it was foolish for him to try to assuage her despair with empty optimism, that the best way to help her tap into her own strength was to reassure her with his love and devotion. With trust in each other, they would stand together and meet this new threat with the same fortitude that had brought them through the trials of the last four years. All these messages from his heart to hers were best expressed by his loving arms around her. "We have to keep faith in our country," was all he said.

*   *   *

In the year 1855 a second son was born to them, and again they chose to name the child Thomas Eldredge Sawyer, honoring the memory of Harriet's father. As the family grew, so did the house that sheltered them. Henry built another bedroom for the children, and Beauty's quarters were enlarged also to include another stall and a paddock where he and a second horse named Prince could exercise. Beauty, now eleven years old, was still Henry's favorite but his love of horses received a fillip when Ambrose rode up one Sunday on a high-spirited gelding and announced that the animal could be added to Henry's stable for very little money. The coal black horse, barely two years old, was a striking contrast to Beauty as they stood side by side nuzzling each other. Henry could not resist him. Harriet smiled upon hearing his rationalization that Prince would "keep Beauty from becoming lonely," and also that they could ride together now. He wanted her to learn to love horses as much as he did.

Try as they did to protect their happiness from the harassment of the problems of the world without, it became harder and harder to withstand the pressures as the years passed. Anger over slavery grew more caustic and moderation seemed to have gone out of fashion. The strident voices heard throughout the land were those of violence and hatred drowning out all restraint and reason. Passions thirsting after bloodshed to settle the score held sway, and the Kansas Territory became the battleground for a guerrilla border war. Ruffians and ne'er-do-wells from Missouri itching to provoke a fight drifted across the border of the territory and found what they were seeking. These raiders stirred up trouble in their struggle to keep Kansas open to slavery while guns came from New England abolitionists to support the settlers who wanted Kansas free. Every act of aggression was met with fierce retaliation. Inevitably the clashes took lives, and back East in the halls of Congress politicians struck out boldly and began to utter such sentiments as the desirability of the South's departure from the new union.

Lawrence, Kansas was the scene of a bloody attack by a pro-slavery contingent. Revenge came in the massacre of five pro-slavery settlers at Pottawatomie Creek by abolitionist firebrand and fanatic John Brown, his four sons and two other followers.

Fear gripped the southern slaveholders—fear that their pleasant plantation life and their flourishing agrarian economy made possible by the system of slavery were in danger of disappearing. Another fear was ever-present: slave insurrections. The 1831 uprising in Virginia led by Nat Turner put constant terror in southern hearts that more bloody slave revolts would follow if control over the slaves were relaxed.

In 1857 the plight of a Negro slave Dred Scott drew the attention of the whole country when his case finally went to the Supreme Court of the land. Dred Scott had been taken by his master to live in Wisconsin and Illinois, both free of slavery, and after living there for some time, Scott sued for his freedom. Chief Justice Roger Taney spoke for the Court when he decreed that

97

Scott had no power to sue because he was not a citizen of any state. Taney decreed, furthermore, that *implied in the Constitution was protection for slavery everywhere* so that it could not be excluded legally from any territory. So now the country was being asked to accept the Dred Scott decision of the Supreme Court alongside the concept of "popular sovereignty" established in the western territories.

The following year's senatorial race in Illinois brought two politicians into the election arena to debate these inflammatory issues: Abraham Lincoln and Stephen A. Douglas. The two battled each other in debates that focused the whole country's attention on the invidious canker of slavery.

Although the South's economy remained strong because of the world's voracious appetite for its cotton, in 1857 a business depression was felt in the North, which section demanded from the Federal government protective tariffs and a homestead act to alleviate it. The weak government of Democratic President James Buchanan was ineffectual in dealing with these sectional problems. In fact, it appeared to be doing nothing as the nation was sucked into the vortex of approaching armed conflict.

In 1859, the downward trend towards tragedy was exacerbated by John Brown who, having decided the moment had come to incite a slave insurrection in the South, with only a small band of followers raided the Federal arsenal at Harper's Ferry, Virginia. His intention was to use the captured weapons to arm the slaves who would come forward. The plan fizzled when the slaves did not appear; John Brown was captured, tried, convicted of treason, and hanged.

Fear ignited and fanned the flames of passion in the South. To the land of Dixie the abolitionists had spoken loudly and clearly, said the southerners. There was no basis left now for healing the rift; it seemed that there was not even a desire to find a peaceful solution.

Henry and Harriet Sawyer watched these developments that were slowly but steadily eroding the security and serenity of their lives. They tried to maintain a kind of detachment. Their lives had something of a rote to them and there was satisfaction to be derived from this. True, there was little variety from day-to-day, but life hummed along pleasantly with the knowledge of what to expect from it. They had never thought of questioning the necessity for hard work. They had not resisted it, rather welcomed it. Nor had they ever stopped to even ponder if they were happy. Happiness was not a goal they pursued; it was the result of many things that went to make up each day, and in the case of Henry and Harriet Sawyer happiness came as unconsciously as breathing. They had never been taught to expect life to give them anything. One was born, one grew up, one went to work. Sometimes life was unfeelingly cruel, other times it gave good fortune unstintingly. That's the way it was.

Far away from their sheltered part of the country the political campaigning went on with increasing momentum. A desperate intransigence held the South in a strait jacket: it would not, could not, release its grip on the bondage of four million human beings who picked its immensely profitable cotton crop for the whole world's consumption and performed every kind of labor that was necessary to maintain the pleasant way of life so cherished by the southern slave-holding society.

The country grew more and more polarized as the presidential election of 1860 drew near; there was a split in the Democratic Party resulting in the nomination of two candidates—Stephen A. Douglas for the northern wing and John C. Breckenridge for the southern wing. The new Republican Party was a mix of members of the former Whig Party, people who wanted the territories to remain free, homesteaders who wanted free farms on the frontier, and business interests that asked for higher protective tariffs for northern industry. Immigration had brought many hundreds of thousands of Europeans to northern cities who provided the cheap labor for the burgeoning Industrial Revolution there. The tremendous western expansion had created a link between itself and the northeast in commercial endeavor.

At this stage of his political career Abraham Lincoln was a "moderate" on the subject of slavery: he was against it in principle, considering it an evil that had to be contained and ultimately eradicated, but he thought that the Federal government did not have the power to interfere with it as it existed in the southern

99

states. He did believe that slavery should not be allowed in the western territories.

Both publicly and quietly in private around the country a warning was being voiced: if the Republican Party's candidate Lincoln were elected in November, would the South remain in the union?

Believing fiercely in states' rights, the South looked upon each state as being sovereign. It denied the Government's right to preserve itself or the union. Each state could decide for itself, with no intervention from outside, when or if it would withdraw from the union. The power of each individual state was supreme.

Lincoln was elected by a solid majority in the Electoral College but with less than a majority of the popular vote. Shattering events to the union followed quickly. South Carolina was the first state to secede on December 20, 1860 and the cotton-producing states of Mississippi, Alabama, Georgia, Florida, Louisiana, and Texas followed without delay.

Henry had been correct in his assessment of New Jersey's politics: the state did not support Lincoln in the election. They were, indeed, living in the "middle"—in the North geographically and in the South politically.

By February 1861 a new nation called the Confederate States of America came into being and adopted a provisional constitution. It elected Jefferson Davis of Mississippi as President and Alexander Stephens of Georgia as Vice President.

Peace was no longer an option. The stage was set for war. Henry wondered where his adopted state of New Jersey would ultimately place its support.

road, driving them back to the barnyard where they would spend the winter.

Henry still felt a little dazed by what he had seen. Suddenly, inexplicably, he felt a tweak of homesickness. He wished he could share his delight and tell his family about the barrier island paradise.

11

With a heavy heart at the break-up of the Union and the added sadness of leaving his home state, Lincoln boarded the train in Springfield, Illinois on February 11, 1861 for the twelve-day journey to Washington for his inauguration. Hostility and treachery were abroad and so great was the fear for his safety that a detective's warning of a rumored attempt on his life when the train passed through Baltimore convinced him of the advisability of complying with a subterfuge to get him through the dangerous area in the dead of night secretly. The ruse worked

and he arrived safely in the capital, quietly and without fanfare, very early in the morning. He rode from the train station to Willard's Hotel where a flag flew to welcome him to the Presidential Suite.

Ten days later he was in an open carriage with ex-President Buchanan proceeding along Pennsylvania Avenue to the Capitol for the ceremony. Bands played and flags fluttered in the chilly air. Washington at this moment in history—March 4, 1861—was filled with all manner of Southern sympathizers, spies and persons of evil intent toward the new administration. Rather rudimentary precautions were taken to safeguard Lincoln and to ensure that the day's ceremony would proceed without mishap. There were soldiers along the rough cobblestoned route of the

President's carriage, and cavalry was nearby. Sharpshooters were stationed on rooftops and at the Capitol itself.

In his address to the 25,000 persons assembled there, Lincoln confirmed his refusal to acknowledge the acts of secession, calling them unconstitutional, and stated his firm resolve to "preserve, protect and defend" the Union. Since the southern states still lived under the Constitution, he reasoned, slavery was protected in those states by the Constitution.

The Southern bombardment of Fort Sumter in the harbor of Charleston, South Carolina and its subsequent surrender on April 13 were described with emotional fervor in the newspapers that reached Cape Island, New Jersey. On the ocean front drive and along the roads and passageways where stood the town's houses, shops and churches, flags were unfurled with patriotic ardor.

When, on April 15, Lincoln called on the far-flung northern states to send 75,000 men from their militias for the defense of the country, his regular army numbered only 16,000 men who were scattered over 2000 miles of frontier Indian country and along the coast. Ironically, the strongest armed forces were the militias of the seceding states. The northern militias called up were to serve for ninety days. Lincoln's appeal to his loyal governors met with a response of patriotic fervor far surpassing his expectations: an estimated 200,000 volunteers rushed to answer his call.

Enthusiasm for the impending conflict grew apace, and the race to "join up" was swept along like a brush fire in the wind. To the unsophisticated young men who answered the call to arms, the whole idea of war was a glamorous picture painted in an aura of excitement, romantic adventure, and boisterous love of country. The spirit of war was intoxicating. It spread to every dwelling, inflaming every male inhabitant (and a few females) with the desire to whip the Secessionists. The audacity of the attack on Fort Sumter outraged the populace and inspired a display of heretofore unconscious devotion to country and desire to defend it. It was a delirium of patriotism. The brutalities and sufferings of war were unknown. The exhilarating call to country was in every young heart. Whipping the Secessionists would be a three months' lark by which time the war would certainly be over. Ah, it was a great time to be alive!

Henry, riding Beauty on his way home from work, dismounted before a building to read a poster. Under a drawing of the American flag and the heading "A War Proclamation" was the exhortation: "All Patriots and lovers of their country, step forward at this most important crisis and aid your beloved country. Preserve the Union, Protect the Constitution. With united effort we shall render aid to crush the Rebellion and restore the Laws to their protecting influence, enabling the Citizens of this great Republic once more to meet on terms of harmony and friendship, banishing the demon Rebellion and ambitious Traitors, who have brought this evil day upon us. Young men of Character, Energy and Capacity are invited to come forward for the glory of the country."

Next to the poster was another painting of "The Spirit of '61" showing a woman defiantly holding the flag in one hand and a raised sword in the other, captioned with the verse:

"Up with the Standard and bear it on.
Let its folds to the wind expand.
Remember the deeds of Washington
And the flag of our native land."

As he stood staring at the posters, it seemed that their impassioned messages were directed at himself. He was deep in thought when he heard familiar voices in conversation behind him. Turning he faced Nathaniel and Jacob Eldredge who were also studying the posters with rapt expressions, their eyes glazed and jaws gaping.

"Jacob and me, we're goin' to the church for the recruitin' session," Nathaniel stated. "John and Robert are goin' too. We're all joinin' up."

Henry followed the two brothers along the road that led to the church. Flags flew from every rooftop, and attractive young girls holding smaller flags were stationed on the steps of the church. Strains of "Yankee Doodle" played by a brass band and issuing forth from the church brought a rush of patriotism surg-

103

ing through his body as his feet automatically marched to its beat. He was swept along by the crowd of young men, pushing and struggling up the steps to gain a favorable space in the church. John and Robert Eldredge joined their cousins and stood shoulder to shoulder looking up at the pulpit where the minister was preparing to speak. Wrapped around the pulpit was a banner reading "For God and Country" and beneath it was a long table where sat prominent citizens of Cape Island with sign-up sheets before them.

The minister rose dramatically to his full height, and when he stretched his arms out wide to embrace the assembly, the band ceased its playing and a hush fell over the room.

"Citizens of Cape Island and surroundings in the state of New Jersey, we are called upon by our President to come to the defense of our country in its hour of peril. So blatant was the attack on our Union and so base the treachery of those fomenting it that no further deception is needed to inspire the hearts and minds of our countrymen to rally to the fight to save hearth and home from desecration."

Cheers and applause followed, and the minister raised his hand to restore quiet. "Our President calls for help. The nation cannot wait. God expects every man to do his duty!"

Thunderous applause broke out again. With difficulty the speaker brought it under control long enough to end his appeal: "Don't wait. Sign up tonight for ninety days' service to our beloved Union. Save it from the Rebel traitors who would rent it asunder! This is a just and holy war."

The band was playing the "Star-Spangled Banner" now. The excitement over the adventure of going off to war was palpable in the crowd. Henry looked at the volunteers pressing in around him, many of whom he had come to know in the thirteen years he had lived here. There were young farmers, fishermen, carpenters, masons, students, lawyers, old soldiers and youngsters of questionable service age.

Nathaniel and Jacob, John and Robert were in the front rank of signers, and when they reached the table beneath the pulpit, it took only a matter of minutes to write their names on the papers. With jubilant smiles on their faces and their arms clasped about each other, they departed.

Henry was elbowed and shoved by the crowd. In the enthusiasm restraint was cast aside. Pushed along by the throng, Henry found himself in the line next to a young boy who looked about ten years of age presenting himself at the table.

"How old are you, sonny?" the man at the table asked him a little playfully.

"I'm ten, sir," the youngster replied proudly, standing tall and throwing his shoulders back.

"And what will you do in the army?" continued the questioner, smiling a trifle patronizingly.

"I'm going to be a drummer, sir. My grandpa was in the Mexican War and he says the army always needs drummer boys. So that's why I'm joining up."

The band was playing "Red, White and Blue" as Henry followed the boy down the line and wrote his name on the register. Once outside in the cool night air, he untied Beauty and held the reins lightly as they walked along together. He did not mount the horse for some time; he wanted time to think and welcomed the slower pace home. His decision to sign up had not been entered into rashly. His patriotism was closely linked to gratitude for all the good things that had happened to him in his life thus far and an earnest desire to show his appreciation in a tangible way. It was as simple as that.

When at last he swung up into the saddle, he patted Beauty's neck and spoke to him softly: "I'm goin' to miss you, boy." The horse's neck bobbed up and down with each step as he hurried homeward towards his box of oats. "But you'll have to stay behind and help the family."

When Henry walked in the door that evening a little later than usual, Harriet knew instinctively what he had done before he announced it: "I've joined up."

She remained calm and reached up to put her arms around him. "When will you go?" she asked softly, putting her hot cheek against his cool one that smelled fresh from the night air.

"Soon. A day or two."

Nine-year-old Louisa sensed that something important was happening. "Where are you going, Father?" she asked.

Henry sat down on the floor in front of the crackling fire with Louisa on one side of him and Thomas on the other. "Our country is in trouble, and President Lincoln has asked for help. Because I love my country and want it to stay the way it is for the sake of all of us, I'm going to help her right now. It means I have to go away from home for awhile."

Louisa looked up at him with questioning eyes: "Are you going to be a soldier?"

"And shoot a gun?" Thomas wanted to know.

Henry paused momentarily. "Yes, I am going to be a soldier. And while I'm gone, you must be very grown up and help your mother. She will be very busy looking after you and our house and the horses."

"I'll feed the horses," said Thomas excitedly.

"That's fine, Thomas. And don't forget to keep their water pails full, especially with summer coming on."

"I can help Mother in the garden," Louisa offered. "Last summer I learned how to tell the weeds from the vegetables."

After the children had gone to bed, Henry and Harriet sat together as they did every evening. Henry spoke with deliberation. "This is something I feel compelled to do. I've thought about it a lot. I don't like leaving you and the children, but this country has been good to me—to us—and I must help to defend her now. Every man who is able should go." Then, taking Harriet's hand in his, he added: "It's only for ninety days. I'll be home by mid-July. It won't be a long war."

12

As one of the very first volunteers from the State of New Jersey—and a man whose maturity of thirty-one years and unflinching loyalty to his country spoke well for him—Henry was selected to carry dispatches from New Jersey Governor Charles S. Olden to Secretary of War Simon Cameron in Washington; telegraphic and postal communication was deemed unsafe because of the Rebel hold on Baltimore. In the nation's capital at this time conspiracy and intrigue lurked behind every door in every government building. The city was riddled with Secessionist

hangers-on in the government scheming to aid the Rebellion before departing Washington for their home states. The seceding states were busily seizing Federal property within their borders—customhouses, arsenals, mints, forts. Surreptitiously, vast sums of money, arms and ammunition were sent south.

Southern Congressmen and members of outgoing President Buchanan's Cabinet were in collusion in all manner of infamous plots to help the southern cause. Buchanan's Secretary of War John B. Floyd from Virginia, Secretary of the Treasury Howell Cobb from Georgia, and Secretary of the Interior Jacob Thompson from Mississippi used their good offices and positions of power to carry on their murky treasonous dealings without cen-

107

sure. The new Administration found arsenals and coffers empty and was powerless to exact retribution from the rebellious states.

An eerie quiet descended on Washington as it awaited the arrival of the first troops being sent to protect it. Surrounded by hostility, the city held its breath. Feeling cut off from the outside world, the ten-square-mile rectangle known as the District of Columbia girded itself for an assault by the enemy. Rumors swept along that troops from nearby Virginia and Maryland would attack the capital, set it afire, take possession of public buildings, assassinate the President or take him south as a hostage, and, finally, lower the national emblem and raise the southern flag. Once in control of Washington, the Confederacy would have the prestige required to enable it to demand recognition of foreign powers which it desperately wanted.

The close proximity of the enemy was felt at the Long Bridge over the Potomac River: a guardhouse had been erected at the Washington end and over the bridge was Alexandria, Virginia, where a Confederate soldier stood. After dark the fires of enemy forces south of the Potomac could be seen from the capital, and a Confederate flag flying over Arlington Heights, Virginia was visible also.

The appalling vulnerability of Washington to attack and the frightening unpreparedness of the North as a whole haunted Lincoln night and day with the agony of impending disaster. The general disbelief that the South would make good on its threat to secede had left the nation so assailable that where to begin to prepare for actual war was the problem baffling all its leaders. One-third of the officers in the Regular Army were southerners, West Point-trained, who had abandoned the Army to return to their home states, leaving the supply of officers available to the Union sorely diminished. Even Colonel Robert E. Lee, when offered the field command of the Union Army by Lincoln, resigned his commission out of loyalty to his beloved Virginia. Thomas J. Jackson followed suit.

How to train for war and provision with arms, uniforms, food and transport the mass of men coming from all over the North? Theoretically, each state would provide for its own militia, but the ability to do this varied drastically from state to state. Many a man would leave home wearing a homemade uniform and hand-knit socks and carrying a smoothbore musket of antique vintage.

In the absence of any New Jersey infantry in Washington at this time, Henry became attached to the 25th Pennsylvania Volunteer Infantry, but his earliest service was with the Cassius Clay Battalion. Formed in Washington by the formidable Kentuckian Cassius M. Clay and numbering several hundred men, it was a motley group put together hurriedly and armed for the immediate defense of the capital. Their duties comprised patrolling the city night and day, preventing the assembly of conspirators, guarding against conflagrations, and preserving the secrecy of war preparations from the spies and traitors swarming in the city.

On the 18th of April, 460 Pennsylvanians became the first volunteers to reach the capital. Composed of five well-trained and disciplined militia companies from Lewistown, Allentown, Pottsville, and including a battery of artillery from Reading, they marched into the city having been stoned by an unruly mob on their way through Baltimore. They were all armed and equipped. At the same time came 300 regular cavalry from the former command of General David Twiggs who, through a confused set of circumstances, had surrendered them to the recently seceded state of Texas which had subsequently released them and sent them North.

The arrival of the first troops created a ripple of excitement that expelled somewhat the fear gripping the capital. They were escorted by the fur-hatted Clay Battalion as they began their march down Pennsylvania Avenue to the executive mansion to pay their respects to their Commander-in-Chief. Henry, marching alongside the Pennsylvania boys, was conscious of an audible undercurrent of Rebel sympathy in the onlookers all around him. The city was far from secure. It needed more troops desperately. Henry stiffened his back and tightened his grip on his carbine, watching closely for any open hostility other than the swearing and the oaths of defiance that assailed his ears.

President Lincoln greeted the young Pennsylvanians with

impassioned gratitude: "The capital opens its thankful heart to you, its first defenders. We rejoice in your arrival and take comfort in your fidelity to our flag, our Constitution and our troubled Union." His voice trembled and tears came to his eyes as he closed his greeting: "God bless you boys."

Detachments of the newly arrived troops were sent at once to guard the Long Bridge, the arsenal and the navy yard, while the cavalry was mounted and patrolled the city's streets.

No military barracks having been set up, the Pennsylvanians were billeted in the chambers of the House of Representatives where they lounged on the velvet carpeting and gawked at the marble surrounding them and the profusion of red and gold and bronze in the furnishings. Henry had never seen anything quite so impressive in its solemnity. Every Representative had his own armchair and desk, snuff box and spittoon. The smell of bread baking led him to inspect the basement vaults where he found a crude kitchen, stores, and a Negro in attendance at the ovens. The chimneys from these ovens came up through the terrace in front of the Capitol and gave off smoke and the fragrance of yeast.

When darkness came, Henry walked down the steps of the Capitol to report for guard duty at the door of Willard's Hotel, traditionally the center for social life and diplomatic intercourse in Washington. In the warm conviviality of Willard's public rooms could be found a mix of all the factions of Washington society at any time—state governors, generals, office-seekers, artists, clerks, statesmen—everyone jockeying for some political advantage.

The warm April air that greeted Henry's nostrils as he walked under the gaslights on Pennsylvania Avenue was heavy with odors from the stagnant canal. He tried to distinguish the various entities that made up the whole: sewage, rotting animals, decaying swamp vegetation. In all his life he had never encountered anything so offensive, so nauseating, so overpowering. And this was only April! He hated to contemplate the degree of foulness which the steamy months of summer would produce.

He turned back to look up at the Capitol and tried to visualize what its dome would look like when it was completed. The

110

moonlight was shining on a large crane positioned on the marble base of the building and silhouetted against the sky. The ten-foot high iron sheets that someday would form part of the dome were now forming a barricade on Capitol Hill for protection in case of street-fighting.

A horsecar rattled by on its tracks, its bell ringing and its stove smoking. Another member of the Clay Battalion stood at the door of Willard's. "All quiet here tonight," he noted. "I'm told that last week there were a thousand guests. Now there are only forty. All the southerners are packing their trunks and taking the Acquia Creek Steamer home."

The hotel doors swung open and Henry turned for a quick look at the sumptuous parlor and barroom within. Just then a horse-drawn carriage driven by a Negro pulled up at the same moment that a woman in expensive dress emerged with two small girls from the hotel amidst a flurry of boxes piled high in the arms of a Negro maid. Her long dark green velvet wrap set off her fussily coiffured golden locks visible from under her bonnet held in place by matching velvet ribbons. She spoke to the servant: "Be careful, Mattie, with my hat box. Put it on top of the others." And then addressing the children, she said: "Come along, Sue Ann. Take Melanie's hand. And watch the mud. This *awful yellow Washington mud!* And that dreadful smell from the river." She puckered up her face: "Oh, how glad I'll be to be back home in Virginny."

Henry caught the disdain in her southern drawl. As the boxes were crammed into the carriage, her husband came out of the hotel. A servant holding the door for him spoke: "Goodbye, Senator. May you have a safe journey home. Will you be returnin' to Willard's?"

The grim-faced man turned back momentarily to acknowledge the farewell. "Goodbye, James," he said. "Some day, yes, perhaps some day. But the city has changed. It's not the same place it was before . . ." He did not finish.

The family arranged themselves inside the carriage and the woman looked back at the hotel. "Imagine! Soldiers guardin' Willard's!" she gasped. "What's the country comin' to? So many changes since the new people came. I *will* miss dressin' for the

111

balls, though. I hope when we get home to Virginny people will still be havin' parties." And off they went into the darkness.

Leaving Willard's Henry continued on his rounds in the city. Lining the unpaved streets were boardinghouses, brothels and saloons from which issued raucous laughter. Everywhere was a feeling of a young, untamed city which had not had time to finish its dressing for the outside world. Not only was the Capitol missing its dome but the shaft of the Washington Monument rose, unfinished, from its base of white stone blocks.

The voices around him were mostly southern, and Henry was conscious of the angry, furtive looks and the shrinking away from him of passersby who quickened their step as he neared.

He checked out the massive stone, palace-like Treasury Building inside which howitzers now gave the building a siege-like feeling. In the cellar were stores of grain and hundreds of barrels of flour, pork, beans and sugar.

In front of its neighbor, the White House, a few soldiers were having a subdued conversation and Henry joined them. "We hear 700 boys from the 6th Massachusetts Regiment may arrive tomorrow. They got rough treatment in Baltimore when their train arrived. A mob of Rebel sympathizers attacked them when they were going through the city. They got showered with stones and bricks, beaten with clubs and muskets and planks torn out of the bridges. Everything anyone could find to fight them with. Pistols too. They lost some men killed and some wounded. In the end, they had to fire on the mob. Fortunately, they were all armed."

One sergeant spoke up: "Maryland must be in a bad way. Lots of Rebels. The state can't decide which side it's on. Guess no more troops from the North will come through her borders. Too risky."

The following morning the bruised Massachusetts militia arrived carrying thirty-six of their wounded to their quarters in the Senate chambers. They were full of stories about their dramatic passage through Baltimore. "But we weren't as bad off as some of the boys who came down from Philadelphia and got to Baltimore when we did. About 800 of them arrived in the city with no arms or uniforms. They weren't organized at all, but they thought they could be of some help to Washington. They got pretty battered before the police sent them back to Philadelphia."

"Where were their arms?" one Pennsylvanian wanted to know.

"None available," was the answer. "Buchanan's War Secretary Floyd stripped the North and sent them all South."

The city slept more confidently that night, secure in the presence of the Massachusetts Regiment and the knowledge that other troops were nearing the city.

Indeed, Washington had reason to rejoice when the 7th New York and the 8th Massachusetts and 1st Rhode Island regiments all arrived in the city after surmounting the difficulties put in their way in Maryland. Most trudged all day and all night on foot from Annapolis because the railroad tracks and bridges between Baltimore and Washington had been torn up by the Rebel sympathizers. The 8th Massachusetts with many mechanics and railroad men in its ranks knew how to repair the railroad and to put the locomotives back together again that the Marylanders had dismantled.

How the sight of these regiments did gladden the hearts in the capital! They took up their lines of march on Pennsylvania Avenue to pass in review before the President. The parade to the executive mansion was colorful and the whole atmosphere surrounding it was one of jubilation. The three regimental bands played "The Star-Spangled Banner" and drums rolled. Banners were unfurled along the marching route. All of the populace who had waited patiently but fearfully turned out to cheer those who had come to save Washington. It was a glittering display of well-drilled and well-outfitted troops. Having marched overland for many hours to reach the city, the soldiers, upon closer inspection, revealed the strain brought on by their exertion and sleep deprivation. The posh 7th New York, comprised of men of an elevated social standing and distinguished in drill and discipline, wore elegant uniforms and marched with a self-assured, proud step.

A boisterous hurrah went up as a company of cavalry swung into view. The commander was the youthful and wealthy William Sprague, Governor of Rhode Island, who had raised the regiment and paid for it himself. Wearing a hat turned up at one side and sporting a yellow plume, the handsome, twenty-nine-year-old Sprague made a dashing figure with golden epaulettes shining on his uniform. He led a company of the 1st Rhode Island regiment mounted on beautifully caparisoned, high-stepping horses which brought an enthusiastic cheer from the excited onlookers. Government officials breathed a sigh as the Rhode Island artillery battery passed. In front of the White House one of the Rhode Island cannon boomed a salute to the President.

Amidst the celebrating multitude were numbers of Secessionists who looked on unobtrusively, later slinking back into the side streets.

The troops took up temporary quarters in government buildings—in the rotunda of the Capitol, in the House of Representatives chambers and the Treasury Building where they slept on the floor, on chairs and benches. Arms were stacked in the rotunda. They were given a ration of hard bread and salt pork. The strictest discipline kept them at the ready for attack.

From its period of fear and desolation, Washington became a city of vitality and movement. In the streets the rattle of the horsecars was drowned out by the thud of cavalry, the marching of troops and the drumbeat of the tattoo. Soldiers were everywhere, there were constant collisions of drilling troops, and more volunteers came every day from all over the North into the train depot. With the restoration of the telegraph the city lost its feeling of isolation.

There were some one hundred Kentucky militiamen camping out in the East Room of the White House, cooking their dinner in the fireplace and singing. Smoke issued forth from the open door as the animal being roasted gave off delicious odors that permeated throughout the President's residence along with banjo music. Lincoln's boys entered into the fun of having these colorful guests in their home and played games with the Kentuckians.

There were momentous happenings outside Washington at this time, perhaps the most important of which was the imposi-

114

tion of the northern blockade of southern ports. The economic survival of the South depended on its overseas trade to sell its cotton and tobacco. In European markets it could exchange these products for munitions which it needed desperately. It had not enough arms for all the men who were joining up. By bringing an end to the flourishing trade, the blockade was intended to ultimately cripple the South's ability to make war.

More Southern states seceded: Virginia left the Union on April 17, Arkansas, Tennessee and North Carolina followed in May. The Union hold on the border states of Kentucky, Missouri and Maryland was precarious.

Immediately following the secession of Virginia, the U.S. Government arsenal at Harper's Ferry, Virginia found itself inside hostile territory. The small contingent of forty-three men stationed there set fire to the arsenal and armory and departed for safety. Harper's Ferry, whose tumultuous history had begun two years earlier with the exploits of abolitionist John Brown, was now in the hands of the Secessionists under the command of Thomas J. Jackson. This was the spring of 1861. It would continue to be a sensitive trouble spot that later in the coming conflict would again see the Stars and Stripes flying over it.

Within Washington itself the population was filling up with not only soldiers but also hundreds of job-seekers from the North. The President, setting up his new administration, was besieged by these would-be office-holders. Often he stood at his window looking out on the bustling activity and the new faces. It was a colorful sight that met his eyes. He watched the drilling of the Zouaves—the regiment of New York volunteer firemen—dressed in their billowing red pantaloons, spotless white gaiters, and red fezzes while, unconsciously, his feet kept time to the beat of the drums.

In the early months of the war, regiments from northern states did not have a standard uniform. Massachusetts and Pennsylvania boys arrived in the capital wearing blue, those from Wisconsin and Iowa were in gray, Vermont boys wore gray trimmed in emerald, and Minnesota troops could be distinguished by their black trousers and red flannel shirts. It was some time later before all the northern soldiers were clad in the regular army's light blue trousers and dark blue blouses. Lincoln looked down on the splendid horses of the cavalry going by, and the smell of these animals brought back sharply memories of his rural boyhood. These days he did not allow himself the luxury of memories very often but when he did, they brought a certain tranquility to his spirit.

He smiled at the way the soldiers had made themselves "at home" in adapting to their strange accommodations. Hundreds of white tents were now pitched in the parks for the volunteers. Lincoln laughed aloud at a cow being milked there by a Vermont farm boy while the smoke from the cook stoves drifted through the air. One soldier had rigged up a mirror suspended from the branch of a tree and was calmly shaving himself while another was hanging up washed clothes on a makeshift clothesline. He could see quite clearly from his window at the White House the daily butcherings of cattle and hogs in President's Park. The carcasses hung on hooks and their blood spattered the white stone blocks at the base of the unfinished Washington Monument.

One of Henry's evening patrols took him by a Negro neighborhood at the edge of the city. The singing of hymns reached his ears as he drew near the shantytown where lived a thousand free Negroes most of whom had escaped from Confederate states. The light of bonfires revealed their tumble down shacks and tents. The capital was home also to thousands of slaves whose presence was a constant irritant to abolitionists in the city and a sensitive problem for Lincoln to whom slavery was abhorrent but who, at this time, was trying to preserve the Union at all costs and, therefore, kept a low profile on the subject.

When in May 1861 sufficient troops had made their way to Washington, been drilled and armed to secure its safety, an attack was made on the city of Alexandria, Virginia across the Potomac on the 14th. On the day that northern troops pushed the Confederates out of the city, Henry was in the company of some soldiers who came across something none of them had seen before—a slave pen. Their curiosity was aroused by sounds of distress coming from behind the walls. To knock down the high iron gates and doors, they took up heavy pieces of timber nearby and used them as battering rams. Inside they discovered all the Ne-

116

groes of Alexandria crowded together without regard to age or sex or physical condition. The intent of the Confederates had been to ship them all South, but to frighten them they had told them that they were going to be sold to Cuba by the Yankees to pay for the war. At the sight of the Yankee uniforms, they began to scream in terror. Weeping and wailing by mothers holding babies in their arms, old men and women shrinking away from the strangers, and young children hiding behind their parents created a scene of consummate fear. The soldiers were able finally to quiet them and convince them that they meant no harm. Their fears were further allayed at the news that the southerners had left the city. Although against orders, the northern soldiers left the gates and doors of the slave pen standing open, much to the astonishment of the captives.

One day as Henry was patrolling the streets he was witness to a tearful meeting of a father and his little son, both wearing army uniforms. The latter, dressed in a knee-length coat with a short cape attached to it that covered the shoulders, was a drummer boy with the Eighth Michigan Regiment and was en route to Port Royal, South Carolina via Washington where his father had been stationed ever since answering Lincoln's first call for volunteers in April. They met only by chance when, returning from the Washington Navy Yard where his regiment had received their arms, the boy saw his father at a distance and ran to greet him. The father, unaware of his son's enlistment, expressed both shock and joy at seeing him.

"Charlie! Charlie Gardner! What are you doing here?" He embraced his son and held him close to him.

"I wanted to help my country, just like you, Father," the boy blurted out, throwing his shoulders back proudly. "I'm a drummer boy. I take the place of somebody else who can carry a musket."

"But you are only thirteen years old!" his father remonstrated.

"Thirteen-and-a-half," Charlie corrected him.

Their reunion lasted only a few minutes. Charlie kissed his father and turned to run back to join his regiment which had tarried long enough for the brief encounter of father and son. Char-

117

lie's father watched him go, sadness and disbelief mingling in his face.

Henry felt obliged to say something to comfort the man. "You can be very proud of him."

The father, watching the boy's regiment disappear from view, answered: "I wonder if I will ever see him again."

As spring warmed into early summer, the humid heat of the capital bore down on its inhabitants. Dust whirled up from Pennsylvania Avenue, and when even a slight breeze blew from the south, it carried into the windows the putrid odors from the canal. Heads ached from the heavy oppressive atmosphere, and mosquitoes and gnats vied with flies for entrance to the open windows.

Lincoln suffered some of the symptoms of ague ("Potomac fever" the natives called it) which afflicted the capital's residents in the summer: dryness and heaviness in the eyes, a heaviness in the whole body, malaria-like shivers, headache. One evening, to relieve the stress of his physical problems, he decided to pay a visit to the Soldiers' Home, which had been suggested to him as a cool retreat from the stifling heat of the White House. He mounted his horse and rode out of the gate of the executive mansion where he was met by eight mounted cavalry. The 150th Pennsylvania Regiment (the "Bucktails") had been permanently assigned to guard the President. "Good evening, Mr. President," the commanding officer addressed him quietly.

Lincoln acknowledged the greeting. "If one tries hard, one can detect a fragrance of jasmine in the air tonight above the offerings from the canal," he said with a hint of a smile.

As they set off, the 7th New York regimental band was playing "Columbia, the Gem of the Ocean" on the south lawn. The troopers, with sabres drawn, took up their positions, closing in on all four sides of him, shielding him totally. He made light of the organized effort to protect him, but, as they rode along 15th Street in the gathering dusk, he was gratified to see standing on guard at every street corner mounted cavalry.

Upon reaching the drive which led back to the stone Soldiers' Home, Lincoln dismissed the cavalry escort and commenced the ride through the dark woods alone. He relaxed at the

sound of the crickets reveling in the summer air. There was no moon, and no stars lit his way, but the horse plodded, unhurried, seeming to know the way.

In the stillness of the night a shot rang out and a bullet whizzed by the President's head striking a tree behind him with a dull whack. The terrified horse lunged forward, almost unseating his rider, and dashed through the gates of the Home in panic. From his post in front of the Home, a soldier jumped out and grabbed the horse's reins and quieted it with his voice and his hands on the animal's neck. "Slow down, boy. Quiet boy. Easy now. It's all right. There now."

Then to the President he spoke with great concern: "Mr. President, are you all right, Sir?"

A somewhat flustered President assured the soldier that he was unharmed.

"Sir, you really should not ever be out in public without an escort. Even with all the troops in the city at present, these are unsettled times. And you, Sir, are always in danger."

Lincoln dismounted and collected himself. The soldier tied the horse securely after rubbing his hands all over the animal's head and neck and speaking reassuringly to him in soothing tones.

"You must go inside quickly, and may I suggest, Sir, that you spend the night here and return home in daylight?"

As the soldier opened the door of the Home for the President to enter, he said to him: "I'll see to the matter of the rifle shot, Sir."

Lincoln safely inside, turned to speak to the soldier: "I'm obliged to you, sergeant. By the way, what is your name?"

"Henry Washington Sawyer, Sir. Clay Battalion and 25th Pennsylvania Volunteer Infantry."

"I'll remember you," Lincoln answered soberly, studying the younger man's countenance.

13

By July 1861 the capital bristled with troops, untrained but straining for action. They had joined up to fight and they had had enough of waiting. Throughout the North the impatient outcry was: "Forward to Richmond! Forward to Richmond!" The ninety-day service of the first volunteers Lincoln had called for would soon expire, and the prevailing sentiment was that an attack should be made to utilize those troops before they went home.

General Irvin McDowell, a Regular Army officer, was given the command. His enemy was the army of General Pierre G.T. Beauregard who planned and executed the attack on Fort Sumter, and who was now in position only twenty-five miles from Washington at a place called Manassas Junction in Virginia near a stream known as Bull Run. McDowell's force was made up of inadequately trained but enthusiastic volunteers; most had received only superficial training with little target practice or mock combat, many going into the fight just three weeks after being organized. They were commanded for the most part by men without any experience of war who had secured their posts through political favor. A serious problem for General McDowell was a lack of sufficient supply trains—wagons, horses, mules, and harness—the organization of which had fallen far behind schedule. He had neither maps for the coming campaign nor trustworthy reconnaissance officers. With no organized artillery, no commissariat and no staff to aid him, he was not prepared for combat.

General Beauregard's spies in Washington kept him well-informed. Uniquely gifted for espionage proficiency were a number of ladies with southern sympathies. They employed their powers of persuasion and all the feminine artifice at their command. Secret messages were hidden in extraordinary places on their persons: underneath hoop skirts and inside rolls of long tresses tucked at the back of the neck with a comb. Oftentimes they appeared on horseback at enemy picket lines, asking for permission to cross over to see relatives. Inevitably they wangled their way through the lines, carrying vital information to southern officers they sought out. Invariably these ladies seemed to be well-endowed with physical beauty, seductively attractive figures, pleasant personalities and flirtatious ways to which men of influence and position in the North were likely to succumb and reveal valuable information. Beneath their ample bosoms beat hearts so passionately for the southern cause that they did not flinch in the face of dangers attendant to their roles as spies.

The notorious Rose Greenhow, famed for her intimate relationships with many important Washington personages, carried on her treasonous activities in the capital quite openly and dispatched a message to Beauregard giving the exact time for the beginning of hostilities, the numbers of troops involved, and the routes they would follow. Beauregard had the help of brilliant soldiers such as General Thomas J. Jackson (who earned his nickname "Stonewall" in this opening battle of the war), James Ewell Brown "Jeb" Stuart and Joseph E. "Joe" Johnston.

McDowell set off from Washington across the Potomac bridges with some 35,000 raw recruits. Cheering, flag-waving crowds had seen them off as they marched away to war down Pennsylvania Avenue in Fourth-of-July-parade fashion. Swinging on the tips of their guns were bouquets of flowers given them by pretty young girls who had kissed them goodbye. They knew nothing about war but their hearts were light and they felt energized by the thought that, at long last, they were actually going to fight.

It was not long before McDowell's fears were confirmed: he was going into battle without firm control over a mass of men, untried, unused to hard physical training, and undisciplined. Since they had not learned how to fight in the training camps, they would have to learn on the battlefield. Marching had not been part of their training. They became exhausted quickly carrying their heavy packs in the July heat and many fell by the wayside with sunstroke. The temptation to plunder houses and farms along the way proved too strong to resist. Fields of ripe blackberries lured them into breaking ranks for a juicy feast, and they left their line of march to drink from every stream and to remove their shoes and bathe their burning feet.

They took off after various prizes along their route—chickens, pigs, honey from hives—whose capture was cause for raucous merriment on the part of the cheering onlookers urging them on. War was still a kind of sport to these neophytes with their youthful, innocent zest for life and their ignorance of what lay ahead. Later, when bullets began to fly over their heads, they stood awestruck at the strange noise they made.

There was no accounting for the number of women who went to war to be near their husbands or simply to satisfy an urge of patriotism. One feminine warrior of Bull Run was Kady Brownell, wife of Sergeant Robert Brownell serving with the 1st Rhode Island infantry. Commissioned by General Ambrose E. Burnside to be the "regimental daughter," she was the official color-bearer for her company of sharpshooters. Wearing a short skirt, trousers and a red sash, she presented an astonishing picture carrying the heavy standard at the head of the regiment as they walked into enemy fire with bullets whizzing all around.

Even with the leadership of such stalwarts as Burnside, Samuel P. Heintzelman and William Tecumseh Sherman, the Battle of Bull Run went badly for the Yankee forces and they ultimately fell apart and could not be rallied. Their retreat became a rout when they turned, threw down their guns and raced back towards Washington.

The spectacle of thousands upon thousands of frightened soldiers fleeing for their lives was made all the more dramatic by the fact that witnessing it were many sightseers from Washington who, out of sheer curiosity, had taken to their light carriages with picnic baskets full, deciding to treat themselves to a ringside seat at the first battle between the blue and the gray. It was Sunday and a holiday mood had descended on these revelers whose numbers counted in Congressmen, many ladies and some Union officers. The picnickers opened their wicker hampers on the hillside near Bull Run, within sight of the smoke and within earshot of the battle raging. The fancily dressed ladies wore floppy hats to shield their faces from the scorching sun and held field glasses to their eyes, squinting for the action they had come to see. Having had no previous encounter with war, they looked upon it as entertainment that would provide a little excitement to their lives.

It was not long before the retreating soldiers came into view and sparked fear amongst the convivial spectators. The picnic came to an abrupt end. Soldiers and sightseers became entangled in one noisy, pell-mell rush towards safety. Ambulance drivers, forsaking the wounded, unhitched their horses from the wagons and galloped back towards Washington. Riderless horses, eyes blazing with fear, snorted by the mob. Confederate skirmishers, following closely behind, fired into the back of the moving mass of men, horses and wagons. No one was on the sidelines in the panic that ensued.

The yelling, struggling, fighting enveloped all who found themselves on the road. The wheels of gun caissons rolled over bodies, and all authority and rank ceased to exist as officers and soldiers fought each other with bayonets for empty places in ambulances and wagons. Futile attempts were made by some officers to bring their men under control with swords and cursing. As they ran, soldiers dropped everything they were carrying—muskets, haversacks, canteens, clothing. The light carriages of the Washington society picnickers were smashed as they became enmeshed with heavier wagons, and their occupants took to the road on foot and became part of the frenzied mob on the run.

The soldiers streamed back to Washington totally ignorant of where their officers were or how to form their regiments again or even where they would sleep that night. Lincoln looked out of the White House window and saw the disorganized mass straggling along in the heavy rain down Pennsylvania Avenue. They were not an army, he thought, but a staggering rabble out of control. Dirty, unshaven, and many devoid of uniforms and shoes, they presented a forlorn picture for their Commander-in-Chief. The desire for liquor to ease their disgrace was strong and they stormed every establishment where it was sold.

On duty with the Clay Battalion in Washington throughout the Bull Run debacle, Henry had missed the army's initial combat. Now he was witness to its shattering aftermath. Drunken soldiers emerged from every tavern, collapsed in the streets not knowing where to go—and not caring.

Lincoln watched women serving hot coffee to soldiers who sank wearily down on curbstones and flopped up against lamp posts. Others were bandaging the wounded. In his solitude Lincoln expressed dismay out loud: "What will the country say?"

The catastrophe at Bull Run made a clear statement to the North: the struggle to save the Union would not be easy. It would be long and bloody. The job of rescuing the northern army from disaster was given to General George B. McClellan, a West Pointer who had won acclaim in successful battles waged in western Virginia. He would take over from General McDowell now and organize the troops into the Army of the Potomac. He did this by demanding rigorous training and drilling of the men, giving them a new pride in their army and self-respect. They responded to his discipline and high standards of military service with unswerving loyalty and renewed spirit. They called him "Little Mac" with great affection as he instilled in them a new professionalism in their soldiering. Trusting him unconditionally, they would go anywhere he asked, do anything he requested.

At the time that Henry's three-month service came to an end immediately after Bull Run, General McClellan was issuing a call for cavalry in the Army of the Potomac. Henry entertained no notion of leaving the service. With his many years of experience with horses it seemed to him a natural that he could best serve his country in the cavalry. He left Washington and was mustered out of the 25th Pennsylvania Infantry Regiment at the end of July. Ten days elapsed before his next service began, and he went home to see his family.

Harriet's face wore a woeful expression when he announced his intention to re-enlist. "The country needs me. I can't turn my back on her now. She needs every able-bodied man in the country." He tried to explain. "Bull Run was a catastrophe and taught us a lesson. There's a new general now in Washington who is organizing the Army of the Potomac and he wants cavalry. I'm going to join up again. I'll take Prince with me, and I'll need another horse. Ambrose can find me a good one, I'm sure."

"How long will you be away this time?" she asked plaintively.

There was no way he could soften the blow. "I'm signing up for three years," he answered, stroking her cheek to ease the pain of his words.

She fought back the tears that welled up. "Three years!" she exclaimed. "But I thought the war was going to be over quickly. Everyone said the South would never fight."

"That was foolish, reckless talk of people who didn't know what they were talking about. Their army is better trained than ours. They have fine officers. And an excellent cavalry. And what's more, they're fighting now on their own soil—Virginia." He paused momentarily. "Soldiers fight differently when they're defending their own homes and land. It's going to take a lot of hard fighting to win this war." That was all he said on the subject. They would talk more but what had been said was enough for now.

Harriet changed the subject brightly. "A letter came for you yesterday from Pennsylvania," she announced, handing him an envelope.

Henry glanced at the handwriting. "It's from Ma." He read it quickly. "Thad and Si have joined up," he said. "For three years. I wonder how Pa is going to run the farm alone. Ma says he's planning to turn all the crop land into pasture. That way he can probably manage it by himself. He's not getting any younger." He turned back to the letter. "Thad got married and Si and his wife are expecting a baby next month." As he placed the letter back in the envelope, he mused: "I wonder if Thad and Si and I will meet up somewhere in the army. Wouldn't that be a twist of Fate?"

Henry went out to the stables he had built for Beauty and

Prince. The horses whinnied when he opened the stable door and ran up to him. Henry rubbed the soft muzzles and patted the necks fondly. "You're both in good shape," he said to the animals as he bent down and lifted their hooves to examine them. He spoke to the black horse. "Prince boy, are you ready to go to war? You're in the best years of your life right now, you're strong and healthy, and you can help your country. I need you, my good fellow." He patted the big rump and ran his hand down the sleek flank.

Then, putting his arm affectionately around Beauty's neck, he spoke into his ear. "I'm sorry I can't take you with me, boy, but you'd better stay home and enjoy this quiet. You and I have had many good years together, haven't we? Life in the cavalry would be too hard on you, boy. You're seventeen now, you know."

He saddled Beauty and rode to Ambrose's house to transact the business about the second horse he needed, and two days later Ambrose appeared leading a chestnut gelding behind the horse he was riding. The new horse was a two-year-old, strong and spirited, named Thorn. Henry examined him carefully and pronounced him sound. "He'll do fine," he said to Ambrose. As the two men stood discussing the horses, Henry grew serious for a moment. "The regiment is going into camp outside Washington next week. I don't know how long we'll be there before we go into the field for active duty. I'd like to have you with me then. If I can arrange it, will you come? I'll have to be honest with you . . . there will be danger."

Ambrose was thoughtful. "I'd like to do somethin' to help ma country," he said simply.

"That would surely be helping," Henry said firmly. "I'll let you know when the time comes."

Harriet assembled a few things of her own handiwork for Henry to take with him. There was a blanket she had made for their bed, an embroidered "housewife" sewing kit with needles, scissors, pins, buttons, thread and quinine, a pair of woolen socks she had knit, and a decorated folder containing stationery and stamps. Included also were rolls of bandages, an antidote for foul water sickness, and woolen undergarments to ward off ague.

Ezekiel Eldredge had a saddle and bridle for Thorn, and Jeremiah Eldredge offered Henry an extra carbine he didn't need. The four Eldredge cousins who had joined up the same night as Henry three months ago were all in training camps.

*   *   *

In the early months of the war, the Federal Government looked upon the whole idea of cavalry as a frivolous, expensive and unnecessary appendage to its military force. It did not share the Confederate view of the important role that troopers played in the organization of an army. Rather, citizen-cavalry was assessed as a "luxury" beyond the government's means of support. To mount and equip horse soldiers required a great deal more money than the furnishing of infantry units. There was the belief, too, that novices on horseback would not appreciate the necessity of caring for their mounts properly. The general feeling in Washington was that the war would be won quickly anyway, far more speedily than a cavalry could be recruited and trained.

But the First Battle of Bull Run, fought and lost less than a month before, had altered the thinking in the War Department. It was clear that the success of the South at Bull Run had depended to a great extent on the strength of its mounted troops. Bull Run had spelled out clearly the devastating truth that the war was not going to be short-lived, and Union military strategists began to talk of their need for more than 20,000 horsemen for their eastern campaigns. Lincoln called upon the states again.

On August 4, the President authorized Colonel William Halstead of Trenton, New Jersey to raise a regiment of volunteer cavalry from that state. It was to be a private regiment, not under state control, assigned to the War Department, to be known as Halstead's Horse. The aged Halstead, a prominent New Jersey lawyer and Washington politician, quickly filled the regiment with more than 1000 men—mostly American-born but also numbering quite a few German and Irish immigrants. Within a month twelve companies arrived in Washington and proceeded to build their camp on Meridian Hill outside the city. Henry was mustered in as Second Lieutenant in Captain Robert Boyd's Company D, for three years.

127

Upon arrival at the stretch of cleared ground which was to become Camp Keystone, their first of several training camps, shelter tents were pitched and the men were given lumber and saws, hammers and nails, to begin the task of building their own barracks. Amateur cavalrymen, many were also amateur carpenters. Henry's skills and years of experience were stretched to the utmost in teaching the novices the fundamentals of house construction. Many an oath rent the air as hammers hit thumbs.

During this time they became accustomed to shortages that affected their every comfort. There were not enough tents or blankets, uniforms or shoes. At night the men wrapped themselves in their horses' blankets and in quilts and comforters sent from home.

There were many complaints about the food which was cooked outside their tents over open fires by the men themselves whose culinary skills left much to be desired. Often the soup was burned, and sometimes the beef was so tough that hours of boiling could not tenderize it.

"My Ma never gave me moldy bread and I don't intend to start eatin' it now," said one young trooper in disgust.

Another looked at the maggots that came to the surface as the bacon was sizzling in the skillet in the rain. "I don't want none o' them. I only eat meat that comes on four legs."

One morning a soldier announced: "Here comes the bread for the week," as a wagon drawn by a mule and full of loose bread pulled up. The driver shoveled the bread out of the wagon onto the ground.

Occasionally, the standards of the food were raised by the arrival of a farmer from the countryside nearby with a wagon loaded with fresh vegetables, apples and peaches, and chickens. "This here will keep you'uns a coupla days," the farmer offered.

Morale depended on the supply of coffee more than anything else. Each mess had two kettles, one for meat and vegetables and one for coffee. If the men had plenty of coffee to drink, the grumbling ceased.

But trouble of a more serious nature descended on the encampment from the very beginning. The weaknesses in the field and staff officer corps were blatantly apparent. They were mostly men of social and political standing without any army experience, and their judgment on matters of training and drilling the men seemed to rest on winning popularity with the troops. Lack of discipline showed up in the slackening of drills, in the currying for favor among the officers, the lack of respect for authority, and in the cliques within the officer corps. Officers were guilty of giving into public pressure instead of enforcing orders, and then there was old Colonel Halstead who was ill-prepared for his military responsibilities and could hardly cope because of the infirmities of age.

Disregard for elementary sanitation created a slovenliness in attitudes and habits. It was not long before the sick lists grew. Everyone was coming down with measles, and there were the ever-present diarrhea, dysentery and typhoid. Small wonder with the open trenches serving as latrines!

Very early in the regiment's formation there were not enough horses and there was not enough forage or tack for the horses they had. A worse problem was that few of the men knew anything about caring for them. They had never fed them or groomed them, and many could not even ride. The equestrian skills of these northern farm boys, such as they were, had been learned sauntering about on large draft horses bareback on their farms. Many, seduced by the recruiting posters showing dashing troopers on beautiful horses, had joined up because of the elitist reputation that the cavalry enjoyed, the glamour and romance surrounding it, and also because of the popular impression that it was an easier way to go to war than on one's own feet.

What Henry saw when he looked at the men assembled for drill was a mixed bag of country boys: along with the predominance of farmers were merchants, mechanics, store clerks, carpenters, day laborers and machinists. Since, in the North, horses were usually driven rather than ridden, he assumed that most of the men before him now had neither ridden a horse for pleasure nor really cared much for the animal. He was sure that none of them had the remotest idea of how much time would be required to look after his horse and keep it in good working condition. As he scrutinized the troops, Henry wondered also how many of them had ever fired a gun. From their general demeanor and

129

their conversation they did not impress him with their knowledge and experience with firearms. There were accidents with firearms in their hands. It was certain that they would need a great deal of target practice, but at the moment the need for proper firearms, ammunition and blank cartridges (to accustom the horses to firing) had not been filled by the Ordnance Bureau. Marksmanship training would have to wait. First, the men had to learn to ride.

Henry took his duties as an officer very seriously and was appalled at the laxity in command around him. Drilling seemed to be a haphazard, lackadaisical, take-it or leave-it affair. He was determined that the men he trained would never be guilty of abusive handling of their mounts and would learn to keep uppermost in their minds their horses' welfare. His training of the cavalry recruits began with the insistence that their most important duty was to love, honor and have pride in their horses. He showed the men how to "talk" to their horses with their hands, bringing reassurance to the animals through touch. He taught them how to examine hooves. "That's the first thing you do every day. Cast shoes have to be replaced immediately. It's important, too, to watch your horse's mouth," he cautioned. "If you see him tossing his head a lot or going with his jaws set against one side of the bit, the chances are the curb is too tight and needs to be loosened. If his jaw becomes injured, he may need a nose band or a temporary string bridle. Horses can react violently to the pain of the bit. They can start to bolt and become unmanageable and end up being called 'vicious.'

"When we go into action the thought that you must keep in mind at all times is how to spare your horse. His back must be watched carefully. After many hours of being ridden, it will get sore from the rubbing of the saddle. Careful saddling will do a great deal to prevent sore backs. You will dismount at *every* opportunity on the march, remove the saddle and massage his back whenever there's time to do so. You will lead your horse at regular intervals on the march, especially when the road goes up or down a steep hill. You will keep him at a walk. Only when in action will you ride faster. Watch for swellings on his back; no matter how small, they are significant. Give your horse a chance to nibble grass or get a few swallows of water on the march. A good horseman knows his horse so well that he will be able to anticipate what his reactions will be to work, food, water, weight carried and the nature of the terrain being ridden. With good care and consideration, he'll serve you well for many miles."

He continued: "Now, is there anyone who doesn't know how to swim?"

A few of the men nodded.

"Well, you'd better learn. You're going to have to cross swollen rivers with strong currents and you've got to be able to make your horse swim them too when he doesn't want to."

During the first few weeks at Camp Keystone the regiment saw no service beyond the practice field and picket line. Gradually horses arrived from quartermaster depots—900 of them in varying stages of physical health and stamina. The Government paid $110 and up for cavalry mounts, and unscrupulous contractors sold the Government spavined horses, animals that were going blind, and many afflicted with diseases, such as glanders and the heaves. All of these problems had to be sorted out by the cavalry struggling to organize itself into a reliable fighting force.

Henry sat up straight on the back of Prince as the men lined up alongside their mounts for drill practice. He was silently amused at the feeble attempts to mount. All manner of pulling, tugging, struggling, jumping in place, and gasping preceded the successful trips to the saddles, and once having gained their seats they clutched the horses' manes or hung on desperately to the saddles. Some of them were quite rigid with fear of the animals under them. As he gave commands to "trot" and "gallop," Henry watched, his stomach quaking with laughter, as the recruits' faces registered sheer terror. Would these greenhorns ever learn to ride well enough to go into action, Henry wondered.

The physical examinations these men had undergone at the time of their mustering-in were cursory at best, Henry assumed, for there were many varying specimens of manhood and levels of physical fitness before him now. There were a dozen robust boys he guessed to be no older than fifteen or sixteen whose lies about their age had passed by careless mustering officials unimpressed by the rule about the requisite eighteen years of age. Although the desired weight of a cavalryman was 130 pounds, this restriction was not binding. There appeared to be room for everyone in Halstead's Horse. Fat, muscles, and brawn in giant proportions were in good supply. There were also several Mexican War veterans of indeterminate age whose advanced years were flaunted in snowy white beards.

At first none of the men had all the Government's regulation equipment of a trooper. Shortages of uniforms meant that the men appeared wearing all manner of substitute apparel. It was difficult to view them as a single fighting unit; the colors and materials of their garb were as varied as the states and cities from which they came.

Theoretically, the trooper's uniform consisted of a dark blue canvas-lined jacket, a blouse, heavy trousers, a change of underwear, a shirt, stockings, boots and a pair of spurs. His hat was a stiff, broad-brimmed, heavy black felt that resembled a Pilgrim father's hat, complete with black ostrich feather, and pinned to the front were the crossed sabers with insignia and company letter in brass. However, the choice of hat was very often a matter of personal or regimental preference. For comfort and practicality the forage cap with its high crown and the McClellan style low-crowned kepi were more popular.

He was furnished with an overcoat that he strapped across the pommel of the saddle and a rubber poncho and blanket for himself that he carried across the cantle of the saddle. He had a canteen and haversack. His weapons included a three-and-a-half-foot long saber, a saber belt and a steel scabbard four feet long, a carbine and a carbine sling and holster, one or two revolvers with holsters, two cartridge boxes, and gun tools. For his horse he was supplied with a saddle blanket, a saddle, saddlebags, surcingle, nose bag, lariat, curb bit and bridle, halter, watering bridle, curry comb and brush, and a 14-inch-long iron picket pin which would be driven into the ground in bivouac and linked by rope to the horse's halter, allowing him room to graze but holding him fast.

Many men who enlisted brought their own horses and accouterments which did not always include saddles and bridles. The soldier who brought his own horse to war received forty cents a day from the Government for the use of the animal; his feed was also supplied. If he was killed in battle, the owner received his appraised value, but no payment was made if he died of disease, starvation or overwork. When saddles were finally in good supply, they were of inferior quality, being covered with rawhide rather than leather.

The most serious shortage was in cavalry weapons. Men tended to bring with them a conglomeration of weapons of every description from home: single and double-barreled shotguns, squirrel rifles, fowling pieces, pistols, heirlooms from the Mexican War, and muzzle-loading flintlock muskets. This shortage obtained for the better part of two years; because of the cavalry's being "new" to the army, provision had not been made for it when it came into existence in the Army of the Potomac. Sabers were in such short supply that often sticks or branches had to be substituted for guard duty.

After two months in Camp Keystone, Halstead's Horse was moved across the Potomac to a new camp—Camp Mercer, Virginia—which was quickly nicknamed "Camp Mud" because of its low-lying, soggy surroundings. Troubles of many kinds followed the regiment here: soldiers contracted diarrhea, dysentery, and typhoid fever and died, and Colonel Halstead's health failed in the face of disputes amongst his officers forcing him to depart Camp Mercer on medical leave.

Here began a new chapter for the regiment. Governor Olden appointed a new lieutenant colonel: Joseph Kargé, a thirty-eight-year-old Polish officer with years of cavalry experience in Europe. A military man, schooled in the rigid discipline of the Prussian cavalry, was what the floundering regiment he now commanded needed. Kargé bore down on officers and men alike, tightening discipline at every turn. Initially, he met stubborn resistance; he was not used to the independent spirit of the American volunteer who rebelled under his strict tutelage, but he did not give in to their complaints. He personally directed them on the drill field. Their former hours of idleness in camp were replaced by drilling in mounted and dismounted formations, hour after hour.

"I will personally examine your carbines and pistols. I want to find them clean and your sabers sharp!" he bellowed from his horse.

His demands for excellence in performance paid off; the men responded by giving of their best and he rewarded them by fighting a battle with the quartermaster on their behalf. He demanded uniforms and weapons, rations and forage. He also appealed to the citizens of New Jersey for blankets for the troops, proving to the men his sincere concern for their welfare.

Kargé, determined to sort the wheat from the chaff in the corps of field and staff officers, rid the regiment of all those guilty of incompetence and dishonesty in the performance of their duties.

There came another change of campsites, this time to Camp Custis near Fort Lyon, one of the southernmost defenses of Washington. These would be their winter quarters; out came the hammers yet another time, and the men constructed wooden decks for their tents.

Gradually, the men recognized the value of the vigorous training program that had been forced on them. Along with their grumbling over the military formality enforced, they began to feel pride in the regiment and to be conscious of their progress in becoming a fighting force. They were better marksmen, they wielded their sabers with assurance, and their drilling in the field had improved daily. All this had happened in two months under Colonel Kargé.

14

The months of December and January moved slowly for the men of Halstead's Horse. Winter doldrums and the mounting restlessness from the absence of active duty brought on a resumption of bickering, infighting, insubordination and intoxication among the officer corps resulting in their arrests and desertions amongst the men, all of this sparking rumors that the regiment was going to be disbanded. But in February there came a large dollop of good fortune. It was three-fold. First, the State of New Jersey recognized Halstead's Horse as its first regiment of volun-

teer cavalry to be known as the First New Jersey Cavalry and would henceforth furnish the regular stipend to support the families at home. (As history unfolded, the 1st New Jersey was the first to enter the field and the last to leave it.) Second, Colonel Halstead was relieved of his command permanently. Third, replacing the old colonel was an English soldier of fortune, one Colonel Sir Percy Wyndham, who presented a picture of dashing soldiery with a black moustache that measured ten inches end to end. Twenty-eight years old, Wyndham came from a military family of long lineage. At the age of fifteen he had been a participant in the revolutionary "Students' Corps" in Paris, and had gone on to serve with distinction in Italy, France and Austria before coming to America to throw himself wholeheartedly into the battle to save the Union. He arrived at a very opportune moment. The War Department and General McClellan welcomed him with warm enthusiasm. His extensive military experience, and particularly his skills in cavalry operations, recommended him highly to Governor Olden for the commission of Colonel of the regiment. Wyndnam was to serve in conjunction with Lieutenant Colonel Kargé, and it was hoped that the combined leadership of these two seasoned European officers would solve, once and for all, the problems of the regiment. His youthful energy, personal magnetism, self-confidence and air of authority were qualities needed by a leader who was to rescue the faltering regiment from dissolution.

In his first meeting with the troops he let them know that he expected from them obedience to orders and thorough military discipline. The men, having first experienced the toughness of Kargé and seen the results of such discipline, found Wyndham agreeable and were buoyed up by his command.

Sir Percy's determination to pull the regiment into an efficient fighting force quickly succeeded by his reforms in the officer corps. He got rid of the "dead wood"—all those he deemed lacking in leadership—and replaced them with junior officers who had served responsibly.

"Sawyer, I'm promoting you to 1st Lieutenant, Company D," he said to Henry one morning. "I like the way you're handling drill practice. We are well-armed and well-mounted but a great deal more practice is required before we're ready to take the field."

Wyndham had set the highest standards for the regiment and to achieve them he put into practice a merciless drilling regimen, hour after hour, over and over, shifting from marching columns into fighting formation, maneuvers, saber practice, and quick saddling of the horses. He inspected the horses carefully to ascertain if the saddling was done properly. Whenever he came across sloppiness, he gave vent to his wrath on the unfortunate horseman, prefacing it with a habit of twirling his enormous moustache between his finger tips. Wyndham's technique was to so train the regiment by rote that it would respond instantaneously to any commands it was given and to execute them perfectly. Time and time again the regiment was ordered out to prepare for a march and went through the drill of packing and saddling quickly. On each occasion they believed that this time it was for real and that they were on their way to take the field, but each time they were disappointed to discover that it was merely another practice. They had been volunteer soldiers now for seven months and, with each passing day, the desire to meet the enemy became more urgent. They felt self-confident that they were truly ready for combat after these months of vigorous training.

In March 1862 word came that McClellan was finally on the move from Washington to begin his Peninsula campaign with the ultimate goal the capture of Richmond. He was moving more than 75,000 troops and their equipment in 400 transports down the Potomac to Fortress Monroe from which point they would march overland to attack the Confederate capital. To the dismay of the 1st New Jersey Cavalry it was clear that they had been left behind. What they did not know was that Lincoln, obsessed with the conviction that Washington must never be left undefended, had forbidden McClellan from taking McDowell's 1st Army Corps (to which the 1st New Jersey Cavalry was attached) away from the environs of the capital. They could not move until the arrival of replacements from western Virginia. The men of the 1st New Jersey began to fear that the war would be over before they ever saw action.

To take their minds off their bitter disappointment, Wyndham sent them on picket duty and scouting missions which brought them under fire for the first time, put them in some danger, and provided excitement. The daily picketing was along the Rappahannock where the regiment put to good use the training in marksmanship perfected in the incessant drilling by Wyndham and Kargé. The southern boys facing them across the river were infantrymen from Mississippi and Louisiana whose long-barreled rifles were not very effective against the short-range carbines of the New Jerseyites. When a Texas regiment arrived as a replacement, it suggested a truce along the picket line which relieved that duty of any threatening danger. All the boys on both sides complied happily with the arrangement.

During these days of marking time, they also learned valuable lessons about bivouac that would stand them in good stead in future campaigns.

Henry's sixth sense told him it was only a matter of days before the regiment would be on the move, so he sent word to Harriet that Ambrose should join him. In order to have both Prince and Thorn ready for action, Henry had changed horses every other day. Thorn would be ready for Ambrose when he showed up. Ambrose's duties would consist of caring for the horses, finding forage, and serving as groom and general factotum on the march. During a campaign when Henry dismounted to enter the fight, Ambrose would hold the horses. In his unique role, he would not be armed, nor would he receive any pay.

Life in camp was regulated by the buglers and drummers. These youthful musicians did many other chores in camp—even barbering—but their chief responsibility was to give twenty daily calls. As the commands were sounded on the bugle or drummed, the men responded automatically to their summons and, surprisingly, the horses learned to recognize each one and, with ears up, were eager to do their bidding. Often, a horse that had been dismounted, heard the bugle call and hurried into his place in the line.

The chief bugler of the regiment blew the call for the "Assembly of Buglers" long before dawn, which brought two buglers from each company to Headquarters to sound "Reveille" together. When the men were dressed, each company had roll call. Next was the call to "Stables." All the horses were assembled at the grain pile where their canvas nose-bags were filled with the daily ration of grain. The men then took their mounts to the picket-rope with curry-comb and brush and, under close supervision, groomed them. The men washed up and then answered the "Breakfast Call." "Watering Call" brought all the cavalry back to the picket-rope for the watering of the horses, sometimes necessitating a ride of several miles bareback at a walking gait in search of a stream or pond. "Sick Call" was followed by "Fatigue Call" which was answered by the men detailed to police or clean the camp, to build stables or shelters for the horses and mules, to collect wood and water and, when the occasion demanded it, to bury horses.

At the "First Call for Guard Mount" the five or six men from each company who would stand guard duty that day rode to the inspection point. "Drill Call" was followed by an order given by a sergeant of each company to "Saddle Up" and "Lead Out." When the company was formed, he presented it to the Captain with the announcement, "Sir, the company is formed." The Captain ordered "Prepare to Mount," "Mount," and "Form Ranks" and the company proceeded to the drill ground.

In succession the bugle announced "Recall from Drill" and "Dinner Call." In the afternoon, "Drill" followed "Dinner," then came the second "Water Call," "Dress Parade" of the entire regiment, "Stables Call," "Supper," "Retreat," and the evening roll call. "Taps" ended the day at 9 o'clock.

It was a memorable day—April 18, 1862—when the regiment was ordered out of camp to march at long last and join McDowell's force at Fredericksburg, Virginia. That morning excitement filled the air as the men made ready for the two-day march, gathering up their rations and ammunition and packing saddle bags with personal treasures. Rapid bugle calls brought out three battalions, one by one, 900 horses with saddles packed. When the ranks were dressed and flags were flying, the troops moved out with a farewell cheer to Camp Custis to which they would never return.

As they rode out into enemy territory toward Pohick Church, Virginia, the road was thick with mud from spring rains. Every now and then a horse stumbled, skidded in the slime, and threw his rider into the oozing mud. The long blue column of cavalry, endeavoring to avoid the treacherous terrain for the horses, rode through the trees at either side of the road and broke through fences to get to the fields where footing was safer.

Streams swollen from the rains had to be forded. Henry led Prince gingerly into one of the deeper ones while two other officer friends, Zach and Benjamin, were behind him holding the reins of their mounts. The water moved swiftly and the bottom of the stream was full of large rocks and boulders. The three officers saw their horses safely across and then retraced their steps back to the middle of the current to catch hold of dismounted men who had lost control and were being swept downstream. Grabbing them and helping them to shore, they then went back a second time to seize the reins of floundering horses. By the time riders and their mounts were reunited, there were many soaking bodies and drenched horses, but neither a man nor a horse was lost. Wet clothing was stripped off and wrung out. Proof of the poor quality of clothing sold to the government by unscrupulous textile manufacturers became apparent when these garments made from compressed recycled woolen goods ripped apart and "dissolved" when wet.

Ambrose brought up Thorn and that evening as soft rain fell on the bivouac in Dumfries near the Potomac, he gave both of Henry's horses a thorough rub-down and their forage.

As they tried to make themselves comfortable under rain-soaked clothes, some of the men expressed disappointment that their first day in enemy territory had brought neither an alarm nor a fight.

"'Wonder where Johnny Reb is hidin'.'"

"They musta seen us comin' and took off somewheres."

"Don' you-uns worry 'bout Johnny Reb. He's out there with his eyes and ears on us, ye can be sure o' that. An' when he's ready, he'll let us have a good pastin'."

"We'll lick 'em good, ye jest wait."

Split rail fences, which would disappear altogether as the war dragged on, were all around them now and the men lifted the rails off quickly to make fires to boil their coffee. Each man sat on the ground before his own tiny campfire and poured water from his canteen into an empty tin can with a bit of hay wire to suspend it over the fire. Soon the water was boiling and he shook into it coffee from a little cloth bag carried in his haversack. Soldiers ground their own coffee beans in a bucket using the butt of their carbines to pound them. The meal consisted of a piece of salt pork which they broiled on a stick over the fire and hard tack, a thick, dry biscuit which was the staple of every soldier's diet. It was made chewable by dunking it into the coffee. The men cleaned their knives by stabbing them into the ground, lay back on their knapsacks, filled laurel-root pipes with tobacco, and discussed the day's events while the smoke curled skyward.

Hundreds of little campfires which had lit up the darkness during the meal hour were now dying out and the men rolled out their rubber ponchos to make ready for the night's rest. They slept in their uniforms and they laid their heads on haversacks. Sabers were stuck on end in the ground, saddles and carbines were close by.

Before the bugler sounded "Taps," pickets were deployed and Colonel Wyndham himself officiated at the guard mounting, inspecting the arms of all the men who were to be on the picket-line around the encampment that night. Those on duty spread themselves out in an imaginary line; in advance of the pickets were the vedettes who rode out about 200 feet in front of the line. The vedettes would ride their horses back and forth on their "beat" for two hours before being relieved of duty.

On this night, the first they had camped in open enemy territory, one vedette, an eighteen-year-old farm boy from Pennsylvania, Ebenezer Winterholler, at about three o'clock in the morning heard a scuffling in the underbrush not far away. With his carbine at the ready, he sat still astride his horse and listened. The rain was still falling and there was no moonlight, but he strained his eyes to accustom them to the dark. The noise grew louder and, as he watched, the underbrush parted and an animal emerged, one he recognized from its grunting and snorting: a very well-fed hog. This was the first time Ebenezer had ever been on guard duty and he was perplexed. What was he to do? All the instincts of his rural past rushed to the fore. The hunger for fresh meat set his saliva flowing and the sport of the chase became irresistible. He watched as the hog continued his maneuvers. (Ebenezer was to learn in his service in Virginia that southerners did not fence their hogs in, letting them stray about the countryside.)

He slid off his horse, put down his gun, and began a stealthy stalking of the animal. The hog, alerted by the crackling of a twig behind him, began to trot. His route took him towards the next vedette, another farm boy, Algernon Taggart. Ebenezer was in close pursuit of his quarry when he yelled to Algernon: "Hog com-

141

ing!" Catching pigs in the barnyard was not unfamiliar to these two young men, but grappling with one of these proportions in the dark was a challenge to their strength and ingenuity. After battling it for several minutes, they managed to seize its four legs and carry it, squealing its objections loudly, back to the picket-line. There, with the help of their comrades on the picket-line and some rope, they tied it up, to be dealt with in the morning.

Fortunately for them, there was no officer present to witness their dereliction of duty, and they sped back to their posts as fast as their long legs would carry them. Their horses had not moved.

When Reveille sounded at 5 o'clock the two soldiers returned to the picket-line where they untied the hog and led it back to camp with the rope around its neck. Many were the looks of puzzlement as they passed by, pig in tow. One officer blinked as if seeing an apparition. Ebenezer and Algernon kept on walking with exaggerated nonchalance and called back over their shoulders: "Fresh Secesh ham for dinner."

15

When the 1st New Jersey joined the forces of General McDowell in Fredericksburg on schedule, they found the general impatiently marking time until he received his marching orders to help McClellan close in on the Confederate capital. How to keep all these men gainfully occupied and the restlessness under control until the call came? The idle hours were filled up with activities such as reconnaissance, picket duty and foraging, but the men grew more and more anxious to get into the fight they had volunteered for so many months ago.

About May 1 the Jerseymen met the 1st Pennsylvania Cavalry with whom they became brigaded under the overall leadership of General George D. Bayard who at twenty-six was the youngest general officer in the Army of the Potomac. West Point-trained, Bayard wore on his face an indelible mark of his previous military experience of fighting Indians on the frontier: a scar left by a Kiowa arrow. During the next three years the two cavalry regiments, referred to as the "Twins," would serve together side by side on many a battlefield.

On the morning of May 25 the call came for the brigade to break camp and to move south towards Richmond. With a whoop and a holler the 1st Pennsylvania led out the cavalry with the 1st New Jersey following and the infantry coming behind. They proceeded to within fifteen miles of Richmond where the sounds of the battle raging could be heard. They met up with some of McClellan's army on the outskirts of the capital and were champing at the bit to join the campaign the following day.

But Fate had a drastic change of plans in store. Bayard was ordered to change directions—to the West toward the Shenandoah Valley—and the task he was given was to chase the Confederate General "Stonewall" Jackson and his army of 18,000 who had been rampaging in the valley harassing Union forces far outnumbering his own. Jackson's mission was to save the Confederate capital from capture by drawing strength away from McClellan's army. Stonewall had been meeting with dramatic success; he had stopped the advance of Major General John C. Fremont coming east from western Virginia and then chased Major General Nathaniel F. Banks north and east across the Potomac River.

Washington quaked at the nearness of Jackson's army. He had become famous already for driving his "foot cavalry" (the name given his Valley infantry because of their speed and endurance on the march) unmercifully on long marches with terrifying speed. His army was made up of self-reliant country boys, all rugged outdoorsmen who knew how to ride and shoot and were imbued with robust courage and immovable convictions about the war they were fighting to save their farms and villages. What was Lincoln to do to safeguard the nation's capital? It seemed to him that he had only one option: recall McDowell's 1st army Corps now en route to Richmond and keep it closer to Washington in case of attack.

And so, instead of galloping into the fray at Richmond, the column of cavalry turned around and retraced its steps. It was an incomprehensible setback to the hundreds of cavalrymen itching for the fight. They had waited so long to get into the war and now that they had begun their march, why were they being recalled? In stubborn disbelief they trudged back on the road to Falmouth, disheartened and feeling sorely cheated.

Upon their return to their departure point, the 1st Pennsylvania and the 1st New Jersey were joined by a battalion of the 13th Pennsylvania Reserve Infantry, known as the Bucktail Regiment, some of whom had served in Washington when Henry was on duty there during the opening months of the war. The commander of these sharpshooters was Lieutenant Colonel Thomas L. Kane, a noted abolitionist who had helped slaves escape via the Underground Railroad. The new assignment awaiting the cavalry at Falmouth would test their mettle and that of the horses: the 1st Army Corps was to travel west as fast as it could to meet Fremont's army in the Shenandoah Valley in an attempt to waylay Jackson and squeeze him between their pincers. They must make haste; Jackson, once alerted to the approaching forces, would sense the impending trap and rush south to escape.

The ensuing march westward was a grueling endurance contest. The fast pace was cruel for the horses. The sun baked them during the day, sapping their energy. Their hides glistened with foamy sweat and their breath was labored all day long. Unaccustomed to the rough and stony roads, many of them began to cast their shoes. Every evening the regimental farriers worked tirelessly replacing them. Forage and grain were in short supply. The first day's ride was thirty miles towards Thoroughfare Gap in the Bull Run Mountains, not far from the Blue Ridge which formed the eastern rim of the Shenandoah Valley. The second day's march was even faster but during a shower the horses were allowed to graze briefly along the roadside. Another thirty miles were covered before dark when they passed through Thoroughfare Gap and bivouacked on a hillside in the rain. There was little food that night because of the delay of the wagon trains carrying the supplies so that men and horses went hungry. Ambrose led Prince and Thorn and several other horses in turn to pasture and to a stream where they could refresh themselves. After bringing them back, he examined their shoes carefully. He gave each horse a handful of shelled corn from his pocket.

Before daybreak of the third day, the cavalry was out on the march again, pressing on and forcing the horses to the utmost of their strength—and beyond. They began dropping by the wayside. Men were dismounting at every opportunity and leading their exhausted animals forward. A day of hard riding saw the outfit through Manassas Gap in the Blue Ridge, and beyond it lay the fertile, lush valley of the Shenandoah. Men who couldn't stand the pressure of the march straggled to the rear, catching up later in the night, or simply disappeared.

The problem of food and forage was complicated by the continued failure of the wagon trains with all the supplies to keep up with the marching troops. At the most crucial moment, such as after the men had endured an exhausting march in the pelting rain when every fibre of their being cried out for food and a dry bed, the army wagons had a way of getting stuck in the mud about five to ten miles away on the other side of a stream, leaving the men to face the long night in their soaked garments without food, or tents, axes, or cooking utensils. And there was no guarantee that the next day would see the wagons catching up. It was very possible that another day or two of rain would mire the wagon wheels even more deeply and the men's stomachs would contract even more painfully. Until the wagon trains arrived, men and horses would necessarily go hungry. The cavalry carried as much grain in grain sacks and bales of hay on their saddles as possible, but the increased weight was a burden for the horses.

The village of Front Royal, Virginia was a junction point for various elements of McDowell's corps, and when the infantry brigade of General James Ricketts so filled the roads that there was no room for cavalry, the 1st New Jersey, under the leadership of Bayard and Wyndham, tore down roadside fences and detoured through fields to get around Ricketts's infantry and push on ahead. The sounds of artillery in the distance were proof that Jackson's army and Fremont's had met. Once again the 1st New Jersey were exhilarated over the prospects of the fight which appeared to be only hours away.

At the end of five days of punishing riding, the brigade was near Strasburg, Virginia, where Bayard expected to pounce on Jackson's wagon train. His information was that the train was guarded by only a small cavalry force, but when the 1st Pennsylvania, under the command of Colonel Owen Jones, was sent ahead to investigate, they found the supply wagons well-guarded by infantry, artillery and cavalry. Jones withdrew his troops.

The following day it was the 1st New Jersey's turn to have a look. When Colonel Kargé took Major Alexander Cummings's battalion to view the situation from a promontory above Strasburg, they saw a fight in progress between the cavalry guarding Jackson's train and elements of Fremont's army, but as they watched, the supply trains made their getaway.

Kargé, in his eagerness to succeed where Fremont had failed, sent Major Cummings's battalion down the mountainside to reconnoiter.

"Sawyer," Cummings ordered Henry, "take a platoon down there and find out what the Confederate strength is."

Henry led his men on a noisy charge through the streets of Strasburg expecting to engage the enemy in numbers, but all they found were forty barefoot stragglers from Jackson's army shuffling along, dressed in their homespun butternut uniforms, tattered and dirty, with gaunt faces and slouching bodies worn out from the miles of walking,

Smarting under their failure to capture the wagon trains, Kargé and Wyndham brought their troops into the village.

Wyndham had a personal obsession which now became too hard for him to resist: guarding the fleeting wagon train was the dashing and fearlessly bold Brigadier General Turner Ashby, Jackson's cavalry chief and partisan raider renowned throughout the Shenandoah Valley. His fame in making life miserable for Union forces matched the exploits of the other colorful Confederate cavalry leader, J.E.B. Stuart. Ashby was particularly adept at guarding the rear of Jackson's army with reckless charges against Fremont's pursuing force.

Sir Percy Wyndham was not one to be second best. "I'm going to get Ashby," he announced to Kargé. "He's had too much success. It's time he was brought down."

He set off with a battalion of Jerseymen at a fast trot toward Woodstock, joined later by Kargé. While they waited for reinforcements, shells began flying over them. At long last the 1st New Jersey was in the fight! Confederate guns on a hill about 1000 yards away peppered the woods where the cavalry stood hidden awaiting the arrival of an artillery battery. Once it was in position it began answering the Confederate cannon. The Jerseymen dismounted and crept through the woods, carbines at the ready. As Wyndham and Kargé took an attack column of cav-

147

alry directly toward the Confederate guns, Major Beaumont led a battalion from another direction whose attack was to be synchronized with theirs.

Wyndham's signal to charge sent his and Kargé's troopers off on a wild gallop through fields and over fences towards the enemy who poured shells on them every step of the way. Their advance was slowed and finally halted by Confederate cannoneers who moved to a sheltered position in a woods nearer Ashby's cavalry protection. Beaumont's attacking battalion was surprised by a heavy volley of rifle fire from a field of wheat where a regiment of Jackson's rear guard infantry lay hidden. The shout of Captain Boyd at the front, "Down on your saddles!" saved the men who buried their heads in their horses' necks, and the bullets hit the fence behind them. Beaumont, spotting two Confederate guns poised to annihilate them, withdrew his men quickly to a point of safety.

Wyndham and Kargé reformed the regiment and continued pursuit of the enemy who appeared to be escaping. Beaumont charged ahead of the main body in an unsuccessful attempt to reach the Confederate artillery.

Before the day ended, an artillery battle commenced which had its bizarre moments. A Confederate shell landed on a log cabin inhabited by two southern women who had left the security of their homes up in the hills to come closer, so as to witness the defeat of the Union army by their idol, Stonewall Jackson. The shell exploded inside the cabin and tore off the leg of one and severely injured the other. In the midst of the battle two surgeons from the 1st New Jersey, William W.L. Phillips and Ferdinand V. Dayton, ministered unto the two enemy civilians with an amputation and a binding up of wounds. The sufferings of the two women were magnified by the irony of having their lives saved by the hated Yankees.

Another shell exploded underneath Colonel Kargé's horse throwing both into the air. The animal was torn to pieces but the Colonel descended unhurt.

A regimental bugler—a youngster of thirteen years—was wounded by a shell that came whistling through the air and knocked the instrument from his hand and the boy to the ground, senseless.

The day's fighting concluded when a heavy storm blocked out the enemies, one from the other, and the Confederate artillery and Ashby himself slipped away. That night, the 1st New Jersey, totally spent, bivouacked on the battlefield and ate the remnants of food in their haversacks—soggy hardtack. They could not build fires to dry themselves out or to boil their coffee for fear of revealing their position.

The Jerseymen were joined by General Fremont's troops that evening, and the following morning the entire brigade started out again in the rain on the trail of Jackson. It was clear now that, despite its superhuman effort, McDowell's 1st Corps had arrived too late to catch the wily Confederate general. Nonetheless, he could be chased and harassed for many miles, and this the brigade intended to do.

The first trial of the sodden, hungry men and exhausted horses was the fording of the North Fork of the Shenandoah River swollen by the heavy rains. The 1st New Jersey and the 1st Pennsylvania went first, the horses carrying the ammunition on their backs. Next were Kane's Bucktails followed by Captain James A. Hall's Second Maine Battery. Some of the men got across the raging river by holding onto the tails of the cavalry's swimming horses. But, alas, when Bayard's men were all across and stood on dry land again, off in the distance they spied the long line of Jackson's wagon train looking like prairie schooners pulled by mules and moving along rapidly under heavy escort. They had negotiated successfully the crossing of a bridge over yet another branch of the Shenandoah after which Jackon's rear guard set fire to it. The last of Ashby's cavalry to cross had narrowly escaped disaster as the burning bridge disintegrated close behind them and fell into the torrents underneath them.

Utterly frustrated and miserable in their defeat, the cavalry, infantry and artillery all watched as Jackson's army on the opposite bank of the river escaped before their very eyes. Furious at seeing Ashby getting away, Colonel Wyndham, proud of his equestrian prowess, made a bold attempt to force his horse into the swiftly moving river to set an example for the regiment, but the animal balked at all entreaties. There was no hope now of getting across the river, widening every hour in the unending rains which were soaking bodies and hides. There was no food; all the hardtack, which had been issued five days before, was gone. The brigade's wagon trains were mired in the mud somewhere behind them awaiting the corduroying of the roads with saplings and trees to enable them to proceed.

Fremont's soldiers had been plundering the countryside for food, but until this moment the cavalry regiments had maintained their discipline in refusing to do so. Now, General Bayard, realizing that there would be a long wait for the construction of the pontoon bridges, gave permission for the brigade to "live off the country." Off went the men by the hundreds jumping over fences, running through fields, leaping over streams, and racing into barns to rob them of sheep, cattle, hogs and bags of grain. Breaking into farmhouses, they seized freshly baked bread, pies and cakes off the kitchen tables, chickens pecking around the kitchen doors, and anything else that southern housewives had in their stores: milk, jams, eggs and butter.

Back came the men to their camp along the muddy banks of the river, bowed down by the weight of their prizes. Two turkeys being carried by their feet were squawking noisily, pigs were squealing, sheep bleating, chickens cackling, and the men were whooping in anticipation of their first meal in many days. A youngster with a bag of cornmeal exclaimed: "Corn mush for breakfast!"

Fires were lit from dry wood they had scrounged from homesteads and it was not long before smoke was curling up along the riverbank and the odor of roasting mutton and beef and pork filled the air. It was the first meal they had had since starting the westward trek. Bellies grumbled in contentment as vast quantities of meat were consumed.

Ambrose removed the saddles from Prince and Thorn, rubbed their backs, and then poured out a large measure of oats for them. They neighed with pleasure as they crunched their meal noisily.

Sharing the campfire with Henry and Ambrose were two strangers, infantry soldiers from Kane's Bucktails. One seemed especially adept at basting the chicken roasting before them. Henry watched, fascinated, at the way he mixed up a batch of biscuits in an empty tin, using the ingredients pilfered from one of the farmhouses, then holding the tin over the hot coals. Soon he was handing out hot biscuits with melted butter.

Henry's curiosity could not be squelched. "Are you a chef back in civilian life?" he asked.

The soldier smiled and shook his head. Henry noticed the small hands that held out the biscuits to him. The fingers were unusually thin and short. He could not refrain from studying the frame of the man: his build was slight, his feet small, the features of his face were soft, and the complexion was smooth.

The two Bucktails sat side by side, quietly savoring roasted chicken drumsticks. Henry noticed then the difference in the heights of the two.

Perhaps because Henry, unconsciously, appeared to be staring, the taller of the two infantry soldiers spoke up: "I'm Augustus Sullivan and this is my wife, Frances. We were married two weeks before Fort Sumter." He smiled down at the face next to him.

Henry's astonished expression brought further explanation, this time from Frances. "August volunteered the next day. When he was called for active duty I didn't want to be separated from him, so I came along." She looked up at her husband sweetly and continued: "If he is wounded, I want to be near to nurse him."

Henry, intrigued by her simple courage, asked: "Don't you find infantry life very hard?"

She replied: "It would be much harder to be at home just waiting for him." She hesitated before asking: "Do you have a wife?"

"Yes. And two children. I have not seen them for many months. Almost a year now."

"I'm sure your wife would understand how I feel about not wanting to be away from August."

"Yes," Henry answered slowly, "I'm sure she would."

They ate ravenously of a large purloined apple pie and drank coffee for a long time, huddled under ponchos in the rain.

151

Somewhere in the camp "Rally Round the Flag, Boys" was being sung accompanied by a bugler.

Before leaving the group to check on the horses, Ambrose turned towards the Sullivans and said: "I'm sure the Good Lord will look kindly on you. God bless."

On June 5, after a successful crossing of the Middle Fork of the Shenandoah via the pontoon bridges newly built by the engineers, Bayard's men followed by Fremont's began the march to Harrisonburg, Virginia with the cavalry on the flanks of the artillery and infantry. Quite rightly referred to as the "eyes and ears of the army," the cavalry often took up that position.

On their march up the Valley the regiment came upon scenes of deliberate wanton destruction of fine old homesteads and their contents. Pillage and vandalism by the soldiers who had passed through were abundantly evident. There was about the devastation a haphazard aimlessness. Mahogany furniture of no use to the soldiers was broken, pictures ripped to pieces by sabers, mirrors used for target practice, beds mutilated and their coverings torn to shreds, windows broken, doors torn from their hinges, dishes smashed. Houses and barns were burned down. They saw a church whose pews had been plundered for firewood. A library's book and works of art were strewn over the ground in shreds. An old courthouse bore witness to desecration; its walls were violated and its books of records, deeds, bonds, wills, inventories and mortgages were scattered across the floor. A beautiful garden which surrounded a distinguished residence was filled with ruined contents—broken chairs, cracked tables, book with covers torn off and letters shredded, and broken glass from windows and doors. The carpets of the old house were ruined with mud and other gore and a rosewood piano appeared to have had an ax taken to it, and its keys had been stolen. There was about these abandoned homes a feeling of utter desolation in their misery.

After marching the whole day and into the 6th of June, the brigade spotted something that stirred a surge of hope that they might still catch a part of Jackson's army before it escaped from the valley: southeast of Harrisonburg a long line of his wagon trains was stuck in the mud. Ashby's troopers were guarding it, and this revelation alone was enough to spur Colonel Wyndham to action. This might be his golden opportunity—and his last—to snare Ashby once and for all.

Although his orders from General Bayard did not sanction a pursuit of Ashby, the temptation was all-consuming and he gave into it. Ignoring orders to place his artillery guarding all the approaches to Harrisonburg and to engage nothing larger than a skirmish line in combat, Wyndham took the 1st New Jersey (which now numbered fewer than half its original 800 troopers, the rest having fallen by the wayside under the strain, succumbed to illness or deserted) as well as a battalion of the 4th New York Cavalry on loan from Fremont, and off he went to capture his elusive quarry. Three miles southeast of the town he ran into the enemy. Henry was at the head of a skirmish unit fifty yards in advance and advised caution to the regiment since enemy strength was uncertain. But Wyndham, with Captain Shelmire in command of the lead squadron, could not be deterred, and about 400 Jerseymen, with sabers raised, charged ahead.

Their path lay down a road so narrow that they could ride only two abreast instead of the regulation "moving by fours." They were hemmed in further by rail fences at either side. When he saw ahead a line of Confederate cavalry stretched across his path with a thickly-wooded hill behind them, the reckless Colonel urged his troopers fearlessly down the dangerous road. Now that he had actually seen the "bait," Wyndham went wild with excitement, stood up in his stirrups, ordered platoons to form, swung his saber up over his head and yelled: "Gallop! Charge!"

The horses were weary from two days on the road, but Major Beaumont raced the first battalion uphill after the fleeting enemy, chasing them into the woods. Wyndham and Kargé dismounted long enough to destroy some roadside fences, then led the second battalion after him. Major Jones's third battalion attempted to keep up and secure the flanks, while the New York Cavalry stayed well to the rear in a protective skirmish line.

The foolhardiness of the attack became apparent after the regiment had advanced only a few hundred yards: they had been lured into an ambush by more than 1000 Confederates in the woods. With Turner Ashby leading them, hidden enemy cavalry and dismounted cavalry in overwhelming numbers opened fire on the regiment. The Confederate infantry, sheltered perfectly behind the rail fence, sprayed them with bullets. Three Jerseymen fell mortally wounded.

In the midst of this heavy fire, confusion reigned as the battalions tried to reform in an orderly fashion. Wyndham entered the woods but he did not come out of it. Kargé was unsaddled after having been saved by his men from capture by Ashby's 7th Virginia Cavalry. The flag-bearer who had accompanied the regiment, rallying them into the inferno, now lay wounded beside his horse, and the colors were in the hands of the enemy.

Panic seized the horses as their riders attempted to extricate themselves from the vortex of the fray. As each battalion tried to get away, it became entangled with others dashing to safety. The narrow road down which they had galloped only minutes before became a death trap instead of an escape route. There was no saving discipline, no plan of orderly retreat. It was a case of every man for himself.

The frenzied horses dashed into one another down the road, hooves catching in those of neighboring chargers. Frightened, they plunged in all directions, snorting and screaming in terror, when the general movement down the road slowed momentarily in the rush to freedom. Riders fell off their mounts only to be trodden on by others trying desperately to flee. The noise reached a fury—bullets whizzing by, sabers clashing, fences being broken down, limbs of trees crashing, hooves pounding. In the din could be heard the voices of officers furiously cursing their men and attempting to stop their retreat with threats. But to no avail. The mob was unstoppable. Only exhaustion finally slowed the pace.

When the regiment ultimately rallied, they counted their losses: more than thirty men had been killed, wounded or captured. Colonel Wyndham was, indeed, either dead or a prisoner. Captain Shelmire and Captain Clark were prisoners. The death of Captain Thomas R. Haines grieved the whole regiment. In the heat of battle the young lad had been trying to rally his troopers when he was shot by a pistol and then sabered in the head. Captain Broderick saw him fall and killed the Confederate attacker but could not stop to bring off Haines's body.

When Captain Shelmire was being led away a prisoner, he passed a very young soldier, Jones of Company A, lying wounded on the ground. As he rode by, he heard the boy call out to him: "Captain Shelmire, Sir." The captain dismounted and bent over the dying boy. The youngster looked so in need of comforting that the soft-hearted officer cradled him in his arms tenderly for a few moments before he was obliged to remount his horse and move on.

The 4th New York Cavalry had given the regiment no cover; deserting the 1st New Jersey in its hour of dire need, it had left the scene.

But the disorganized flight of the Jerseymen did not mark the end of the battle. Lieutenant Colonel Kane brought to the field 120 officers and men of his Bucktail Rifles battalion followed by a brigade of Fremont's infantry. By this time Ashby's cavalry had been reinforced by foot soldiers, but Kane's infantry's steady pommeling away at the enemy forced their retreat and allowed the last of the Federal cavalrymen to get away safely. There were two casualties of the day's final combat: Kane was taken prisoner but not before Turner Ashby's hour of triumph was tarnished by the bullet of one of Kane's men that mortally wounded him.

That Wyndham was not present to witness the fall of his adversary had about it a poignant irony, especially since his flagrant irresponsibility in his headlong rush into disaster to satisfy his rash personal goal had exacted such an appalling sacrifice from his regiment.

It happened that at the moment prisoner Sir Percy Wyndham was being questioned by Stonewall Jackson in his tent, news of Ashby's death was brought to him. The general was so visibly affected by the loss of his trusted partisan officer that he brought the meeting with Wyndham to an immediate end, retiring in solitude in his tent.

Henry, occupied with finding his men and organizing them into Company D once again, noticed the Bucktails returning from the field. Quickly scanning the faces of the men trudging along, he looked for Augustus and Frances Sullivan. He thought he had missed them but near the end of the line of infantry he spotted them. Augustus, wounded, was leaning on Frances and walking with difficulty. Supporting him with her slight body, she had her arms entwined about him and her face turned up towards his. Slung over one of her shoulders was his rifle. Henry, mounted on Prince, trotted to the line of soldiers and bent down to speak to Frances. "Is he seriously wounded?"

"It's his leg," she answered. "He has been bleeding a lot."

"Let me help." Henry beckoned to Ambrose nearby who was holding the reins of Thorn. The two men lifted Augustus carefully and draped him across Thorn's saddle. "Take him to Surgeon Phillips," Henry instructed Ambrose. Then he hurried back to assemble his company of men.

On the day following the battle, Captain Broderick with Surgeon Phillips and three men from Company K revisited the battleground to retrieve the body of Captain Haines, beloved by the whole regiment and its only officer to have been killed in battle, all the others who were missing having been taken prisoner. A southern farmer had already buried the body. Haines's comrades removed it from the earth and carried it to the farmer's house preparatory to take it away for a proper burial. The farmer's wife had just finished baking some tantalizing pies which set the cavalrymen's mouths watering, and it was with bitter disappointment that they received a warning that approaching the house were a number of Confederate horsemen. The hungry troopers would not give in so lightly to leaving the delicious treats behind, and with stout hearts they carried off the pies with an almost casual nonchalance.

Thomas Haines was laid to rest in a grave in the churchyard at Harrisonburg. Colonel Kargé gave the eulogy for the young officer who had so endeared himself to the regiment for his devotion to duty and his ultimate sacrifice. The cannon at Cross Keys, Virginia boomed the salute.

The regiment's final battle that June was at Cross Keys two days later. It brought to an end the spring campaign, which had failed in its single purpose—the capture of Jackson's force. He slipped away from the valley forever at Port Republic, Virginia and headed for Richmond to give General Lee a hand in withstanding the attack of McClellan.

Henry pondered over the happenings of the last few days. Why had defeat hounded them at every step? There seemed to be no single answer. Was it the regiment's inexperience in combat? Perhaps there were too many commanders and not enough harmony amongst them. Other circumstances, such as the adverse weather, the long distances of travel for men and horses unused to the strain, shortage of rations and forage, took their toll on men and beasts. The morale of the regiment had suffered a blow by its disappointing performance. The men were weary, downcast and dispirited, the horses spent and thin. They all needed a rest.

Henry could not help reflecting on what he had learned through this first experience in combat. This was, after all, going to be a war in which victory would be determined by human factors such as how many miles soldiers could walk in a day, how much forage they could gather for their horses, how much hunger they could tolerate and how much heat or cold both men and horses could endure.

16

Following McClellan's less than distinguished exhibition of military prowess in the Peninsula Campaign, northern morale plummeted as it had done after Bull Run. In an effort to rally the nation to total war and to a speedy conclusion of hostilities, Lincoln, in July 1862 asked for 300,000 new volunteers to serve for three years. Despite the patriotic entreaties of the state governors for men to join up, there was not the rush to fight for the old flag that had produced the ground swell of volunteers in 1861.

Casualties had taken the gloss off the romantic notions of war. There were not many young men left unemployed on the home front who would enlist for that length of time.

Disheartened by the failure of Generals Banks, Fremont and McDowell to ensnare Stonewall Jackson, the War Department assigned all their forces to Major General John Pope whose military reputation had been established in the West. McClellan's failure to capture Richmond was a shattering disappointment for Lincoln; he was ordered to withdraw his Army of the Potomac and take it north to join Pope's army of 45,000 troops along the Rapidan and Rappahannock Rivers from which point a campaign would be launched. Together they would take on the armies of Robert E. Lee and Jackson.

In August 1862 Henry found himself performing the arduous duty of guarding the rear of the long wagon train of General Pope. This task, for which the cavalry was especially suited, demanded constant vigilance, physical endurance and extraordinary patience as the mules pulled the heavy wagons slowly for endless miles over rough terrain, struggling up hills and often through mud which came up over the wagon wheels.

The wagon train being guarded by the 1st New Jersey stretched out for thirty miles behind the infantry, artillery and the rest of the cavalry. Each wagon occupied eighty feet on the march, even more on bad roads. There were 1400 wagons drawn by 8400 mules. They carried food, forage for the animals, ammunition, clothing, entrenching tools needed for building roads and bridges. Nine thousand animals—mules and horses—ate 200 tons of food daily. Hay, corn, oats and barley had to be carried.

The army's supply of fresh meat went along on the hoof. These 10,000 head of cattle had to be protected as well. The troops and wagon trains so filled the roads that there was no room for the cattle; they were driven by herdsmen on horseback through the fields and woods alongside the roads. As they picked their way through brambles and thorns, they lived off the country, stopping to eat whatever they found, progressing slowly.

In the haversack of every infantryman, artilleryman and trooper at the start of a campaign were six days' ration of hardtack and three days' ration of meat. When the latter was gone, the fresh meat supply came from the herd. The troops stripped cornfields and apple trees as they marched.

The canvas-covered wagons resembled Conestoga-prairie schooners. On the march the canvas cover was drawn closely over front and back. Each wagon had a tool box in front, a feed trough behind, a wooden bucket for water, and an iron "slush bucket" for grease hanging from the hind axle.

The mules that pulled them were driven by teamsters especially gifted in the profanity necessary to keep the recalcitrant animals on the move. This expertise was called into play when a heavy, lumbering wagon broke down or became mired deep in mud and the six mules pulling it had to extricate it. They were able to do this with the help of the large black snake whip which the teamster snapped across their backs, always accompanied by

159

a litany of swear words that had no end. At times like this, the whole train came to a standstill. There were frequent stops and starts, and the cavalry escorting the train grew exasperated with the slowness of its progress. It was the most detested job of the cavalry. The stops were frequently longer than the starts. Virginia mud was a fact of army life that had to be experienced to be believed. Sometimes the wagons following behind the marching columns sank so far into the mud that the only way to save them was by sheer muscular strength. Often it was the Negro contrabands who had attached themselves to the regiment who combined their strength to heave the wagons out of the mire. If there were any fence rails left in the countryside that had not been used for firewood, these were used to pry out mules that had gone down as far as their shoulders.

Marching along with the train were hundreds of men who belonged to the army but never fought: cooks, hospital gangs, quartermaster's people, the "present sick," officers' servants, and habitual "skulkers." The ambulances occupied two miles of the train's length and the artillery batteries four miles.

At the end of the train was a mule laden with all the baggage necessary to prepare a meal for the commanding general and his officers at headquarters: a mess-kettle, frying pan, mess pans, tent poles, canvas, valise, knapsack, haversack, hammer and musket. These implements were piled so high all over the mule that nothing could be seen of the animal except his head, enormous ears and feet.

A somewhat coveted position was that of wagon guard whose duties embraced tending the brake on the wagon as it careened down an incline, as well as gathering forage and loading and unloading wagons, but who enjoyed the special privilege of having his knapsack and haversack carried on the wagon. To be relieved of these burdens on a day's march made an immense difference to bodily fatigue, especially to the legs of the infantryman and his shoulders and back which carried the heavy bags of equipment and bore the indentation marks of the straps.

When the train stopped moving for a few minutes Henry slipped out of the saddle and led Prince to the side of the road in search of some grass for him to nibble. Thorn was being ridden by

160

his friend, Benjamin, whose horse had expired on a long march. Remounts were hard to come by. The cavalry were required to sweep the countryside in search of them, appropriating them from pastures and barns, but these forays into enemy territory did not always yield a prize.

As the August sun beat down on the marching infantry the men discarded everything that was too heavy to carry. They relieved themselves of the burden of blanket rolls, coats, knapsacks, even haversacks. These cast-offs edged the line of march leaving a trail behind that stretched for many miles.

Although the work of guarding a wagon train was boring, it did not allow for indifference on the part of the troopers. The train was always in danger of surprise attack from the enemy. Hundreds of cavalrymen were required to protect its rear and flanks; its unwieldy length and the slowness of its speed of travel increased its vulnerability, as did the onset of darkness. The march did not stop at nightfall. It continued under a starless sky.

The column kept plodding along until three A.M., then halted for a rest. The troopers did not dare unsaddle their horses. Henry, Ambrose and Benjamin threw themselves on the ground with Prince and Thorn standing nearby. They had covered seventy miles. Fully clothed and with boots on, Henry positioned his tired back as comfortably as he could into a hollow.

He had been asleep less than an hour when he was awakened by the lowing of cattle nearby and the muffled commands of what sounded like cattle rustlers. Henry awoke with a start, sprang to his feet, grabbed his carbine, jumped into the saddle, and rode off into the inky darkness towards the sounds of the raid. Following closely behind was Benjamin on Thorn.

Partisan raiders, who numbered in their ranks many deserters and draft-evaders, were feared throughout the countryside. They were nothing less than bandits who robbed and molested at will, respecting neither person nor property. Their guerrilla tactics were the dread of the civilian population as well as of the army. They took whatever they wanted from barns and households. By day they hid in the woods and did their thieving at night. They were master train-wreckers, halting trains and robbing the passengers, then derailing and tearing up the tracks, burning bridges and setting fire to buildings. They had perfected the lightning strike followed by a quick scattering into the woods and hills.

On this night the 1st New Jersey knew not whether the attackers wore the Confederate gray or were partisans from the countryside riding their extremely agile horses that were adept at making their getaway by leaping fences and ditches as easily as deer in an area entirely familiar to them.

In the darkness it was difficult to know exactly what was transpiring, but the noise of the cattle led the troopers to believe the assailants were rounding up some of the herd. Without moonlight or starlight it was impossible to distinguish friend from foe and great care had to be exercised to keep from wounding their own men and the herdsmen. In the scuffle that ensued, southern voices rang out urging the animals on: "Halloo! Come, boy." In the midst of the jangling of metal spurs and the straining of the horses under the attackers, shots were fired to urge the cattle to stampede. Some of them on the edge of the herd broke away and began to run into the woods followed by the thieves. The 1st New Jersey gave pursuit but the unfamiliar terrain slowed their horses and the raiders got away unscathed. It was clear that it was the work of partisans well-versed in nightfighting, over territory they knew well.

When the first light of day broke through at five o'clock, the regiment was in the saddle again after a break of only two hours. The herdsmen counted ten of their cattle missing. Before the day's march commenced, the regimental butchers shot several steer with rifles to have fresh meat for the men to cook that evening.

The cavalry's principal duty was that of protection rather than combat. Along with guarding the wagon trains at the rear, it was also screening the front and flanks of the main body of the marching army from attack. It was perpetually scouting. Because the enemy was constantly attempting to reconnoitre the army's position, the cavalry had to place themselves in every avenue of approach to the main body. Patrols went out to locate the enemy's position and to determine his strength and the nature of the country. When cavalry on patrol were attacked by advance elements of the enemy, skirmishes followed.

The cavalry arranged themselves in two or three concentric lines of posts. The "outpost" was nearest the enemy; it was made up of a chain of vedettes (mounted sentries) posted three miles in advance of the army's main body. The vedettes were so positioned that they could see each other during the daytime and hear each other at night. A second line of pickets was stationed about three-quarters of a mile behind the vedettes, a third line (the main guard) about the same distance behind the pickets.

The hours spent on vedette duty dragged interminably and were so boring that those engaged welcomed a bit of action by the advance of enemy scouts with shots being fired to enliven the monotonous duty.

Along with protecting their own supply lines, the cavalry raided those of the enemy, pursued defeated enemy infantry and took prisoners, captured horses and mules. There was also the unpleasant task of preventing their own frightened infantry from running to the rear when a battle was raging. Fear was contagious and it took only one timid soldier who lost heart and started to run from the spray of bullets to get all those around him to desert their posts and join him in his flight to safety. The officer in charge was forced sometimes to scream at the terrified runaways, "Stop or I'll shoot!" It was the cavalry's job to round them up and force them back into the fight.

Colonel Sir Percy Wyndham reappeared in August having been paroled soon after his capture by the Rebels at Harrisonburg and subsequently exchanged. His arrival was timely for the regiment, which had lost the wounded Colonel Kargé. When Wyndham rejoined the 1st New Jersey, Bayard's brigade was on the north bank of the Rappahannock, having fought hard to gain this position. The brigade was suffering from exhaustion of many days in the saddle and an acute shortage of able-bodied horses. In protecting Pope's army the cavalry engaged in scouting in all directions. They guarded fourteen miles of riverbank. Skirmishing went on all day with Jeb Stuart's cavalry. McClellan's army was moving slowly north and west but had not joined Pope's forces.

The 1st NEW JERSEY Cavalry in VIRGINIA, 1862-63

Opposing picket lines were set up on either bank of the Rappahannock after dark, so close to each other that conversations inevitably took place between the two armies who, by virtue of their circumstances, bestowed informal truces on each other.

"Hey, Billy Yank! You-uns got any coffee and sugar?" came a Rebel voice from across the river.

"Yep," was the reply through the darkness. "We'll trade for your newspapers and tobacco, Johnny Reb."

Fashioning a rude boat out of a plank, the Yankee soldier placed on it a measure of coffee and sugar, then gave the plank a mighty push out into the river in the direction of the voices on the opposite bank. Unloading the gifts, the Secesh then wrapped some newspapers around the supply of tobacco being exchanged and sent the plank back across the stream, calling out as he did so: "Them-uns are pretty new papers. The Sunday morning *Chronicle* from Washington and a week-old *Freeman*. And a Richmond paper too."

Another Southern voice called out: "Whatcha think of this here war?"

A Yankee voice answered: "We're tired of it and we want to go home. Why don't you advance?"

"It's you-uns' turn. We did it last time."

Another Rebel voice shouted: "I got some letters fer some friends up nawth. If'n I send 'em across to you-uns, will ye send 'em on?"

The plank sailed back and the letters, weighted down with a stone, made their way to the Yankee side of the river.

As the two armies bedded down, voices on the northern shore began singing "Yankee Doodle." When the tune ended, southerners followed with refrains of "Dixie." Then, as "Home Sweet Home" began on one side, voices from across the river joined in. The strains of that universally-beloved music floated in the night air, touching the heart of every homesick soldier regardless of what uniform he wore.

Private Caleb Sergeant of the 1st New Jersey's Company K voiced his sentiments about the prohibited fraternization which had been so pleasant: "There are a lot of men over there on the

166

other side of the river that I have no quarrel with, and tomorrow I have to take up my gun and try to kill them. Why? I don't hate them. If the rank and file of both armies were given the chance, they would soon make peace with each other . . . somehow."

Henry was ordered to take a scouting detail of a dozen men to feel out the strength of Jeb Stuart's position. When he was organizing the soldiers, mail arrived and brought a letter from home. "A long time has passed since your last letter," Harriet wrote. "I hope you are keeping well. We miss you every day. We have not gotten accustomed to your absence from home, but we are trying to keep minds and bodies occupied to make the time pass. I have a new sewing machine that sews shoe uppers to the soles. In this way I feel I am helping the war effort from home and that perhaps my work will bring you back to us more quickly. I understand that the government issues soldiers poorly made shoes that come apart after not many miles of walking. I like to feel that my work is helping to correct that problem. I have heard stories that are hard to believe about the government's having only one size boot for all soldiers regardless of the size of their feet and that sometimes mistakes have been made that result in a shipment of shoes all for the right or left foot only. How can this be?"

Henry smiled at Harriet's disbelief in the government's ineptitude. It would be hard for her to understand—Harriet who was a model of practical common sense would find such absurd bungling and inefficiency in high places incredulous. How could she comprehend the situation of Bayard's cavalry brigade at the moment: all their equipment—boots, haversacks, tents, wagon wheels—was forty miles away and the only thing they had in abundance was horseshoes, all size 5's to fit nothing but huge draught horses?

He led his twelve men off in the direction of the Orange & Alexandria Railroad running northeast towards Manassas Junction. The railroad was General Pope's lifeline for supplies and it was subject to raids by the flamboyant Stuart and partisans. Henry, in the lead, urged Prince through a tangle of bushes and dense underbrush to reconnoitre the railroad. They came to a clearing but kept well back from the opening out of sight. From this vantage point they observed enemy cavalry scouting along the railroad tracks. How vulnerable those tracks appeared! They went on for miles, unprotected, at the mercy of Confederate railroad-wreckers and random partisan attacks. From his hiding place Henry counted several hundred troopers. He could hear the jangling of their spurs. They were obviously only scouting as there was no wagon train and no artillery. He wondered where they were going and how far they would follow the railroad. Pursuit was out of the question. Greatly outnumbered, they could only observe and report back to Wyndham what he already knew: the railroad was in grave danger.

Late in August the Second Battle of Bull Run began heating up. Lee had moved his army north to join that of Stonewall Jackson for a concerted effort to defeat Pope. Lee took a dangerous step and divided the army, sending Jackson on a stunning march to encircle Pope. Lee remained in position. Jackson set out on his perilous march with more than 24,000 men most of whom were sick with diarrhea and dysentery, footsore and all ravenously hungry, having had no regular rations for days. They tramped fifty-four miles in thirty-two hours, many of them with bare feet tortured with blisters, and wearing tattered clothing. Slogging their way under a blazing sun, they lived on whatever they could grab along their march: parched corn on the stalk and green apples off nearby trees. Stragglers fell by the wayside but many caught up with the marching column later on.

After leading his men through the western end of Thoroughfare Gap in the Bull Run Mountains, Jackson emerged at the eastern end and marched to Bristoe Station where he called a halt well to the rear of Pope's army. With his inimitable flair for the wondrously dramatic, he climaxed his spectacular march by ripping up the rails of the Orange & Alexandria at this way-side station and sending Jeb Stuart's cavalry on to Manassas Junction to capture hundreds of tons of Federal supplies. Subsequently, Jackson brought his soldiers to Manassas and turned them loose on the spoils. From box car to box car the famished men went running in ribald revelry swooping up cakes, candy, oranges, lemons, lobster salad, oysters, bacon, ham, bottles of Rhine wine and hardtack, stuffing their haversacks along with their mouths. Later that evening, their bodies satiated with delicacies, they stretched out on the ground and lit up purloined cigars and puffed them with a clownish sense of triumph, all the time patting their distended bellies.

News of Jackson's brilliant feat astonished the befuddled Pope who waited in vain for McClellan to arrive with his troops. It was General McDowell's idea to send Bayard's brigade north quickly to plug the western end of Thoroughfare Gap, thus stopping Confederate General Longstreet from following Jackson's route and bringing his 30,000-man army through it. If Bayard were successful, the junction of the two Rebel armies would be prevented.

With Colonel Wyndham in command, what was left of the 1st New Jersey was at the Gap busily engaged in felling trees. The Gap was a narrow defile with rugged 200-foot high mountains covered with rocks and trees forming the sides. The New Jersey's task was to so fill the mouth of the pass with obstructions that the enemy would find its way blocked and be unable to pass through. It was a preposterous assignment for 200 weary troopers to withstand a force the size of Longstreet's with its many thousands of foot soldiers and artillerists, but Bayard thought it was worth the gamble, especially since General James B. Ricketts's infantry division of 5000 men was on its way to lend a hand at the eastern end of the Gap. It was a daunting mission for Ricketts as well since most of his men had never seen combat. How could these young men in the 11th Pennsylvania just off the farms and the city boys in the 12th Massachusetts hope to turn back Longstreet's 30,000 seasoned veterans? As they prepared to go into battle for the first time in their lives, they wrote their names and company and regiment on slips of paper and pinned them inside their uniforms in case identification were needed later on.

With axes the Jerseymen cut down hundreds of trees of all sizes in the pass and dragged them with great effort to the mouth of the Gap and inside it. It was a very hot morning this August 28th, and the strenuous work involved also the climbing of hillsides to dislodge heavy boulders which they rolled down on top of the trees. The men then camouflaged the barrier by throwing earth over it. Hidden along the route that the enemy would have to travel through were dismounted troopers crouching with carbines ready to fire on advancing skirmishers.

Dust was seen rising west of the Gap as Longstreet's leading brigade was starting through. It was turned back by Wyndham's main body, the 2nd New York and 1st Pennsylvania on either flank. They tried a second time and a third, each time being repulsed by heavy fire. Longstreet brought up an artillery battery to blast his way through but it was sent back under a withering shower of cartridges.

When his men failed to penetrate the defenses of Wyndham, General Longstreet devised a plan to send a large body of his men scrambling up over the sides of the gorge on their hands and knees to flank the Federal troops. While Ricketts was engaged in a fierce battle at the eastern entrance to the Gap, the Confederates' climb gave them control of the summit on either side. More Confederates scaled the craggy mountains and slid down to assemble at their base, at the same time that more gray-clad troops came through Hopewell Gap in the mountains six miles away with the intention of flanking Ricketts. When the latter was, indeed, threatened on both flanks, he withdrew his men to safety, realizing the foolhardiness of trying to stave off the attack by an enemy five-fold his numbers. What remained of the 1st New Jersey Cavalry followed.

The retreat route was through the battle area where lay many dead and wounded. Henry led Prince by the reins. He did not see Benjamin or Thorn anywhere around him, and Ambrose had gone to search for them. Overcome by the weight of yet another defeat, Henry walked slowly, his eyes on the ground. The troopers had been in the saddle for many days without rest. The horses were staggering with fatigue, backs sore from the incessant saddling, stomachs rumbling with hunger. Their heads hung low. Many stumbled. Days of endless scouting had preceded the hours of physical labor and the heavy fighting at the Gap. Not only were the men exhausted and hungry, their hearts were heavy with discouragement over their failure to block Longstreet. They did not speak as they rode or walked along behind Ricketts's slow-moving infantry. Suffering from a feeling of fatalism, they had come to believe they were destined only for defeat.

The sun was going down behind Henry as the procession trudged along disconsolately straight east from Thoroughfare Gap on their way to join Pope's main force that would ultimately fight Lee, Jackson and Longstreet near the 1st Bull Run Battlefield. Prince lost his footing and went down on his knees momentarily. He struggled to his feet with Henry's assistance. It was at this moment that a shaft of fading sunlight shone through the trees suddenly onto the face of a Yankee soldier seated and propped up against a tree with his eyes closed and his hands holding the head of another soldier lying across his lap. Henry had grown numb to the sight of wounded and dead soldiers, but when he looked at the pitiful picture these two presented, he stopped for a moment before them. They seemed to embody all the human tragedy of war. Something about them arrested his attention. Their faces were covered with the grime of war, hair disheveled, uniforms torn, and on the recumbent soldier was a large blood-stain across his chest. He was motionless, either unconscious or dead. Henry studied the two men, then crouched down before them for a closer look. As he lingered a few moments, the seated one opened his eyes. Looking up with the sunshine in his eyes, he squinted at Henry whose face suddenly contorted into wide-eyed shock.

"Thad!" he gasped incredulously. "Is it really you? Are you all right?" He extended his hand and touched the arm that held the wounded soldier. "Is it Si?"

The man he had called Thad answered softly: "Henry . . . I can't believe it . . . after all this time . . . Si's hurt real bad. . . . Help me."

Coming across his brothers in this place and in this state after a separation of fourteen years so unnerved Henry that it left him momentarily weak, incapable of thought or action. When he had recovered himself, he continued to ply Thad with questions, one after another. "Did you get hit too? . . . How long have you been here? . . . What's your regiment?"

Thad took a deep breath and began to answer, a few words at a time. "A bullet just grazed my arm." He pointed to a hole in his sleeve. "I was lucky. . . . But Si took a shell hit. . . . We're both with Ricketts . . . the 11th Pennsylvania. . . . He charged the Gap . . . drew back. . . . I saw Si fall . . . dragged him back this far . . . couldn't go any further. Not sure he's still alive." With eyes full of pain, he looked down at his unconscious younger brother. "Oh, God, he just cain't die. He has a son he's never seen." Thad clutched Si's hand tightly, bringing it to his own heart.

Henry knelt on the ground and felt for Si's pulse, then placed his head on his chest. He pulled Si's shirt back exposing a deep chest wound which was still oozing warm blood. "That's a good sign," Henry remarked hopefully. "He's breathing." His face mirrored his feelings of helplessness. Where would they find a doctor, let alone a field hospital?

Turning to look up at Prince whose head was drooping, he asked Thad: "Can you help me lift him onto the horse?"

Thad laid Si's head gently on the ground, then stood up with difficulty, leaning against the tree for support until the dizziness in his head cleared. Henry lifted Si from under the arms while Thad picked up his feet, and together they laid him, face down, across the saddle. As they walked alongside Prince, Thad held Si's head up to keep it from bumping against the hard saddle with each step of the animal.

They followed the retreating army. "This was our first combat," Thad continued, speaking slowly, and catching his breath at intervals. "Most of the 11th is farm boys . . . we joined up together with a lot of fellas from farms around ours."

"How is the farm? How are Ma and Pa?" There was so much Henry wanted to know that his questions came tumbling out faster than Thad could answer them.

"They're older," Thad said. "But they're well. Pa turned all his crop lands into pasture, mostly."

"Ma wrote me that you were married."

"Yep. Emma and I live with Ma and Pa. Until the war is over. And so does Si's wife, Hanna. And the baby."

The procession slowed to a stop momentarily and just then Ambrose appeared alone. "I can't find Benjamin or the Thorn horse anywheres," he announced to Henry, his face tormented with anguish. "I looked for them everywheres," he continued. "I swept the whole field where the fightin' was done, clear back to the Gap and there's jes no sign o' them."

Henry's face clouded. "We may still come across them, Ambrose. They may even be ahead of us. You've done all you can do right now." And then, nodding toward Thad and Si, he added: "These are my brothers. I came across them after the battle. One is wounded pretty bad."

Ambrose looked closely at Si. "If he was ridin' nex' to the horse and not on top o' that saddle, he'd be more comf'table. I can carry the saddle." With that he brought Prince to a halt, undid the girth, and while Henry and Thad lifted Si slightly, Ambrose slipped the saddle out from underneath him and placed it across his own shoulder.

The retreating army marched along slowly with darkness approaching. The brothers, feeling despair and exasperation at the slow speed, were at the mercy of circumstances they could not alter. They must simply plod along, hoping somehow to find help. It was a ghastly, sickening route they followed. On either side were the mutilated bodies of the dead, the wounded who cried out in pain for a drink of water, the corpses of horses that had gone down with their riders, some having fallen beside them and others on top of them.

In the fading light, soldiers with crude stretchers could be seen moving amongst the fallen. Their shadowy figures moved quietly in the dusk, searching for the living. Henry left the line of march to speak to one of them.

"Is there a hospital up ahead?" he asked.

"Not a hospital," the man replied, "but a house where we're laying the men out on the grass until a surgeon comes."

There was only faint light remaining when the little party came upon the relief station the soldier had described. The house was situated up on a hill, and the ground that sloped down to the path of the retreating army had been spread with hay to bed down the 3,000 casualties. Candles flickered all over the hillside as moving figures carrying water buckets and dippers could be distinguished bending down to minister to the bodies on the ground. Henry and Thad lifted Si off Prince's back and carried

173

him a short distance. They were debating where to lay him when a feminine voice behind them said quietly:

"Put him right here." A plain-faced woman with her heavy hair knotted at the back of her head and wearing a long calico skirt held a lighted candle in one hand and with the other smoothed out the hay where Si's head would rest. All around them men were moaning pitifully and begging for water. Their calls were answered by other women who were washing and binding up wounds, applying compresses and ripping material to fashion makeshift slings.

"This is our brother," Henry explained to the woman. "A shell hit him in the chest. We've brought him quite a ways. On a horse."

Handing the candle to Henry, she asked him to hold it well above the dry hay while she crouched beside Si and tore his shirt back gently to expose his wound. Candlelight shone on the faces of the two brothers highlighting the lines in their foreheads and the gaunt worried eyes which had seen no sleep for many hours. The nurse felt for Si's pulse. With her face full of compassion she looked down at Si, brushed the hair back from his damp forehead and stroked his cheek.

Looking up at Henry and Thad, she said: "I'm sorry. It's too late to help him now. He is at rest."

Henry grasped the candle tightly as if to coax strength from it, then it began to shake and he gave it back to the nurse. Thad looked down at his brother. A sob escaped him as he crouched beside Si putting his own head on Si's shoulder. "Oh, Si," he cried, "to die so far from home!"

Henry sank down next to Thad and put his arm around him. "At least, he didn't die alone, Thad, like so many of these men all around us are going to die."

As they lingered beside Si, stroking his arm and face, a passing nurse called out: "Miss Barton? Is Miss Clara Barton here?"

The woman who had attended Si was still standing nearby. "Here I am," she answered. Before turning away from Henry and Thad, she passed behind them and laid her free hand momentarily on the head of each of them. "God bless," she murmured

174

softly and disappeared into the darkness with the nurse who had summoned her.

As Henry and Thad kept their vigil beside Si throughout the night, they heard "Miss Clara Barton" being called for by voices all over the hillside. "I wonder who she is," mused Henry. "Everybody seems to know her and wants her attention."

Against the background of the cries of the wounded lying on the hill, the two men talked for many hours about their brother, remembering happier days on the farm when they were growing up. "Do you remember that spring of 1848 when I rode away from the farm on Beauty and you and Si both gave me gifts? I wish I had had a chance to tell him how many times I have used his jack-knife. I've used it to cut everything from branches over a trail to tough beef. I've stirred my coffee with it and I've killed a snake with it." He drew it out of his pocket and showed it to Thad. "I've even trimmed horses' hooves with it."

They sat there until dawn; sometimes long periods of silence passed and then one of them would recall something else about their dead brother to reflect upon. It was a time of grief but it was also a time of healing as they shared memories of their boyhood on the farm and talked about the experiences each had had in the past fourteen years.

When morning came, although they had not slept they felt strengthened by the wake for their brother. The three set to work digging a grave under a tree using a strange combination of tools: Henry's cavalry sword, a fence rail with a pointed end from along the roadside, the handles of Henry's tin dipper and frying pan and a rusty tool they found in an out-building of the house on the hill. The ground was rock-hard, and digging with these clumsy implements was slow-going.

With Si's jack-knife Ambrose fashioned a cross with two small twigs fastening them with a lace from Si's boot. Underneath it, on a piece of wood he carved:

Silas Thomas Sawyer
11th Pennsylvania

"I hope one of us survives this war so's to tell Hannah that he died a hero and how we buried him ourselves," said Thad as he looked at the grave covered with the dry earth of Virginia and marked with Ambrose's cross. They lingered a few moments as the sun rose upon the scene. "I wish this was Pennsylvania," Thad continued. "We're leaving him so far from home. It's hard to say goodbye knowing we'll never see this place again."

Looking around at the devastation of the countryside and at the hundreds of bodies lying on the nearby hill, Henry spoke: "He'll not be alone, Thad. He'll be in good company. There are a lot of Pennsylvanians here who'll be alongside him."

They turned away from the grave and resumed walking, Ambrose carrying the saddle to give the sores on Prince's back time to heal. Eventually they caught up with soldiers from their regiments, and Thad and Henry, walking with arms around each other's shoulders, had to bid each other goodbye.

Benjamin and Thorn were never seen again and were presumed lost, killed in action, in the Battle of Thoroughfare Gap.

17

Although President Lincoln wrote the Emancipation Proclamation in July of 1862, it was not issued publicly until September, because he wanted the nation to receive it at a favorable psychological moment—after a victorious battle. The military defeats of the summer, climaxed with the crushing losses of Second Bull Run, made him hold off until after the Battle of Antietam September 17 which, although it ended in something of a "draw," became a turning point of the war when Lee's campaign to win a decisive victory north of the Potomac failed.

On September 22 Lincoln presented to his cabinet the final draft of the preliminary Proclamation of Emancipation. He did it with grave doubts about how it would be received by the country the next day, especially the border states where conflict over the issue of slavery was always rife but where slaveholders, nevertheless, had chosen to remain inside the Union. Their loyalty was at best tenuous, however. What would be their reaction to the bold course he had set the country on—from which there was no turning back? Would it push them over the brink into the Secessionist fold?

Until this time in history the Administration vowed the war was being waged only to save the Union. Now it declared forthrightly that, henceforward, the war would be fought to liberate the slaves in Rebel states and that freed slaves could now enlist as soldiers and sailors. All this was to take effect on January 1, 1863:

"All persons held as slaves within any state or states, wherein the constitutional authority of the United States shall not then be practically recognized, submitted to, and maintained, shall then, thenceforward, and forever, be free."

Thus stated, the Proclamation applied only to the states in rebellion. It did not empower the government to free slaves in border states or any states within the Union.

The shock ripples of the Proclamation were felt throughout the land. Although northern abolitionists spoke out fiercely against the institution of slavery, they did not speak for the North as a whole. There was sympathy for slaves as such but it was a different matter to contemplate what the effects of freeing them would be. It was one thing to liberate more than 3,000,000 souls but what would the consequences of this daring act be? What would happen to them then? Where would they go? How would they survive, suddenly free, in a robust America unprepared for admitting them into its society?

Antagonism toward the black race infiltrated the North and the West, sometimes finding expression in brazen violence of the type which erupted amongst Irish dock workers in Cincinnati who beat and stoned free Negroes (working for less pay than they were) and drove them through the streets while the police looked on passively. In Brooklyn, a tobacco factory employing two dozen black women and children was attacked by Irish-Americans who tried to burn it down. In southern Illinois where hands were needed to harvest the crops, the War Department shipped in a group of contrabands who were promptly driven out by angry natives of that state.

Within the ranks of northern soldiers there was everything from an undercurrent of prejudice to outright hostility toward the idea of black freedom. They had no love for slavery but most of them had no love for slaves either. It was all right to go to war to risk one's life to save the Union and to fight treason, but now they were being asked to shed their blood and give their lives to free an entire segment of the population with whom they would ultimately be forced to associate and compete.

Henry listened to views expressed all around him, sometimes furtive (when Ambrose was present), at other times belligerent and scurrilous. When escaped slaves gravitated to the army on the march, Yankee treatment of them ranged from indifference to contempt to brutality.

"I'm for freeing the whole lot of them," one Vermont soldier remarked to Henry, "as long as I don't have to live with them."

"Emancipation is not worth the blood being spilled for it," said another Pennsylvanian. "Too many good men have been killed and a lot more are going to die to set them free."

The Negroes became the natural scapegoats for the disgruntled soldier who blamed them for the horrendous loss of life in the long and bloody campaigns.

"I thought I joined up to save the Union and to keep slavery out of the territories, not to free the niggers!" exclaimed an Ohioan.

From a Bostonian: "I can see what will happen when they're all free to go wherever they want. We'll have three million semi-savages overrunning the North and taking our jobs."

"They'll work for whatever pay they can get," added another city dweller. "What will *that* do to our wages?"

"I don't care if'n they're free. I jes don't want 'em to be equal," a Michigan lad ended the conversation for the time being.

Henry heard them out and then commented quietly: "The best friend I've ever had is Ambrose. Whenever I need help he is right there. He comes from a family of freed Negroes who have worked hard and honestly all their lives. They have proved to me that, given a chance, Negroes become outstanding citizens and patriotic Americans." He wanted to say more but let it go at that. There would be other opportunities for him to speak his feelings on the subject and he would make the most of them.

In the South the Proclamation was received with varying degrees of fury including threats to execute any Union soldier captured after January 1st.

Despite the rumblings and outbursts of anger, Governor John Andrew of Massachusetts got permission from the War Department to raise a black regiment. Prominent abolitionists became officers and enough men from northern states enlisted to create two black regiments—the 54th and 55th Massachusetts.

President Lincoln, sensitive to the antagonism throughout the country, toyed with the idea of establishing a colony for freed slaves in Central America as a way of solving the problem, but it was attacked as being racist and inhumane. What is more, the Negroes whom he queried about the proposition of leaving the country for a peaceful spot showed no enthusiasm.

*   *   *

After the appalling carnage of the Battle of Fredericksburg in December 1862, the defeated Union Army went into camp along the Rappahannock to lick its wounds. Winter descended on it and the Confederate Army encamped across the river. Oppressed with the malaise of defeat, the northern troops felt this was the season of the year that was the hardest for a soldier to bear. The enforced inactivity gave him time to reflect on his miserable state and to feel the cruelty of the harsh winter.

On one of these dreary winter evenings, Henry wrote to Harriet: "Almost two months have passed since I was wounded at Aldie. It was on October 31st when the 1st New Jersey fought some of Stuart's finest troops bravely with pistol and sword, but we took a heavy toll of horses and riders. I was the last rider to withdraw from the scene but not before a pistol ball penetrated my abdomen. Unfortunately, I was thus rendered disabled for some time and was in a field hospital. I am now a captain, as of October 1st.

"To the Sanitary Commission belongs much credit for gallant service in hospitals. The heroism and self-sacrifice of these intrepid and philanthropic women, these noble women, are familiar to all of us who have received their kindly ministrations. Their work alleviates suffering in field and city hospitals and on the dreadful hospital boats. They comfort the dying and pray with them during their last moments of life. In their self-forgetfulness and angelic devotion to the sick and dying are manifested a Spartan-like spirit of heroism and gentle charity. There are many hundreds of these women whose shining deeds hold them in honor equal to the nation's fighting men."

In the absence of battles to fight, the energy of the men went into improving their winter quarters. Through their individual ingenuities they built and furnished their huts with materials scrounged from the countryside. The zing of axes and the crash of falling trees reverberated in the air as the men dragged the timber "home" to split it into slabs for the walls of their winter dwellings. Nobody knew how long it would be before orders came to move on, but in the meantime the men meant to be as comfortable as possible and installed refinements of their own making to effect these changes from the primitive to the furnished state. The log walls were put together with mortar of Virginia clay and over all a shelter tent roof was erected. Even windows were installed and the very handy ones built fireplaces with chimneys. Surrounding farms were stripped of every usable old board along with every bushel of wheat and corn, every cow, horse and pig surrendered by farmers at gunpoint. When food was running short, Captain Walter Robbins of the 1st New Jersey was sent out by Colonel John Kester to reconnoitre the countryside. With a few men Robbins swept the area thoroughly and, not finding sufficient provisions outside the enemy lines, this gallant officer ventured inside the enclosure of the enemy's pickets. With unabashed courage and daring he held the Rebels at bay while capturing every turkey, chicken, goose, duck, pig and sheep about their camp and carrying off his prizes before their very eyes without losing one man. Upon his return to his own lines, Robbins handed over to the mess the ingredients for two days' delicious feasting.

As winter wore on, the wood supply disappeared and it was necessary to search a long distance for it. After the snow came the mud, growing deeper and deeper. To prevent the horses from standing in it, their stables had to be corduroyed—laying logs four inches in diameter side by side across the mud to lift the horses out of the mire. This job became the fatigue duty of many a private.

To while away the hours that the rain pelted their tents or the snow blew in the cracks, the men wrote letters, balancing their hard tack boxes on their knees for writing desks. Those who were not letter-writers indulged in games such as euchre and cribbage. Reading material was at a premium and any book that found its way into camp was passed along through many hands. Chequers and backgammon occupied some soldiers. The illiterate did not enter into games but lay on their blankets, smoking their pipes and talking.

As daylight faded, game-playing within the candle-lit tents gave over to sociability and reminiscences about home. The candles were held in unique candlesticks: bayonets were unfixed, the points stuck in the ground with the shank holding the candles. Visits from soldiers who joined up in the same hometown brought gossip and news reported in letters from families. In some tents vocal or music supplied by a banjo or violin helped to pass the evening hours.

Domestic chores done at home by wives and mothers now had to be performed by the soldiers. There came a time when the need for cleanliness in one's clothes could no longer be ignored. Standards of personal hygiene varied drastically, and oftentimes weeks went by before some men took note of the condition of their bodies and their clothing. An infestation of lice would force them into a vigorous scrub of their persons and to the task of washing their clothes. For the latter chore, the camp mess kettles served the men well. In them meat and potatoes were boiled, soup was cooked, tea was brewed and apples were stewed. These chores done, the kettles were transformed into laundry tubs in which water was boiled to accept the soiled clothing of the soldiers. Any entrepreneur amongst them could make a business of doing camp laundry; customers were easy to find.

Men brought out their "housewives" in the evenings to do their mending jobs; these attractive little cases supplied by a wife, mother or sweetheart contained the necessary needles and thread and a thimble for mending garments and darning socks. The only socks worth darning were hand-knit ones from loved ones. In the government-issued socks, large holes appeared after only a day's march leaving the toe end wide open, enabling the soldier to pull them on from either end.

The camp barber plied his trade in winter months inside the tents. Often his skills were subject to question when the job was done with a primitive razor and the man's appearance was appraised by his fellowmen. Many soldiers just allowed their hair and beards to grow, unchallenged, for months on end until the heat of summer.

Picket duty in winter was the job every soldier abhorred. When temperatures dropped low enough to freeze the ink in ink bottles and to make solid blocks of ice in canteens, it was unmitigated misery to shoulder a gun on the picket line and remain there vigilant for hours with nothing to occupy one's thoughts except the cold seeping into every bone and the hunger twisting one's stomach.

Picket duty could last three days but in the severe winter weather it was usually held to one. Pickets reported for guard-mounting in the cold air which turned their breath to frost, had their arms inspected by the commanding officer, passed in review before the highest ranking field officer of the day, then started for the picket posts. The latter were the assembly points for four men; from here they took turns going ahead to serve as vedettes for two hours. In extreme temperatures at night, pickets at the posts were allowed to warm themselves with small fires. Often as not, they had not eaten anything but hardtack in twenty-four hours, and as they paced back and forth bending their heads into the wind with snow collecting on their beards and eyelashes and with carbines at the ready at all times, their minds were filled with anticipation of hot coffee when they came off duty.

Nighttime pickets were subject to raids by not only the enemy but also by roving bands of partisans. The infiltrating enemy was always attempting to replenish his supply of horses; since every cavalry trooper who lost his horse was required to find a new one or go in the infantry, horses were the universally coveted prize. Partisan outlaws armed with double-barreled shot guns for shooting squirrels and rabbits, often stirred up trouble in surprise attacks and stole whatever they could get their hands on of Federal war materiel. Highly sought after were Sharp carbines and ammunition, Colt army pistols, sabers, McClellan saddles, bridles, blankets, rubber ponchos, and, of course, horses.

The line to be picketed was so long—twenty-five miles of the

Rappahannock—that duty of three days on and three days off was normal in fair weather.

A lieutenant in Henry's company, Birdsall Cornell, went out on picket duty in a blizzard that February. The snow was blowing so hard against his face as he rode his horse out to the line of vedettes that he could not open his eyes to the sting of the icy particles. He shouted through the storm to Private Jacob Youmans, the vedette riding next to him: "This is just the kind o' night Johnny Reb would come callin' on us, thinkin' we'd not be expectin' him."

As their horses picked their way along in the dark, stumbling now and then, the two soldiers kept heads bent to the storm and carbines resting on their thighs. Upon reaching the imaginary line for vedettes, they separated, one to the right and the other to the left, and took up their positions. Here they stood in the darkness, brushing the snow off their mounts, patting their furry necks and speaking soothingly to them. Birdsall beat his hands together to warm them while Jacob whistled to keep his spirits up and to ward off the sense of danger. The horses became restless and their riders let loose the reins to give them freedom to move about. Although it was against orders they dismounted and began to tramp up and down heavily, stirring up the circulation to keep their feet from freezing.

How long they remained on vedette duty there was no way of telling exactly but after a period of perhaps two hours each rider turned his horse and rode back to the picket post for his relief, guided to the spot by the smell of smoke from the small fire at the post where the relief men were huddled trying to keep warm.

Dismounting, Birdsall and Jacob stood talking to the reserve men, their faces glowing red in the firelight. Suddenly, from out of the darkness came a scuffling of horses' hooves, gunshots ringing out, and boisterous yelling as the little group was encircled, their horses' reins snatched from their hands while bullets whizzed by their heads.

"I be a-thankin' ye, Billy Yank," shouted a southern voice. "This here hoss'll make me a nice remount. Now Johnny Reb won't have to go into the ol' infantry!"

From the stunning speed with which the surprise attack

184

was executed and the horses with all their accouterments whisked away, it was evident that the Confederates were working in conjunction with raiders who were locals, intimately familiar with the lay of the land and expert at this kind of nighttime guerrilla ambush. That the pickets had escaped death at the hands of the outlaws seemed small recompense to them at the time for the loss of four horses that had carried them through more than a year of active service. At first light the men would be forced to search the unfriendly countryside for remounts. They would have to go farther and farther afield since Virginia had been picked almost clean of horseflesh. They commiserated silently on how far the search would be and how long it would take to train mounts and replace those they had lost. Sloshing through eight miles of snow and mud back to camp, weary in body and spirit, and shivering from the cold, they were full of self-recrimination for having been so disgraced.

Sir Percy Wyndham's temper had a short fuse for one individual who stalked him intermittently while he commanded the troops protecting the capital. This annoying gnat was Captain John Singleton Mosby who enjoyed the reputation of being the most enterprising partisan leader in the service of the Confederates. Wyndham refused to credit him with this status, looking upon him as a common bushwhacker and horsethief, vowing publicly to put an end to these incursions. With his troopers he scoured the countryside looking for Mosby's hideaways. They uncovered several guerrillas hiding in their homes in outlandish places—under beds and inside hoop skirts not being worn at the time. But Mosby was not subdued and continued his infuriating rampages on Wyndham's supply line and outposts. His men practiced stealthy hit-and-run tactics; after wreaking havoc and thieving, they chose not to stand and fight but escaped on their skillfully-trained horses. Mosby stated his intention openly to capture the Englishman inside his headquarters. The plan fizzled when Wyndham happened to be absent that evening; captured instead was Brigadier General Edwin H. Stoughton—an act which caused great embarrassment to the Union high command.

After accepting full responsibility for the catastrophe at

Fredericksburg, General Burnside was relieved of command of the Army of the Potomac in late January 1863 and "Fighting Joe" Hooker assumed it. He was aghast at the low morale of his force of 100,000 men who had lost faith in themselves and who still smarted under their mishandling by the generals who had led them. They looked with disgust on their incompetent leaders, such as Pope and McDowell, who had wasted so many young lives through bumbling stupidity at Second Bull Run. They needed someone to trust, to restore their pride, confidence and self-esteem, someone who knew how to be a leader. They needed another McClellan. Desertions were increasing at a frightful rate. In his resolve to solve the problem, Hooker began by giving furloughs to veterans of two years' active service. Later, furloughs were awarded to those regiments that were showing discipline, care of arms and horses, and denied those that were neglectful. "Dead wood" was weeded out of the officer corps and replaced with younger men who were promoted. Rations improved and included fresh vegetables and soft bread to replace the tiresome hard tack. Hooker also arranged for the immediate delivery of express boxes of food sent to the soldiers from home. Previously, they had been allowed to spoil sitting for days on wharves.

There was also more clothing and new arms—some of the army's first repeating rifles taking the place of single-shot carbines.

The men were sensitive to these efforts to make life in the army as bearable as possible and they began to feel that "Fighting Joe" shared some of General McClellan's affection for them. Before long they were lifted out of the doldrums by drills, inspections and reviews that restored their sense of professionalism in the service to their country.

For the cavalry Hooker brought about a revolutionary change. On February 5 he consolidated the 11,400 troopers into one corps under the command of General George Stoneman. Previously General McClellan had chosen to organize them by attaching the twelve regiments of cavalry singly to as many divisions of infantry. He believed that the volunteer mounted troops lacked the leadership and training to be capable of a large-scale independent operation separated from the infantry. And so the cavalry was scattered throughout the army and made to serve under commanders of brigades, divisions and corps of infantry.

Opposing it was the Confederate cavalry organized effectively early in the war into a brigade under the command of Jeb Stuart. Later it grew into a cavalry division of four brigades with five batteries of horse artillery—an extremely powerful fighting force for which the Union cavalry was no match as it was originally organized. Suffering from fragmentation, it lacked the cohesiveness to empower it to meet the Confederates on equal terms.

Then too, the Confederate trooper was a different kind of man from his northern counterpart. Typically, he was young, eighteen to twenty-two, and he came from the wealthy land-and-slave-owning class. A high-born gentleman, he was an experienced horseman who had grown up "at home" in the saddle; at foxhunts in the rolling hills he leapt fences with grace and believed whole-heartedly in his superiority as an equestrian. His horse was a splendid animal, the finest product of generations of southern horse-breeding. He rode off to war on the best horse in the family's stable, adorning himself in colorful trappings, such as a sash and a black felt slouch hat topped by a black ostrich feather. He cut a dashing figure—the personification of the popular romantic notion of the daring cavalier in wartime. He felt the tangible importance of what he was doing because he was fighting for his own home and fireside in his own country, surrounded by a sympathetic citizenry everywhere campaigns were fought on southern soil. His morale was high, his self-esteem enhanced by the confidence that his leaders believed the cavalry to be a highly valuable branch of the service. It was natural for him to become a proud, stouthearted soldier who believed in his military superiority over his enemy and in his own invincibility.

In a letter to Harriet, Henry shared some of his observations and conclusions about the enemy: "The Army of the Confederacy is made up of the flower of the South. The colleges were deserted, all professions suspended, offices abandoned, and the plow left in the furrow. Students and those with professions entered the

Confederate service. Those with native talent, the educated, and those with high moral standards entered the Army of Northern Virginia. This enlistment made the army of Virginia the flower of rebellion. Fighting for what? An independent confederacy of which the cornerstone is human slavery and an aristocracy intended to be far in advance of England's social system. The lower southern classes have been taught that they are fighting for home and firesides. That army developed an efficiency unsurpassed in ancient or modern times. Such is the material opposed to our Army of the Potomac, with most of our West Point officers on the Rebel side, with a superior system of militias having prepared them for this emergency, with such an army on their own ground, choosing always their time and place on which to deliver or accept a battle."

*   *   *

By the spring of 1863 the Union Army found itself facing a dangerous shortage of manpower. The men who had enlisted in 1861 for two years and those who had served in nine-month militias organized in 1862 were all due to go home soon. Over the past seven months the losses suffered from disease, combat and desertion (averaging 200 a day) had brought the number of able-bodied soldiers to a precarious low. Lincoln, in private, bemoaned the desertions and the inordinate number of men on furlough granted by company officers, the absentees outnumbering the recruits. He cited whole regiments with two-thirds of their men absent. He despaired of the army desertions, considering them to be the most serious evil the country had to deal with. In the Battle of Antietam, he pointed out, McClellan had 180,000 names on the army rolls. But of these 70,000 were absent on leave, 20,000 were in hospital or detailed for other duties, leaving some 90,000 to fight the enemy. After two hours, 30,000 men had straggled or deserted, which left the General with 60,000—about the same number as the Rebel Army had.

Volunteering for army service was nearly at a standstill. The ebullient patriotism and the desire for adventure characterizing the first men to answer Lincoln's call in 1861 had been battered by the grim realities of the string of northern defeats in the field. The glamor of war had ceased to be. There were few men now unemployed in the North where the economy was spinning along healthily.

The inevitable enactment of a conscription law for all men between twenty and forty-five came about in March. Exemption for physical or mental disability kept some men out of the service. Others pleaded that they could not leave a motherless child, an orphan brother or sister, or a destitute parent. To avoid being drafted one young man pleaded that he had lost his front teeth, which would make it impossible to bite off a cartridge. Some draftees fled to Canada or the West, others just disappeared into the backwoods.

There were two other ways to escape the draft. One was to hire a substitute and the other was to pay a commutation fee of $300, which bought exemption—a sum often representing a year's wages for a laborer. Inherent in these two processes were countless loopholes for fraud and injustice. But there were other ways that draftees could buy their way out of serving. Money to help them came from their hometown treasuries and from factories and businesses and railroads (that needed their labor), political machines currying favor, and from draft insurance societies, which offered a $300 policy for a premium of a few dollars a month.

Whereas hiring a substitute to fight for oneself or paying a fee to avoid service were methods designed to help men elude conscription, the bounty system came about as a way to stimulate volunteering. It became the practice of cities or towns or private individuals to pay a bounty to a volunteer and also to a veteran for re-enlistment when his tour of duty expired. It was a way to fill the quotas when Lincoln called for more troops. A "bidding" war often resulted and bounties rose to $300. Later in the war additional bounties were offered by the states and swelled the recruit's reward to $1000. This amount of money could support a family left behind for a very long time.

The pre-bounty veterans of 1861 and 1862 viewed with contempt the bounty volunteers who came into the service in 1863 and later. These seasoned soldiers had borne the brunt of two years' hard fighting for a cause they believed in, with no finan-

189

cial incentive to join up. They looked with disdain upon the men who were in it for the money.

The "bounty jumpers" learned how to collect several bounties by deserting from one town to another, assuming a different name, collecting another bounty, and "jumping" on to a third. Oftentimes as much as $1000 could be realized by this scheme. But they earned the undying scorn of the veteran troops who watched them desert or allowed themselves to be captured by the enemy when the fighting began. When a battle commenced in all its fury and bullets were zinging overhead, the voice of a veteran of two years' service could be heard admonishing the bounty enlistees to "get in there and do your $300 worth of fighting."

Nothing made soldiers happier than payday, and nothing caused more grousing amongst them than the laxity with which their pay was meted out. Often five months of active service passed before they received it. This delay was hardest on the veterans who had been serving since the beginning of hostilities and were trying to support families at home, whereas the new recruits enjoyed large bounties for their enlistment. Five months found almost all the men out of money and deep in debt.

The debts were owed the sutler—an institution of this war without whom the hardships of army service would have been even more dire. The sutler was a civilian traveling merchant dealing in groceries and dry goods who had permission to set up his tent near the encampment of the regiment to which he was assigned. The sutler's tent provided the men with all kinds of luxuries—at a price. He sold pies and molasses cakes, lemons, sugar and other goodies they had hungered for after many months of eating hardtack and salt pork. "Rallying on a sutler" was a popular sport with the soldiers who looked upon him as a "sharpie" charging them outrageous prices for his goods. When his tent was mobbed by the soldiers who lifted the baked items when his back was turned, he objected: "I have a family to feed." However, often he trusted them until the next pay day to settle their accounts. This was not done individually but by the paymaster who deleted the sutler's account before the soldier received his pay.

Still, the sutler made life more pleasant by providing such

precious delicacies as butter, cheese and condensed milk which soldiers bought at outlandish prices in desperation to have something that tasted good and reminded them of home, even though they knew full well that they were being gouged at the hands of an extortionist. The sutler provided them with self-raising flour to make pancakes and fritters, tobacco to while away the evening hours, and dry goods such as army regulation hats, cavalry boots, flannels, socks and suspenders. He was a "convenience" and the men traded with him, all the time resigned to the knowledge that they were victims of his rapacious nature.

Subtracted also from the soldier's pay before he received it was his clothing account with the Government. A soldier got forty-two dollars a year allowed him for his clothing, including guns and equipment. At the end of the year he had to settle up with Uncle Sam's Quartermaster. If any of his equipment was lost or destroyed or if he used more than forty-two dollars' worth, the balance came out of his pay.

Often, when all his debts were paid, the soldier was left with a paltry sum for himself, especially when the paymaster decided to pay him for only two months' service and to "retain" the rest until the next pay day.

18

Near the end of April 1863 General Stoneman took his new cavalry corps on a trial run. They crossed the Rappahannock and turned south into the Virginia countryside. The "liberated" cavalry rode off like cowboys on a riotous expedition, ripping up railroad bridges, destroying whole trains, burning railroad cars full of provisions waiting in depots, and wrecking lines of telegraphic communication. One of their main objectives was the rounding up of all the serviceable horses that could be found in enemy sta-

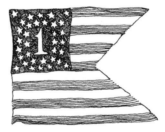

bles and pastures. Many Negroes astride their masters' best horses, rode out to greet the troopers and followed along with them, their horses becoming remounts for the cavalry.

Colonel Wyndham took two regiments of cavalry and made the James River canal his target. They galloped recklessly—a manner favored by the flamboyant colonel—and set fire to four bridges, canal boats loaded with food and forage, and a warehouse of tobacco, then battered down the locks and gates. After putting the canal out of service, they captured 140 horses and mules.

Henry, under Wyndham's command, led a detail of men in tearing up a section of a railroad. Using crowbars and levers, they pried up railroad ties and set them afire in a roaring blaze, then laid the rails on the flames, the better to bend, twist them around trees, and render them useless.

In another part of Virginia along a different railroad, cavalry swooped down, guerrilla-fashion, and torched storage sheds and trestles, wrecked two locomotives and tenders and captured 175 mules and horses.

Judson Kilpatrick, dubbed "Kill-Cavalry" for the brutish way in which he drove his cavalry, stormed his way into another part of the state destroying a railroad depot and telegraph wires, burning bridges, running a train of cars into the river, setting fire to a thirty-wagon train full of bacon and a depot where were stored 60,000 barrels of corn and wheat. He captured and paroled 300 prisoners. All of this destruction was carried out in a five-day rampage entailing a ride of 200 miles.

These raids ended on May 7 when the exhausted but elated cavalry corps came back to the north bank of the Rappahannock. It had become a revitalized fighting force, and the nation now acknowledged its ability to conduct an independent mission and work as a self-contained unit. For the first time the troopers found themselves made useful and elevated to a station better than that of watchmen for the army. No longer would they be tied to the slow-moving divisions of infantry and endless miles of wagons. Quite suddenly they were imbued with long-buried self-respect and self-confidence.

Following the Confederate victory at Chancellorsville in early May 1863, Lee prepared for his summer campaign in the North, intended to draw the fighting out of Virginia into the farmland of Maryland and Pennsylvania which would provide food and forage aplenty for his long-suffering troops who were eating sassafras buds and wild onions to protect themselves from scurvy and whose horses were dying of hunger. In June he moved his army away from Fredericksburg west toward Culpeper Court House, Virginia. The entire Army of Northern Virginia numbered now 80,000 strong. Lee's plan was to clear the foe out of the Shenandoah and then advance north across the Potomac into enemy territory. His cavalry had been strengthened by the addition of brigades and by fresh horses brought back by soldiers who had been on leave for the express purpose of finding remounts.

There were now just over 10,000 troopers and horse artillery gunners drawn up between Culpeper and Kelly's Ford.

Commanding the rejuvenated corps of cavalry was Jeb Stuart who, to show off their brilliant horsemanship of which he was extraordinarily proud, planned a military review and a gala social event on the plains of Brandy Station, Virginia for the local citizenry and invited guests on the fifth of June. Gathered along the two miles to the parade grounds on this sunny afternoon were hundreds of spectators who came out to applaud the elegant horsemen as they rode by to the accompaniment of bugles and three bands and with battle flags waving. Witnessing the colorful spectacle at the parade grounds were crowds of guests from near and far—military officers and their beautifully dressed ladies—who watched and responded enthusiastically as the cavalry regiments went through their drill. The handsome horses with their resplendent riders performed a mock charge accompanied by twenty-four guns of the horse artillery. The audience shouted rousing cheers of delight. The celebratory mood of the review lasted many hours and was climaxed by a ball that evening on a lawn in Culpeper that was lit by torches and Chinese lanterns.

The pride and vanity of Jeb Stuart were inflated by the praise heaped on him for his brilliant cavalry genius and "glory shone all about him."

Because General Lee was unable to attend the magnificent pageant, a second review was held for him on June 8, after which Stuart moved his brigades nearer the Rappahannock for the launching of the northern invasion.

General Hooker was uncomfortable with the knowledge that three brigades of Confederate cavalry were assembled near Culpeper. What was the reason for their presence, he wondered. Were they screening the next movement of Lee's main army or were they contemplating a raid? He ordered General Buford to find out. On June 5 the latter reported back that what appeared to be the Confederacy's entire cavalry was in Culpeper County and that its numbers seemed very much increased. Hooker, convinced that Stuart was about to lead his cavalry on a raid to the north, ordered General Alfred Pleasanton, who had replaced

Stoneman because of illness, to take the cavalry across the Rappahannock, smash the Confederate cavalry amassed there and destroy their trains and supplies.

While Stuart was enjoying the adulation in his headquarters at the top of Fleetwood Hill near Brandy Station, the Union cavalry corps prepared its attack to catch him off-guard. On the morning of June 8, while the Confederates were entertaining General Lee on the parade grounds, Pleasanton's cavalry was making ready to march. The corps was divided into two commands: one under General John Buford consisting of the First Division and the Reserve Brigade, and the second led by General David McMurtrie Gregg made up of the Second and Third Divisions. The cavalry was to be reinforced by 3000 men of two infantry brigades: General Adelbert Ames's to Buford, General David A. Russell's to Gregg. This would bring Pleasanton's strength up to 11,000.

The attack was to have several prongs. After crossing the Rappahannock at Kelly's Ford the following day, Gregg's division and Russell's infantry were to march northwest seven miles to Brandy Station. Gregg's other division under Colonel Alfred Duffie would proceed due west six miles to Stevensburg, four miles south of Brandy Station. Buford would bring his men and Ames's infantry across the river at Beverly Ford, seven miles north of Kelly's Ford, and with the cavalry in the lead would march four miles southwest to Brandy Station. At this point he would meet Gregg and together they would advance toward Culpeper where, it was thought, they would find Jeb Stuart. (What they did not know was that Stuart had moved his troopers away from Culpeper to Brandy Station so that the spot where the Federal cavalry expected to join forces was actually right in the middle of Stuart's camp.) Colonel Duffie, once at Stevensburg, would provide flank protection for the main force as it marched toward Culpeper.

With one important exception, all went according to plan. Most of the cavalry and the two infantry brigades reached their respective fords after nightfall on June 8 and remained hidden in the nearby woods, the cavalry holding their horses during the night. To keep their presence secret there were no bugle calls and fires were not lit. There was no coffee, and the men's supper was cold hardtack and pork and water. They were set to cross the fords at 3:30 A.M. on June 9. Henry was with Wyndham's brigade made up of the 1st New Jersey, 1st Pennsylvania and the 1st Maryland Cavalry. Only Colonel Duffie's division coming from its camp in Warrenton, Virginia was tardy in getting to Kelly's Ford and upset the carefully laid out plans of Gregg to have him lead the crossing before dawn. He did not arrive until 7 A.M., which delayed Gregg's crossing until broad daylight.

At first light on June 9 thick banks of fog came rolling over the Rappahannock shrouding the activity along its banks. Buford's lead column under the command of Colonel Benjamin F. Davis with the 8th New York Cavalry (and Captain George A. Custer, then of the 5th United States who attached himself to Davis's force) got across Beverly Ford but in so doing stirred up picket fire from a company of the 6th Virginia nearby, awakening Jeb Stuart at his headquarters on Fleetwood Hill three miles away. Confederate sharpshooters held off Buford's attackers while Stuart's horse artillery and reinforcements of Confederate cavalry formed a strong battle line at a protected spot with higher elevation behind a stone wall at St. James Church.

After fording the river, Gregg followed Colonel Duffie on the road toward Stevensburg for four-and-one-half miles and then turned northwest toward Brandy Station. It was late in the morning when Gregg's brigades—Wyndham leading on the left with Henry commanding the 1st squadron and Judson Kilpatrick on the right—were riding toward Fleetwood Hill. Fleetwood was the prize they sought where they hoped to seize Stuart's confidential papers. With Fleetwood in the hands of the Federals, Stuart's forces now engaged at St. James Church would find themselves between two lines of Federal fire. His escape to Culpeper would be blocked. Fleetwood Hill sloped down towards the Rappahannock for one-and-three-quarters miles and with a width of one-half mile. It merged into a wide, gently falling high plateau—a stretch of ground ideal for a cavalry engagement.

As the Federal cavalry neared Fleetwood, the hill looked bare of troops. It was true that only Major Henry McClellan was there with some orderlies and a lone lieutenant who had a single six-pounder howitzer. When McClellan spied the Federal cavalry coming on, he sent the lieutenant with his cannon to the crest of the hill to fire on them, and he also dispatched an orderly to Stuart for help. At the sight of the gun, the approaching cavalry misjudged the situation, thinking the Confederates to be strong in number; they halted their advance on the hill and sent for an artillery battery to be brought up to support them.

From the scene of fighting with Buford's force several miles away, Stuart sent back successive waves of his cavalry—the 12th Virginia and the 6th Virginia and the 35th Virginia Battalion—to Fleetwood. Each in turn rode back at a thundering gallop to charge the Federals head-on on the hill. In the vanguard of Federal troopers was the 1st New Jersey in perfect formation, with flags and guidons flying above the column of squadrons. It took the full brunt of the charge.

Many months later, Henry told Harriet what his feelings had been when the regiment was drawn up, waiting for the bugle to sound the charge, as the Rebel cavalry approached in a cloud of dust: "For a moment only, an awful silence fell upon the field. This is the time that tries the courage of the bravest for, once in the heat of battle, the average soldier forgets all danger in the turmoil and excitement of the hour."

There ensued the clash of cavalry that destined the Battle of Brandy Station to become the most important cavalry engagement in Civil War annals and firmly established the Federal cavalry as a force to be reckoned with for the duration of the war.

Stuart sent up the brigades of William E. ("Grumble") Jones and Wade Hampton as further reinforcements, and with their savage yell with which they began every charge—a blend of a piercing, sustained shriek, a blood-curdling scream and a Hi-hi-Hi yip-yip—the Rebels stormed into the melee with drawn sabers flashing in the sun like streaks of flame and the hooves of horses pounding on the hard earth, sending up clouds of dust that enveloped all the combatants. They were met by the Federal cavalry on the gallop with sabers swinging and every man shouting with jubilant confidence in his own invincibility as their flags flew above them. The swordsmanship the 1st New Jersey had learned from Europeans Kargé and Wyndham stood them in good stead.

Proper military formation began to waver on both sides and it became a hand-to-hand fight between squadrons, smaller groups and lone individuals battling each other fiercely for possession of the artillery guns. Men rode in every direction, their identity erased by the dust and powder smoke swirling over them. Curses and yells from both sides filled the air, and everywhere could be heard the din of pistol shots, the snort of horses and the screams of those that were shot, the plunging to earth of their enormous bodies, the bang of metal on metal as the bloody sabering grew in intensity, and the shrieks and groans that resonated when blades slashed into flesh. Grape and canister fell thickly and riders without horses and horses without riders ran everywhere in confusion. Men who were thrown up in the air when their horses were shot out from under them came down to earth, dazed, but still rallied to fight from behind their mounts' carcasses, steadying their pistols on the saddles.

Lieutenant-Colonel Virgil Broderick had one hundred New Jerseymen on the hill when he gave the order to "Charge!" Henry on Prince was at the head of his squadron, taking ravines and ditches at a gallop. All around horses' flanks were covered with white foam that made their sides glisten in the sun. Bravery and gallant heroism were the order of the day. When Broderick's horse was mortally wounded and staggered to the ground beneath him, his orderly, farrier Private James Wood, leapt from his own horse to supply a remount for the officer. In so doing the younger man was taken prisoner by a careless Rebel who did not move fast enough to prevent Wood from seizing a carbine lying on the ground and pointing it at his captor. Although the carbine was empty, the intrepid Wood took the man prisoner, then got back in the battle as soon as he could grab hold of a horse with empty saddle.

Seeing Broderick unhorsed a second time and surrounded by a crowd of Rebels about to cut him down with their sabers, Henry was overcome with a surge of loyalty. "Oh, my God!" he exclaimed aloud as he pulled Prince's reins up and reversed his direction to go to the aid of the imperiled officer. As he did so, whistling through the smoke came a shell that flung the valiant Prince over on his side, never to rise again, at the same time that Henry felt the blast of a bullet in his ear shattering his head and another tearing open his thigh. He fell with his faithful Prince, but before losing consciousness he saw in a flash Major John Shelmire lying inert nearby across the body of a Rebel, Broderick also prostrate on the ground, and the regimental guidon being grabbed from the enemy by a little troop of the 1st Pennsylvanians.

The Battle of Brandy Station went on for many hours with both sides fighting to exhaustion and with only a few horses left standing, incapable of further exertion. Pleasanton ordered the withdrawal of his forces. The retreat of the Union cavalry across the Rappahannock was orderly and unhurried. Stuart's dispatches, which Pleasanton wanted, had been seized from his headquarters before he had gotten back to Fleetwood Hill.

Pleasanton was criticized afterwards for his indecisive leadership that failed to achieve an overwhelming victory over Jeb Stuart. But there was agreement on both sides that the Federal cavalry had "turned the corner," proving themselves a match for Stuart's men. No longer did they feel inferior to the horsemen in gray; they gained self-confidence and an esprit de corps that would embolden them on every battlefield that lay ahead.

In the Battle of Brandy Station, Stuart took more casualties than he had ever suffered before in one engagement. Enormous was the satisfaction amongst the Federal cavalry for having embarrassed the swashbuckling Stuart by catching him unawares and stunning him into recognizing them as a formidable adversary he would have to reckon with from this day forward. The vanity of the mighty cavalier was stung, and the brilliance of his reputation in the field was tarnished by the less than enthusiastic reports in southern newspapers that spoke of the recent battle as a "disaster" for the Confederacy.

One Confederate casualty at Brandy Station, whose wounding and subsequent capture by the Federals would have a direct bearing at another point in time on the destiny of Henry Sawyer, was Brigadier General William Henry Fitzhugh (Rooney) Lee, the twenty-six-year-old second son of Robert E. Lee. He was shot in the thigh while leading a cavalry brigade in a final charge. Convalescing at the home of a relative not far away, he was discovered, captured and imprisoned by the Federals in Fortress Monroe.

19

For more than a night and a day Henry lay unconscious on the hard floor of the church. Finally, his sore and stiffened body began to stir, and he raised one hand to his head. Before opening his eyes he was aware from the sounds and smells around him that he was not alone. The hot, oppressive air in the church, fetid with odors of bodies, blood and septic wounds, reached his nostrils, bringing a ripple of nausea through his body. His lips and throat were still parched from the smoke of the battle he had been through several days before.

Next to him on the floor a groaning man tossed and turned, jarring Henry into wakefulness. He opened his eyes slowly and saw in the distance a lone candle shining in the darkness. He tried to move but every bone and every muscle refused. Turning his head toward the suffering man, he whispered softly, "Where are we?"

No reply.

Henry extended his hand with difficulty and touched the man's arm lightly. "What *is* this place?"

There was a murmur followed by a gasp of pain.

In the faint light of the candle Henry could make out a Yankee uniform on the man. "I'm Henry Sawyer. 1st New Jersey Cavalry."

After a long silence came a voice stating quite clearly, "Gideon. Gideon Adams. 1st Pennsylvania."

Henry raised his head long enough to have a look around, then sank back onto the floor and listened to the voices around him. He was confused; southern dialect seemed to predominate.

The two male patients who had carried him to this spot approached now and stopped by Gideon Adams.

"Where are we?" Henry asked the men.

"This here is Culpeper. You'uns is in Culpeper, Virginny, Yank," one of them answered.

"But this place? It looks like a church," Henry insisted.

"It was. Onc't. But now it's a hospital. A *Confederate* hospital," he stressed.

That explanation of his whereabouts gave Henry pause. A Yankee officer in a Confederate hospital was not exactly the role he'd choose for himself. "How did I get here?" he asked.

"Ye came in with a bunch o' wounded from Brandy Station. Ye was one o' the lucky ones who made it out alive."

"What day is it?"

"About the 11th o' June, I reckon."

The two men carried Gideon Adams away and Henry lay back on the floor trying to remember what had happened to him. He felt his sword next to him and fingered it, attempting to initiate the recall of events that had brought him to this place.

Recollections of the battle drifted back slowly, muddled and painful, until the harsh truths began to etch themselves clearly in his mind. Fleetwood. Stuart. Prince. Shelmire. Broderick. Wyndham. He sighed and shut his eyes as if to keep the memories at bay. Lying motionless for some hours, trying to relieve the stress and despair weighing on his mind, he slipped into a troubled sleep.

The quiet was disturbed by the return of Gideon. Henry was roused by the groan which escaped the man as he was laid with exaggerated gentleness on the floor by the two men who had carried him away. The sleeve of Gideon's shirt had been torn off, and a blood-soaked bandage was drawn over the stump of his arm.

About his person was the smell of chloroform and whiskey. Groaning, he covered his eyes with his good arm.

"Ye're next," one of the bearers said to Henry.

He was picked up, one man carrying his feet and the other grabbing hold under his arms and lifting his shoulders. As he was borne through the aisle of the church, he caught sight of the cross on the altar. He was carried into a room where the doctor, holding a scalpel between his teeth, was standing by a table and another man was wiping blood off of it with a rag. The only light in the room came from a few candles, and as he was laid on the table, Henry made note silently of the doctor's mien. Above his bare torso with its massive shoulders was a haggard face with sweat dripping down in rivulets. Blood smeared his face and the hair that hung over his brow and covered his burly chest and arms. A gray-striped apron was tied around his waist and knotted in front much like a butcher's. Threaded suture needles were pinned to the apron. The blood of many patients before Henry was congealed on the apron in a black mass. Dark eyes, sunken in their sockets, looked down at Henry, and as the doctor bent over him, taking Henry's head in his hands, he smelled whiskey on his breath.

"Hundreds of our own I been doctorin' fer days. Now here comes Yanks. Some on our side are aimin' to kill ye on the field, the rest of us are s'posed to put ye back together agin," he said brusquely. "The whole thing don't make sense to me."

Henry considered how he should reply but, unable to think clearly, he remained silent.

"Southern boys come in here, prayin' to God Almighty to save their lives and to help them win this war. Then the Yanks lyin' on the table are askin' that He lets 'em win the war so they kin all go home to their loved ones. Now I ask myself, 'What's God to do in this case? What side is He on? Is He wearin' blue or gray?'"

All the time he was talking the doctor was cleaning out the bullet wound in Henry's right cheek using a sponge that he dipped in a basin of water blood red in color. He swayed somewhat as he worked, his body jarring the table as he leaned heavily against it.

"Now ye was lucky, Yank. The bullet went clear through yer neck and came out the left side o' the spine. In a few weeks ye'll be back on the field shootin' at our southern lads. Unless, of course, they put ye into prison fer a spell and give ye time to think."

While he talked the doctor dabbed the wound with a rag soaked in whiskey and chloroform. Then, ripping a piece of material from a linen tablecloth, he wrapped the makeshift bandage roughly around Henry's head. "Let's have a look at the leg." The blood in the thigh wound had adhered to Henry's uniform when it dried, and as the doctor pulled the trousers down, the wound commenced to ooze blood again. Henry winced. The doctor, breathing heavily as he worked over him, several times put down his instruments and wiped his head with the back of his bare hand.

"Well, I guess we've fixed ye up as best we kin fer now. If the wound suppurates, the maggots'll clean it out," he said, finally.

Henry was at a loss for words, but he felt it was imperative that he respond in some way. He managed a simple expression of gratitude. "Thank you, sir, for your trouble."

The doctor waved his hand to the two attendants while he turned his back on them and reached for a bottle in the cabinet. Henry was carried from the dimly lit room, back to the darkness of the church, where he was laid in the same spot next to his sword. Gideon writhed in agony in his delirium. Henry spoke to the men placing him on the floor. "Isn't there a bed somewhere for him?"

"Everythin's full up," one answered. "We got room fer only a hundred here and now we got over 300, includin' all you' uns. This is the best we kin do fer'im."

The moans of pain all around him bore down on his sensibilities, suffocating him with such anguish that he cupped his hands over his ears to shut them out. He closed his eyes, hoping that sleep would bring a respite from the suffering of all the unfortunate ones lying around him. He felt no enmity in this place. There was a certain fraternity amongst the wounded.

How long did he lie there? Minutes? Hours? His mind was muddled but he was conscious of his hands being pried away gently from his ears and off in the distance a soft, southern voice speaking to him, "Soldier, here's some cold lemonade for you."

Henry opened his eyes to see a woman with a large frame hovering over him and holding a pitcher and a cup. He could not believe his eyes or his ears. She stood there in the candle-lighted gloom like an angel with her sweet, feminine entreaty. Stooping down to his level, she poured a cupful and held it to his lips, cradling his head in her other arm.

"Thank you, ma'am," he whispered to her.

She turned towards Gideon who was raving in unconsciousness, and Henry, noting her look of distress, said to her, beseechingly, "Are you a nurse? He's in a very bad way. Just lost his arm."

She looked dismayed. "No. Oh, if only I *were* a nurse! But I'm just a Virginia homemaker trying to help wherever I can. My husband and sons are all away in the war."

A shaft of embarrassment shot through him from the humiliation he felt. A southern woman giving aid to a Yankee officer while her own husband and sons were on a battlefield fighting against all he believed in! When he recovered his composure sufficiently, he continued, "I was just fearful that he won't make it if he doesn't get some care soon."

"I'll do what I can," was her response. She disappeared into the remote darkness of the church and returned momentarily carrying a basin of water and some cloths. Kneeling down on the floor next to Gideon, she bathed the sweat from his forehead and cheeks and applied cool compresses. Then, removing the bandages from his arm, she bound it with fresh pieces. Her face was contorted as she worked. Appalled at the ghastly savagery of the surgery, she kept swallowing hard to fight back the nausea. Gideon rolled from one side to the other as she nursed him tenderly. After the wound had been dressed, she slowly removed what was left of his shirt and stuffed it and some other rags inside his jacket to fashion a pillow for his head.

Watching her soothing manner, Henry forced himself to speak again. "Ma'am, if he were able to say it himself, I know he'd want to thank you for your kindness." He paused for a moment before continuing, "It's a special gratitude because of you being who you are and we being who we are."

She turned towards Henry in the dim light and laid a hand on his head. "I pray to God every night that if my husband or sons should find themselves in a Yankee hospital, some northern woman with a sympathetic heart would find it within herself to care for them as best as she was able." She rose with some difficulty and looked down at Henry, "You know, this is *not* a women's war."

20

On the evening of July 3, 1863 the prisoners stumbled off the train and walked from the depot through the streets of Richmond. They were a motley lot of officers, some limping on bloody bare feet, others with head bandages, all trudging footsore and battle-weary, carrying their personal effects slung over their shoulders and backs. Gaunt, hollow-eyed, unshaven faces bore the ravages of months of war. One man walked with crutches, his injured leg swathed in blood-soaked bandages being considerably shorter than his good one. Several sleeves dangled empty

from shoulders. Uniforms were torn and dirty, hair disheveled, shoes almost destroyed from months of marching and fighting. Consciously or unconsciously, the men had adopted the mien of captives: stooped and with heads bent they were silent as they proceeded on their way, glancing up only occasionally to see where the road led. Guards jostled them rudely to keep them in a four-file column.

Along the busy thoroughfare were gathered the curious local citizenry—white and black, women and children, and an occasional wounded Rebel soldier on crutches. The white women wore drab clothing and bonnets, which shielded their sullen countenances, but from those partially hidden mouths came invectives loud and vulgar and obscene.

"Yankee pigs!" railed one scowling woman, pointing an accusatory finger at the passersby. "May you rot in hell!"

The ranting passed along from women to children who glared, stuck out their tongues, pointed fingers, and shook their fists. All along the route from the train depot to the prison the soldiers were taunted, reviled, insulted by the women who walked beside them gesticulating abusively. "Johnny Reb will beat ye all, nigger lovers . . . General Lee will fix ye fools once and fer all."

The soldiers seemed oblivious to the tirade raining down on them. Their march followed the Lynchburg Canal and there was considerable activity around them that is always present at a commercial waterside. After a mile of walking they came to a three-story brick building which looked like a storehouse, old and somewhat dilapidated, situated by the Kanawha canal. Nearby flowed the James River. The street signs identified the spot: Twentieth and Cary Streets. From one corner of the building hung a small sign reading: "Libby & Son, Ship Chandlers and Grocers." And on the end facing the prisoners was written clearly: "Libby Prison." The marchers came to a halt.

Henry Sawyer, his head wound still bandaged, looked up at the windows of the second and third floors and saw the emaciated faces of inmates looking down. There were no panes in the windows, only iron gratings covering them. As the prisoners stood waiting to be admitted, a piece of paper fluttered down from one of the windows and landed beside Henry's foot. Furtively he retrieved and read it: "Hide your greenbacks." The warning was whispered along the ranks, and surreptitiously Union currency was stashed away in the lining of caps, coats, and inside shoes of the men who wore them. With an affected nonchalance Henry reached down and slid five much-prized U.S. notes underneath the tongue of his boot while a soldier with long unkempt hair next to him folded one into a small square and stuffed it quickly inside his ear, pulling his tousled locks over it. Another soldier who bent down to tie a bootlace, with his face thusly hidden, tucked a greenback under a cud of tobacco in his cheek. It would not be long before they learned through firsthand experience what they had been told by soldiers who had escaped from

Rebel prisons: northern greenbacks (worth much more than southern graybacks) could buy a prisoner almost everything from the guards—extra food, favors, even escape.

The prisoners filed into the building, some of them taking a last look over their shoulders at the outside world they were leaving. Henry felt a sinking sensation in his stomach as he left the warm fresh air and entered the dank darkness of the Libby. Except for the Confederate hospital, which he had recently left, this was his first incarceration of the war. The official greeting, which he received along with his compatriots in tatters, was not long in coming.

"Strip them clean!" bellowed Captain Dick Turner, inspector and commissary officer of the Libby, flinging his arms out toward the prisoners. The guards were quick to obey. Their search was rough and thorough, reaching inside pockets, sleeves and trouser legs, inspecting all body parts, and rifling haversacks for hidden treasure. Henry's bootlaces were ripped out, three buttons torn from his jacket and his faded, ragged toilet kit grabbed. The contents of the latter were paltry, inconsequential except for a solitary valuable—the jack-knife which Si had given Henry the day he'd left the farm so many years ago. The guard who discovered it leered slyly at Henry as he slipped it into his own pocket, glancing stealthily around him.

"Thought you was goin' to hang onto this, right, Yank?" The man was rough and there was about his person a stale odor. " 'spect ye planned on doin' a little diggin' with this, right, Yank? No sech luck. Johnny Reb'll take care o' this fer ye. Ye won't be needin' this here in ol' Libby."

Anger flushed Henry's cheeks. For a moment he considered protesting physically for his possession, but he knew such an act was pointless. What possible chance that this fiend was capable of any appreciation of sentiment?

The villain sneered and ran his hands roughly down the full length of Henry's back feeling for hidden booty. The greenbacks Henry had pushed under the tongue of his boot had gone undetected thus far. Perhaps if he were lucky he could one day buy the knife back from this uncouth culprit if they chanced to meet. And deep down inside him Henry was certain that they would meet.

209

The compass that had been given Henry by Thad on that memorable day in 1848 when Henry said goodbye to his family had been smashed when he was first wounded. Henry was certain that the compass, stored in the upper pocket of his jacket, had saved his life when it deflected a bullet from his chest.

Prisoners all about him were submitting to the indignities of the guards. An officer who protested at the search promptly received a blow to his face from Dick Turner. "Swine!" Turner cursed the officer, his blue eyes turning steely and vicious as he lowered the blow.

The guards were openly frustrated that their searches had yielded such meagre prizes. The captives had been so thoroughly denuded of all valuables in previous searches that at this point they were like picked chickens. Every watch had been stolen, rings and personal trinkets taken, all writing materials and personal journals pilfered, and any "excess" clothing such as hand-knit socks or sweaters had been appropriated long ago. One man's torn trousers were held up now by a piece of cord, his leather belt and buckle having been seized the day before as he boarded the train.

As the guard shoved Henry on and confronted the next prisoner in line, Henry was conscious of a hand slipping something light into his trouser pocket. He did not turn around instantly but waited a few seconds. Then his eyes met those of Gideon Adams, now undergoing a search by the same infamous guard. He looked straight into Henry's eyes imploring him for silence. Henry turned and walked on. Feigning disappointment in the results of their search, the guards abused the unfortunate lot of prisoners despicably. "Damned sons of bitches! There ain't a trinket on 'em. They're a lousy lot o' rabble! Scum!"

Henry mused silently about how many of their pockets jingled with trinkets such as his jack-knife!

Gideon came alongside him. Surreptitiously, Henry reached into his trouser pocket and drew out a nail file.

"I reckon this may come in handy," Gideon whispered to Henry with a faint glint in his eye as he took the file back with his lone hand. "You never know how long we may be here. We might want to leave before they're ready to say goodbye to us . . . and this might hurry us along . . . if we took to digging."

Henry forced a weak smile, remembering his jack-knife.

The prisoners were pushed ahead toward steep wooden stairs with no landing, customary in warehouses. As he waited his turn to mount them, he shot a glance off to one side of the room he was leaving and his gaze came to rest on captured Union regimental flags hanging upside down on the walls. The sight of these noble banners sent a shooting pain through his heart as he visualized what their capture had meant in terms of human life squandered on the field. For a fleeting moment Henry heard the cries of the wounded color-bearers, saw the flags rent by the shells fall, only to be picked up from the ground by other boys younger than the fallen and carried above their heads through the smoke and fury of battle. Hung there upside down to demoralize the prisoners, these standards had the reverse effect upon Henry who, unconsciously, stiffened his backbone as he trod heavily up the stairs.

At the top the newcomers were greeted boisterously by the inmates starved for news from the outside world. Officers from General Robert H. Milroy's Eighth Corps and Colonel Abel D. Sreight's 51st Indiana swarmed over the "fresh fish," pelting them with questions: "What's yer regiment? Did ye come across any 51st Indiana Infantry? Any news from Gettysburg? Where did the Rebs capture ye? Were ye at Bull Run? What happened to the 1st Pennsylvania? I was with the 1st Maine. Any sign of them? What of Kilpatrick? How far north did Lee get?" On and on they pummeled the new arrivals with queries until one seasoned prisoner cried out: "Give 'em air!" and the initiation ceremony died down.

There was a smell of burning food in the atmosphere as Henry found a space in the room that he was to share with twenty other officers. This was their mess and barracks and "recreation" area all rolled into one. The walls were naked and the room bare of any furniture. Three inmates sat on the rough floor sharing a blanket while the man in charge of cooking for the day leaned over a smoking, broken stove. He turned and addressed Henry, "Hope you like burned cornmeal coffee."

211

"How's the food?" Henry wanted to know.

"You won't get fat," the cook for the day responded. "Today you'll get rice soup. No salt. There's nothing at night."

Henry studied the man's physique. Over six feet in height, he was stooped and his shoulder blades pushed out his shirt. His arms and hands were bony with fingers like sticks. "Have you been here long?" he asked the man.

"Since Fredericksburg. 'bout six months. I've lost count. Just as well," he added grimly.

Henry's face registered shock. "Have there been no prisoner exchanges in that time?"

The man shook his head. "Only one or two. Special cases. Special favors. There's lots of talk about exchange all the time. You'll get sick of it. Men get their hopes up. Then nothing happens."

Henry's face expressed dismay, his hopes shattered by this revelation.

He walked across the filthy floor of the room towards the window, but as he neared it one of the men under the blanket warned him sharply: "Stay away from windows. Sentinels outside the Libby have orders to shoot any face that looks out. 'Few days ago we lost a man standing out there in the middle. He caught the bullet meant for the one looking out who jumped back."

Henry stepped back into the suffocation of the room with its burning odors and approached the wooden trough, which was supplied with water piped in from the nearby canal. He took a drink of the lukewarm, yellowish liquid. "After a rain we get a lot of the bottom of the canal," explained an inmate who had observed Henry's grimace at the foul taste.

He threw his haversack down on the floor and his jacket on top of it. Then, smoothing them out, he lowered himself onto this self-styled cushion next to an officer on whose bare ankles large sores like boils had formed. Both ankles were swollen from scurvy. The luckless victim was aware of Henry's observations, and he offered an explanation: "Sometimes the Sanitary Commission sends boxes with pickles in them to Libby prisoners. Vinegar keeps scurvy under control. The last box we opened had nothing in it but some old newspapers from New York. The guards had stolen everything out of it." He looked depressed. "All we eat is cornbread. Scurvy gets a hold here. Like the sailors at sea for months who don't get any vegetables or lemons."

"Who is the Commandant here?" Henry wanted to know.

"He's another Turner. Not the one you just met. That's Dick. He's a brute. The Commandant is one Captain Thomas Turner. A West Pointer but a rebel through and through. We hear he's never even been in the field. Not to be trusted, either. They're quite a pair, those two."

"Does it do any good to complain to him or the surgeons?"

"The Commandant?" The sick man gave vent to an expletive. "Turner says 'rats for rats.' That's his philosophy. Starve us and we can't cause any trouble." He turned to the officer lying on the floor next to him.

"Hey, Rufus. The captain here fancies we should go to Turner and curtsy and ask him for a glass of lemonade." Both men slapped their knees and guffawed.

The man called Rufus elaborated on the joke. "I kin jes' hear Turner askin' the guards to bring up a silver tray with cold lemonade for all of us. 'With the Captain's compliments. All ye can drink, boys. Plenty more where this came from. We'll bring it to ye every afternoon at tea time so's to cure that nasty ol' scurvy ye're all gettin'. Drink up now.' "

They continued their joke but their laughter trailed off sardonically.

An officer across the room from Henry asked him about his head wound: "Where'd you get yours?"

"Brandy Station. Virginia," he answered. "A big cavalry battle June 9th. 1st New Jersey Cavalry taught Jeb Stuart a lesson. He was putting on a show for the ladies and we took him by surprise."

"How'd you get to the Libby?" another asked.

"I lost my horse. That was the worst of it. He'd brought me through twenty-five engagements. Been with me since February '62. He caught a shell at Brandy Station. Rebs picked me up and took me to hospital in Culpeper. I was there about three weeks, then they loaded those of us who could walk on the train for Richmond. On the train I heard rumors of a big battle going on up in Pennsylvania at a place called Gettysburg not far from the Maryland border."

The men listened to him with rapt attention. News from beyond the miserable confines of the prison was nourishment for their fighting spirit. "Where's McClellan now?" one wanted to know.

"Nobody knows. Meade commands the Army of the Potomac now. Just relieved Joe Hooker. Vicksburg is heating up. Stonewall got his at Chancellorsville. By mistake one of his own men shot him."

"Lee keeps winning. Our generals are no match," offered one man sitting in a dark corner. "Even Little Mac couldn't defeat him."

The conversation ended there and each man took some wheat bread for his lunch which had been distributed by the Negroes that morning. Henry looked around at the cadaverous figures in the mess. He wanted to ask so many questions: how many months of imprisonment had it taken to turn them into these walking skeletons? Was the Commandant indeed such a monster that he was slowly but steadily starving them? Had there been attempts to escape? No prison had ever been built that held inmates who did not try to escape. He would get his answers in time, he felt sure.

Henry lay down on the floor with his head on the crumpled up haversack. The smell in the room was a mix of unwashed bodies, burned food, and excrement. He closed his eyes and thought of the countless nights he had lain on the hard ground under the stars with Prince and Thorn standing nearby, nights when he had shivered with the bitter cold, when his stomach had rumbled with hunger and his body had ached from hours in the saddle and the tension of combat. But nothing about that discomfort had come even near the wretched state in which he found himself at present. He must not lose control and guide his thoughts away from this hell to hold onto his sanity. What would he think about instead? The war? The war that had been his whole existence for over two years? His horse? Prince, the noble companion. No. Thinking about Prince brought too much pain. Shelmire and

214

Broderick? The two officers who had gone down with him on the field, men he had followed with loyalty and devotion. Sir Percy with his ridiculous moustache and clear blue eyes, a genius in his own right? What had become of him in the smoke and carnage of Brandy Station? Henry had heard his command to charge, then lost sight of him. In the ensuing holocaust, he'd heard a shout: "Wyndham's taken a ball in his leg." But that was all. Was he lying in a hospital or a prison or in the ground with others of the regiment? And Ambrose? What had become of him after Brandy Station?

*   *   *

During the Battle of Brandy Station, Ambrose had remained in camp looking after the spare horses, and that evening when Henry did not return with the troops that crossed the Rappahannock and came back into camp, Ambrose questioned some of the soldiers to find out what might have happened to him. One New Jersey trooper had seen him go down with his horse, but in the midst of the battle raging he could not tell if he had been killed, nor could he name the spot where Henry had fallen. Early the next morning Ambrose set out to find his friend.

On foot he crossed Kelly's Ford, then made his way over the pockmarked earth which had borne the brunt of the desperate fighting the day before. As he trudged up Fleetwood Hill under the hot sun, he examined the face of every fallen soldier wearing the blue uniform. The bodies were heavy and bloated. The gruesomeness of this horrible scene overwhelmed him and he felt a sickening revulsion coming over him. He searched quickly until the scorching temperature finally forced him to sit down briefly to gather his strength.

Nearing the close of the day, he gazed across the battlefield, wondering where next he should go. Just then, as he was aware of the sun going down, he smelled something strange. The Confederate burial detail had finished their work not a great distance from where he stood, and the acrid smell of burning horseflesh still hung in the air. He started walking in the direction from which it came, and in the twilight he found the spot where warm ashes from a large fire still smoked, and the ground

215

bore remnants of the battle so recently fought there. The burial detail had done their job thoroughly in clearing away the casualties—except for one that had escaped their notice. In the gathering darkness Ambrose spied the lone black heap lying on the field. He approached it carefully and knelt on the ground beside it, placing one hand on the cold flank and running his fingers through the black mane.

"Prince!" A sob burst from his throat. "I'd have known you anywheres."

His hand found the wound on the animal's bulging side. "What happened to you, boy?" he whispered. "I hope you died quick and di'n't suffer long. Where's your masta? Poor boy. You-all can't tell me nothin'." Ambrose felt the ground around the carcass for clues to Henry's fate, but there was nothing, only holes from shells and heavy fighting.

It was dark now and Ambrose could not make his way back to the regimental encampment until daylight. He had eaten nothing all day, nor had he had anything to drink. Lying down on the earth next to the fallen Prince, he stretched out and looked up at the stars filling the sky above. What had happened to Henry? Was he killed? Wounded and captured? Taken prisoner?

What should he—Ambrose—do now? Without Henry's presence he had no place in the cavalry. He would be a lone Negro without any status in an unfriendly countryside in constant danger of capture. He lay the rest of the night mulling over the predicament in which he found himself. Where could he go now? Home? How could he make his way there through territory unfamiliar and hostile? Could he hide somewhere until the war was over? Question after question with no answers forthcoming. In loneliness and despair he stretched out his arm to Prince, a steadfast friend through all the hardships and danger of the war. With his hand on the animal's body he became silent for awhile, as a measure of repose came to his tormented brain, and he gathered up his thoughts.

"Lord, you brought me this far. You won't drop me now, I know that for sure."

He lay quietly on the hard ground for many hours before

sleep came. The sun nudged him into wakefulness early to be on his way back to camp.

Standing up, he looked down at the horse and spoke to him one last time. "I don't like to leave you here alone, boy. But there's nothin' I can do for you now." He looked at his empty hands. "I can't even bury you." Turning away sadly he walked back the long way he had come.

*   *   *

Henry's head pained him suddenly, so sharply that it made him wonder if his thoughts had provoked the wound. He would think of happier things. Louisa and little Thomas. What were they doing at this moment? He saw the cottage he had built with his own hands, the flowers Harriet had planted and coaxed into bloom, and the sea with its ever-changing cloud effects and winds. These pictures brought a measure of tranquility to his senses. He heard the groans of the inmate with scurvy and slowly he felt himself drifting off into merciful sleep.

A short time later a slapping, swatting sound awakened him from a nightmare in which he was administering aid to the prostrate Prince on the field. Dazed, he struggled back to the reality of the present. The noise which had so rudely startled him was a clap of flesh upon flesh by a nearby officer in pursuit of vermin on his person. Henry rolled over and witnessed for the first time a spectacle that was a daily recreation at the Libby: "skirmishing." The officer tore off his clothing in a frenzy, stripping himself to the skin. Kneeling on the hard floor he bent over his ragged uniform and inspected it with his fingers, inch by inch, seams and folds and buttons and buttonholes, shaking it and crumpling it and then unfolding it again for a further examination. When at last he discovered the tiny white louse lurking inside the collar he extricated it and crushed it between thumbnail and fingernail, a vehement oath escaping his lips. There followed an exploration of his own naked body aided by a buddy who covered the area of his back. A nibbling predator was found hiding in the crack between his buttocks and was quickly brought to ground. The victim plucked another offender out of the space between two of his toes and its demise was rendered similarly between fingernails. A careful perusal was then made of the man's head, his friend making his way through each strand of hair to the scalp, separating the hairs meticulously. A bite in his armpit brought a further inspection of that hairy hollow which yielded yet another small prize.

Henry watched this performance, appalled at the misery suffered and at the hopelessness of a "cure." If they were forced to live in filth without sufficient water and soap to maintain even a low standard of hygiene, what chance was there to avoid this pestilence? No physical suffering he had endured in his months of military service out in the open at the mercy of the extreme whims of nature had ever brought him near the hideous wretchedness being dramatized before him now.

There was no medicine to apply to the bites. The man who had sustained the attack of the vermin simply pulled his clothes on, thanked his buddy and sat down again on the bare floor to await a further assault.

Henry rolled over on his back again and stared hard at the wooden ceiling above him. Cobwebs hung down from the rough rafters of this old warehouse and his eyes lit upon a spider busily at work on the intricate construction of its trap. Henry watched, mesmerized by the machinations of the industrious little creature. An unwary visiting fly blundered into the web, tried to retrace its steps, became helplessly entangled and ceased its struggles when the spider approached. Henry thought how like the unfortunate invader he was at this moment, caught in the prison web and at the mercy of Commandant Turner. He closed his eyes to shut out the final anguish of the luckless, innocent trespasser. He would not give up the idea of a prisoner exchange. He could not. That thought must be always in front of him, like a candle in the darkness.

21

While the Battle of Brandy Station was being waged in Virginia, an event occurred in another part of the country that would have a dramatic bearing on the life of Henry Sawyer.

Following his disastrous defeat at Fredericksburg in December 1862, General Ambrose Burnside lost command of the Army of the Potomac and was sent (banished) to take charge of the Department of the Ohio. The area embraced the states of Ohio, Indiana, Illinois and Kentucky and, on the surface, was comparatively peaceful, devoid as it was of all but sporadic armed conflict and this in the border state of Kentucky. But be-

cause much of the population was of southern origin and its sympathies lay with the Secessionists, it was not without its troubles.

The genial, bewhiskered General Burnside, whose thick beard grew up to his ears bringing into common use the term "sideburns" to designate such an arrangement of facial hair, arrived in Cincinnati, his ego more than a little deflated by Fredericksburg and anxious to salvage his reputation. Proclaiming fiercely that he would ferret out all disloyalty in the civilian population, he adopted the tactics of a military man trained to deal with the enemy. He let it be known at the outset that any sympathy shown for the Rebellion "either expressed or implied" would forthwith be considered as treason and would not be tolerated. He promised punishment for any aid given the Secessionists by citizens of the Department of the Ohio.

It was during the spring of 1863 that he locked horns with the Copperheads. These citizens of northern states who were pro-Confederate in their sympathies and bitterly opposed to the war being waged by the Lincoln administration, favored peace at any price. They took their name from the badges they wore pinned to their lapels, which were made by cutting the head of Liberty out of the big copper pennies last issued in 1857 by the Federal Government. Some opponents thought the choice of name given to the whole movement was very apt, suggestive of the sinister qualities of the snake of the same name that lies quietly waiting to strike.

Most vocal of the Copperheads was one Clement L. Vallandigham whose violent opposition to the war was fueled to the point of explosion by the Emancipation Proclamation. His fiery speechmaking throughout his campaign for the Democratic nomination for the governorship of Ohio brought him directly into the domain of General Burnside who, riled, took stern action. He sent soldiers to arrest Vallandigham in his home and imprison him. Amidst riots of Vallandigham's supporters and the burning of a Republican newspaper office, he was tried in a military court and found guilty of expressing sympathy for the Secessionists and of trying to weaken the government's efforts to suppress the unlawful rebellion. Ultimately, the good offices of Lincoln were sought to smooth out the fracas, which he endeavored to accomplish by banishing the miscreant to the Confederates.

In early June 1863 Burnside's witch hunt for southern sympathizers in his Department led him also to the offices of the strongly Democratic *Chicago Times* which, ever since Lincoln's Proclamation, had turned its big guns on the Administration in Washington. Although its editor had originally supported the North and opposed secession, when the sensitive issue of slavery was placed on the anvil of the conflict, the newspaper reneged and went on the attack. The paper spoke to the many northerners who were devout anti-abolitionists, and its message was characterized by bitter invective. When Burnside stopped the paper's publication with soldiers, again Lincoln had to come to the rescue and quiet the uproar of its editor and readers who shouted that freedom of the press had been suspended by Burnside's militancy. In effect, Burnside received a slap on the knuckles and an entreaty to be more perspicacious.

On the 9th of June—the same day the Battle of Brandy Station was being fought in Virginia—two officers wearing Yankee uniforms rode into Fort Granger, Kentucky, which had been built to secure the line of communication of Union General Rosecrans in Tennessee. The two captains presented passes and orders from the Adjutant General at Washington, all properly countersigned by General James A. Garfield, then chief of staff to General Rosecrans. Their orders from the War Department in Washington confirmed that they were to make a minute inspection of the command, lines of defense and forts of General Rosecrans's department.

Colonel Baird, in command of Fort Granger, promptly mustered his command and the thorough inspection was carried out. The two officers were graciously entertained at lunch and lingered on at the fort until twilight when they took their leave. In their saddlebags were their written notes concerning the fort, its garrison strength and its weaknesses, which had been pointed out to them with meticulous detail.

As they were riding out of the precincts of the fort, Colonel Wilson of the 1st Kentucky Cavalry was riding in. Passing them in the gathering darkness, Wilson caught only a glimpse of the departing officers but something about their demeanor aroused his suspicions. Hastening to Colonel Baird, he asked quickly: "Who were those officers I saw riding out of the fort?"

"Captain Corbin and Captain McGraw. War Department sent them."

"Let me see their papers," Colonel Wilson demanded brusquely.

Colonel Baird produced the letters written over the signatures of the Adjutant General and General Garfield. Wilson held them up for close examination, squinting at the signatures as though looking through a microscope. He shook his head, looking puzzled and troubled. "I don't like the looks of this," he said to Colonel Baird. "There's something not quite right about all this." He paused then looked piercingly at Baird and asked slowly: "*Just what* did they see here?"

"They were taken on an inspection of the whole fort. Just as the letters instructed."

"Guns? Troops? Everything?"

"Yes."

"Did they reveal anything at all about themselves?"

Colonel Baird looked down at the ground thoughtfully. "Well, Corbin did say he'd been at West Point. He's Regular Army. I questioned them and their answers seemed to ring true. Nothing out of line. Very sensible."

"All the same," Colonel Wilson continued, his mouth growing taut, "I mean to have a closer look at Captains Corbin and McGraw. If they're not who they say they are, they've got their nerve coming through our lines. The Rebs have been trying their luck at recruiting in Kentucky. Lots of sympathizers here."

Wilson picked up the letters again and scrutinized them. "The way things are back in Washington," he said, "it would not be hard for anyone to get his hands on a piece of official letterhead from the War Department. And signatures are easy to forge. I would not be at all surprised, Colonel Baird, if we have intercepted a couple of Rebel spies. Now all we have to do is catch them!"

He hesitated not a moment longer, dashed out, and on the run ordered ten men to mount at once. "We have a chase on our hands," he shouted at them. "Not a moment to lose. Those two officers . . . well, we're going to bring them back. They have a fair head start on us and now they have the dark as well." His face took on a grim expression. "I'll wager they're on a fast gallop and won't stop until their horses give out. We aren't coming back without them, understand?" he barked at the men who were saddling their mounts and swinging up into their stirrups, guns at their sides.

They rode off like a posse at a desperate speed into the darkness with Colonel Wilson in the lead.

The pursuers fanned out to cover a larger area and spurred

their horses to a hard gallop, some following the track through the dark forest, others crossing fields and streams, and the rest riding furiously up and down rolling hills. Hooves pounded in the night. The blackness was relieved only by distant lightning. After an hour's desperate chase, they came together again far from the fort just as a summer thunderstorm broke over them. Taking shelter under some trees near a rocky stream, they let their horses drink and rest momentarily. The inky darkness was lit up now by flashes of lightning coming in rapid succession. Thunder rumbled in the heavens above as the cloudburst drenched them. In one instant when the sky was streaked with silver, Wilson caught sight of something metallic shining on the opposite bank downstream from where they huddled. He squinted hard through the rain and flashes of lightning only seconds apart.

"What *is* that over there?" he asked pointing to the silver shining in the shadows.

"A stirrup perhaps, sir," one of his men offered.

"Or a sabre," countered Wilson slowly. "Let's have a look." They left the cover of the trees, riding their mounts cautiously down the embankment into the stream, holding their guns at the ready. Another illumination of lightning revealed clearly the glint of sword and stirrup.

The crashing of the thunder blotted out the ensuing scuffle of horses' hooves on the stones of the stream bed as the two hunted men began their escape, plunging into the darkness and urging their horses up the embankment with curses and whips. Following hotly on their heels raced the eleven would-be captors, the storm drowning out their cries which sounded like the baying of hounds nearing their quarry. The darkness was filled with the sounds of horses straining as they splashed over rocks and up stream embankments, their riders spurring them on to greater and greater speed.

The chase came to an end in a field when Corbin's horse stumbled in a hole and fell, throwing his rider over his head. McGraw stopped to lend a hand to his comrade. There was no hope of escape from the field. They were surrounded quickly by Wilson and his men who came charging ahead. "Your names?" Wilson shouted at the two.

"Captain Corbin. Captain McGraw," came the fierce replies.

"The General Commanding requests your return to the fort." His men began disarming the two captives. They pulled away, resisting.

"What's the meaning of this?" Corbin bellowed.

"The meaning," Wilson began slowly, "is that the General has a few questions he wants to ask you."

Corbin protested but Wilson was firm. The escort rode on both sides and behind the two men with Colonel Wilson in the lead. The storm had passed over and the ride back to the fort proceeded uneventfully, silence having fallen on the riders.

The countenances of the captives did not betray any fear. When compelled to dismount, they remained outwardly cool and unconcerned. But when Colonel Wilson approached the men on the ground and asked to see Corbin's sabre which he had been allowed to keep while on horseback, Corbin blanched, grasping the hilt of his sword firmly. "You have no right to my sabre," he challenged defiantly. "You are breaking all Army regulations. I will report these insults to the War Department in Washington." His eyes blazed with contempt.

Colonel Wilson persisted and at last Corbin drew his sword. Wilson took it in both hands and carried it to the light. On the blade was an inscription. Wilson read it aloud: "Captain Williams, Confederate States Army." Turning towards the two men, he added tersely: "I charge you both with espionage against the United States of America."

"How dare you?" yelled Corbin. "The War Department will hear about your insolence. I demand my immediate release!"

Wilson strode up to Corbin and peered into his face. "I know you," he bellowed at the indignant man. "You're not Corbin. You're Williams. I knew you at West Point, didn't I? You were Lieutenant Williams. You deserted the Regular Army and went south . . . with all the others who betrayed their country. I knew you well. All traitors," he finished icily.

After further questioning of McGraw there was nothing left for him but a confession: he turned out to be one Captain Charles Peters, a cousin of Lieutenant Williams, on the staff of General

Bragg whose forces were not far away, a constant harassment to General Rosecrans's army.

The guilty men were suddenly quiet. Their espionage was clear. The notes they had written were in their saddlebags. The information they had recorded was clearly of inestimable value to the enemy.

General Garfield was duly notified and the matter was laid before General Rosecrans. A court-martial was convened at midnight. The two men were found guilty of spying and their immediate execution was ordered since there was reason to believe that an attack by the Confederates on the fort was imminent. General Burnside concurred that justice was about to be done; he would be glad to be rid of two more perpetrators of treason.

At dawn the following morning, June 10, 1863, Williams and Peters sitting in a cart astride their wooden coffins were driven outside the fort to a staunch cherry tree. They were hanged without further ceremony and their bodies, under a flag of truce, were sent back across their own lines.

In Richmond sometime later, Colonel Robert Ould, Confederate agent for the exchange of prisoners, read about the executions in the newspaper. Incensed, he contacted his Union counterpart, Colonel William H. Ludlow, at his headquarters at Fortress Monroe, Virginia, informing him that the Confederates would retaliate, selecting two captured Federal officers of the same rank as the spies for execution.

Colonel Ludlow responded quickly: "I must remind you that Captains Williams and Peters were executed as *spies*. Should the Confederates decide to execute brave Union officers captured on the field of battle, then the United States Government will have no choice but to retaliate in turn."

22

The wrath of the South exploded over the execution of the two spies. General Burnside added fuel to the already blazing fire by justifying the fate of the two men with his statement that his firmness was in keeping with his determination to "quit handling the Rebellion with gloves." Revenge by the enraged South embraced the custom of man for man, rank for rank. For spies Williams and Peters it took a novel twist inside Libby Prison.

On July 6, 1863, only a few days after Henry Sawyer's arrival there, all prisoners with the rank of captain were mustered and marched down the stairs. The seventy-five men thus assem-

bled on the ground floor were in high spirits, suspecting that the reason for this meeting was to inform them of a prisoner exchange they were soon to be a part of, or that, perhaps, they were to be paroled. Elated, they began singing "Home Sweet Home," clapping each other on the back, their hopes rising with their voices. Henry's thoughts of Harriet and his children brought a lump to his throat. The poor man afflicted with scurvy had tears in his eyes. Bent over with emotion, he was comforted by a fellow officer's arm around his shoulder.

The officer in charge, Commandant Turner, faced the group holding a paper in his hand. When he began to speak the captains grew silent. "This is an order received today from Jefferson Davis." A deafening hush followed his opening words. He read on: "To Captain Turner. I hereby order you to select by lot two

Union officers with the rank of captain for immediate execution by hanging, in retaliation for the execution of two Confederate officers hanged by General Rosecrans in Tennessee."

A terrible stillness descended on the room. The announcement—only a few words that had required less than a minute to utter—knifed through the air like a sheet of lightning. The men looked frozen where they stood. An icy cold blanket of doom hovered in the atmosphere. They could taste it, smell it, feel it closing in around them. There was a slight movement in their ranks, a cough, and then a bold outcry: "This cannot happen!" yelled an officer, outraged. "We are military personnel. Soldiers. Those two Rebs who were executed were guilty of espionage. We aren't *spies*! We were captured on the field."

An uproar of support from all the officers broke out. "Captured on the bloody battlefield!"

"What about the articles of war? How can Jeff Davis ignore them?"

"If he does, the North will do him one better! Bastard!"

"Stinking bastard."

"This is unjust. Unfair. We are innocent men. We've done nothing to deserve this cruelty. We're guilty of no *crime*."

"It's barbarous! Just like the Rebel swine to think of some fiendish torment like this. And they call themselves 'southern gentlemen!' "

"Where's their honor?"

"Where's their sense of justice? Right and wrong?"

"Southern aristocrats! Foul pigs!"

"Wait until ol' Abe gets wind of this! Jeff Davis'll rue the day he sent that letter!"

The prisoners swarmed over Captain Turner with fists raised but the guards stepped in quickly and beat the mob back. "Ye're prisoners of war!" bellowed Captain Turner. "Don't forget it! Ye have no say in what happens to ye. Jeff Davis has the final say. What he says goes. And he says it's an eye for an eye and a tooth for a tooth. And the drawing by lot will take place now, right here, jes' like his order says. 'For immediate execution by hanging.' That'll teach your Yankee officers a lesson. Maybe they'll show our southern boys more respect next time."

The men were in revolt. Anger rumbled through their ranks as the guards herded them into a large hollow square formation for the drawing of lots. When they protested physically, the guards pushed them roughly into lines with blows to heads and bodies as the tormenters saw fit. There was no recourse left to them but to accept their fate. No voice could be raised in their defense.

"Now write yer names on the papers," Turner continued to shout above the uproar. It was clear from the clumsy manner in which the guards handled the papers that this was the first time they had been called upon to serve in such a capacity. They fumbled the collection of the slips of paper, dropping one here and there, stooping to retrieve them and stuffing each one awkwardly in the box. The noisy protest of the men continued unabated until Captain Turner held up his hand as if to make an announcement. Clutching the box in his other hand, he entered the hollow of the square which they had made. "Now I'll leave it to all of ye to choose someone to draw the lots. He'll draw two names. Only two. That's all."

The men quieted down. Everyone seemed to be waiting. "Come on, now," insisted Turner. "Speak up. Who's going to do the drawing?"

The silence prevailed, heavy and oppressive. At last Henry was moved to speak. "I suggest that since this is such a grave matter—a matter of life and death—and that you are asking one of us to select two of our number *to die,* it's a task rather for a chaplain."

Upstairs in the prison were three captured chaplains imprisoned with other men from their regiments. Henry's suggestion met with general agreement and the chaplains were summoned from above. When informed of the proposal put to them, they all refused to perform the assignment. No amount of reasoning could persuade them that this odious undertaking fell within the orbit of their responsibility to the men.

Henry then singled out the eldest of the three, a Rev. Joseph T. Brown, with whom he had talked briefly since his arrival at the Libby. The white-haired man was chaplain of the 2nd Maryland Infantry regiment. "Rev. Brown," he began solemnly and kindly, "we have no one else to turn to. We need your help. You have served God all your life. We are helpless, caught in this dreadful situation from which there is no escape. We are all afraid. God knows we need strength to face the terrible truth about to be revealed to us. Can you accept this responsibility, consider it as a duty to your fellow men in your service to God? Surely, He will not hold you responsible for its outcome."

The Rev. Brown, his emaciated frame trembling slightly, reached out to Henry and grasped his outstretched hand. He did not speak but nodded his assent to Henry's request.

Henry stepped back into his place in the square of prisoners. As Turner extended the box to the chaplain, a death-like stillness settled on the group. "Draw one name," Turner commanded.

He did so and, unfolding the piece of paper, he read softly but clearly the name: "Captain Henry Washington Sawyer. 1st New Jersey Cavalry."

Henry's face turned ashen. For a moment he could not see or hear or feel. What were those words that Rev. Brown had spoken? His mind was a blank. Then the numbness in his limbs gave way to a desperate shiver passing through his body. His military experience had taught him how to mask his feelings before his men and how to control fear in time of danger. That self-possession saved him now. He looked straight ahead and did not speak.

Rev. Brown reached into the box and drew the second name. "Captain John M. Flinn, 51st Indiana Infantry."

A gasp escaped the second condemned man. His body went limp and he began to shake. The soldiers at either side supported him. Rev. Brown approached the frightened Flinn and took hold of his arm. "I am sorry, my son. May God bless you and give you courage to face this ordeal." His face bore the anguish in his heart.

The prisoners crowded around Sawyer and Flinn attempting to console them but feeling woefully ill-prepared to offer any comfort other than a sympathetic slap on the back as their farewell. Embarrassed, they turned away and dispersed upstairs, leaving the two desperate men facing Turner and several guards.

Captain Flinn, a Roman Catholic, asked to see a priest to administer the last rites. In a short time two priests appeared from outside the prison walls and took him aside for counsel. Henry watched as the two southern clergymen endeavored to quiet the doomed Flinn with gentleness and compassion, and he reflected on how easily the painful political differences could be surmounted by the humanity of man to man. He thought to himself, what is all the bloodshed of this war accomplishing?

Henry and John Flinn had not long to dwell on their miserable plight; under an escort of twenty Rebel soldiers and a lieutenant commanding they commenced their march to Camp Lee. The name rang out like a death knell to the two men for Camp Lee was well known as the site for all military executions. Here deserters from the Rebel army were hanged, and here Union spies met their doom.

The harshness of the Confederates in dealing with their own people was nonetheless tyrannical than their treatment of Yankees. No southerner with opinions about the inflammatory issue of slavery which differed from the popular Confederate one dared to express them without fear of reprisals. If he spoke out against the belief that slavery was a Divine institution, that it was destined to be the cornerstone of a new dynasty to be established in the South, he did so at great risk to his personal safety. There was a strong sentiment abroad in the deep South that this was no place for a republic, that what was needed was a strong military government with but two classes, Aristocracy and Slavery, with the poor whites making up the army.

Henry and Flinn tramped along the streets of Richmond in the company of the two priests with a boisterous crowd of the curious citizenry of Richmond in their wake. With arms reversed the escort marched to the death-tap of a single muffled drum. The two prisoners kept their eyes on the ground to avoid the glares of the local populace gathered to witness their torment. With every beat of the drum Henry felt his hope being extinguished rhythmically, bit by bit.

As they dragged along a carriage passed them, then stopped abruptly. Its occupant was Bishop Lynch of Charleston, South Carolina, who was in high favor in the South, having successfully run the blockade and secured recognition for the Confederacy in Europe and returned with that of the Pope as well. Seeing the two priests walking with the prisoners, Bishop Lynch leaned out of his carriage to ask: "What is the meaning of this?"

As the priests stepped aside to speak to the Bishop, the line of marching men continued on its way with the taunting beat of the drum. The two clerics presented the facts quickly to their superior who listened attentively, then shook his head in disbelief. "It can't be," he said. "Tell them not to lose faith," and he ordered the carriage driver to proceed in haste.

As the gates of Camp Lee loomed up in the distance, two scruffily dressed civilians, unshaven and dirty, came alongside the group of marchers and marched with them. "So, ye're off to Camp Lee, are ye?" one jeered, pointing at Henry and Flinn.

His companion took up the theme. "They'll have a nice little party for the both of ye when ye git thar. You kin bet yer life on that!" His fiendish laughter sent a shudder up Henry's spine.

The obscenities continued: "Comin' from ole Libby, are ye? Bet ye'd like to be goin' back thar right 'bout now. Wahl . . . two Yankees less means two Yankees won't need no feed . . . that's more for us Rebs." Two of the escort, annoyed, pushed the men away as their voices trailed off in horrible ghoulish screeching.

The end of the march was near and feet were slowing with weariness when suddenly a Confederate officer, well mounted and riding at desperate speed, overtook them at a gallop as the entrance to Camp Lee loomed up directly in front of them. He handed a dispatch to the lieutenant in charge of the prisoners and the group came to a halt. Henry looked up to study the expression on the officer's face as he read the dispatch to himself. At first the man seemed puzzled with his face contorted in a frown. Then the muscles in his jaw relaxed. In that fleeting moment Henry allowed himself the sweet ecstasy of hope. He did not even breathe. His heart seemed to stop beating momentarily and he put out a hand to Flinn. "John," he whispered, "something's happened. Maybe . . ."

He did not finish before the lieutenant gave the order: "By fours, right about."

Never before had Henry performed a military evolution with

greater promptness or joy. They were headed back in the direction from which they had come, and it had all happened in that split second of the "right about." The agony of spirit he had suffered on the long march was suddenly lifted, but he checked his elation quickly: was it realistic to allow himself to take heart from this mysterious interruption? He told himself that it was foolish to place so much import on that brief happening. But still he could not suppress the courage that kept leaping up inside him with every step back towards Libby Prison. His legs, which a moment before could hardly move with fatigue and despair, now seemed to take on life and energy anew. He felt as if he could walk across the state of Virginia and back again.

Henry leaned toward John Flinn. "John, I'd say your Bishop had something to do with this change of plans. I don't know what to make of it but at least we're headed *away* from Camp Lee." Henry's jovial mood brought a slight smile to his companion's face.

They were marched back to the office of Provost Marshal John Henry Winder, Commander in Chief of all Confederate military prisons. Although their incarceration in Libby Prison had been of only a few days' duration, they had been thoroughly indoctrinated on the reputation of the provost marshal. His treatment of Union prisoners had won for him epithets "brute" and "monster" and "tyrant." No man was more hated and more reviled for the suffering and starvation in the prisons he administered. No figure was the object of more imprecations than Winder. The accounts of his inhumanity to the men within the walls of his prisons were rife in the Libby.

Henry shuddered at the thought that he was about to make the acquaintance of this individual. Winder's opening salvo befit his reputation.

"Bishop Lynch has seen fit to intervene," he said sarcastically. "What gives a cleric the right to stick his nose into a military matter I don't see, but you've got a ten days' reprieve—only ten days, you understand—for Flinn here 'to prepare himself for absolution.' That's what the Bishop asked for," he scoffed contemptuously.

Henry's newfound hope was short-lived. The blow that had

smashed it came crashing down on his whole frame. All that they had won, then, was a temporary respite, merely ten more days for contemplation of their inevitable demise!

John Flinn looked despondent and his shoulders slumped.

Having delivered the initial shocker, Winder followed it with a warning: "Don't delude yourselves with any false hopes about escaping your sentence. Retaliation is what has been ordained to show the Yankee generals that they can't treat our valiant Confederate officers so shamefully. Retaliation will be enforced. Your execution is set for July 16th. It will take place on that date."

The whole prospect of a hanging filled Henry with such revulsion that he forced himself to speak out. "May I ask a favor, that we be shot in place of hanging?" Somehow it seemed to him a more honorable death and one more becoming to an officer.

"Indeed not!" Winder's voice thrashed out. "That would not be retaliation. And retaliation is what is called for here, man for man. You will die by hanging." His voice resembled a bark.

Hopeless as their situation appeared to be, Henry did not totally despair. If their case could only be brought to the attention of some individual highly placed in the Federal government there might be reason to have faith in their ultimate escape from this invidious sentence. What was it that the prisoner had said when lots were being drawn? 'Just wait until ol' Abe gets wind of this . . .' Perhaps he was right. But how could they get word of their plight to the President in time?

Henry took courage and addressed the provost marshal: "May I be permitted to write a letter to my wife?"

His request was considered and grudgingly granted by Winder—under certain conditions. The letter would not be "private" but would be scrutinized by various officials along the route of its delivery.

Henry sat down at the table in Winder's office. Picking up the pen, he placed it on the paper but did not write. How could he tell Harriet all the things he wanted to say to her, the feelings deep in his heart, when his words of affection would be subjected to the callous eyes of countless indifferent readers on their way to her? How could he break the news of his impending fate without breaking her heart? Well, she had always been strong and intrepid in the face of every danger and tragedy they had encountered in their life together. He would put his trust in her now—and in God.

He began to write:

Provost-General's Office
Richmond, Virginia, July 6, 1863

My dear wife:

I am under the necessity of informing you that my prospects look dark. This morning all the captains now prisoners in the Libby Military Prison drew lots for two to be executed. It fell to my lot. Myself and Captain Flinn of the Fifty-first Indiana Infantry will be executed for two captains executed by Burnside.

The Provost-General, J.H. Winder, assures me that the Secretary of War of the Southern Confederacy will permit yourself and my dear children to visit me before I am executed.

You will be permitted to bring an attendant; Captain Whilldin, or Uncle W.W. Ware, or Dan had better come with you. My situation is hard to be borne, and I cannot think of dying without seeing you and the children. You will be allowed to return without molestation to your home. I am resigned to whatever is in store for me with the consolation that I die without having committed any crime. I have no trial, no jury, nor am I charged with any crime, but it fell to my lot.

You will proceed to Washington. My government will give you transportation to Fortress Monroe, and you will get here by a flag of truce, and return the same way. Bring with you a shirt for me. It will be necessary for you to preserve this letter to bring evidence at Washington of my condition. My pay is due from the 1st of March which you are entitled to. Captain Thomas Ford owes me fifty dollars—money lent to him when he went on furlough. You will write to him at once and he will send it to you.

My dear wife, the fortune of war has put me in this position. If I must die, a sacrifice to my country, with God's will I must submit; only let me see you once more, and I will die becoming a man and an officer; but for God's sake, do not disappoint me. Write to me as soon as you get this, and go to Captain Whilldin; he will advise you what to do. I have done nothing to deserve this penalty. But you must submit to your fate. It will be no disgrace to myself, you or the children; but you may point with pride and say, 'I gave my husband;' my children will have the consolation to say, 'I was made an orphan for my country.'

God will provide for you, never fear. Oh! It is hard to leave you thus. I wish the ball that passed through my head in the last battle would have done its work. But it was not to be so. My mind is somewhat influenced, for it has come so suddenly on me. Write to me as soon as you get this. Leave your letter open and I will get it. Direct my name and rank, by way of Fortress Monroe. Farewell. Farewell. And I hope it is all for the best. I remain yours until death.

H.W. Sawyer
Captain, First New Jersey Cavalry

A cold shudder passed through him. His head was bowed as he put his signature to the letter. Reading through what he had written, Henry hoped that his explanation to Harriet had not been too harsh and that he had not conveyed too strongly the despondency he felt. He hoped, too, that she would discern his clear appeal for help. He handed the letter to Winder who waited impatiently, drumming his fingers on the table.

The provost marshal handed the open letter to a junior officer with orders for its dispatch, then turned to the two condemned men. "You'll be going back to the Libby now. Only you won't be going back with the same status as before." He paused, then added grimly: "You're going back as condemned prisoners with a ten-day reprieve before your execution. You'll be in isolation as befits such as yourselves. There's no escape from the dungeon, so forget any ideas you may be entertaining along those lines."

A dungeon was exactly what it was. They were led down the dark stairway into the cellar and pushed into a tiny cell that smelled of many foul odors—excrement, vermin, damp. Henry could not believe that this cell was to be their accommodation for ten long days and nights. It was vault-like; in the darkness it seemed to measure approximately six by eight feet. There were planks on the ground for them to sleep on but Henry guessed there would be little sleep for either of them when he heard the furtive scurrying of rats as the guard opened the stout iron door and shoved them inside. A tiny finger of light penetrated the darkness through a kind of skylight. When Henry brushed against the cold wall he felt water running down it. The guard banged the door behind him.

John Flinn sank down onto a plank and put his head in his hands. "My God!" he groaned. "You have forsaken us."

Looking up at the speck of daylight, Henry put his hand on Flinn's shoulder. "John, I am not giving up yet," he said quietly. "We have ten days. This is hell but we have both been through hell before in this war and we can stand it for another ten days. I still have hope that somehow we'll be saved."

"What makes you think that?" Flinn responded with a touch of scorn in his voice. "Nobody knows we are here. How could we expect any help?"

"I can't rightly explain it," was Henry's response, "but if my letter gets through to my wife I think we have a good chance."

"It'd take a miracle," Flinn answered lugubriously, "and there aren't many miracles in this war. I haven't seen one in two years of fighting."

"If you've been fighting for two years, John, and you're still alive, I'd suggest that miracles have been happening to you every day!"

"I guess you're right there," agreed Flinn with a faint smile on his face.

Shortly thereafter there came a rattling at the door and a guard presented them with their rations: cornbread and water. The cornbread was dry and tasteless. "You know, John," Henry said as he stuffed the bread into his mouth, letting some dry crumbs fall on the damp floor, "if I make it home again and my wife Harriet ever serves me cornbread for dinner. . . ." His voice trailed off into the darkness. A soft chuckle came from Flinn's corner.

As they sat in the darkness with their thoughts, they became aware that a door was opening in a part of the cellar next to their cell. There was a sound of wheels, something heavy being pushed by men who were exerting great strength to move their load. Although Henry could not hear what the men were saying, he could make out two distinct voices that were uttering expletives. Suddenly there was the sound of something sliding down and landing on the floor with a mighty thud, then receding wheels and finally the door being shut.

"What can that be?" John wondered aloud.

"Sounded like a cart being emptied," answered Henry.

"I wonder what was in it." Silence followed.

They sat in the darkness without a word passing between them. Suddenly, there was a pounding on the door followed by a demanding voice: "Sawyer? Flinn?"

Neither man answered.

The door was opened with a jerk. "Sawyer? Flinn?" It was the rasping voice of the guard. "Answer when ye're called, ye bastards! Ye're goin' to be hearin' from me often. More than ye like, I reckon. When ye're asleep too I'll be callin' on ye. That is, if ye ken sleep in there with them varmints runnin' over ye and nibblin' yer toes."

He slammed the heavy door and his ghoulish laughter could be heard echoing in the cellar as he climbed the stairs leading up to the main floor of the prison.

Only the weakening shaft of light coming through the skylight told the two captives that night was approaching. They went through the ritual of preparing for bed. There was no covering for the planks on which they were about to lie down and attempt to sleep. There were no blankets to cover them and no pillows. Both men sank down onto their planks with a sigh that came from aching muscles and empty stomachs. Henry's large frame hung over the sides of the plank. Shivering in the dampness, he sat up, bent his legs and pulled them up to his chest as if to warm himself.

Flinn on his plank began his rosary prayer: "Holy Mary, mother of God . . ."

Henry listened and closed his eyes. "God Almighty," he prayed silently, "if you see fit to help two prisoners in their sorry plight, that would be most merciful. Guide my letter into the hands of my dear Harriet, and sustain her when she receives its painful message. Help her to act wisely and speedily. Protect her from all harm on her journey to this hateful place. You hear prayers from many men on both sides of the battlefield in this war. How can you answer all of them when men are set against one another? I do not ask for any special favors, just an audience for my thoughts. And courage. Deal with my problem in your infinite wisdom. Amen."

As they lay quietly waiting for the blessing of sleep, Henry felt the tread of something small on his lower limbs. He swept his arm out and knocked a rat off his foot. At the same moment Flinn swatted another off his back.

"John," Henry offered, "we'll have to take turns at this. One rests while the other stands guard. You go first. I'll be on guard. They'll return, I'm sure of that."

Time passed and again came the banging on the door, followed by the bellow: "Sawyer? Flinn?" As before the captives did not respond. When the door was pulled open by the guard, Henry spoke before the man could berate them.

"We need some blankets," was all he said.

The guard laughed contemptuously and was in the act of slamming the door shut when, in the pitch blackness, Henry reached under the tongue of his boot for the Yankee greenback hidden there and shoved it into the man's hand. "Will this get us two blankets?"

The guard did not reply but stuffed the money into his pocket, bolted the door behind him, and the two prisoners heard his footsteps growing fainter on the stairs.

It was Henry's turn to rest and he laid his body on the hard plank, easing it down gently. He was aware that his head wound was throbbing. Touching the bandage with his fingers, he could feel the dried blood on the outside and he realized that the wound had not been dressed since his arrival at the prison. Well, there was nothing he could do about that now. He let himself drift into a reverie. The last battle at Brandy Station . . . Broderick and Shelmire . . . and Prince . . . Loyal Prince . . . Jet black Prince swishing his long tail in the smoke and noise of battle . . . Prince standing over him while he stole a few moments rest on the ground between battles. . . . His faithful friend who was his constant confidant, whose disposition never altered even when forage and water were non-existent. It had been devastating to Henry to watch the animal grow thin from the lack of sufficient food and from overexertion. He had watched helplessly as the sores appeared on Prince's back from days of relentless saddling. There had been no way to treat the sores so that they could heal completely. He mounted the saddle every day and rode until nightfall, always with the hope that a respite in the fighting would allow him to remove the saddle for a spell so the sore back could regain its health. Sometimes Prince had winced when the saddle was lifted onto his back. On these occasions Henry had spoken gently to him, patted his neck, and scratched behind his ears, and this affectionate attention had calmed the animal.

Thoughts which drifted through his head gave way to a kind of peace as he edged onto sleep. He was slipping away, suspended between consciousness and the dream world, when a snuffling noise and a tugging at the bandage on his head wound startled him. Attracted by the smell of the blood, the loathsome intruder had managed to get by the watchful Flinn and was gnawing with its sharp teeth at the filthy rag that covered the wound. Thus rudely awakened, Henry sat up with a start, knocking the rodent to the floor of the cell. It scuttled away noisily.

Anything approaching sleep was out of the question now. He sat up with his head buried in his hands. How long he had remained in this position with eyes closed and mind empty of any thoughts save the misery surrounding him he did not know, but in the distance he heard footsteps. Were they real or in his subconscious? He could not tell. But suddenly the door opened, this time preceded by no abrasive shriek from the guard, and two blankets were pitched onto the floor. No conversation passed between the inmates of the cell and the donor of the blankets. The door closed noisily and the footsteps receded.

"The power of the purse!" exclaimed Henry to Flinn as they wrapped themselves up warmly and stood up to stretch the stiffness out of their limbs. "Did you hide any greenbacks?"

"I stashed away only two inside my sock the day we arrived here. I am sure they will come in handy before we leave this hellhole," he said grimly.

Henry looked up at the skylight. "Well, John, we have survived one day and one night here already. Look! It's getting light. By my calculations this must be the seventh of July."

23

Henry's letter to his wife was sent out of the Libby under a flag of truce. With the envelope left unsealed enabling all curious eyes to read the contents, it arrived in Cape Island, New Jersey three days later. Normally, Harriet Sawyer read his letters in the privacy of her home but today her heart leaped at the sight of the familiar handwriting; so great was her anxiety to read his words that she sat down on a bench outside the post office, putting her market basket beside her. A bonnet shielded her face from the warm July sun and from passersby.

For more than two years Harriet had steeled herself for bad news. With her children looking over her shoulder, she had traced on a map her husband's engagements described in his letters and had scoured the newspapers for every account of the 1st New Jersey Cavalry in action. Almost every family around her had been informed of the death of a loved one lost on the battlefield, and Harriet felt a foreboding closing in on her. Was Henry's luck running out? His last letter written in May from U.S. Ford on the Rappahannock was filled with despondency:

"Our cavalry defense is not worth a damn. It will be entirely useless if the Government doesn't provide better for us. For twenty days our horses have not been rested for one day. A great many have died for want of food and devastating hardships. We have some days not a mouthful to give them. And their backs are all in sores, putrefying, being saddled so steadily. We are all short of rations. And I have to go without any supper tonight, for Lieutenant and myself have not even a cracker. We have coffee but that is all. And what is left from supper I shall have for breakfast, which is nothing. I hope we shall get some rations for tomorrow's dinner.

"Well, this is soldiering . . . in reality, and no mistake. I do not consider this a bloody war but I do think there is a bloody lot that has the management of it. But finding fault will not make it any better. But we have so much useless, severe and hard service that is not of the least advantage, which is enough to make anybody swear.

"What is before us I cannot say, but I think that thirty days will find us under the guns of the fortification of Washington again. All the two-year men and nine-months men are leaving us, which will amount to 50,000 men, and it is doubtful whether we can hold our position with the force left.

"Our whole army is in good trim, in fighting condition, with the exception of the cavalry which is worn out.

"But here we are, if they keep us out here on this duty two weeks longer, we shall not have any horses left. My Prince has a sore back. But I hope we shall see better times yet.

"You need not look for me before August, as I see no chance whatever. It is getting dark and I must quit. I would give a horse to spend the night with you.

"Thousands of men are being dragged from their families unwillingly so I ought not to find any fault, for withal, I haven't yet paid for it."

Puzzled by the unsealed envelope now in her hand, she drew the letter out carefully. She did not stop reading until she reached the end, conscious only then of the weakness in her entire frame. The bad news had come at last . . . the inevitable . . . she shared in the tragedy now with all the wives and mothers and sisters and sweethearts around her. She felt dazed and for a moment her brain went numb with despair. She forced herself to read the letter again, stopping at certain passages to find answers to her questions. What had the two Confederate officers done to bring death upon themselves? Why was it necessary to follow that horror with yet another execution? Why was Henry in Libby Prison anyway? The mention of the "ball that passed through my head in the last battle" was testimony to his having been wounded yet again. Where had he been captured? Was he shielding her from the fact that he was dangerously ill? These unsettling thoughts raced through her head, each one overtaking that preceding it, until Harriet closed her eyes to keep from swooning. She wanted to cry to relieve her anguish, but it was not the time for tears. *Henry was not dead.* It wasn't sadness she felt. It was terror—sheer, cold, paralyzing fear that she might be too late.

She read through the letter a third time, slowly, repeating the specific instructions Henry had given her. ". . . bring the children . . . go to Captain Whilldin . . . proceed to Washington . . . then to Fortress Monroe . . . bring a shirt . . . preserve the letter as evidence." She looked hard for the most important fact: *how much time was there before his execution?* Perhaps even now she would not be there in time. There was much she *didn't* know, but one thing she was certain of: she must hurry. There was not a moment to lose if she were ever to see her beloved again and feel his strong arms around her. Oh, God, how she needed that strength now.

Gathering up her basket, she put the letter into the pocket of her long skirt and hurried away from the post office. So many thoughts crowded into her mind that she struggled to sort them all out clearly. First, the children. Louisa eleven and Thomas eight. Twice in his letter he had mentioned his desire to see the children one last time. Second, Captain Whilldin. She ran along the dusty road to his house, her skirts and her bonnet ribbons flying out behind her. Arriving at his door out of breath she discovered to her dismay that he was not at home. There followed a moment of indecision in which she struggled to compose herself for all the tasks immediately ahead. Henry had instructed her to have Captain Whilldin or Uncle W.W. Ware or Dan accompany her but there was no time to try to find them. If she were to be ready for the ferry that afternoon, she could not use the precious time that remained to search for the men. She must go alone.

"Washington," she began to talk to herself out loud as she turned towards her home. "The fastest way is by rail from

Milford. We'll take the ferry across the bay to Lewes. Then the stage to Milford. The train to Washington. We should be there some time tomorrow."

Harriet opened the gate and came up the path to the cottage where the children were playing in the garden with their pet rabbit. "Children," Harriet began, trying to keep her voice from quaking, "I have had a letter from your father."

"Oh," Louisa interrupted, "is he coming home?"

"No. He is in prison in Richmond, Virginia. He wants us to come to visit him." Harriet tried to keep her voice calm and reassuring.

"Was he wounded, Mama?" Louisa asked, her anxious blue eyes studying her mother's face.

Harriet paused a moment. "Yes, but he was well enough to write the letter, Louisa. He wants us to come right away. It's a very long trip."

"When will we go?" Thomas asked as he stopped stroking the rabbit's ears.

"This afternoon," Harriet answered. "We have to catch the three o'clock ferry. We must get food ready and a change of clothes. Louisa, you can help with the basket."

The children sensed the urgency in their mother's voice. Louisa followed her into the kitchen and sliced the loaf of fresh bread she had made the previous day. She buttered each slice and cut pieces of cheese and cold chicken, wrapping everything in a clean towel. There were strawberries in a bowl that had been picked that morning in the garden. And apples, the last of the winter's supply. She found a jar of pickles and some cake from the baking the day before. She fit them all into the basket, leaving space for three hard-boiled eggs and a bottle of water.

"Thomas," Harriet instructed, "the rabbit will have to stay in the hutch while we're gone. He will need lots of food. Find all the fresh clover you can in the field and stuff the hutch full. And make sure he has plenty of water." Then she added slowly, "I don't know when we will be back."

"Are we going to take Father a present?" the little boy asked.

Harriet looked down at him and smiled. "Yes," she answered, patting his curly head. "That would be very nice. What

243

would you like to take him, Thomas? Something he likes especially."

Thomas thought hard, his little brow furrowed. "He likes licorice," he announced brightly. "There are licorice drops at the shop."

Harriet responded, "Licorice drops would be just the thing, Thomas." She handed him a few coins. "Run along and buy some for Father." She watched him run down the path, his thin legs gaining speed as he turned out the gate and his hands clutching tightly the coins. A sick feeling stirred her stomach as she watched her little son go off on his errand. She had a mental picture of the poignant scene when Thomas would present his gift to his father.

Several hours later, basket in hand and shawl around her shoulders, Harriet walked with her two children to the ferry slip. Both Louisa and Thomas, dressed in clean clothing, carried small parcels containing their requirements for the journey. Inside a bag over Harriet's arm were some current newspapers full of accounts of the battles at Gettysburg and Vicksburg. She knew that soldiers in the field were always short of news about what was going on in the rest of the country. The newspapers were wrapped around some treats from her kitchen: coffee, lemons, pickles, white bread. "He's tired of hardtack and cornbread, I'm sure of that," she mused to herself.

The sun shone down on the little party as they waited for the ferry boat to take them across Delaware Bay to Lewes. The sea was sparkling and seagulls were crying and swooping across the waves. The beauty of the scene made Harriet's heart ache anew for her husband. She wondered if he would ever see his beloved Cape Island again. "How often I think of the natural beauty which surrounds our home," he wrote in his letters from the field. "I hold that picture in my mind at all times and it helps me to endure the smell of gunpowder and the noise of battle which envelope me constantly. I dream of the time when I can stand by your side with our children and look out on the broad Atlantic and know that I shall never be forced to leave you again." For one fleeting moment Harriet succumbed to despair, her face growing sad as her hope flagged.

244

Her thoughts were interrupted by Thomas's excited tug on her arm. "Look, Mama, there's the ferry."

The little steamer landed its passengers on the quay, and Harriet and her children watched silently as they filed by carrying baskets and parcels and small cases.

"Will we be on the ferry long?" Thomas wanted to know.

"Not very long. Just across the bay to Delaware. Then we'll ride the stage to Milford which will bring us to the train."

As she said these words the journey ahead loomed up in her thoughts as of interminable length. A voice inside her kept nagging away: "Will we be in time? What if we are too late?"

Several hours later when the little group were settled in their rail seats, Harriet closed her eyes, trusting that sleep would eventually come. She had memorized Henry's letter. His handwriting appeared before her now: "You will proceed to Washington . . . My government will give you transportation to Fortress Monroe . . . It will be necessary for you to preserve this letter to bring evidence at Washington of my condition . . . I have done nothing to deserve this penalty . . . I die without having committed any crime . . ." His words kept echoing in her head . . . ". . . proceed to Washington . . . my government . . . bring evidence to Washington of my condition . . . I have done nothing to deserve this penalty. I die without a crime . . ." over and over again until her ears rang. *What was Henry trying to convey to her* as he wrote from prison? Was there a message hidden there? ". . . Washington . . . my government . . . preserve the letter . . . evidence of my condition . . . I have done nothing . . . I die . . . no crime."

The words pounded away. Suddenly, as if a chord had been struck, she understood the full import of his letter. She wondered now why it had taken her so long to read between the lines and why she had not seen the clues in the first reading. Her course of action was clear: "Go to President Lincoln for help." That was the message that fairly screamed at her now.

"Go to President Lincoln for help." Of course, that was it. Two years had passed since Henry's military service in Washington when he had spent his first three months guarding the Capital city and had been in almost daily contact with the President. But would Lincoln remember Henry now after two years of war with its defeats, the rising casualties, his frustrations with his incompetent generals and the political burdens of his presidency weighing down on him? How could he be expected to remember a friendship with a lone sergeant back in April 1861—even one who had intervened to save his life?

Harriet clung desperately to the hope that President Lincoln *would* remember and that she, Harriet Sawyer, would somehow be able to gain admission to the Capitol. If only she could secure an audience with him long enough to show him Henry's letter, she was sure he would help her. His kindness and compassion were legendary. And Henry's plight was one that she was confident would move the great man to use his extraordinary powers against the blatant injustice of the cruel fate that awaited the condemned men.

The train rattled through the countryside, stopping occasionally to take on passengers, but the children slept in their seats and did not waken. Harriet, relieved now by knowing exactly what her mission in Washington would be, fell into a light sleep as well. Her hand clutched tightly the bag in which the all-important letter lay.

The railroad station in Washington was alive with activity: soldiers marching, businessmen hurrying and jostling one another, here and there a drunken civilian leaning against a wall and a veteran of the war walking on one leg as a grim reminder that the conflict was not far away. The children, holding each other's hands tightly, kept close to their mother's skirts as they emerged from the station into the daylight of the nation's capital. Inquiring directions to the Capitol building, Harriet guided the children onto a horsecar—a novelty which brought smiles to their faces as the car with its bell ringing jolted along amidst the bustle of the teeming city. They opened their eyes wide to the strange sights around them. Soldiers were everywhere: regiments filing through the streets, soldiers on guard on the doorsteps of buildings, groups drilling on the lawns between government buildings. Cavalry troopers rode by and Harriet strained her eyes to catch sight of the insignia on their uniforms, unconsciously looking for the 1st New Jersey Cavalry.

The noise and the dust from the unpaved streets came

through the windows of the horsecar. "Mama, what is that awful smell?" asked Louisa, screwing up her nose.

Harriet smelled it too but did not know that the odor was a mixture of the reeking swamps that surrounded the city and the sewage in the open canals. "It's just a city smell," she replied. "This isn't Cape Island," she added gently, patting the child's hand.

They passed the base of the Washington Monument under construction with soldiers encamped on the grounds around it, boarding houses, many saloons, Willard's Hotel with carriages pulled up before its doors and elegantly clad ladies emerging into the sunshine. Into the windows floated more odors of the city—a blend of sweating humanity, heat and horses. The horsecar paused to take on passengers in front of a large private residence that had been converted to a hospital; taking the air at the upper story windows were wounded soldiers with bandaged heads and bodies. Louisa called her mother's attention to a soldier leaning out who had an arm missing.

Harriet had read that the dome of the Capitol was unfinished. From the horsecar window she caught sight of it looming up ahead and gathered the children up to a light at the next stop. Looking up at the impressive structure, she felt very small and insignificant. As she mounted the steps of the building, a child on each side of her, she felt her spirits go limp. She grew timid about the prospects before her, a little shocked at the bold, audacious thing she was about to do. Imagine anyone having the temerity to come off the street unannounced and expect to gain admittance to the President's office! How had she ever arrived at this absurdly impossible scheme to rescue her husband?

Pausing at the top of the steps momentarily to catch her breath and to regain her courage, she approached the soldiers standing guard at the entrance to the Capitol. To their inquiry into the nature of her business, she answered: "I have come about a matter of extreme urgency," she began slowly, trying to control her nerves. "My husband, an officer in the 1st New Jersey Cavalry, is in Libby Prison." Then, turning her back on the children, she added softly: "He has sent me word that he is to be executed. I *must* see the President." Her voice quaked slightly.

247

The soldiers looked at her anguished face and at the two young children. "As you can well imagine, Madam," one of them replied, "President Lincoln is an extremely busy man."

Harriet was quick to respond. "I understand that fully. But my husband was stationed here in the Capital at the beginning of the war, from April to July 1861, and he made the acquaintance of the President. In fact, they saw each other every day." When one of the soldiers seemed about to interrupt, she finished quickly: "He was the President's bodyguard on many occasions. He rescued the President one evening from an attempt on his life."

The soldiers listened to her story, then one of them asked: "What is your husband's name and what was his unit in 1861?"

"He is Henry Washington Sawyer and in 1861 he was with the 25th Pennsylvania Volunteer Infantry. He was in the Clay Battalion, too."

One of the soldiers departed into the darkness of the Capitol with her information, leaving her with the other guard. "You have had a long journey?" he inquired.

"Yes," she answered with a sigh. "We have been traveling since yesterday. From Cape Island, New Jersey."

The soldier looked down at Louisa and Thomas. "I have two children at home just about your ages. I haven't seen them in a long time," he added wistfully.

"Do they live in New Jersey too?" Louisa asked softly.

"Oh, no. They live way up in Vermont. Much farther than New Jersey. I sure would like to see them again. And my wife."

"How much longer will you serve?" Harriet asked.

"I'll probably be here 'til the end of the fighting. I was wounded at First Bull Run and can't go back to the field again, but I can serve here alright."

Harriet sympathized: "I'm sure this is just as important as fighting battles. After all, you're safeguarding the President."

Just then the other soldier returned and beckoned her to follow him. Harriet's heart was pounding hard as she walked through the door, buoyed up by her initial success. Inside the Capitol was a welcome coolness from the sweltering sun. She followed the soldier into an office where he instructed her to sit on a long bench. The children, subdued by the strangeness of the room, sat very still on either side of her and did not speak. They held their parcels tightly and looked up in awe at their surroundings: the high ceilings, the marble floors, the comings and goings of uniformed servicemen walking briskly.

The excitement coursing through Harriet's body from the realization that she had actually not been turned away at the door made her hot and cold. She tried to contain her anxiety and to keep her body from trembling, but it seemed that every moment she sat waiting to see the President was bringing Henry that much nearer to his frightful end. She clutched the letter in her two hands, smoothing it repeatedly on her lap.

Allowing herself a moment of prayer with her eyes closed, she was startled by a voice announcing: "Mrs. Sawyer, Mr. Lincoln wishes to see you. Will you come this way, please?"

Harriet, grasping the hands of the two children, followed the secretary to the door of the President's office. Lincoln rose to greet her, his huge frame towering above her as he extended his hand. Then, smiling down at Louisa and Thomas, he placed a hand on the head of each child. "What's your name, laddie?" he asked the youngster.

"It's Thomas, sir."

"And how old are you?"

"I'm eight, sir."

"I have a son named Thomas, too. He's ten. I call him Tad because he looked like a tadpole when he was born. His head was too big for his body." The President laughed softly, then paused a moment, and added: "Once upon a time I had four boys but the Lord saw fit to take Eddy and Willie home and look after them in Heaven. I do miss them."

Sensitive to the suffering in Lincoln's expression, Thomas, without any prompting from his mother, said very quietly: "I'm sorry, sir."

Harriet thought that she had never seen a face that expressed such inner misery. There was a haunting sadness in the eyes, in the gaunt hollows of the cheeks, in the cavernous lines that furrowed his countenance. The burdens of the war had left their mark on this man for all the world to see. Overcome by his

249

gravity, Harriet forgot momentarily her own troubles and her heart reached out to him in sympathy and understanding. She wanted to touch him, to let him know that she shared his anguish.

He was not alone in the room. "Mrs. Sawyer, may I present Secretary of War Edwin Stanton," he announced motioning to the gentleman across the room.

After greetings were exchanged and all were seated again, Lincoln addressed Harriet: "I understand you have in your possession a letter from your husband with some very grave news. It must be very personal but I wonder if you could let me see it."

Harriet produced the letter and the President took it from her gently. She studied his face while he read the contents, hoping to find some hint there of his resolve to help her. Louisa and Thomas remained silent the whole time, and the only noise in the room was the ticking of the grandfather's clock behind the President's chair. Harriet was aware that her own heart was beating twice for every tick. She felt that it might come through her chest, it was pounding so like a hammer.

Lincoln held the letter up and addressed her: "May I share this letter with Mr. Stanton?"

"Of course," she answered quickly. Stanton reached out for it and went back to his chair.

"My dear Mrs. Sawyer," Lincoln began. "This is a shocking state of affairs. A dreadful situation in which your husband finds himself through no fault of his own. My heart goes out to him and to you and your children. This war is full of injustices and atrocities and, unfortunately, I cannot attempt to right all the wrongs done to our brave soldiers. Their sufferings grieve me and in most cases I am powerless to alleviate them. However," he paused, "in this instance I will try to help two valiant officers who have been serving their country for more than two years. I do remember your husband's loyal service at the beginning of the war when the capital was rife with treason and the lives of many of us were threatened regularly." The President's somberness gave way to a flicker of a smile. "And I do recall something very special about your husband. It seemed to me that I had never met a man who was so fond of horses. Am I right?"

His remembering touched a soft spot in her heart. "Yes, you are right, Mr. President. He has had horses all his life from the time he was a small boy. He took two of his horses with him when he enlisted in the cavalry."

Lincoln's face regained its gravity after this exchange. "The important factor in the situation confronting us is haste. We have no time to lose."

He turned away from her and addressed Secretary Stanton who had replaced the former War Secretary Simon Cameron: "Mr. Stanton, what is your reading of this? We are confronted by a situation in which a dangerous precedent is about to be set, that of the lives of soldiers captured in the field being equated with those of spies. *This must never be allowed to happen.* Have we any cards to play?"

Stanton thought for a few moments before he responded: "Yes. We hold an ace, Mr. President." He stopped, letting the impact of his words sink in. "We have a very . . . er . . . *valuable* captive from the Confederacy," he continued with great satisfaction. "He is a member of a First Family of Virginia and connected with someone high in authority with the Secessionists." He smiled with obvious pleasure in having private information to reveal to his chief.

"Who is it?" Lincoln demanded eagerly.

"None other than Brigadier General W.H.F. Lee, son of General Robert E. Lee. He's known as 'Rooney' Lee. He was captured after being wounded in the cavalry battle at Brandy Station June 9th."

Stanton finished speaking and the President remained very thoughtful for a few moments. When he spoke his words came deliberately and emphatically. "If a threat to hold the life of General Lee's son in ransom for those of Captain Sawyer and Captain Flinn would fail to convince the Secessionists of our resolve in this matter, then what other hostage could do so?" Silence fell on the room. "I am hopeful that this bold action will bring the Confederates to their senses."

He turned towards Harriet: "Mrs. Sawyer, I am going to do all in my power to save your husband and Captain Flinn. They are brave men who deserve the gratitude of our whole country. Is it possible for you to return here tomorrow at this time? I will be able to tell you then what has been achieved."

Harriet thanked the President and promised to return the following day. She gathered up the children and was almost at the door when he spoke again: "Do you know anyone in Washington? Where will you spend the night?"

A trifle self-conscious of being a stranger, Harriet answered quickly: "Oh, we'll be fine, Mr. President. Not to worry about us. But thank you all the same."

She was in the act of shepherding the children out the door when the President recalled her: "There is a boarding house near here that is respectable. Mr. Stanton will make the arrangements for you to stay there if you wish."

She blushed in embarrassment. "Thank you very much. You are very kind."

Following her departure Lincoln sent for his Chief of Staff General Henry W. Halleck and the two men sat and discussed long into the night the action of the Confederates towards Sawyer and Flinn. Incensed by their cruel injustice to the innocent officers, Lincoln and Halleck debated many courses of action. Finally, in the pre-dawn hours they decided on a strategy to rescue the prisoners from impending death. It was a plan which would make an abiding statement to the Confederates about their treatment of Union prisoners of war from this day forward. In the person of General W.H.F. Lee, fate had provided Lincoln with a "gift" of inestimable value to the success of the plan. He was going to gamble with men's lives. The stakes were high.

The next day, July 11, to Colonel Ludlow, Union Agent for the Exchange of Prisoners of War, went the following order from Washington: "The President directs that you immediately place General W.H.F. Lee in close confinement and under guard, and that you notify Mr. Robert Ould, Confederate Agent for the Exchange of Prisoners of War, that if Captain H.W. Sawyer and Captain John W. Flinn, or any other officers or men in the service of the United States, not guilty of crimes punishable with death by the laws of war, shall be executed by the enemy, the aforementioned Lee will be immediately hung in retaliation. It is also ordered that immediately on receiving official or other au-

252

thoritative information of the execution of Captain Sawyer and Captain Flinn, you will proceed to hang General Lee as herein above directed, and that you notify Robert Ould, Esquire, of said proceedings, and assure him that the Government of the United States will proceed to retaliate for every similar barbarous violation of the laws of civilized war. Signed, H.W. Halleck, General-in-Chief."

Upon receipt of this order, Colonel Ludlow sent off the following official warning to: "Hon. Robert Ould, Agent for Exchange of Prisoners, Richmond:

"Sir, I am directed to inform you that General W.H.F. Lee has been selected as hostage for Captain Henry W. Sawyer, 1st New Jersey Cavalry, and Captain John W. Flinn, 51st Indiana volunteers, who, you inform me, have been chosen by lot for execution. Upon information being received of the execution, by order of your authorities, of these officers or any other officers or men in the service of the United States, not guilty of crimes punishable with death by the laws of war, the Confederate officer above named will be immediately hung in retaliation without giving you other or further notice. Signed, W.H. Ludlow, Lieutenant Colonel, and Agent for Exchange of Prisoners."

It was on July 15th—the ninth day after the drawing of lots in Libby Prison—that the Richmond newspapers published President Lincoln's order that placed the fate of the renowned hostage squarely in the hands of the Confederates themselves. The official pronouncement touched a very sensitive chord. Abuse of the vilest kind was heaped on the head of Lincoln, on all Yankees and the whole northern populace.

When Henry Washington Sawyer's letter to his wife was published earlier in the Jersey City, New Jersey *American Standard,* public indignation had been aroused. Now, only a few hours before the scheduled executions, a battle of words was unleashed in the newspapers both North and South.

The *Daily Fredonian* of New Brunswick, New Jersey reported that they would not take place because of the threat of severe retaliation announced by the North towards the famous southern captive. "As Jefferson Davis does by Sawyer and Flinn, so shall we do by Lee," the paper slammed home.

253

The *Richmond Examiner* entered the fray, casting aside the importance of Lee in the drama: "It is hoped that the Executive (Jefferson Davis) will see fit to give the order for the executions (of Sawyer and Flinn) immediately; and as we now have over 500 Federal officers in our hands, besides 6,000 privates, it is in the power of the Government to carry retaliation to a very bitter extreme. The people call for the death of these two Yankees and it is useless to delay their deaths any longer."

The *American Standard* snapped back: "The *Examiner's* statement was 'evidence of atrocious vindictiveness on the part of the Rebel leaders.'"

Outside Libby Prison enraged mobs gathered and chanted for the executions. Some noisemakers hurled stones at the bars covering the openings that served as windows and had to be restrained by the soldiers guarding the prison.

When Harriet Sawyer returned to Lincoln's office, she was informed of the President's action to effect the release of the two condemned men. She was told that passage to the Union-held Fortress Monroe near Norfolk, Virginia had been arranged for herself and the children. "It is my understanding," Lincoln said, "that at Fortress Monroe you will proceed under a flag of truce up the James River to City Point. It is hoped that at City Point the Confederate authorities will permit you to continue your journey to Richmond and thence to Libby Prison." Lincoln looked kindly at Harriet as he continued: "I wish I could give you my complete assurance that the long journey you are embarking on will meet with success, but I cannot. I fear that the Confederates may put a few stumbling blocks in your way once our plan for the son of their favorite general is revealed by the newspapers." He shook her hand and held it. "I wish you a safe passage and I hope sincerely that you will be reunited with your husband. He is a brave man. Please convey to him my deepest gratitude and that of the country for his courageous service."

"Thank you, Mr. President," was all that Harriet could murmur, so overcome with gratitude was she. Her eyes filled with tears as she added, "And God bless you, Mr. President."

24

When Harriet Sawyer and her children steamed up the James River towards City Point, Virginia, the date was July 16th—the tenth day of the reprieve from General Winder. Although there was no way she could have known that this was the date he had set for the execution of the two prisoners, she felt in her heart that precious time was slipping away quickly. Twice in his letter Henry had asked her to write as soon as she received his news and this she had not done. She had not taken the time to compose

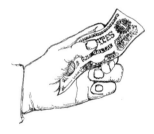

her thoughts for him and to put them down on paper. In her own mind she believed—at least, *hoped* all along—that they would be reunited before a letter could reach him.

She stood at the railing of the small steamer and above her flew the flag of truce by which her safety was pledged. Clutched in her hand was the official letter over the President's signature requesting a safe passage for herself and the children from City Point to Libby Prison in Richmond, and in her bag was Henry's letter which was open for all eyes, hostile or friendly, to read.

For the first time in her life Harriet saw slaves at work. From the steamer she observed numbers of them on the wharves engaged in hoisting heavy burdens onto their backs and carrying them while an overseer shouted and gesticulated at them.

It was fortunate that President Lincoln had prepared her for the reception which she received from Confederate authorities to whom she handed his letter and that of her husband. Richmond newspapers' reports of the threat to the life of the famous southern prisoner had inflamed public sentiments. Everywhere in the South vile abuse was heaped on the head of the President, the Secretary of War, and General Benjamin "The Beast" Butler in command of Fortress Monroe.

On this morning consternation over the exchange of communications between the two governments was at its peak. When Harriet presented her letters, Lincoln's request on her behalf was flatly refused. She was not even permitted to set foot on land. The officials' minds were closed to any appeal she could put forth.

"But my husband is under sentence of execution," she pleaded. "Every minute brings him closer to the end. His only request was that I bring our children to see him *one last time.*" Her voice broke in anguish. "It does not seem to me to be an unreasonable request of a man who is about to die for no crime committed but simply because of the anger of one government against another." She stopped to gain control of her shaking voice. "We have come a very long way. Is it *possible* that we are to be turned away? For what reason? I do not understand." She paused a moment before adding very quietly, "I do not understand the thinking of men."

The blunt denial was the pronouncement of an individual of very short stature who puffed himself up rooster-like in his attempt to impress her with his importance. He took obvious pleasure in delivering the bad news. "Confederate States of America War Department ruling, ma'am. That's all I can say. Mr. Ould, Agent of Exchange, says landing at City Point is forbidden. His word is final."

Harriet tried not to let his smug, self-satisfied air fluster her. She drew a sheet of paper from her bag and addressed the official, looking him squarely in the eye: "If I write a letter to my husband, can you *assure* me that it will be delivered to him *without fail* at Libby Prison?"

He shrugged his shoulders, then nodded assent rather casually.

Harriet tried to keep her hand from trembling as she wrote what she feared might be her last letter to Henry. Most of all, she wanted to reassure him not to give up hope. She told him about receiving his letter dated July 6th, of her journey to Washington with Louisa and Thomas, of their audience with the President and Secretary Stanton, and of their promise to help. "Mr. Lincoln *did* remember you and your service in Washington," she wrote. "He holds you in the highest esteem and extends to you his personal gratitude." Stopping momentarily to ponder just how candid she should be concerning the naming of the renowned hostage, she decided to refrain from adding anything of a jarring note which might imperil her letter's safe delivery into his hands. "Today is July 16th and I am writing this letter at City Point. It appears that this is to be the end of our journey for we are refused permission to proceed further. It is hard to bear that we have traveled this far to see you only to have the success of our endeavors thwarted at the very end. My heart aches for you, but I am trying to be brave for the children. They are here by my side, anxious to see your dear face. Do not give up hope. There are many who are trying to help you. I hope that God will grant you the courage you require to see you through this ordeal. May the love of your family sustain you through all the anguish you are suffering. Your loving wife, Harriet E. Sawyer."

Harriet read the letter through again and carefully affixed to it Henry's name and rank as he had instructed her to do. Handing the letter to the official, she realized that the chances of Henry's receiving her message depended on the disposition of the unpleasant individual facing her. She must do nothing to antagonize him lest this attempt to communicate with her husband be aborted. Harriet grasped his hand for a fleeting moment and implored him with tears in her eyes: "Will you *promise* me that there will be no delay in the delivery of this letter to my husband?" She faltered slightly before adding: "*Even one day* could make all the difference."

The expression of torment on Harriet's face moved the man. "I'll see to it, ma'am," he responded a bit begrudgingly.

Harriet thanked him and then remembered a further request. "We have brought with us a few things for my husband," she said, slipping the bag off her arm and extending it to him. "Some old newspapers, some sweets, a bit of food from home. And he asked especially that I bring him this shirt. Is it possible that these trifles could accompany my letter safely to Libby Prison? And *hopefully* arrive in his hands?"

Thomas, listening carefully and remaining silent throughout the long exchange, suddenly spoke up: "Sir, do you like licorice drops?"

The man's countenance softened as he looked down at the boy. "I reckon I do, sonny. 'Don't know as I've ever had one.'"

Thomas reached for the small packet in his pocket and held it out to the man. "Here . . . try one, please, Sir."

The man popped one into his mouth. "I'm thankin' you, sonny."

Thomas looked up at the man. "Will you give the rest to my father, please, Sir? He's very fond of licorice. It might make him happy." He shoved the packet of sweets into the man's hand. The official, a little dumbfounded by the child's innocence, fumbled at being caught off guard in a moment of weakness that shattered his brusque exterior.

"I'll do what I can, sonny," he said. And to Harriet he spoke in a hushed voice: "I shouldn't be promisin', ma'am, but your case seems hard." Pausing a moment to survey his immediate surroundings lest there be witnesses to their conversation, he added: "'Course there's no guaranteein' your husband will get your gifts, prison life bein' what it is. They'll pass through a lot of hands before they reach your husband, ma'am. I hear tell that life in ole Libby is not all that sweet. Prisoners get hungry and guards are mighty curious about what's in packages and oftimes they aren't fully responsible . . . if you know what I mean, ma'am."

Harriet responded, "I do. But thank you for trying. I am deeply obliged to you for your kindness. Goodbye." She extended her hand to the man to ease his embarrassment. Was it the "weakness" in his character that he had betrayed by helping her that flustered him, she wondered? He turned away from her quickly, hiding the letter and the bag under his coat, looking furtively over his shoulder to see if his civility towards her had been detected by any observers.

The little party watched him go. "Mama," Louisa asked softly, "do you think Father will get our presents?"

By way of answering Harriet put her arms around both children and hugged them closely to her. "I think so. I hope so," she whispered.

There was no course left to her now but to go home. She had tried to do everything Henry had asked of her. That she had failed at the eleventh hour to bring the children to see him would grieve her for many days.

The steamer took them back to Fortress Monroe, and from there they made the return journey to Washington and then home. When she opened the door to her cottage in Cape Island, its familiarity and security welcomed her. She sank heavily into a comfortable chair—Henry's chair—and sighed as she said to her children: "Oh, isn't it good to be home!"

Louisa brought her mother a cup of tea and sat on the floor beside her. "Mama," she said, stroking her mother's hand, "Mr. Lincoln is such a good man. I think Father is going to be all right. Don't worry."

Harriet, looking down at her daughter with a sudden awareness of her maturity, fondled the blond curls gently. "I think you are right, my dear child. We have done our best. Our very best. That is all anyone can do in times of trouble. Now we must keep faith and hope in our hearts." She bent down and kissed Louisa on the brow.

*   *   *

Following the sharp interchange of communiqués between the Union and Confederate Agents for Exchange of Prisoners, an order was sent from Washington to General Benjamin F. Butler to place General W.H.F. Lee, then in Fortress Monroe, in solitary confinement so that he should suffer the same conditions of imprisonment as the men for whom he was hostage.

In the Libby dungeon the two condemned officers knew nothing of the turmoil outside the prison walls stirred up by the newspapers' inflammatory accounts. They were in total isolation from the affairs of the outside world.

One day, to break the appalling silence of their cell, Henry said: "I have never heard the whole story of how you managed to gain admission to the Libby, John. All I know is that you were with Colonel Streight on some kind of raid."

John Flinn, disturbed from a deep reverie, responded: "Mules."

"Mules?"

"Yes. Mules in Alabama." Flinn, who had been lying on his plank, pushed himself up to a sitting position to tell his story. "Streight took command of the 51st Indiana Volunteers in September of 1861. His territory was Tennessee and Kentucky. He came through the Battles of Shiloh and Perryville. I joined up in December of 1862 just before Stone's River. It was a few months later in April when we grouped in Nashville for a raid through the hills of northern Alabama toward Georgia. We set out to knock hell out of the Rebel railroads. There was trouble from the very beginning though. And it was because we were riding mules. We became a Mule Brigade! We were 2000 strong, mostly infantry. Some so-called expert in the army convinced Streight that mules would be better than horses in the rough terrain of the Alabama mountains. The mules were a problem right off because a lot of them were almost dead at the start and had to be left behind. It took a day for men and mules to get to know each other and Streight hadn't counted on that. Have you ever ridden a mule, Henry? They can be so danged cantankerous that no matter how hard you whip 'em they dig their feet in and won't budge an inch. You can yell, kick them in the ribs, beat the hell out of them. They just stand like statues. They don't feel anything. Because of the damned mules, Streight fell behind in his arrangements to join up with General Dodge in Eastport, Mississippi, and Dodge ran right into the Reb cavalryman, Colonel Roddey, instead, who pushed him twenty-three miles to Bear Creek, Alabama. When Streight finally arrived in Eastport and found that Dodge had left, he decided to press on and catch up with him at Bear Creek. In the midst of all this chasing around after each other, again the mules caused a problem. They brayed so loudly that Roddey's cavalrymen were tipped off as to their whereabouts and the stupid asses let themselves be stampeded! Four hundred of the cussed beasts ran away! Streight got replacements of the mules in Tuscumbia, Alabama and with 1500 men he started out after Nathan Forrest. We chased General Forrest and Roddey and their cavalrymen across those Alabama hills and met them at Day's Gap and Hog Mountain and finally at Lawrence. That Forrest is a shrewd one, though. He has a bag of tricks always ready. He tried one on us that we discovered later—too late. He made his troops look like a lot more than they were. He appeared to have a long train of guns but it was really only one section of artillery going round and round. It seemed to Streight that we were greatly outnumbered. He surrendered. That was May 3, this past spring. Yep, Forrest was a hero that time. He sent us prisoners back to Virginia. Officers went to the Libby, the men to Belle Isle and Castle Thunder. I guess one place is as bad as another," he finished.

"I hear Streight is at the Libby, right?" Henry asked.

"Yes. Up on the top floor. He's itchin' for an exchange."

"Aren't we all!" Henry agreed.

Since their incarceration in the dungeon on the sixth of July, they had tried to keep track of the days with small gravelly stones they found on the floor. They felt like stones to the touch but in all probability the hardened droppings of rats were mixed in. Every morning both men placed one in their pockets so that they could cross-check the passage of time. On the morning of July 16th they counted ten stones each and waited for the cell door to open, wondering who would be the purveyor of the bad news. Would General Winder himself, perhaps, take satisfaction in announcing to them that the fateful moment had arrived? Or would it be the same guard who for ten days had been their only human contact—this faceless, nameless being they knew only by the putrid odor of his body and the rasping voice with which he barked his orders at them?

Sawyer and Flinn were sitting on the damp planks waiting for the events of the day to unfold. "John," Henry began, feeling the growth of his beard, "even if we didn't count the pebbles, I'd almost be able to tell you how many days we have been here from the length of my beard." He ran his fingers through the heavy growth, rubbed his face and scratched his head, combing the tangles out of his hair with his fingers. Everything about his person was cause for revulsion. His body had not been bathed for more than ten days and every part of him stank and itched. Everything about dungeon life created self-loathing and reduced the victim to the status of an animal. And yet, Henry reasoned to himself, no animal ever lived in such depravity or allowed its body to become the repository of such filth. The stench from the bucket holding their excrement befouled the air and no fresh air found entrance to the vault-like surroundings.

There came the day's first banging on the door and the presentation of the first cornbread and water. Henry lifted the dry bread to his lips with his dirty hands and the smell of them so sickened him that he was unable to swallow. He waited for a few minutes before trying again. Conscious of the weakness in his limbs he forced himself to down it with the meagre offering of water.

Flinn spoke now. "Perhaps the time has come to see what another greenback will produce in the way of victuals." Reaching deep down inside his sock he drew out a note from its hiding place.

They sat on their planks listening for any strange sounds that might signal a change in the day's proceedings. But all they heard was the same noise which had occurred on their first day in the cell, that of wheels turning under the weight of a great load being pushed by men who were straining to move it forward. It was all happening in the room next to their cell. There was the same swoosh of something heavy being emptied out and sliding onto the ground, then the banging shut of the door and voices trailing off.

"What *can* that be?" Henry wondered aloud, the kind of question that does not expect an answer.

An amount of time that felt like the morning passed and the guard was at the door. He had no purpose except to disturb them lest they had fallen asleep. "What is in the room next to us?" Henry challenged the man. "We heard noises of something being dumped."

The guard swore. "Don't ye be botherin' yerselves about that," he said belligerently. "What's in there won't be causin' you'uns any trouble. Nor nobody else neither. Jes' damn Yankees that won't be goin' nowheres 'cept in the ground some day when the diggers see fit to put 'em there." He waited for a moment before his finale: "They're the lucky 'uns."

It took a few seconds for the import of his words to sink in. Then John Flinn called out to him: "We want some meat like the other prisoners get."

The surly voice came back in the darkness: "Ye git no meat 'cause you'uns isn't ordinary prisoners. Ye're condemned. No need to waste good meat on them'uns that's goin' to die anyways."

Flinn leaned forward and pressed the greenback into his hand. "Bring us some meat," he demanded, "and some potatoes and vegetables and coffee."

The door slammed behind the man and they heard his feet mounting the stairs.

They waited in silence, both men visualizing a plate piled high with slices of roasted meat, potatoes swimming in brown gravy, and fragrant steaming vegetables in such abundance that they hung over the edge of the plate. Their salivary glands began to function and the never-ending gnawing of hunger in their bellies subsided momentarily as a sensation of general well-being swept over them at the thought of the hot coffee following the meal.

During the ten days they had shared each other's company the condemned men had filled the hours with talk on every subject from personal family matters to their war service. They had discussed their boyhoods, parents, siblings and vocations before the war, their wives and their children, and their enlistment in the service.

They compared regiments and officers, their victories and their defeats, wounds suffered, hospital experiences, and their capture. They talked about their beloved country, the issue of slavery, Lincoln, politics, their plans and hopes for the years following the war—if they survived it.

Both lapsed into silent reveries they did not wish to share

263

with each other. Henry talked to Harriet in his thoughts, telling her the many things about her that were poignantly dear to him now, things that he had never mentioned to her when they were together in peaceful times. Why had he been so remiss, he wondered? He wished that he could tell her how he loved her high forehead and the way she fastened her hair back so that he could kiss her brow when she looked up at him. He would like to say to her how much her womanly gentleness and quiet presence reassured him every day when no conversation was even necessary to feel the flow of love passing between them. His love for her had deepened during the painful separation the war had forced on them. The thoughts which brought his fevered spirit the only repose during the endless hours of darkness in this hell were thoughts of Harriet and his two children. Everything he dreamed about his life after the war centered around her. If he survived this ordeal, he wanted only to be with her and to love her for all the time the Lord gave him.

Inevitably, his thoughts wandered to others who were close to him . . . Thad . . . Si . . . Ambrose. He wondered about men who had fought side by side with him . . . and the leaders of the regiment, Kargé and Wyndham. He found himself thinking of Frances and Augustus Sullivan. Had Augustus survived his wounds? Were they still together? Then, there were all those men he had taught how to ride and given instructions on the care of their horses. How many had fallen with him at Brandy Station? What officers were left and where was the regiment fighting at this moment?

A muffled sound outside their cell roused them. They anticipated the usual banging to announce the guard, but it did not come. Instead the door opened rather slowly and he reached in in the darkness. In his hands were the offerings elicited by the greenback: a piece of meat, bread and a container of coffee.

The prisoners could not discern the exact quantity in the dark but to their fingers it felt paltry. "Is this the best you could do for one greenback?" John complained fiercely. "That's the last bribe you'll ever get from me, you swine!" He swore again at the man who made no comment before leaving as surreptitiously as he had come.

In the dark they pulled the piece of meat apart with their two fingers much as two children do pulling on the wishbone of a chicken. Stuffing it in their mouths they chewed hard for awhile, then extracted the masticated wad and stuffed it in again. Finally, having subdued its toughness, they swallowed hard. There were two mouthfuls each. Their stomachs, long unused to such fare, grumbled and rumbled at its arrival.

"This must be white bread, John," Henry said. "It's soft and it doesn't crumble."

They pulled the hunk of bread apart and ate it greedily, washing it down with the lukewarm coffee, taking turns tipping the container to their lips.

Silence followed the meal. Disappointment was heavy in the air and sleep was the only alternative to despair. They lay down on the planks and pulled the blankets over them.

Lying there they could hear two sounds: one came from their disgruntled stomachs, the other from outside the prison walls. Voices very faint and far off, a muffled eruption of anger being vented by many people, came to them. Both men stared up at the tiny skylight and listened intently to the distant outcry. There was no suspicion that they were the cause of the furious uproar around the exterior of the prison, that the enraged populace of Richmond was demanding their immediate execution and heaping vitriolic invective on Lincoln's head for his abominable actions against one of Virginia's noblest families.

The fading light told them that evening had come. July 16th, with all its expectations, was nearing its end and they were still alive. What had happened to Winder's warning? Henry recalled his words: "Don't delude yourselves with any false hopes about escaping your sentence . . . your execution is set for July 16th and it will take place on that date."

There was no more food that day. With difficulty the prisoners stood up and leaned against the damp wall for support. They stretched their legs and arms, bent their backs, did a few strengthening exercises to limber their weakened muscles and to rid themselves of the appalling stiffness they felt throughout their bodies. But they could not continue the exertion for long. Their frames were depleted of all reserve energy and they were

265

overcome by an all-embracing weakness which made their legs tremble under them.

Sinking down onto his plank, Henry ran his hands up and down his arms and legs and felt the bones just under the surface of his flesh. Stretching out, his body creaked as it reached its full length on the wooden board. A sigh of pent up anguish escaped him. "Death would be a welcome relief." He did not say the words but he thought them to himself. He wanted to keep on fighting back but he was losing his grip. There was a strange lightness in his brain. Trying to hang onto his resolve not to give up hope, he clenched his fists, but the determination to hold fast to life was fading perceptibly, and he seemed powerless to bring it back. There was not a part of his physical being that was not contorted in wretchedness. Hunger swept through his body like an electrical current, his throat and mouth were sore from dryness, his head ached and his eyes hurt as if sand were irritating the eyeballs. The dampness of the place had penetrated his bone marrow and his nerves were on edge. The hopelessness of his situation and the squalor enveloping him had driven him near the edge. A merciful balm akin to sleep rolled over him slowly like a wave on the beach, pulling him back from the precipice.

The following morning the guard's first visit was not to deliver rations but to escort to the cell a Catholic priest and a minister. In the darkness, voice was the only indicator of age: these men were older than the prisoners. The sparseness of space inside the vault forced the four men to stand. While the priest talked to Flinn in hushed tones, the minister introduced himself to Henry.

"I am Reverend Moore of the Presbyterian church. I have been given permission by the prison authorities to visit you daily if you wish."

"Daily?" Henry exclaimed with incredulity. He found the whole situation rather humorous in a sardonic kind of way. "Who gave you permission, Reverend?"

"General Winder. Only yesterday."

"Yesterday?" guffawed Henry. "We were supposed to be *dead* yesterday! I think you're wasting your time here, Reverend," he finished rather sourly.

"If you believe in God, my son, then my time is not wasted. My mission is to bring hope where there is despair. I find despair all around me these days. In my church, in the city, in the country."

His unctuous manner irritated Henry who thought he detected an identifying accent also. "Are you a southerner, Reverend Moore?" he asked pointedly.

The churchman was taken aback slightly. "Not by birth," he answered carefully. "My father was a Presbyterian minister in Carlisle, Pennsylvania. His congregation educated me for the ministry." He paused a moment as if weighing his words. "After my ordination I received a call to a church in Richmond. I answered that call and I have lived here ever since. That was quite a few years ago," he added.

"Then I presume that you are sympathetic to the southern cause," Henry continued. "A Secessionist even?"

The Reverend Moore halted in his tracks. He was not prepared for such aggression from a doomed prisoner. "In my years of living in Richmond and ministering unto the needs of the southern people," he said, deliberating between his words, "I have learned a great deal. Some of my . . . er . . . *northern* ideas have changed . . . I believe they were wrong."

"Do you believe that slavery is wrong? Or is that one of your *northern* ideas that changed?" Henry went on the attack.

The venerable reverend tried to retain his calm. "I see the slaves on my wife's plantation. They are well cared for, they are not hungry, they are not abused. Rather, they are happy folk who feel secure and who sing and dance at the end of the day to express their joy in their good fortune at having kindly masters. I have come to see the validity of the southern system of benevolence to the ignorant slave. I believe it to be of Divine origin. It protects them and looks after them from birth to death. Northerners are blind to the social welfare system that the slaves enjoy."

Henry girded what strength remained in his loins to confront his visitor. He spoke slowly and with great effort. "Reverend Moore, I am first and above all a patriot. I love my country with all my heart and soul. I have given two years of my life fighting to defend her and to preserve our precious Union. I hate treason and disloyalty and weakness of resolve. We—you and I—are far apart in our basic beliefs about many subjects, I fear. We could not agree on how to preserve our republic, nor could we *ever* find common ground to discuss the plight of thousands of human beings with skins of a different color who, through no fault of their own, find themselves in bondage. Because you chose to be a man of faith, your *professional* duty is to teach the love of God and charity for all human beings. I find it impossible to marry this faith to your pronouncements on the subject of slavery and make any sense of it at all." He drew a long breath before finishing: "I can see no purpose in our further association and I would be very grateful if you would not suffer me with another visit from your good self. Good day, sir."

Henry sat down weakly on the wooden plank, uttering not another word. The Reverend Moore pushed open the cell door and left the dark surroundings, followed shortly by the priest. Outside the waiting guard clanged the door shut.

*   *   *

Seven weeks passed before Sawyer and Flinn were released from their dungeon hell. One day in August 1863, supporting each other and carrying only their blankets, they crawled feebly up the stairs at the behest of the guard. They had endured days and nights of suspense and bewilderment, hovering between life and death, fearing death one moment and inviting it the next. Why had their execution failed to materialize? That was the question they pondered on end during the soul-destroying, tedious hours they spent in the dank darkness of their cell. Had someone highly placed in the government intervened?

They had grown weak and at times senseless. The deprivation of food and activity had rendered their bodies useless. The bones, now so close to the surface of their flesh, made lying down or sitting excruciatingly painful.

As they reached the top of the flight of stairs on their knees, they attempted to stand up by holding onto each other. They squinted, barely able to open their eyes to the light. Grasping arms, they stared at each other, their faces almost touching.

"John!" Henry gasped. "You've gone gray!"

It was true. On the day he entered the dungeon Flinn's handsome countenance was framed with hair and a thick beard that were jet black. He put his hands to his face now, felt his matted beard and ran his fingers through his tangled hair. The hollow eyes gave him a ghostly appearance as he peered closely at Sawyer's face. "You're the same," he said, shocked. "Nobody will recognize us."

The two bedraggled officers stood at the top of the stairs hanging onto each other's emaciated frames and began to laugh. It was the first laugh that had been elicited from either body in many weeks, and it caused a strange pull of muscles in the gut that contorted their faces in pain. The moment of levity was a release but it was short-lived. The guard, who had opened the heavy iron door of their cell for the last time and led them up the first flight of stairs, pushed them now towards the second. They must mount these and yet another flight to reach their former quarters on the top floor. Looking up at the thirty-seven stairs they felt the wobble of their legs, and the ordeal of mounting all those steps appeared as an impossible challenge. There was only one way they could climb them: on their hands and knees, pulling their bodies up slowly, resting, then another pull. They counted each one aloud as they proceeded. At the top they were out of breath and lay on the floor gasping for a few moments. Slowly they lifted their heads and squinted through sore eyes at the surroundings they had left such a long time ago. It took minutes for their eyes to focus as they strained to see familiar faces. What their fellow prisoners saw shocked them speechless: the ravages of the dungeon etched in the ghastly cadaveric faces, the pinched features and the deep sepulchral eyes.

"My God! Henry Sawyer, is that you?" exclaimed a voice finally from across the room. "We thought you were dead long ago."

The voice was that of Gideon Adams, his acquaintance from the Culpeper Hospital and the officer for whom Henry had hidden the nail file in the guards' search. "Is that you, Gideon?" Henry answered in a hoarse whisper, rubbing his eyes.

Gideon stood up and went to his friend's assistance. Placing

269

his lone arm under Henry's armpit, he lifted him to a standing position and supported him. Henry struggled to speak coherently: "No, I'm not dead but more dead than alive," he said. "I stink, Gideon," he laughed softly. "Haven't washed since the sixth of July." His voice was gravelly and he faltered between words.

Joseph, the officer who had skirmished for lice on his body the day Henry arrived at the Libby, got up off the floor to help Flinn. "John Flinn! I never would've known you," he gasped. "My God, what have they done to you?" Joseph's voice expressed horror at the skeleton of a man he was about to lift. Helping John to his feet and putting his arm around him as he led him to a vacant corner of the room, he eased him down gently to the bare floor.

Flinn rested his head against the wall behind him, keeping his eyes closed. "I couldn't have hung on much longer," he whispered. After a few minutes' silence he added: "Is there any coffee?"

Joseph rose and fetched him something from the stove. "It never saw coffee beans," he laughed, "but it's warm and wet." He lifted the cup gently to John's lips. He drank it with long, grateful draughts, and sighed.

The officers crowded around the two men pommeling them with questions about their incarceration in the dungeon and expressing dismay at their gaunt countenances and broken bodies—so eloquent a testimony to their treatment for the past seven weeks. The stifling heat in the room mixed with the body odor of the two men was oppressive and nauseating.

"What I would give for a bath in a tub of warm water!" said Henry with emotion. He began ripping off his filthy ragged clothing besmirched with mildew.

"Being August the water is pretty warm now," encouraged Gideon as he helped Henry to the wooden washing trough which contained some rather yellowish water. "My wife sent me some soap in her last box," he continued. He went to his corner and brought forth the fragrant luxury. "The guards stole everything else. Don't know why they left the soap behind. I reckon you need it more than I do."

Sawyer and Flinn stood naked before the trough while their

bodies were supported and scrubbed with the muddy water from the canal and the bar of precious soap. They leaned over the trough for the shampoo of beards and tangled hair. One of the officers brought out a pair of hidden scissors and cut their fingernails and toenails under which an accumulation of filth had collected. The same scissors were used to trim inches off their hair which had grown wild and unruly. Their scalps were inspected closely for vermin. Next came shaves for both men, the razor being wielded by one Nathaniel who was a doctor in civilian life. He clipped off the matted beards, trimming the remaining stubble neatly. Their clothing was discarded and they were both dressed in cast-offs of different sizes scrounged from the officers' haversacks. The effect of the mismatched uniforms was humorous and both men managed a chuckle at the absurd picture they presented.

When Henry sat down on the floor finally in the spot which he had claimed to be "his" the day they arrived at the Libby, he looked around him. It was then that he realized the officer with scurvy who had been on the floor next to him was not there. "Where's Matthew?" he asked.

"Dead," came the answer. "The scurvy finally got him. Just a few days ago."

There were new faces around him Henry observed. Prisoners had arrived after him from Gettysburg and faraway Vicksburg. "The tide of the war is turning," said a stranger sitting next to him. "The Rebs are on the run. Meade is pushing them hard. It won't be long now before Lee surrenders. Then we can all go home!"

"I don't think so," countered another newcomer whose legs were swathed in bandages. "The Rebs fight fiercest when their backs are to the wall. They have the advantage of fighting on their own soil to defend their own homes. Nothing girds a soldier to valor like an enemy treading on his home land. And don't forget another strong point in their favor . . ." He paused a moment waiting for their close attention. "Every man in the Confederacy is in its service. There are *no bounty men* in their ranks. No, on the contrary, the war is far from over. I predict a long haul before peace comes." He paused again. "And peace won't come with the end of the fighting. Their cause is too deeply ingrained."

The moment of solemnity was interrupted by the appearance of Sergeant George, a member of the prison staff who was reputed to be an easy mark for obtaining favors if they were elicited by bribes. He was carrying a small paper bag when he approached the group of officers with John and Henry sitting in their midst. "This here is for Henry Sawyer," he announced, holding the bag up rather playfully over their heads. He seemed to be waiting for something as he dangled the object tantalizingly out of their reach. Gideon rose and, with a swoop of his long arm, snatched the bag from his clutches, much to the displeasure of the simpering toady. "Give me that!" Gideon's booming voice sent the man fleeing.

Henry put the bag on his lap. It felt very light and inside was nothing but an envelope with his name written in a familiar feminine handwriting. He squinted at it in disbelief. Then, recognizing that it had been written by Harriet's hand, he felt his heart leap and skip a beat. He brought the letter close to his eyes and began to read it slowly, savoring each word and lingering at the end of each sentence. When he reached the end, his eyes were moist. Her words answered so many questions that had been troubling him for many long days and nights in the dungeon. He knew now why their lives had been spared, that President Lincoln had intervened, and that, for the time being at least, they were "safe"—whatever that meant when one was a prisoner of war. Suffice it to say that they had received a kind of promotion from the status of "condemned." Perhaps they could now even dream about a prisoner exchange.

Henry had been right in his assessment of Harriet. He had her to thank for everything. With her keen intelligence and perspicacity she had interpreted the subtle instructions in his letter to her from Winder's office and had acted boldly with her usual fortitude and integrity. She had done her best as she always did. He closed his eyes tightly in gratitude, and when he opened them at last he looked again inside the bag. It was empty except for a small packet of paper lying in one corner.

It contained one licorice drop.

25

Daily life in prison had two ever-attentive companions: hunger and boredom. The idle hours stretched to infinity, and keeping them company was faithful hunger, gnawing, gnawing, gnawing. There was one topic of conversation which captivated the men in their misery: prisoner exchange. Men sat together on the floor eating their rations and expressing their opinions endlessly on the subject dearest to their hearts. Many of them had entered the prison confident that their stay would be of short duration.

Captured on the battlefield and forced to march often more than a hundred miles to this spot, many of the men arrived in Richmond with their spirits buoyed up by the hearsay that the Libby was only a stopover point. Exchanges were going on all the time in prisons in different parts of the country, they had heard, and many soldiers talked with certainty that soon they would be back in service with their regiments. At night when they laid their heads to rest on pillows fashioned of their own boots, the talk of exchange went on in whispers until they fell asleep, and oftentimes the subject made inroads in their dreams.

Exchange of prisoners had been going on since early in the war although none of the men in the Libby had a very clear idea of exactly how the system worked. In July 1862 the Dix-Hill cartel for the exchange of prisoners had been signed, both sides agreeing to discharge prisoners on parole ten days after their capture. A parolee promised on his honor not to take up arms against the enemy until he was part of a formal exchange.

Lieutenant James M. Wells of the 8th Michigan Cavalry, who read history in civilian life, seemed to be well-informed on the subject. He began by telling a group of listeners about his capture in Georgia. "A Reb soldier took my high-top boots and gave me his shoes in return. They were so ragged I had to tie them on my feet in order to keep them on," he said. When he arrived at the Libby in October he was wearing trousers that were six inches short in the legs and made of a green material similar to that covering billiard tables. The seat was big enough to fit a small elephant. "We were marched over a hundred miles before they crammed us into open freight cars and shipped us to Richmond. The Rebs kept us quiet for two weeks on that journey out in the open by telling us we were on our way to Richmond for a prisoner exchange."

He explained then what he had learned about exchange in history: "The cartel of exchange of prisoners is based on the one drawn up during the War of 1812 between America and Great Britain. Every prisoner has a 'value' determined by his rank. A brigadier general is 'worth' twenty enlisted men in exchange, a colonel is exchanged for fifteen men, a major for eight, a captain for six, a first lieutenant for four, and on down."

Every day they anticipated the arrival of Dick Turner with the news that a boat was waiting for them at City Point where many exchanges took place. They would be released from this odious place and breathe free air again. Dick Turner did come often but never with news about prisoner exchange, only with orders—new regulations about prison life laid down by the other Turner—which he took malicious delight in delivering.

Days passed and the summer slipped away. When September arrived and there had been no exchanges, the men grew impatient and sullen. They began to feel bitter at having been forgotten by the leaders in their government who were letting them sit here half-starved in this squalor.

Attempts were made by some to explain the government's

stand. In defense of its seeming inaction one officer reasoned that it was to the Federal government's advantage *not* to exchange before the autumn campaign ended since the release of a large number of well-cared-for prisoners from northern prisons back into the Confederate forces would be a great advantage to the South. It sounded logical to some who heard this argument, but still the feeling of being forsaken was like a sore that would not heal.

The reality that was hardest to bear, however, was that of "special" exchange when a captive from both sides would mysteriously disappear from the confines of prison. It happened via the "exchange bureaus" whose agents—General Samuel A. Meredith for the Union and Robert C.S. Ould for the Confederates—had established a degree of cooperation which allowed privileged prisoners to walk out. Morale amongst the men left behind plummeted when this happened. Their sufferings were greater, their hunger deeper as they chafed under the injustice of the practice.

And, as so often happens when questionable ethics become a factor in human relations, the sense of honor of the men, which had been displayed in a hundred different ways on the field of battle, began to erode. A fighting soldier's loyalty to his country knows no boundaries as long as he feels its sense of justice and integrity. Let him see those virtues become tarnished in the actions of his government and his own moral fibre weakens. It happened that way in the Libby. Men began to bow and scrape to the Rebs for special favors, always with exchange in mind. They gave away any item of their personal possessions to the guards if it had the power to persuade. To have one's name put at the top of the supposed "list for exchange," money, of course, curried the highest favor.

With the arrival of prisoners from the Battle of Chickamauga in the fall of 1863 the rations at the Libby diminished and worsened. There were now over a thousand mouths to feed. There was only bread made from corn, and meat was replaced by sweet potatoes and cabbage. Sometimes the offering consisted of half a potato. There were days when the men received three tablespoons of rice or small beans. The quality of the rations was disgusting: there were worms in the beans and the vegetables were rotten. Prisoners who formerly had used their hidden cash to obtain better food from the guards, dug deep into their pockets and found them empty.

The cartel for exchange had ceased to be effective during that summer, and exchange of officers had dwindled to nothing. Hardship was not confined to Libby prisoners; conditions in all the prisons in Richmond deteriorated to a degree that alarmed Provost Marshal General Winder who feared he could not quell an uprising of over 11,000 starving, ill-housed captives with his insufficient number of guards. His appeals to his government for more staff were not answered nor were his urgent demands for increased rations for the luckless men. Reports of overcrowding, starvation, and lack of even basic sanitation, blankets, tents or other shelter on Belle Isle—the small island in the James River—circulated through the northern newspapers, and great was the outrage of the populace who demanded retaliation in northern prisons unless the appalling suffering of their loved ones in the South were ameliorated.

Scandalous stories of prison life drifted through the lines to enrage northern families: soldiers were so hungry that they sold their clothing and blankets to sutlers for food, ruffians among the prisoners robbed, beat and even killed weaker inmates, supplies sent from northern homes to relieve the suffering of the captives "disappeared" along the way, official consignments of clothing sent from the Federal Government to the prisoners were diverted to Rebel troops.

Worst of all was the bitter cold at the end of 1863 and the beginning of 1864. Men tried to keep out the wintry blasts that blew in the open windows by stuffing bedding and rags into them. They slept fully-dressed, wrapped in their blankets (if they had any), but many prisoners perished from the cold. If there was a stove in the room, there was no wood to build fires or to cook their rations. When reports came through that more than 1000 officers in the Libby slept on bare floors without blankets and that they were in dire need of hats, shoes, socks, shirts and overcoats, the Federal Government answered the call for help by sending 500 blankets to the senior officer among the prisoners, General Neal Dow, for his personal distribution to the most needy. This mission of mercy was followed by another shipment of 1000 suits and 1500 blankets. This time General Dow was permitted on parole for the purpose of distributing the clothing and blankets to the prisoners on Belle Isle.

When the General returned to captivity in the Libby in November he told the shocking truths about Belle Isle to all who gathered round: "The island is a wretched place," he began. "It is low-lying and unhealthy in its situation in the river. We think that sleeping on the floor in this Hell is inhuman, but the boys on Belle Isle are far worse off. There are about 6000 of them there and only about half of them have tents. The rest sleep out in the open on the ground with no blankets and only ragged clothing covering their bodies. You wouldn't believe it unless you saw it for yourselves. They're being kept alive in conditions unfit even for animals. Lying on the ground in filth, some without even pants or shirts or shoes. There's no fuel. No soap. They're all dirty and starving. Ten of them die every day but I'd say that by Christmas—a little over a month—they'll be going at the rate of 100 a day. Those who haven't frozen to death will die of hunger, and disease will take the rest. Dysentery and diarrhea are what they all have in common."

His horrific descriptions cast gloom over the men, but Dow had not yet finished with his distressing news: "Everyone in Richmond is in competition for whatever food is available: the civilian population, the Reb army and the prisoners are all hungry," he went on. "Hardly any meat is left to divide up. It is going to get worse, too. The talk on the outside is that the prisoners are going to be moved out of the city to take the pressure off. Winder is afraid the lid will blow off with so many starving prisoners confined in inhuman conditions. I'm told he lives in constant dread of a break-out."

Henry asked: "Where are the prisoners going?"

Dow replied: "Some say the move will be south, maybe to Georgia, and that already Winder has sent his son to select a location."

The Confederates blamed the food shortage on the northern blockade and the overcrowding on Lincoln's opposition to the cartel for prisoner exchange. Lincoln was opposed to the cartel on principle for it gave official recognition to the Confederacy whose existence he was not anxious to acknowledge. Talks on the thorny subject of exchange bogged down on a number of issues on which both sides stood pat and refused to negotiate. Highly inflammatory was the question of Negro prisoners. The South insisted that they would not be treated as prisoners of war if captured, considering them southern "property" who must be returned to their masters. To a southerner it was unthinkable that a former slave could be considered the equivalent of a white in a prisoner exchange. They were threatened with execution, as were the Union officers commanding them.

And as the war progressed, Lincoln also found prisoner exchange to be counterproductive to the war effort. Large numbers of Union prisoners on parole were a burden. On their honor they could not engage in combat or any kind of military duty with a deleterious effect on the enemy; most wanted to return home while they waited to be formally exchanged, and many expected that they would be mustered out permanently and never return to active duty. In addition, there was also the possibility that a battle-weary soldier in the field could gain welcome relief from combat by letting himself be captured with the expectation that parole and exchange would follow. There were others—the "deserter types"—who found surrender to the enemy as an attractive way out. Lincoln was convinced that there was more loss than gain for the North in the cartel agreement.

The collapse of the prisoner exchange was exacerbated by the revelation of irregularities in the parole of the 30,000 southern captives taken at Vicksburg in July. When it was discovered that a good many of these parolees were turning up again as captives after the Battle of Chattanooga four months later, the Confederates were accused of having arbitrarily returned them to duty after Vicksburg without their being officially exchanged.

Autumn crept into winter. Now and then a canal boat arrived from City Point, sending scuttlebutt sweeping through the Libby that there were packages from home aboard. Excitement ran feverishly through the prison as men allowed themselves to hope. They waited patiently as the packages made their way through "inspection" in the nearby warehouse and finally to the

Libby itself three days later. Upon opening them on the prison floor surrounded by their fellow inmates, the recipients were never sure what had been in them originally when they were packed by loving hands at home; usually there were large empty spaces inside attesting to the light fingers of Rebel guards who had had the first look at the contents.

One such delivery of packages happened on a bleak day in November when winter's chill was at the open windows. Stomachs were empty and pulling, and disgruntlement with prison life was palpable in the room where Sawyer and Flinn sat. Every newspaper had been read and reread until it was in shreds. Nathan, an officer captured at Chickamauga, who had arrived at the Libby only a month before and whose physical health was more robust than that of the officers around him, was sitting with a tablet on his knees doing pencil sketches of some of the faces from the battle scene so fresh in his memory. He was an artist in civilian life.

"How'd you keep that tablet away from the guards when you arrived?" Henry asked him.

Nathan smiled. "As a matter of fact, a guard did seize it and was going to keep it," he answered. "A little flattery and an appeal to the man's vanity worked wonders: I offered to draw his picture if he gave it back. Evidently he liked it because he offered to keep me supplied with pencils whenever I need them." They chuckled together.

A guard arrived on the scene at that moment and summoned a few of the prisoners by name to collect their packages from the warehouse. When they returned with them everyone watched as the contents were brought out. There were hand-knitted wool socks which had somehow escaped the guards' attention by being wrapped inside old newspapers, boxes of raisins and dried prunes, containers of homemade jellies and green tomato relish, sweets, loaves of fruit bread, sweaters, shirts, newspapers and other reading matter, and letters in feminine handwriting and juvenile printing.

That was the way it happened on a "good" day. In early December 1863 prisoners began to look forward to Christmas boxes from home. They saw off in the distance a boat arrive on the ca-

279

nal and waited for the announcement that there were packages below. But days passed into weeks and they heard nothing. Finally word came that there were boxes for some of the men. Carrying them up the stairs and placing them on the floor in full view, the men opened them to look for their Christmas goodies. Most of the boxes had been rifled of anything of any worth; the only food in them had rotted and the smell of it assailed the little assembly of heart-broken prisoners. Angry oaths aplenty followed and the names of the two Turners were shouted with a vengeance throughout the cheerless, frigid room.

John Flinn had never recovered from his stint in the dungeon, either physically or mentally. He was a ruin of a man, his body depleted of its vigor and ability to rejuvenate itself, and his spirit broken. His mood was perpetually afflicted with moroseness and hopelessness. Unfortunately, his Christmas box was one of those that had been the object of the guards' theft. Unable to be consoled, Flinn simply lay down on the bare floor with his face buried under the blanket that had been so dearly bought during his dungeon stay. The spirit of Christmas that had flickered momentarily in the grim surroundings had thusly been snuffed out by the inhumanity of the infamous Turners and their ilk. Their cruelty, like the dampness in the walls of the Libby, penetrated the spiritual marrow of every inmate.

So absorbed was Henry Sawyer's mind with the proposition of exchange that he wrote a letter to the Governor of New Jersey in November on this very subject:

"To His Excellency Joel Parker, Governor of New Jersey," it began. "To the active restless spirit of a soldier a few hours' restraint of liberty is annoying and painful, but months of confinement approximate death itself. While in this confinement it occurred to me I could not better entertain a vexing, weary hour than by writing a brief line to the Chief Executive of my gallant little state, and I trust, my dear Governor, you will pardon my presumptuousness in so doing.

"I have been a prisoner of war in Richmond within a few days of five months. It has been my privilege to be in the field of active service since the first hostile gun was fired in this cruel war. I have been with the Army of the Potomac in its varying fortune in every campaign until my capture. I have tasted much of the bitter experience and misfortune of war, yet until my present captivity I have escaped the hands of the enemy. On the 9th June last, at the fight at Brandy Station, I was wounded and left on the field senseless; when I again recovered consciousness I was a prisoner in the hands of the enemy. I lament my capture more than all my other trials of the war. The memory of the fight at Brandy Station shall ever give me pride, and I bless the day I identified my military life with the 1st New Jersey Cavalry. I thank God I have now good health and hopeful spirits although, as you may imagine, my experience for the past few months has been most trying. My continued absence from my regiment has not lessened my interest in its welfare, and I have been much concerned for some time since hearing that Col. Wyndham had left the service. I have ever regarded him as a most excellent soldier and regret his retirement. His retirement will, I imagine, create a vacancy in one of the field positions of the regiment. Now I ask Your Excellency to consider any claims I may have for promotion. You may appreciate that I have the normal ambition of a soldier. I trust and have confidence in your fairness and discretion in considering my past service record and experience.

"It is perhaps not necessary for me to remark that I, in common with my brother officers in confinement, am most anxious on the subject of exchange. We have long been hopeful but have thus far been disappointed. If your direct offices could in any way hasten the day of our deliverance, you would place many soldiers under lasting obligation.

"Hoping your health is good, I am, Governor, Your Obedient Servant, H.W. Sawyer, Captain, 1st New Jersey Cavalry."

One other subject received equal attention in the prisoners' thoughts and conversation: escape. As hope for exchange grew dim, the focus turned on escape, especially for the healthier, stronger prisoners. Colonel Abel Streight of the 51st Indiana Infantry, whose imprisonment was one of the longest of the officers, mused perpetually on the subject. Because Streight and his raiders on mules had had the temerity to penetrate so deeply into the southland before their capture, they had been treated harshly by the Turners and the guards. Streight had tried once to get away by offering a gold watch to a guard. That personage betrayed him at the eleventh hour and turned him over to the Turners who sent him off to a cell in the dungeon and gave him only bread and water for three weeks. But this punishment had not daunted him and he talked openly about escape plans with any company in which he found himself.

There had been a few escapes from the Libby by individual prisoners noteworthy for the audacity with which they were carried out. The success of these daring attempts energized those left behind. One man hid himself in a hospital cart underneath a pile of corpses, and when the cart was left unattended outside the prison awaiting the burial, he emerged and took flight. Another dressed himself in a stolen Rebel uniform and walked down the stairs to the ground floor, nonchalantly passing the guard and strolling into the office to ask directions to a certain Rebel officer's headquarters outside the Libby. The Reb took the greatest pains to give explicit directions, even accompanying him to the outside door and pointing the way. Seeing the two together, the sentinels outside were not suspicious and let the escapee pass without notice.

For days on end the Libby prisoners roamed throughout the building looking for possible escape routes. At night they were constantly on the prowl inspecting windows and doors and feeling the walls which partitioned the rooms. From the two upper floors where they were incarcerated, they stared out of the windows, looking down at the ground below studying the position of the prison. The Libby stood on its own with a sentinels' path going around all four sides. The nearest building was a warehouse which looked to be some fifty feet away. On the other three sides were streets and beyond one of them—Canal Street—was the Kanawha Canal, parallel to a tow path and the James River. Some prisoners gazed at the canal and at the river in the distance and considered the chances of an escape via the sewers into one of those waterways.

Every effort was made to enlist the help of Negroes who worked in the Libby and could bring information from the outside world. One Negro laborer did bring news from Belle Isle prison: a bold and complex plan had been laid for a general uprising in all the prisons in Richmond. Whispers estimated that as many as 20,000 prisoners who were spread out all over the city would be involved. A breakout would begin in each prison simultaneously when the signal was given. Prisoners would overpower their guards, take their arms, and escape to the Tredagar Iron Works where guns and ammunition in ample supply awaited them.

The plan did not stop there. Prisoners were to take over the city and the Confederate Congress in session, and to capture President Jefferson Davis. They were to "hold on" until reinforced by Union troops then in Virginia. All was in readiness for the breakout, each prison knew the signal and what its assigned duties were. The fateful night arrived and the whole plan fizzled like wet fireworks when it was revealed to prison authorities by a traitor inside.

The Richmond newspapers were ecstatic in their reporting of the attempted prison break that failed. "Southern womanhood has been saved from dishonor," the headlines screamed.

Officers inside the Libby brooded over the failure and began to plan anew. Through that aborted attempt there came the realization amongst the group most enthusiastic about escape that a plan would succeed only if those involved were of unquestionable integrity. A small number of prisoners became well-known to each other during their nocturnal reconnaissance of the prison, and fifteen of them formed a secret association. They decided on tunneling underneath the vacant lot to the warehouse fifty feet away.

Major A.G. Hamilton of the 12th Kentucky Cavalry and Colonel Thomas E. Rose of the 77th Pennsylvania Volunteers were the instigators of the tunnel plan and they guarded the secret closely from the majority of Libby prisoners, their conviction being that the fewer who knew about the tunnel the greater the chance for its success.

The two top floors of the prison held the men in rooms named for Streight, Milroy, Chickamauga, and Gettysburg. On the first floor under these two lofts was a kitchen where the men had free access to stoves for cooking their meals; behind the stoves were fireplaces never used. It was in this area that the escape exercise had its beginning. Rose and Hamilton determined that a hole could be cut through the bricks of one fireplace large enough for a man to disappear through it. From that point they would have to cut into the thick solid wall separating the kitchen from the hospital on the other side, taking care that the incision would not penetrate the hospital side of the wall, then to cut downward four feet and, finally, to cut through the wall again, thereby reaching the cellar below. The whole passageway from the kitchen to cellar would resemble a "Z" in shape. Once in the cellar (also known as "Rat Hell") they would embark on the actual tunnel itself.

Rose and Hamilton waited until after the playing of "Taps" each night and then descended to the kitchen darkness, removing the bricks carefully and commencing the digging. Their work could be carried out between ten P.M. and four A.M. only, the hours that found the kitchen empty. One rusty jack-knife and a chisel which the two men had secured and hidden were their only tools. They took turns using the crude implements, one cutting, the other standing guard. At four o'clock came the morning call by the prison sentinel—the signal for the two men to stop their work and to replace the dislodged bricks carefully in the fireplace, leaving no evidence behind that anything was amiss. Hamilton and Rose started their secret operations in mid-December 1863, concealing them from the authorities and from all but the selected number of prisoners.

Boredom in prison life was relieved every now and then by entertainment which came about spontaneously. General Neal Dow, a politician before the start of the war who had succeeded in passage of the famed "Maine Law" banning liquor from his native state, was one of the Libby's most illustrious orators. On the subject of prohibition he was an indefatigable speaker. His temperance platform had about it always an element of the ridiculous for his audience whose only drink was the murky canal water and who had long since forgotten the taste of alcohol. Nonetheless, General Dow held forth for many an hour castigating the evil of drink, reminding his listeners that his words would have meaning for their peacetime lives. "Total abstinence from alcohol" was his crusade; he drummed his message into the ears of the prisoners as they lay about on the floor of the Libby, grateful for any diversion that would occupy their minds. The majority listened respectfully, restraining their urge for ribald commentary, because of the General's admirable war record with the 13th Regiment Maine State Volunteers and the wounds he had received at Port Hudson, Louisiana before his capture.

The lectures on the sins of alcohol were lightened by singing. It mattered not the quality of the voice; a rich tenor could inspire a weak bass. The opening refrain of a Negro spiritual or a familiar Irish ballad sent voices soaring from every corner of the room. Favorite Christmas carols were sung over and over again, verses repeated until the tunes died out from hoarseness of the throats. Feet tapped in time to the Rebel favorite "Dixie," with one prisoner beating out the catchy rhythm on a makeshift drum. As the opening line "I wish I was in de land ob cotton . . ." was sung, a ripple of laughter spun across the room. They gave vent to their homesickness in "Tenting Tonight on the Old Camp Ground" and "Weeping Sad and Lonely."

The dread of facing Christmas within these grim walls was perhaps the inspiration for the formation of the Libby Prison Minstrels. With blackened faces the performers sang songs, told jokes, danced, clowned, presented funny skits and even had the prisoners hooting with laughter at a spoof on prison life under the villainous Turners and Sergeant George. Guffaws and belly laughs reverberated throughout, and for a few moments the starkness of that Libby prison Christmas was forgotten.

Serious discussions took place some days on topics raised rather casually. An officer named Phineas, a learned professor from Massachusetts, presented some interesting facts on the subject of prisoners of war throughout history. "Being a prisoner of war is one of the oldest conditions in human experience," he stated. "Since ancient times, long before the birth of Christ, prisoners taken in war have been the concern of warriors and legislators alike. Roman and Carthaginian generals 200 years before Christ exchanged prisoners in the Punic Wars. Down through the ages codes and laws evolved which provided for prisoners—justice, kindness, even pity, fair play, humanitarianism, mercy and charity being the goals." He stopped a moment before adding his final summing-up: "It seems only in our 19th century that warfare has changed to struggles for victory at all costs, and the tradition of humanitarianism by the victor for the vanquished has given way to cruelty. Hence, the appalling conditions under which we exist at present."

In a single evening many diverse occupations kept men's minds employed. Chequers and chess were played with pieces of wood or bones scrounged from the kitchen. Decks of cards, torn and grubby from months of use, were brought out from haversacks for whist. A man was engrossed in his Bible while those around him amused themselves by telling tall tales of life before the war. One officer, Francis, started a round of jokes with one from his Kentucky farm: "Would you believe it when I tell you I've got a dancin' pig on my farm?"

Jeers followed. Then he continued: " 'Course what I didn't tell you is that he only dances after a drink o' corn liquor. Give him a dose o' good Kentucky moonshine and let a little tune on the banjo begin, and he's off whirlin' 'round in circles liftin' his trotters up in time to the music. Sure as I'm sittin' here."

Robert from New York City laughed: "Don't let old General Dow hear that tale. He'd have something to say to that pig, all right!"

"Does your pig have a hangover the next morning?" asked Henry who was half listening to the banter as he wrote a letter to Harriet.

One tall story after another followed, each more outlandish than the last, and then the laughter ceased as the desolation of their situation weighed down on them and the cold mist from off the James drifted in through the windows.

Some of the men became serious as they talked openly about battle experiences. One Captain Algernon Applegate, a cavalry trooper whose leg was shattered at Gettysburg, reminisced about his fright when he first came under enemy fire months before. "I was so afraid, I wanted to skedaddle out of there," he said. "I started to pull my horse back and then I heard the voice of an officer behind me yelling, 'Steady there!' I looked back and he was glaring straight at me. The fight was getting worse and the grape was falling all around me. After a few minutes I decided I wanted no part of this and edged my horse over to the side near a woods. But I heard the officer yell again, 'Steady!' He was still watching me. I tried a third time to get away from that hell of powder and bullets all around me, but no matter how often I tried to run, that damned officer was staring me down. So I finally gave up and decided the only way to get him off my back was to get back into the fight. Which I did."

"What happened?" Captain Watson Stackhouse, a Chickamauga vet, asked.

Algernon smiled as he replied, "That cured my shaking nerves. After that I never tried to run. Guess I have that officer with his watchful eyes to thank for that."

Devotionals took place regularly; men brought their Bibles and gathered for inspirational readings and prayers. From their experience in the ministry during pre-war years, preachers offered homilies: "Within these walls we are one large family living daily with suffering, despair, pain and loss of hope. Lord, help us to show compassion and encouragement to one another. By our actions let us show our faith in God. Lord, help us through times of loneliness and danger. We put our trust in Thee and Thy loving kindness. Amen," preached Jacob, a reverend from Tennessee.

There were many hours of every day that passed in thoughts of home and nostalgia for the past. Letters from loved ones were read again and again as if for the first time and put away carefully to be brought out yet again when spirits sagged. Men closed their eyes to their surroundings and let their minds drift on to pleasanter times and to reminiscences of loved ones far away.

Henry Sawyer thought about the farm he had left fifteen years ago, his mother and father whom he had not seen since then, and his brothers. He thought about Si lying in a grave far from home and he wondered if Thad was perhaps a prisoner now, lying on some filthy floor dreaming about his boyhood days, too. He also thought about all the horses he had known in his thirty-four years. There was the Percheron team Rob and Willy. Then came Flash, the pony that was his sixth birthday present from his father. He had learned to ride bareback, gripping the brown, furry body with his knees. Flash became his closest friend and together they rode over the farm, through the woods and down the country lanes. Henry recalled it vividly now. In the woods they came upon deer and Henry reined Flash in gently as they waited quietly in the shadows of the great trees for the appearance of the cautious does with their fawns. He knew where the rabbit holes were, where squirrels and chipmunks hid, and deep in the woods was a marshy pond where a beaver lived amongst the sunken logs. These happy memories lifted his spirits. He pondered the changes that fifteen years and the war might have wrought on the landscape of his childhood.

His next horse was Beauty, the noble, handsome, faithful friend who brought him off the farm and who played such an important role in the adventures of those thirteen Cape Island years that remained at once poignant and joyous in his memories of Harriet and their children. He wondered about Beauty now. Oh, there would be many stories to hear when he got home! Days and evenings of stories by the fireside.

Visions of Thorn and Prince on the battlefield brought him such anguish that he shut them out of his mind quickly. Their loss was still too close to think objectively about them.

There was one memory of horses, though, that brought instant comfort to him. Early in his life something had happened which erased his casual affection for horses in general and replaced it with a devotion that was rooted deep in his soul. There had been an accident on the farm when he was only five. One of his favorite places to play with his brothers was in the hay mow upstairs in the barn under the great roof. In the summertime haying season the horses pulled the wagonloads of freshly cut timothy up to the sliding doors of the big barn where it was pitchforked up onto the floor of the loft above the animals' stalls. The soft pile of hay grew higher and higher with each load until the sweet-smelling grass reached almost to the stout wooden beams stretching across from one side of the barn to the other. It was from this height that Henry and Si and Thad loved to jump into the hay, sinking way down over their heads into its softness. There was nothing quite as much fun as lining up next to one another on the beam and springing off it together, flying through the air and coming down into the embrace of the pile of hay that was still warm from the summer sun that had dried it for days. The contest of the three boys was to see who could jump the farthest. The delightful sensation of soaring out into the openness of the barn kept them clambering up onto the beam time and time again for another try, with shouts of "I'm an eagle" and "I'm a black hawk" ringing up to the rafters and sending the frightened swallows scurrying from their nests.

On this particular August afternoon Si and Thad were not there to play. They had gone with their father to a neighboring farm to help with the threshing. Boys of even seven and eight were given chores to do on those occasions, but Henry was too small to be of any real help. He preferred to while away his time playing with the twin lambs that had been orphaned in the spring. "You can have 'em as pets," his father had said when the ewe died. "You'll have to feed 'em regular on a bottle to keep 'em alive 'til they go onto grass." Henry had named them Reuben and Rachel. Now they were six months old, very fat and weaned from the nursing bottle. He filled their water bucket with fresh water and brought them clumps of sweet purple clover and alfalfa from the other side of the pasture fence. As he sat on the fence looking at them he felt a rush of pride at how healthy they looked. It was all because of his feeding them for many weeks with bottles of warm, foaming milk from the days' milkings that Reuben and Rachel had survived and grown so fat and frisky. Hopping down off the fence, Henry patted their soft backs and stuck his fingers down into the wool, flicking a couple of ticks off their ears. He laughed at them, remembering how they had tugged at the rubber nipples so hard that Henry had had to hold onto the bottles with all his strength, one in each hand, as they sucked the warm milk.

The afternoon was very hot, the sun beating down ripening grain and drying grass. Perfect threshing weather, Henry's father had commented at breakfast. All was quiet in the barnyard as the animals rested in the shade of the apple trees along the fence. Henry was alone. Blackberries were ripe and his mother was in the house making jelly. He could smell it as he walked slowly up the path to the kitchen. She opened the door to him. "Here's somethin' ye like a lot, Henry," she said, offering him a piece of fresh bread spread with butter and the clear black sweetness. He champed it down quickly and licked his fingers. Sensing that he might be a little lonely, she suggested, "Why don't ye fetch the book Grandma gave ye last Christmas and I'll read it to ye."

Henry brought the book to her with a smile and they sat on the porch swing together turning the pages illustrated with drawings of uniformed British soldiers riding horses and other soldiers not so well-dressed carrying muskets. His mother explained that the story was about the American Revolutionary War and these were the soldiers who fought on both sides. Henry liked the horses best and gazed at them a long time, not wanting her to turn the pages too quickly. "Some day when ye go to school ye'll learn about the war," she said. "It happened not very long ago. A little over fifty years. That's all. It was a very important war, and after it was over our country began to grow strong. Grandpa fought in it. He can tell ye all about it."

"Is that why Grandpa limps?" Henry asked.

"Yes. He was with General Washington at Valley Forge. That was a terrible winter, and many of the soldiers froze to death." She took hold of his face and turned it gently towards hers. "Ye are named for General Washington, Henry, a very brave soldier and father of our country. Your father and I gave ye his name so's ye would never forget what he did." Henry listened intently and looked back at the picture book. There was a drawing of General Washington seated on a handsome horse. Henry thought he looked very brave, indeed.

After awhile his mother went back to her work in the kitchen and Henry wandered idly down the path towards the barn, stopping to look in at the Percherons who stood in the quiet coolness of their stalls enjoying their leisure. They were not tied as they would be later on when his father returned in the evening and forked the fresh hay down into their mangers from the hay mow above and put oats in their feed box. They had come into the barn now seeking shade and were standing side by side and head to tail, their two long tails swishing back and forth chasing horse flies and deer flies off each other's flanks. Sitting on the open steps leading up to the hay mow, Henry wondered if they were conscious of how clever they were in adopting that closeness which enabled them to protect each other from the bites of their predators. Did their tails work thusly without having to be told to sweep off the flies, he mused, or was each swish of the tail an answer to a command the horse gave it? He would have to ask his father about that. His father knew everything about animals.

Henry climbed the stairs slowly to the hay mow where the results of the previous day's work in the hay field were piled high. It was the highest pile of hay he had seen all summer and it covered the whole floor, even the open chutes leading down into the horses' mangers. "Whew!" was all he could gasp. "I wish Si and Thad were here."

At the top of the stairs was a pitchfork leaning against the barn wall. It was much taller than he was but he grasped it and scooped up a forkful of the fresh hay and pushed it down the open chute into the manger below. The Percherons stirred and responded immediately to the unexpected treat with a soft whinny. Henry could hear them pulling the hay out of the slots in the manger and chewing it with slow, rhythmic crunches of their enormous teeth. He sensed their contentment in their chewing.

Dropping the pitchfork over the opening of the manger he looked up to the top of the pile of hay and whistled softly as he'd heard Si and Thad do when something impressed them mightily. "Well," he thought to himself, "I'll have a jump even if they're not here."

He climbed up to the big beam over the hay and sat there a moment in the stillness and semi-darkness of the barn pondering how far he would be able to jump and how far down he would sink. The first jump into a new pile of hay before anyone had trampled it down was always the most fun. Today there would be no contest with Si and Thad. He usually lost because they were taller and their legs longer. He stood up very straight to his full height, bent his legs, and sprang with all the strength he could muster in his muscles. He sailed through the air, crying out to the swallows he disturbed from their perches high up under the roof of the barn: "Look out! Here I come!"

As he descended he overshot the pile of hay and landed with a heavy thud on the pitchfork which he had left lying across the open chute to the manger. His feet came down on the end of the sharp steel tines bringing the long wooden handle upright with full force whacking him sharply on the forehead and knocking him off balance. His body flew head first down the open chute and into the manger where it stuck, quiet and motionless.

From the depths of his unconsciousness, he could hear somewhere off in the distance the frantic whinny of the Percherons. The sound of their cries seemed very far away and yet very distinct. Running round and round the barnyard, kicking up dust, snorting and screaming, their tails flying out behind them, Rob and Willy spread the alarm. Henry had never heard them holler like that. He could not move from his upended position but he was regaining his senses and what he heard from the barnyard was their rousing call for help.

How long it seemed before his mother answered their frenzied summons! He was conscious of her voice in the barn. "Henry! Henry! Where are ye?"

He struggled to free himself from the chute where he was wedged and she heard him.

Her footsteps up the stairs were quick. He felt the tug at his overall legs as she pulled him backwards and upwards out of the chute and laid him on the floor.

"Henry! Henry!" she cried over him, gently pushing the hay away from a large lump on his forehead. "Child, whatever in the world happened to ye?" There was a bloody trickle above one of his eyes as he opened them and saw her frightened face. She spoke softly to him. "I heard the horses and knew somethin' must be wrong in the barn. They were goin' wild. Sounded like two stallions goin' crazy." She kissed him tenderly. "Now I see all they were tryin' to do was bring help to you."

Henry tried to speak. He whispered, "Ma, it was the pitchfork. I should've stood it up. Pa'll be mad. He's always told me not to leave pitchforks lying around."

There was a dull pain in his head as she gathered him up in her arms and carried him carefully down the stairs. He could see the Percherons watching with an expression of perplexity in their big eyes. He had never noticed those eyes before, so full of feeling. As his mother cradled him in her arms, Henry reached out to stroke the two horses, caressing them on their velvety muzzles with his fingers. They licked his hands in return and he felt their warm breath. Willy whinnied softly and Rob nuzzled Henry's hand for more attention.

"Oh, Ma," he said, "aren't they beauties? Tell Pa to give 'em a bit more oats tonight."

26

One day, not long after Henry's reverie about his horses, an extraordinary happening occurred in the prison. He was in the kitchen; from force of habit he went there every morning to make his breakfast coffee out of roasted cornmeal. After it was brewed, he could hardly swallow it, but at least it was hot and that was comforting. On this particular morning prisoners huddled about the stove attempting to start a fire with wet wood. Black smoke curled up and the men cursed bitterly. One whittled shavings from a piece of wood, lit them and attempted to light the fire with

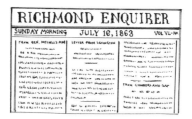

the bright flames. More smoke resulted. While the attention of everyone was focused on this operation, Henry stood back a ways from the stove and leaned against the wall.

Suddenly, a guard appeared in the kitchen with a Negro pushing a cart laden with rations for the inmates. There was a barrel of meat (probably mule meat, which the indeterminate flesh they received now had been dubbed by the prisoners), which he lifted from the cart and set down in the kitchen. While the guard busied himself with inspecting the provisions, the Negro approached Henry. From underneath his jacket he brought forth a newspaper, folded many times, and thrust it furtively into Henry's hands. Underneath his breath he said hurriedly, "'This here is for Massa Henry Sawyer. Tell 'im it's from Ambrose."

He did not linger long enough for Henry to respond but turned back abruptly before the guard could notice, and together they disappeared.

Henry was so startled he could not move. He blinked, wondering if he had seen an apparition. No, the newspaper in his hand bore testimony that, indeed, the figure who had placed it there was of flesh. Because it had been delivered by stealth, so by stealth he must retain it. He shoved it quickly inside his shirt and as he did so he was conscious of the excited pounding of his heart. Ambrose! Where was he? In Richmond?

Henry drank his ersatz coffee, all the time marveling at his good luck in having been in a position to receive the newspaper from the stranger. Walking up the stairs to his corner, he found that he was alone, the rest of the prisoners being in the kitchen. He drew the newspaper out of its hiding place, sat down on the hard floor with a groan, and opened the crumpled folds to scan the front page. It was the *Richmond Enquirer* for July 16, 1863—the date set for his execution. He read: "To City Point today came Mrs. Harriet Sawyer on a boat from Fortress Monroe to see her husband, Henry W. Sawyer, one of two Yankees being held in Libby Prison and condemned to die in retaliation for the execution of two brave Confederate officers by the failed General Burnside in the North. Mrs. Sawyer was refused entry to the city of Richmond—justifiably in the face of her President's scurrilous threat towards the gallant southern officer now held captive in an abominable Yankee prison. Rightly, this northern woman was sent home. Why should she receive even a measure of southern hospitality when the leader of her country flaunts his power in the scandalous treatment of the son of our esteemed Commander of all Confederate forces? Gallant young General W.H.F. Lee, who fought valiantly until wounded and captured, now languishes in prison where he is fed on sweepings we would not offer our good southern hogs, and must suffer the further ignominy of being named hostage for Sawyer and John Flinn in the Libby.

"What further vile vindictiveness can the malevolent gorilla in Washington initiate? Is there no limit to the depths of infamy to which he will stoop? The insults to one of our noblest southern aristocrats pay tribute to the malignity which fuels the brain of the monster in the capital. . . ."

Stunned, Henry laid the newspaper down wearily and shut his eyes momentarily. Playing on his sensibilities staccato-like were myriads of truths and revelations. Now at last he knew the answer to the question that had haunted him for almost five months: why had his execution promised for July 16th not taken place? Here, before him, was the whole story. But who was this Negro who had managed to smuggle in the paper from Ambrose? And where *was* Ambrose at this moment?

He thought, too, of how many months of emotional strain he had endured before these facts finally reached him. Old newspapers published in Richmond made their way inside the prison walls quite frequently and were passed along through hundreds of hands to all eyes hungry for news of the outside world. Why had Fate been so capricious as to choose to withhold the newspaper of this particular date from the Libby—the 16th of July, so important to his life and that of John Flinn? The coincidence was just too incredible to grieve over.

John Flinn. Henry remembered him now. He must be told the news immediately. Seeking him out, Henry found him on the floor drinking his coffee. He whispered: "John, read this story. Read it and weep for joy! You'll never believe our good fortune!" He handed the newspaper to his friend and sat down next to him.

Flinn was silent, his face betraying no emotion as he read. Henry was shocked at the hollow eyes and gaunt cheeks he beheld. Finishing the newspaper account, John looked up and spoke slowly: "This is good news. All we have to do is hold on 'til the end of the war." He paused for a moment before adding: "I'm not sure I'll be able to do that."

"Of *course* you will, John," Henry insisted. "Think of it! The life of General Lee's son being held in ransom for ours! That's something you'll tell your grandchildren about. We're safe, John! We don't have to worry any longer about that damned Winder and his fiendish plans for us. And we may *not* have to wait until the war is over either. Exchange could come any day. If Rooney Lee complains loudly enough about life in the Yankee prison, somebody might just unlock his cell door. And if that happens, well, the door of the Libby will open to us, too!"

The two prisoners sat and did not speak for a few moments. Then Henry closed their discussion. "We have President Lincoln to thank for all of this, John," he said. And silently to himself he added: "And Harriet."

*   *   *

During the five months of his imprisonment, Henry had found the only way to shut out the grim reality of his degrading existence was to so immerse himself in silent thought that he could affect a state of near-unconsciousness of his surroundings. In this manner the hours were consumed, sometimes almost pleasantly in nostalgia about his family, other times in fabrication about the future and often in conjecture about cavalry friends with whom he'd bonded in danger and combat. A good many of these bouts of reverie came to an abrupt end with the troubling question that nagged him: where is Ambrose?

What *had* happened to Ambrose in all these months since the disappearance of his friend at the Battle of Brandy Station? After a fruitless search of the battlefield and the discovery of Prince's body, he retraced his steps to the camp of the 1st New Jersey and arrived there in a very troubled state. In the absence of Henry, what was he to do? Was there a job for him still with the cavalry?

A friend, Eli Winterholler, a blacksmith with Company K, saw him walking into camp looking dejected and worried. He greeted him: "Whatsa matter, Ambrose?"

"Henry Sawyer is missin," he answered. "I found his horse . . . dead . . . but nothin' else to tell what happened to him. When the soldiers all came back from the big battle, one o' them told me he'd seen both o' them go down together. I looked all over that field and there's just no sign o' him anywheres."

"Well, that probably means he was wounded and captured. Maybe taken to a hospital."

"A Rebel hospital?" Ambrose looked dismayed. "That's no good thought," he answered, shaking his head.

Eli was thoughtful and quiet for a moment before presenting

another option. "Maybe he's a prisoner." He put his hand on Ambrose's back and continued: "I'm sure you'll find him . . . somehow . . . Now what are you going to do?"

"I'd like to stay with the cavalry," he replied, "if they'll have me . . . I don't have any place else to go . . . I could keep on takin' care o' the horses and I can do buildin' and fix things when they break."

And so, when later that June the Union Army followed Lee north into Maryland and Pennsylvania, Ambrose went along with the 1st New Jersey to fulfill his avowed intent "to do something to help his country." He looked after many horses, groomed them, inspected their shoes nightly, led them to springs often far away, doctored the saddle sores on their backs, and tracked over miles of ravaged Virginia countryside en route to the North searching for forage. He worked earnestly and tirelessly and often with Eli, his closest friend, who sensed about him an ever-present melancholy over the loss of his friend.

Following the Battle of Gettysburg, the war turned south again through Maryland and into Virginia, and Lee's army was pursued throughout the summer and into the autumn as it retreated toward Richmond. In late November 1863 the 1st New Jersey was in bivouac near Mine Run, Virginia, north of Richmond, when a bag of accumulated mail came in one day. In it was a large envelope for Ambrose addressed to him "in care of the 1st New Jersey Cavalry." He recognized the handwriting as Harriet's; the lessons she'd given him in reading and writing had enriched his life in countless ways and at this moment enabled him to learn some news vitally important to him.

"I do not know if you will ever receive this letter," she began, "because I do not know where you are. But the information it contains is of such import that it merits my endeavor to convey it to you. Recently the enclosed newspaper came into my possession, and although the news is old, it is new to me and, I would guess, to you as well. Henry is a prisoner in the Libby Prison for officers in Richmond. I have had only one letter from him, in early July, and no word since. It is my feeling that he himself is probably unaware of the facts contained in this newspaper article. After reading it, you will realize how much his mental anguish would be relieved if he could be informed of these truths concerning his imprisonment. Can you think of any way they could be delivered to him?"

Overjoyed to know that Henry was alive, Ambrose was filled with such unspeakable gratitude that he bowed his head and was silent a moment. Henry *not dead* but a prisoner! The fear that had sat like a stone on his heart all these months vanished with the reading of Harriet's letter. He opened the newspaper—the *Richmond Enquirer* for July 16, 1863—and found the article that he read through slowly, carefully, once, twice, a third time. Harriet's words "can you think of any way . . ." absorbed his thoughts completely. He, Ambrose, must find a way to be the messenger of this good news.

That evening, while they worked together repairing the shoes of a cavalry horse, Ambrose told Eli that he had received word that Henry was in Libby Prison.

"How did you hear?" the astonished Eli wanted to know.

Ambrose pulled the newspaper from his pocket and handed it to the farrier. "His wife sent this to me from Cape Island, New Jersey. She wants me to figure out a means o' gettin' this news to him. It's important to his peace o' mind. She's sure he can't know the full story. There's lots o' big words in that article I can't make out but I can see that it's real important that he understands what's happenin' to him in that there prison." He paused. "You'll understand better after you read it." Eli put the newspaper in his pocket.

Lee's army retreating southwards was encamped not many miles away, and on the 27th of November there was a partisan-like raid on the 1st New Jersey in bivouac by a sizable number of Confederates. There followed an extraordinary sequence of events which could not have been foreseen by any of the actors in the drama. Ambrose had gone off in the late afternoon to forage some distance from the regimental encampment. Virginia had been virtually picked clean of all fodder for animals, necessitating longer forays to find it. In his absence the enemy cavalry came in at dusk—quietly, not with their usual ghostly yell—and swooped down on a group of horses, which had been tethered for the night. Noiselessly, they untied the animals, and with lightning speed each mounted Rebel grabbed hold of a horse or two and, with a thump to their rears, succeeded in getting about thirty of them running. Simultaneously, in another part of the camp the rattatattat of gunfire commenced around the commissary stores. The Rebels, suffering from shortages of horses and food, were staging a desperate and dangerous raid to acquire both.

The noise of the horses' hooves startled Eli who ran out just as they became frightened and started to stampede. In his effort to stop them, he did not think twice before leaping on the last horse just as a Confederate officer came up behind him and yelled: "That's fine, Billy Yank. We'll take you along with us." Eli, who was unarmed, turned to see the man pointing his revolver at him. There was no recourse but to obey the Rebel command.

When Ambrose returned many hours later, he found the camp in an uproar. The theft of the valuable horses and a week's supply of hardtack and bacon had been carried out with such daring and bravado as to be an infuriating embarrassment to all. Searching for Eli for an explanation of what had happened in his absence, Ambrose found that his friend was missing. He covered a large area around the camp to determine if he had been shot, but there was no trace of him. As Ambrose trudged back to camp, uppermost in his mind was the thought that it seemed to be his lot in life to be always searching for someone he couldn't find. Then there came the moment of devastation when he remembered: the newspaper from Harriet was in Eli's possession.

A few days later, in Richmond about seventy miles away, Eli was in the process of being admitted to Belle Isle Prison. He was aware of the necessity of getting rid of the newspaper before he was searched by the guards. For Ambrose's sake he felt an obligation to attempt to forward the paper to Henry Sawyer in Libby Prison not far away. He looked around at the guards and noticed one Negro prison attendant who was given to some civility not displayed by the guards who pushed and bullied the prisoners. As he approached the man, he dug down into the depths of his trouser pocket and retrieved one lone greenback lodged there. Pressing it quickly into the man's hand, he implored most earnestly under his breath: "Please see to it that this paper reaches Henry Sawyer in Libby Prison. It's *very* important. Tell him it's from Ambrose." Pulling the crumpled newspaper out of his other pocket, he passed it furtively to the Negro, then turned away and got back into the line of prisoners.

27

One particularly bleak day in January 1864 when the desolation of his surroundings bore down on him heavily, Henry composed a letter to Harriet following a fruitless visit to the office of the Commissioner of Prisoner Exchange: "I had the pleasure of a walk in the fresh air," he wrote. "You have no idea how weak one gets after such a long confinement, for this walk nearly tired me so much that I would not be able to walk a mile further. I am very sorry to inform you that no exchange will take place. You must do

the best you can without me and always have hopes that something will occur to effect my release.

"These are hard times here with us. It is a heavy sacrifice that we are making but withal it becomes us to bear it and to do so without grumbling. If I retain my health I shall feel thankful, and I hope to do so by the thoughts of the future—when I shall be delivered from this imprisonment with its monotonous days and dreary nights, its cramped accommodation, its uncertain duration, its eternal round of unchanging employment or, rather, none at all. I say the thoughts to escape from such conditions and to enjoy what circumstances for the last three years have denied me, the tranquility and joy of home with the affections of my family, are what will buoy me up. May God speed the day when we all shall be permitted to return once more to our happy and peaceful homes. I send you much love and my prayers for you and the children."

*   *   *

With the coming of the new year the tunneling operation under the Libby proceeded in earnest. The passageway having been opened up from the kitchen fireplace to the cellar below, the digging commenced on the tunnel itself under the vacant lot with the objective being the warehouse fifty feet away. The wall through which the tunneling began was five feet thick. Using clamshells, knives and their fingernails, the men bored a hole about two feet in diameter nine feet below the surface of the ground. The problem of what to do with the dirt thus excavated was solved by using a wooden spittoon sequestered from one of the prison rooms above; a cord was attached to it so that the digger could fill it with dirt and it could be pulled back out to the cellar opening by his helper who emptied it and concealed the dirt under some straw. The work was tedious and soul-destroying in its slow progress.

Light for the digging operation was supplied by candles stolen from the prison, but at times the air became so foul as to extinguish the flame. The body of the man digging almost filled the passageway, and the problem of the air supply grew more serious as the tunnel lengthened. Whoever was digging had to back out often to breathe.

From the thirteen prisoners in whom he had confided his plan weeks before, Colonel Rose now formed work details of five men to help with the digging, and he decided to risk employing them during the daytime hours. A day of work was followed by two of rest.

Although correct measurements of distance covered and the angle of excavation were impossible to determine while underground, the weeks of digging convinced the men that they must be nearing their goal. From the upper windows of the Libby they looked down during the daytime at the vacant lot separating them from the warehouse and tried to estimate how far the tunnel had gone underneath that stretch of ground. The decision was made one night to make a slight detour to establish their exact position: they would dig straight upwards and have a look above ground. The chisel being used went straight through the earth suddenly and came out directly under a street lamp within earshot of a sentinel passing there. Only by quick work of the excavator of the moment who stuffed his shirt in the hole and camouflaged it with dirt did he escape detection. He did have time to reconnoiter the area with a glance: an additional fifteen feet of tunneling would bring them to the warehouse.

The daytime work became too risky for the diggers since their fellow prisoners could not account for their absence at the guards' roll call twice daily. To safeguard the whole project the workers went back to nighttime shifts only.

One morning in the first week of February 1864 Colonel Abel Streight sat in a corner of his prison room attempting to waken himself with a tin cupful of the vile-tasting brew of chestnuts and rye that passed for coffee. He sat alone, leaning up against the rough brick wall and feeling rumblings in his empty stomach. A Negro day laborer appeared; he came sporadically to clean out the mud that accumulated in the trough from the canal water that was pumped into it. It was from this trough that the men drank and washed themselves. Streight watched idly as the Negro lifted the mud out and dumped it into a bucket, and he engaged the man in conversation.

"Where do you come from?" he asked.

"I live in Richmon', sir," was the reply.

"Are you a freed slave?"

"Yes. I was with Massa Van Lew's family up there on top o' Church Hill, but before the war Miss Lizzie set us all free. Ma mother and father and sisters and brothers. Nine of us."

Streight's interest was aroused. "Is this Miss Van Lew a southern woman?"

"Oh, yes, sir! But she doesn't think like a southern woman. She thinks different. She's a fine woman. Yes, sir, a good woman. Sent some colored folk up north to school, she did."

"And who is there in the family now?"

"Jes' Miss Lizzie and her mother and Miss Lizzie's sister. Her brother is away. Massa Van Lew he died a long time ago. It's a big house for jes' three womenfolk. Lots o' empty rooms now.

Before the war the family had big parties. The house was always filled with visitors. There were big balls and banquets. But Miss Lizzie doesn't entertain anymore. Maybe it's her views on the war that makes her life hard right now."

"Yes, I see," answered Streight thoughtfully. Then he continued: "Just exactly where is this house?"

The Negro shrugged his shoulder in the direction of the street in front of the prison. "Straight up Church Hill to the top. It's the biggest house up there."

When the Negro disappeared Streight had much to ponder. He filed all these timely revelations away carefully. "One never knows when this kind of information will be very useful," he thought to himself.

In early February a few of the prisoners who had been entrusted with the secret of the tunnel quietly undertook a regimen of physical training to prepare themselves for the exertion of the escape and its aftermath. Not one of them knew how far away the Union lines were or the nature of the terrain they would have to cover that first night and all the nights thereafter. To strengthen their weakened bodies, long walks inside the Libby and moderate physical exercises were embarked on. The men went walking round and round the rooms; nobody thought this behavior odd. The other prisoners, lying on the floor or propped up against the walls, hardly noticed them. When they were not moving about, the men who were "going out" carefully appraised their personal belongings to decide which they would take with them.

There was one observant inmate who became aware of the subtle undercurrent of preparations going on about him. Henry noticed Captain Terrance Clark of the 79th Illinois and Major George H. Fitzsimmons of the 30th Indiana in guarded consultation nearby. Summarily the pair were joined rather casually by Captain John Gallagher and Captain W.S.B. Randall, both 2nd Ohio, who lived on the floor below. The little group huddled together talking candidly. Henry could not hear their conversation but his intuition told him that something was astir. He could feel it in the air. He said nothing to arouse their suspicions that he sensed the intrigue, but he watched and kept his own counsel.

Colonel Rose began one last solo marathon early in the morning of February 8, 1864—the seventeenth day of digging. He worked ceaselessly all day long and far into the night. At midnight, suffocating from the deadly stench and his strength almost gone, he broke through the ground and saw stars in the dark sky above him and breathed the cold, fresh air. He climbed out from under a shed next to the warehouse. After a hasty reconnaissance of the immediate escape area—determining such things as the exits from the yard, gates to be unlocked, paths of the sentinels—he crawled back through the tunnel to the cellar and announced the good news that the goal had been reached. It was three o'clock in the morning of February 9th.

The rest of the day was spent in making preparations for the getaway that evening. Colonel Rose and Major Hamilton envisaged an orderly plan of escape enabling a certain number of prisoners to follow them out that evening and many more to flee at later dates. They suggested that parties of fifteen men should leave together, allowing a generous time lapse between each departure. Darkness came early still and at seven o'clock on the 9th the working party who had dug the tunnel assembled in the kitchen and descended the passageway for the last time. The fireplace bricks were replaced after them and Colonel Rose and Major Hamilton led their party into the tunnel crawling on their bellies.

Despite the months of starvation in the Libby, Colonel Streight's frame was so ample that it posed a problem when he began to crawl through the tunnel: his stomach stuck in the entrance and he had to remove his clothing in order to squeeze through.

With the speed of an electric current news of the completion of a tunnel and the escape of fifteen of their number swept through the two upper floors of the Libby igniting the passions of desperate men into a frenzy. Even sick prisoners lifted their feeble bodies up off the floor and, staggering, joined the throng. Only a few thought to grab their overcoats, one slipped his bare feet into the boots of a dozing neighbor, a handful remembered to stuff some leftover cornbread into their pockets. The crowd became an unruly mob. In the stampede of frantic men pushing towards the stairs leading to the kitchen, the weak were trampled on and went down under the crush. Racing down the stairs, the escapees reached the kitchen and began tearing the bricks away from the fireplace.

Panic ensued. Most of the men were in rags and their shoes had holes—if they wore shoes at all. So wild were these prisoners from Chancellorsville, Gettysburg and Chickamauga to reach the outside world that they gave no thought to provisions of any kind. Ill-prepared for such an escapade in mid-winter, they climbed recklessly into the hole, dropped to the cellar floor, and in the darkness proceeded to grope for the tunnel and struggle for first position at its entrance.

What awaited these captives who crawled into the tunnel that night and emerged into the bitter cold darkness outside the Libby? Those left behind were given to wondering, and many hours were spent in imagining the trials which lay ahead for the brave men from Pennsylvania, Michigan, Wisconsin, Indiana, Illinois and Ohio, moving by night and hiding by day, trying to reach a friendly Yankee picket line.

Henry had not been tempted to join the escaping party because of his firm belief that an exchange was in the offing for himself and John Flinn if they had the patience to wait it out. He took comfort in knowing that General W.H.F. Lee was being carefully guarded in Fortress Monroe.

When the roll was called the following morning, the revelation that 109 prisoners were missing brought the prison staff near to apoplexy. With inward glee Henry relished the guards' astonishment that they had been fooled so outrageously. How could it have happened? The fireplace bricks had been restored carefully and the last man to go out of the tunnel had covered the exit in the yard. A whimsical sense of mischief inspired one of the inmates who stayed behind to mislead the authorities by suspending a rope of blankets outside one of the windows. General Winder was furious, the Turners were embarrassed, and the guards were befuddled at how 109 men could escape under their very noses and leave no evidence behind them. Winder accused the guards within and the sentinels without of having taken bribes, and he had them marched off to Castle Thunder where they were locked up.

The Richmond newspapers' stories of the 109 Yankee officers shocked the city out of any sense of security it might have been enjoying.

Henry looked out the window across the vacant lot under which the tunnel had been dug and saw a crowd of curious onlookers gathered below in wonderment and speculation.

For days the Libby inmates waited for news of their friends now on the outside. Gradually, the captured ones began to reappear—singly, haggard, bone-weary, suffering from exposure, all with harrowing stories to tell—until their number rose to forty-eight. Information particularly shattering to the morale of the men filtered through one day: Colonel Rose was back. He had been sent directly to a cell in the dungeon. Upon his release he joined the officers again and told them the exciting story of February 9 and the experiences that followed. He entertained his captive audience for many hours with firsthand accounts of the dangers at every turn of the road, the cold and the hunger, nights of falling into swamps and hiding in the woods, taking refuge in abandoned buildings, following the York River railroad tracks to bridges where hiding places could be found near the river, escaping from sudden appearances of Confederate cavalry, being tracked by bloodhounds hunting them down, hiding in hollow logs by day and trudging through strange country by night, finding shelter and being fed cornbread and bacon in a Negro's cabin, fording the Chickahominy, wading waist-deep through bogs and creeks, wearing soaked clothes that froze on the body, avoiding enemy pickets, being shot at by guerrillas in a forest, lighting small fires to keep from freezing to death, stumbling into thorny brambles and thickets that tore hands and feet and lying there quietly as Reb patrols marched by only a few feet away, creeping with head down through ditches, taking directions from the sun and stars, running stooped over through open fields with bullets whizzing overhead, and, finally, staggering blindly through a sleet storm to reach the protection of a forest where the exhausted spirit caved in under searing hunger pangs in the belly.

Colonel Rose related that he and Major Hamilton had become separated early in the darkness of February 9. Nothing had been heard from him.

John Flinn was curious to know the fate of Colonel Abel Streight. Days passed and he did not reappear which suggested his safe arrival at the Union lines. The guards announced with obvious satisfaction one morning at roll call that two of the escaped officers had drowned. As time went on, prisoners began to count and subtract and the figure they arrived at was fifty-nine—the number who got away successfully and who, hopefully, were rewarded for their bravery by reaching a safe haven.

28

At the top of Church Hill—the highest of Richmond's seven hills—stood an elegant mansion of three-and-a-half stories with wide verandas, tall columns and gardens which rambled on down to a bluff overlooking the Libby Prison below. This impressive structure was home to Elizabeth Van Lew whose father's success as a hardware merchant had endowed her generously with the world's goods. Long before the war the Van Lew home was the venue for entertainment of countless distinguished and

famous visitors—musicians, poets and prominent politicians who dined and danced and partook of the most lavish Southern hospitality. Many were the cultured guests and artists from abroad.

Elizabeth was sent north to be educated and when she returned to her Richmond home from Philadelphia, she was a confirmed and outspoken abolitionist, making her something of a misfit in the southern society into which she had been born. Her strong anti-slavery views were voiced without restraint, but the wealth and social position of her family allowed her some protection from public censure—at least before hostilities began.

Mr. Van Lew died in 1843, and as the country moved steadily on its course toward armed conflict, Elizabeth persuaded her mother to free their Negro house servants. To reunite families, some of whose members had been sold and thus separated, she bought the relatives back from other slaveowners.

Now a spinster in her middle forties, Elizabeth had cultivated assiduously the eccentricities of dress and behavior which had earned for her the appellation of "Crazy Bet." Her peculiar personal habits and appearance offended Richmond society and caused her to be regarded as a silly hysterical woman of questionable sanity. More and more she became the subject of ridicule and scorn—the effect which she desired since being laughed at as a harmless lunatic enabled her to continue her rather unorthodox work. Nothing pleased her more than being mocked by Richmond socialites.

One day in late February she emerged from her mansion with a shabby cloak pulled around her. Her hair was in untidy ringlets that hung in a tangled mass giving the impression of general dishevelment. As she walked from her garden onto the path leading down Church Hill, she mumbled unintelligibly out loud, causing several passersby to snicker and turn away. Over her arm was a basket whose contents were hidden by a cloth.

Making her way in tiny, mincing steps down the hill, she came to the Libby where she asked to see the Provost Marshal.

The guard looked down at her angular face and sharp nose with an expression of disbelief. Who was this odd creature wanting to usurp Winder's time?

Conscious of the man's distaste at having to deal with her, she said quickly: "I have something for him," and she patted her basket.

At the sound of her voice, General Winder appeared in the doorway and beckoned her to enter. "Please come in, Miss Van Lew." Winder, a man of ambition, was acutely aware of the influence of the Van Lew name in Richmond society.

She bustled into his office and threw back the cloak hood from her tousled hair. "I have brought you the calendula shampoo I promised you when we first met a long time ago at my home." His eyes lit up as she continued: "Anyone with beautiful hair such as yours should do everything possible to nurture it and keep it healthy. It is, indeed, your crowning glory! I made the

311

shampoo myself for you." She managed a flicker of a flirtatious smile.

Winder's vanity caused his face to redden under her flattery. "Thank you, Miss Van Lew. And how is everything at the top of Church Hill? Are you finding the shortages of food and other necessities of life taxing your disposition?" His tone was somewhat obsequious.

"When we consider the sufferings of all the boys fighting this war I do not think civilians should voice their complaints no matter how arduous they may be," she replied emphatically.

"Is there anything I can do for you to make life easier?" he asked with a gallant bow. His attempt at ingratiating himself into her favor was more than a little obvious. He was proud of the shock of white hair and the erect bearing cultivated in his army training which contributed to the polished appearance he wanted to affect.

Elizabeth Van Lew looked up at him with her piercing eyes. "Yes, there is something. A very small favor I'd like to ask," she said. "I would like permission to bring a few homemade goodies to the prisoners." When his face expressed surprise, she went on: "Perhaps it is because of my natural womanly tenderness that I like to think there must be some kindly women in the North who are visiting our southern boys in Yankee prisons and bringing them little gifts made by their own hands to ease the hardships of prison life." She continued to peer up into his face. "Do you think me naive, General?"

Her intimacy disarmed him and when he answered her his voice betrayed an uncomfortable fluster. "N-no. Of course not. You are the soul of kindness." He patted her arm. "What things do you have in mind for the prisoners?"

She pulled back the cloth covering her basket and he looked in at an assortment of jellies and pickles, a bar of soap, a few lemons, a loaf of bread, a book and writing paper. Underneath these items and out of sight were some newspapers carefully folded.

"You are very generous, my dear." His flattering tone changed abruptly and he added: "Let us hope that you are correct in your appraisal of northern women."

He led her up two flights of stairs to the Chickamauga floor where the prisoners were lying about on the dirty floor. A smell of burned ersatz coffee filled the room. Recently a mixture of chicory and okra had been substituted for the long-vanished coffee beans. At the sight of Winder and Miss Van Lew the men became subdued instantly. A few stood up, endeavoring to be chivalrous. Elizabeth caught sight of their toes protruding from shoes and bony knees pushing through holes in their trousers.

Turning her back on Winder, she knelt down and put her basket on the floor in their midst, her untidy locks swinging out in front of her face. As she began lifting the jars out she spoke to them very softly: "I live up on the hill nearby. I'll come again." Rising from the floor she whispered in the ear of the nearest soldier: "Read the newspapers." That was all she said before disappearing down the stairs with Winder.

The men were so startled at this bizarre little drama with its incongruous protagonist who came and went so quickly that they could not speak. Finally, one of them spoke: "Who *is* she?"

A guard nearby overheard the question and spoke out: "Oh, that's Crazy Bet," he sneered. "She's a little 'teched in the head. A harmless soul, though. Lives like a recluse up on top of that hill in a big castle-like place."

When the guard left, the men examined the gifts. Colonel Jubal White took out one of the newspapers—the *Richmond Examiner* for February 26, 1864—and unfolded it carefully. On page 3 he came across a short paragraph with a Washington, D.C. dateline that had been bordered lightly in pencil:

"Usually reliable sources within this capital report increasing speculation about a raid on Richmond prisons in the imminent future. Rumors are circulating that the Union Army will attempt to free prisoners on Belle Isle and in the Libby following reports that the thousands of captives held there will shortly be moved out of the Confederate capital to the Deep South to relieve the overcrowding. Still unidentified are those who will lead the raid, but speculations are that the Union cavalry will be heavily engaged."

Dazed, Colonel White put down the newspaper and did not speak for a brief moment. Then, holding it to a fellow officer, he pointed to the paragraph and said: "Look at this."

The newspaper passed from hand to hand throughout the Chickamauga floor. When it came back to Colonel White he took the paper again and examined the article closely. He looked very solemn and spoke slowly: "Do you know what I find to be most interesting about this story? It's not the news itself that may be only a fantastic rumor. No, it's the outline that was penciled around it."

The men were quiet and thoughtful. "You mean Crazy Bet?" one offered.

White nodded. "Why did she do it? Who *is* she, anyway?"

There was silence until White spoke again: "I am beginning to believe that this 'Crazy Bet' is not so crazy after all. Certainly not as crazy as she'd like everyone to think she is."

"You mean . . ."

"I mean it appears that we have a 'friend' on the outside. Call her what you will—spy, informer, Rebel traitor—'Crazy Bet' knows what she is about."

Colonel Josiah Sprague who had been reading the other newspaper—the *New York Times* for February 22, 1864—suddenly spoke up: "See here. There's another penciled story." He began to read aloud softly: "Colonel Abel Streight, 51st Indiana Infantry, one of 109 prisoners who made a break from the notorious Libby Prison in Richmond on February 9, passed through Union lines safely and has arrived in Washington to give a report to the Federal Government on conditions in Richmond prisons.

"Colonel Streight once before attempted an escape from the Libby but was unsuccessful. He gives credit for his recent good fortune to a southern Rebel sympathetic to the northern cause who risked personal safety to hide him and other escaping officers for a week, providing them with food and shelter and aiding them with valuable contacts along the escape route in their final dash from enemy territory to the safety of the Union lines."

The men sat stunned and stone-like. For a few moments no one spoke. At last Colonel Sprague whispered under his breath: "That's our not-so-crazy Bet."

Another prisoner who had broken the loaf of bread in two, brought forth folded greenbacks baked inside. "Lookee here," he said. "These will buy us a few favors."

314

The news of the intended raid swept through the Libby with the speed of a virulent virus infecting all in its path. The subject on every man's lips, it was the cause for colorful and imaginative conjecture. It did not matter that no one could distinguish fact from fiction. All that was important was that now there was cause for hope. There had not been much of that around lately. Everyone waited and watched for a sign.

Elizabeth Van Lew wasted no time in making her next visit to the men in the Libby. Twenty-four hours later she packed her basket again with delicacies from her kitchen shelves and added a few pairs of wool socks and a wool scarf which had belonged to her brother years before. All of Richmond shivered in the brutal February weather but nowhere was it so harsh as inside the prison with windows open to the frigid damp.

She set out from her home in a snowstorm. This morning she had very important news for the prisoners. With her cloak over her head and shoulders she took tiny steps as she descended the hill to keep from slipping in the snow. Two small boys making snowballs behind her back threw one at her disappearing figure, taunting in a loud whisper: "Witch!"

Gaining admission to the Libby, she found that General Winder was absent. To the guard she said sweetly: "Would you be so kind as to escort me upstairs?" Handing him a glass of quince jelly she had planned to give to the Provost Marshal, she continued: "I have a few little things to give the poor men up there. They suffer so from the cold." She pulled back the covering on her basket and showed him the old socks.

Grunting a rough acknowledgment of her gift to him, the guard rather begrudgingly led her up one flight of stairs. She gestured her desire to stop in the section of Gettysburg prisoners. Strangely enough, although she had never seen these men before, they appeared to recognize her and seemed almost to be *expecting* her. Squatting down on the floor, she drew forth from her basket the several pairs of socks, at the same time noting that one of the prisoners was engaging the waiting guard in conversation. Motioning to the prisoners standing near her she said: "Here. Sit down and try these on for size." Immediately three officers sat down on the floor and began removing the ragged covering of their feet. She huddled over them, her cloak still shielding her face, and as they pulled on the socks with exaggerated slowness she whispered in their ears: "Union cavalry under the command of General Kilpatrick and Colonel Dahlgren are outside Richmond. They are coming to raid Belle Isle and the Libby to set you free. Be ready! Pass the word along."

The men listened, their faces expressionless, but as the guard drew near they raised voices of approval of her gifts: "These are a perfect fit. Thank you."

"Did you knit these yourself?"

"The last pair of socks I had were lost at Gettysburg. Somebody took them off my feet when I was wounded on the field. That's eight months ago, right, Ma'am?"

Distributing the homemade bread and little cakes quickly amongst the men, she took her leave as unceremoniously as she had come and followed the guard to the door of the Libby, thence climbed up the hill to her home with the snow gathering on her cloak.

Left alone, the men could talk of nothing else but the news that Crazy Bet had brought. The rumor of the day before was no longer without foundation. Kilpatrick and Dahlgren and Federal cavalry were out there not very far away and were going to rescue them at long last from this Hell.

Obeying her command to "pass the word along," they dispersed throughout the various sections of the prison and, unobserved by the guards, told the good news. As it spread from one floor to another, men began to ready themselves in many little personal ways for the moment when the doors of the Libby would be battered down and they would all go free.

Henry Sawyer confided in his friend Gideon: "You know, Kilpatrick got his nickname 'Kill Cavalry' honestly. All over Virginia I heard about his daredevil recklessness. He knows no limits for pushing his troopers *and his horses*," Henry added with feeling. "Doesn't spare 'em ever. He's a glory-lover. It's no exaggeration to say he's ruthless in the way he drives his men."

Gideon mused: "Let's hope he is true to his reputation then when he arrives at the doors of the Libby!"

By roll call the following morning when the raid gossip was

at its peak, General Winder chose to address the prisoners: "I have today authorized Captain Turner to place 200 pounds of gunpowder in the cellar floor. This is a warning. Should there be any attempt to escape, the charge will be set off." His announcement to the officers created an uproar of protest which sent Winder scuttling away to his office in the lower confines of the prison.

A day passed and then another. The men in the Libby waited and waited. Had something gone wrong? Where was Crazy Bet? Then, on the third day, the former slave from Elizabeth Van Lew's household who had relayed such useful information to Colonel Streight a few weeks before, came to do his work at the Libby bringing with him a Richmond newspaper published on the 4th of March. It brought the heart-breaking news of the failed raid, dashing the hopes of the patiently waiting men:

"Colonel Ulric Dahlgren, in command of Union cavalry troops, was killed last night in an ambush near King and Queen Court House. Colonel Dahlgren was part of a force of an estimated 4000 troopers led by General Judson Kilpatrick whose intent was a raid on the city of Richmond to free the 15,000 prisoners presently held here. The Confederate War Department, learning of the raid in advance, took emergency measures and saved the city from the devastation of enemy troops and prisoners alike.

"Colonel Dahlgren with 100 troopers rode into a trap set by Major General Fitzhugh Lee's cavalry; 92 of his men were captured following his death. General Kilpatrick conducted a raid in the area where Dahlgren met his death, but he, too, failed to carry out the attack on Richmond. He lost more than 300 men and 500 horses.

"Papers discovered on the body of Dahlgren attested to a plan to burn Richmond and to kill Jefferson Davis and his Cabinet."

29

In early March 1864, following the tunnel escape and Dahlgren's aborted raid, Henry Sawyer was aware that some of the prisoners were "going out." Lieutenant Rufus McKean, an amputee from the Battle of Chickamauga, was packing a haversack with his one arm. He had shared space on the floor next to Henry for five months.

"Where are you going?" Henry asked his friend.

"Moving," he answered.

"Where?"

"Not sure. Guards don't say exactly. I get the feeling it's south, maybe Georgia."

"Any word from Winder?"

"No. Just the Turners. They say we're going to the open countryside. Far from Richmond. I guess General Dow was right when he said that there are too many prisoners concentrated here in the city and we make the civilians 'uncomfortable.' How about that!"

Henry was thoughtful for a moment before bidding farewell to his friend. "Well," he said encouragingly, "maybe a change of scene will be a good thing. At least you won't have to smell the canal any longer. Or drink it. Maybe in the new place you'll look out on green fields and southern pines. I wish you well, Rufus." He clasped the lieutenant's hand and helped him with his coat.

As others departed, Henry realized the prison population was shrinking—very gradually but noticeably. There were actual empty spaces on the floor now. He felt a sadness coming over him. The men who were leaving had become his friends. Thrown together at first as strangers, many wounded and all disconsolate, they had shared the frightful cruelties of prison life for months and had somehow survived. They had listened to hours of story-telling from one another's personal lives, to letters sent from loved ones at home, to battle experiences, to whatever subjects anyone wanted to talk about. Their common suffering had welded them together as no other experience could have done. Every time Henry observed an officer gathering together his gear for the impending leave-taking, he thought about the comraderie of war which had bound them together, and he felt a sense of loss. He wondered if they would ever meet again, some time way off in the future when peace had returned to their unhappy land. How long would the war go on, this war which was to have been a short one, the politicians said back in the spring of 1861? How many of these brave men who were departing would manage to endure the unknown brutalities awaiting them in the next prison? Often as he watched them go, he offered silent prayers for their safety.

Always, after the departure of prisoners, there was at least one guard who made a furtive reconnaissance of the space thus vacated for any possessions that might have been left behind. On the day that Rufus left, Henry observed that the guard who was making the search looked familiar. He had a certain malevolence about his expression and bearing that jogged Henry's memory: it was the fiend who had stolen Si's jack-knife the day he arrived at the Libby almost nine months ago. Anger churned like an acid in Henry's stomach at the sight of the man groping in the corner where Rufus had lain these many months. The Devil incarnate, it seemed to him, was at work desecrating the memory of the gallant soldier. Henry watched the unsuccessful search and the evil in the squinting eyes. He had never seen malice and spite enshrined so indelibly in a human face.

He noted the disappointment of the guard in his failure to find any forgotten treasures, and at that moment an idea came to Henry. From his sitting position on the floor he grabbed the leg of the guard's trousers. "You!" he shouted.

The guard stopped at the command.

"Where's my jack-knife? I want it back."

The man tried to free himself from Henry's grasp. "What jack-knife?" was the sullen retort.

"The one you stole on July 3rd when I arrived at this filthy place."

"I don't have it," he snapped back, kicking out the trouser leg in his effort to get away.

"Oh, you have it, all right!" continued Henry glaring at the specimen of sniveling humanity in his clutches. From under the tongue of his own boot he brought forth his last remaining greenback and waved it in front of the face of his struggling captive. "Will this help you to find it, perhaps?"

The guard's beady eyes lit up and he made an attempt to grab the money.

"Oh, no!" exclaimed Henry, pulling it back quickly. "Not until you produce the knife. Now go and find it. And hurry. I'll give you one hour. No knife—no money. It's as simple as that."

The man kicked out furiously. "You can't talk to me like that!" he yelled. "Yer a prisoner. I don't take no orders from the likes of you! I *give* the orders!"

Henry released the trouser leg. "You're right," he answered deliberately. "I am a prisoner but I have one greenback that you'd like to have. There's only one way you're going to get it. Is that clear?"

The man stomped out of the room swearing at the walls and ceiling and kicking everything in his path.

Henry chuckled. He had not chuckled in a long time—probably during his whole captivity—but now he chuckled out loud with the relish of a small boy who has played a trick on someone. After the chuckle he put his head back and laughed long and hard. Months of pent up emotion were released in a torrent of laughter that came as a catharsis to his spirit.

In less than an hour the guard returned and pitched the jack-knife onto the floor next to him. Henry examined it, tested the blades, and rubbed it fondly between his hands. He tossed the greenback on the floor and took pleasure in seeing the guard stoop to pick it up. As he did so Henry warned him, shaking the knife at him: "Now don't ever let me see you put your filthy hands on this again."

The guard stuffed the money in his pocket and slunk away like a beaten animal. He reminded Henry of a fox. As he watched the retreating figure, Henry was conscious of a sharp twinge of remorse, albeit fleeting. What type of individual could be expected to perform the onerous tasks of a prison guard other than one whom Fate has cast into the dregs of humanity? Perhaps he had been too hard on this fellow who performed the unsavory work expected of him to the best of his ability.

Before daybreak one morning in mid-March Henry was jostled into consciousness from a fitful sleep on the floor. In the dim light he opened his eyes finally to focus on a guard crouching over him. "Sawyer?" the man queried. His voice was as rough as his handling. "Sawyer here," Henry replied.

"Git up then," the man continued in a coarse, demanding tone. "Bring yer gear. All of it. Where's Flinn?"

Henry pointed to a corner of the room. "Over there."

"Wake 'im up. Bring 'im with ye. Hurry now."

Henry blinked. "Whose orders?"

"Don't matter whose orders, Yank. Do as I say."

Henry wakened John Flinn. The two men were fully dressed, never removing their clothing for fear of freezing to death. They gathered their few possessions together into haversacks and followed the guard down the stairs, Henry supporting his friend.

On the first floor of the prison they met General Neal Dow who stood with his haversack in hand. Henry felt his heart beginning to pound wildly. Was this the day they had been waiting for? John, looking ashen white, leaned against the wall and hung his head. Turning to Dow, Henry asked: "Sir, what's this all about?"

The general shrugged his shoulders. "I haven't any idea," he replied. "I'm as much in the dark as you are." Then, nodding towards the office of General Winder, he added: "But I reckon we'll know soon."

The Provost Marshal was uncommunicative as he shuffled through papers on his desk in his office. At last he emerged and spoke: "Captain Turner and two guards will accompany you. I'm sending you out before dawn *for your own protection.*"

Just as unceremoniously the three prisoners followed Winder to the door of the Libby. As he opened it to the fresh air of the outside world, hope surged in the breasts of the three men and they stood for a moment breathing deeply and looking up at the few stars still left in the sky. The light hurt their eyes which had grown sore from the smoke-filled kitchen where they spent so much time.

A wagon drawn by a horse was waiting, and sitting in the driver's seat was none other than Captain Thomas B. Turner. Henry wondered silently if this occasion marked their final encounter with the Beast of the Bastille. The three prisoners stepped into the wagon and seated themselves on straw in its bottom. Two guards sat apart from them. Not a word of explanation was forthcoming from Winder. The wagon was pulled away from the prison door and rumbled along Canal Street.

Henry looked back at the grim exterior of the Libby, conscious of a wave of sickness knotting his stomach and, yet, there was something else he was not prepared for: a flash of inexplicable poignancy about leaving this place that had been his hell for over eight months. How was such a crazy emotion *possible,* he asked himself? There was just no understanding human beings, he mused, smiling at the ridiculousness of the painful sense of loss that had swept through him. And yet, his regret at leaving the comradeship of the hundreds of men that had made the misery bearable was real.

Where were they going? Winder's phrase "sending you out" was ambiguous. That could mean that they were en route to another prison far away from Richmond. What had he meant by "for your own protection?" It was all very strange. But in a few moments he grasped the full import of the words. It was daylight now and there was activity in Canal Street. A little group of bystanders watched closely, gesturing obscenely and shaking clenched fists as the wagon passed by.

It was a short distance to the tow path along the James River where a dirty old tugboat was waiting with a number of

Confederate officers aboard. Henry could feel the stares of the Rebels who seemed to be discussing the three of them.

In the rough voices to which Henry had become inured over time, the guards and Turner demanded that they exit the wagon, pushing them impatiently towards the boat. Weakness in their limbs made walking precarious and they stumbled. General Dow, the first to step aboard, received a salute from all the Confederates.

"Name and rank," commanded the Confederate captain.

"General Neal Dow, 13th Maine."

"Captain Henry Sawyer, 1st New Jersey Cavalry."

"Captain John Flinn, 51st Indiana Infantry."

Their departure from the Libby was over. Henry could not comprehend how such an important happening in their lives should have taken place with such speed and without a trace of fanfare. Not before the boat began to glide along the shore did the three men realize fully what was happening to them.

"Where are we going, Captain?" General Dow asked.

"City Point, sir," was the reply.

City Point! The words had a musical ring to them. City Point—well-known as the place where prisoners were exchanged.

Turning to Dow, Henry said quietly under his breath: "Sir, I don't think we're being sent to another prison. I believe we are going to be exchanged."

"You may be right. I hope so," was his reply,

Hope. Hope, long dormant, was alive and well. An ecstasy of happiness and well-being Henry had not felt in many months flooded his heart and soul. He sat up tall and drank in the cool air deeply; with each breath new vitality entered his body and his mind cleared. He could not contain his joy. Turning to John Flinn, he said: "John, I do believe we're on our way out. We've left the Libby behind us. All those months of torture, of being hungry and cold and eating rotten food, they're all in the past. I have a feeling in my bones that there's no more prison life ahead for us."

Flinn smiled weakly. "If you're right, freedom has come none too soon," he commented slowly. "I hope there is strength enough to enjoy it."

Henry studied the wan countenance and the stooped posture of his companion. The man exuded despondency and misery and defeat. It made Henry sad to feel the crushed spirit and the absence of hope. "John," he said, putting an arm on Flinn's shoulder, "you'll be fine. All you need is a change from prison life. We all do."

As the craft moved slowly on the water there was silence amongst its passengers. Although secretly each one desired conversation, they sensed the distance separating them and respected it. After all, reflected Henry, what topic except for the weather and the river scenery could they have discussed amicably? Each individual was immersed in this bloody conflict which had become so acrimonious that no one could keep his perspective anymore. Hate and revenge offered the only common meeting ground. So the officers from both sides kept their counsel and ventured on no intercourse that might have broken the icy silence.

As they neared City Point, they observed two Confederate officers standing on a majestic steamer with "City of New York" written on her bow and flying the Stars and Stripes. Henry had not seen that flag for such a long time and the sight of it blowing in the breeze brought a surge of joy and pride through him. One officer was very tall and distinguished looking with a curly brown beard. As the tugboat neared the steamer, Henry observed that the man, although wearing on his upright collar the three gold stars of a general, was, indeed, quite young—in his middle twenties, perhaps.

Following General Dow, Henry and John were assisted from the boat. As they stretched their emaciated frames to full height, the tall Confederate officer approached the three of them with hand extended. "William Henry Fitzhugh Lee," he said courteously with a relaxed expression on his face. The brand of an aristocratic gentleman was stamped clearly on his person. He had a powerful frame but walked with a slight limp. Pale from months of imprisonment, the face behind the beard was handsome.

"Neal Dow," responded the senior officer grasping Lee's hand.

"Henry Sawyer."

"John Flinn."

The second Confederate officer with Lee was a captain. He approached and gave his name: "Robert H. Tyler."

The embarrassed pause which followed was cut short by Lee who smiled rather jovially at Henry and John as he said with a twinkle in his warm brown eyes: "I guess we should congratulate one another on our escape from hanging. There was a time when certain individuals were anxious to put a noose around each of our necks!"

He spoke with a casual self-confidence in a friendly manner which put all actors in the closing scene of this drama at ease.

"How long have you been a prisoner, sir?" Henry asked him.

"Almost nine months. I believe we fell in the same battle. Brandy Station? I took a hit in the leg." Pausing momentarily for another smile, he went on: "Your fellows have treated me to residence in both Fortress Monroe and Fort Lafayette. I guess they wanted to be hospitable and offer me a little variety to relieve the monotony. Your General Ben Butler is a seasoned host in these matters." The mention of Butler's name carried a certain sting. "The Beast" was definitely not popular with the Confederates.

General Dow spoke up then. "We did not shed any tears when we said goodbye to the old Libby, either. Being a guest for nine months in the Libby is a generous dose for any man."

The geniality which flowed within the group was pleasant to men who had not experienced it for a long time. "What will you do now?" Lee asked them.

"I'm leaving the service," Dow answered.

Flinn and Sawyer responded that they were "going home."

"And yourself?" Dow asked.

Lee replied quietly: "I will return to my regiment."

A multitude of unspoken thoughts trembled in the air. The war was still to be fought and won. The conflict which had brought these men together was far from over. Many more men on both sides would lose their lives. More prisoners would be taken. It would go on and on interminably until both sides were bled dry and their young manhood sacrificed. What would be the end result of all the bloodshed? How long would it take the country to forgive and forget and to get on with the business of peace?

Lee brought their discourse to a close. "I wish you well," he said to Dow, extending his hand to the General and then to Sawyer and Flinn. What more was there to say? He and Tyler stepped aboard the tug which the three Yankee officers had just left. It moved away slowly with its two passengers. Lee turned and gave a final wave of his hand to the three men aboard the *City of New York*, standing under their country's flag.

Epilogue

Late in March 1864, following his exchange, Henry Sawyer was commissioned Major of his regiment. After a few months' furlough at home with his family at Cape Island (now Cape May), he rejoined his command and returned to active duty, serving another eleven months until the regiment was mustered-out and honorably discharged at Vienna, Virginia on July 24, 1865. He left the service with the rank of Lieutenant Colonel. Back home, his early interest in hotels flourished anew, and in 1867 he became the proprietor of the Ocean House in Cape May and operated it until 1873. Three years later he built the Chalfonte Hotel which he owned and managed for many years. It is still in operation today and is the oldest hotel in Cape May. His civic duties embraced service as Cape May City Councilman and Superintendent of the United States Life Saving Service for the coast of New Jersey. Sawyer died on October 16, 1893 from heart failure. The inscription on his tombstone in the Cold Spring cemetery reads:

> A soldier whose deeds of valor and suffering
> for his country have been exceeded by no one.
> An officer of whom his men were justly proud.

His wife, Harriet, pre-deceased him in 1889. His son, Thomas, died at the age of nine years, and his daughter, Louisa, lived to be forty-three, dying two years after his own death.

Following Harriet's death, Sawyer married Mary Emma MacKissic, and from this union the present-day Sawyer family is descended.

Ambrose is a fictional character. One can visualize his continuing service attached unofficially to the First New Jersey throughout the remaining two years of the war as the regiment fought all over Virginia, witnessed the surrender of General Robert E. Lee at Appomattox Court House on April 9, 1865 and took part in the Grand Review in Washington, D.C. on April 23rd. It is easy to imagine Ambrose's fear and trepidations as he made his way home to Cape May, traveling through strange and hostile country and unsure of what awaited him upon his return or of what had befallen his dear friend Sawyer. An ending to the story befitting these two patriots would be their ultimate reunion back home, their friendship strengthened by many months of separation and suffering. One would like to think of them standing together at Beauty's paddock, immersed in reminiscences of their wartime experiences and expressing gratitude that their lives were spared in the long and bloody conflict.

Bibliography

American Heritage Century Collection of Civil War Art. Edited by Stephen Sears, 1974.

American Heritage Picture History of the Civil War. Editors of American Heritage, narrative by Bruce Catton, New York: American Heritage Publishing Co., Inc., Bonanza Books, 1982.

Atlas of the Civil War. Edited by James M. McPherson. New York: Macmillan, 1994.

Battle Atlas of the Civil War. By the editors of Time-Life Books. New York: Barnes & Noble Books, Inc., 1996. By arrangement with Time-Life, Inc.

Bearss, Edwin C. *Fields of Honor*. National Geographic Society, 2006.

Billings, John D. *Hardtack and Coffee. The Unwritten Story of Army Life*. Boston, 1887. Reprinted by Corner House Publishers, Williamstown, Massachusetts, 1973.

Blakey, Arch Fredric. *General John H. Winder, C.S.A.*. Gainesville: University of Florida Press, 1990.

Bradford, Sarah. *Harriet Tubman, the Moses of Her People*. New York: American Experience Series, Corinth Books, 1961.

Bray, John. *Escape From Richmond. Civil War Times Illustrated*, May, 1966. First published in Harper's Magazine, April 1864.

Catton, Bruce. *A Stillness at Appomattox*. Garden City, New York: Doubleday & Co., Inc., 1954.

Catton, Bruce. *Centennial History of the Civil War*, 3 volumes, Garden City, New York: Doubleday & Co., Inc.
Vol. I: *The Coming Fury*, 1961.
Vol. II: *Terrible Swift Sword*, 1963.
Vol. III: *Never Call Retreat*, 1965.

Catton, Bruce. *Mr. Lincoln's Army*. Garden City, New York: Doubleday & Co., Inc., 1951.

Catton, Bruce. *Reflections on the Civil War*. New York: Doubleday & Co., Inc., 1981.

Clark, Champ. *Decoying the Yanks. Jackson's Valley Campaign*.With the editors of Time-Life Books, The Civil War Series. Alexandria, Virginia: Time-Life Books, 1984.

Domschcke, Bernhard. *Twenty Months in Captivity. Memoirs of a Union Officer in Confederate Prisons*. Edited and translated by Frederic Trautmann. Fairleigh Dickinson University Press, 1987.

Dorwart, Jeffrey. *Cape May County New Jersey: The Making of an American Resort Community*. New Brunswick, New Jersey: Rutgers University Press, 1992.

Eicher, David J. *Civil War Battlefields. A Touring Guide*. Dallas, Texas: Taylor Publishing Co., 1995.

Faust, Drew Gilpin. *Mothers of Invention. Women of the Slaveholding South in the American Civil War*. University of North Carolina Press, 1996.

Fisk, Wilbur. *Hard Marching Every Day 1861–1865. The Civil War Letters of Private Wilbur Fisk*. Edited by Emil and Ruth Rosenblatt. Lawrence, Kansas: University Press of Kansas, 1983.

Foster, John Y. *New Jersey and the Rebellion. History of the Services of the Troops and People of New Jersey in Aid of the Union Cause*. Newark, New Jersey: Martin R. Dennis & Co., 1868.

Garrison, Webb. *Civil War Curiosities*. Nashville, Tennessee: Rutledge Hill Press, 1994.

Glazier, Willard W. *The Capture, the Prison Pen and the Escape*. Hartford, Connecticut: H.E. Goodwin, 1868.

Godfrey, Dr. Carlos Emmor. *Sketch of Major Henry Washington Sawyer*. Trenton, New Jersey: MacCrellish & Quigley Printers, 1907.

Guernsey, Alfred H. and Henry M. Alden. *Harper's Pictorial History of the Civil War*. The Fairfax Press, 1866.

Hennessy, John J. *Return to Bull Run. The Campaign and Battle of Second Manassas*. New York: Simon & Schuster, 1993.

Henry, Robert Selph. *As They Saw Forrest. Some Recollections and Comments of Contemporaries*. Editor. Jackson, Tennessee: McCowat-Mercer Press, Inc., 1956.

Hesseltine, William Best. *Civil War Prisons. A Study in War Psychology*. Columbus, Ohio, 1930. Reprinted in New York, 1964.

Klein, Frederic Shriver. *Lancaster County, 1841–1941*. Lancaster, Pennsylvania: The Intelligencer Printing Co., 1941.

Lippincott, George E. *Lee-Sawyer Exchange. Civil War Times Illustrated*, Vol. 1, No. 3, June 1962.

Livermore, Mary A. *My Story of the War*. Hartford, Connecticut: A.D. Worthington and Co., 1889.

Longacre, Edward G. *Jersey Cavaliers. A History of the 1st New Jersey Volunteer Cavalry, 1861–1865*. Hightstown, New Jersey: Longstreet House. 1992.

McDonald, Cornelia Peake. *A Woman's Civil War—A Diary With*

Reminiscenses of the War, From March 1862. Edited with an Introduction by Minrose C. Gwin. University of Wisconsin Press, 1992.

McPherson, James M. *Battle Cry of Freedom: The Civil War Era*. New York and Oxford: Oxford University Press, 1988.

Moran, Frank E. *Colonel Rose's Tunnel at Libby Prison. Century Illustrated Monthly Magazine*. Vol. 35, March 1888.

Nielson, Jon M. *Brandy Station: The Prettiest Cavalry Fight. Civil War Times Illustrated*, July 1978.

Pyne, Henry R. *Ride to War. The History of the First New Jersey Cavalry*. Edited and with an introduction by Earl Schenck Miers. New Brunswick, New Jersey: Rutgers University Press, 1961.

Robbins, Walter R., Major Commanding 1st New Jersey Cavalry. *New Jersey Cavalry 1st Regiment. 1861–1865*. Published for the officers and men at the True American Office, 1865, at New Jersey State Library at Trenton, New Jersey and at the New York Historical Society, New York.

Sears, Stephen W. *To the Gates of Richmond. The Peninsula Campaign*. New York: Ticknor & Fields, 1992.

Shaara, Jeff. *Jeff Shaara's Civil War Battlefields*. New York: Ballentine Books, 2006.

Starr, Stephen Z. *The Union Cavalry in the Civil War*. Volume 1. Baton Rouge, Louisiana: Louisiana State University Press, 1979.

Stern, Philip Van Doren. *Secret Missions of the Civil War*. New York: Bonanza Books, 1990.

Stradling, Lieutenant James M. *The Lottery of Death*. McClure's Magazine, Vol. 26, 1905.

Thomas, George E. and Carl Doebley. *Cape May: Queen of the Seaside Resorts, Its History and Architecture*. Philadelphia: The Art Alliance Press, 1976.

Tobin, Jacqueline and Raymond Dobard. *Hidden in Plain View. The Secret Story of Quilts and the Underground Railroad*. New York: Doubleday, 1999.

Vidal, Gore. *Lincoln*. New York: Random House, 1984.

Von Borcke, Heros and Justus Scheibert. *The Great Cavalry Battle of Brandy Station, 9 June 1863*. Translated by Stuart T. Wright and F.D. Bridgewater. Winston-Salem, North Carolina: Palaemon Press, 1976.

Wells, James M. *Tunneling Out of Libby Prison*. McClure's Magazine, Volume 22, 1903.

Wiley, Bell Irvin. *The Life of Johnny Reb*. Indianapolis: Bobbs-Merrill, 1943.

Wiley, Bell Irvin. *The Life of Billy Yank*. Indianapolis: Bobbs-Merrill, 1952.

Young, Agatha Brooks. *Women and the Crisis. Women of the North in the Civil War*. Published by McDowell, Obolensky, 1959.